I WENT TO
VASSAR
FOR THIS?

A Novel by
NAOMI NEALE

MAKING IT®

June 2006

Published by

Dorchester Publishing Co., Inc.
200 Madison Avenue
New York, NY 10016

ISBN 0-505-52686-7

The name "Making It" and its logo are trademarks of Dorchester Publishing Co., Inc.

Printed in the United States of America.

Visit us on the web at www.dorchesterpub.com.

MORE HIGH PRAISE
FOR NAOMI NEALE!

CALENDAR GIRL

"Hip, sassy, and filled with offbeat characters who will steal your heart."

—*USA Today* bestselling author Katie MacAlister

"Neale's addictively acerbic writing style and endearing heroine make for a deliciously humorous book that is a natural for Bridget Jones fans. Yet Nan's realistically complicated relationships with her family and friends add emotional depth, granting Neale's novel an appeal that reaches beyond the chick-lit crowd."

—*Booklist*

"Beneath the laugh-out-loud antics of assorted characters lies a simple fairy tale with a happily-ever-after ending…. Get this one for the keeper shelf—to read scene after scene for a good laugh on a cold winter night."

—*RT BOOKclub*

"Chick lit and contemporary romance readers will laugh with Naomi Neale's naughty and nice tale."

—*The Midwest Book Review*

"Naomi Neale deftly combines chick lit with laugh-out-loud contemporary romance… If you enjoy romance sprinkled with chuckles, *Calendar Girl* is a delightful way to spend your reading time."

—Curled Up with a Good Book

Other books by Naomi Neale:

**CHRISTMAS CARDS FROM
        THE EDGE** (Anthology)
THE MILE-HIGH HAIR CLUB
CALENDAR GIRL
SHOP 'TIL YULE DROP (Anthology)

ACKNOWLEDGMENTS

Kate Seaver originally approached me with the idea for this book's setting. Without her encouragement, it never would have been written. I'm also deeply indebted to Joe Cherry and Tom Franklin for their many contributions. You guys are the best! To Patty Woodwell, many thanks as well. My life would be infinitely poorer without our vicious online games of canasta and your expertise on exploding kitchen appliances.

Chapter One

An eye for trends. That's what the boys at Motive had said when they'd plucked me from my sedate business school and tossed me into the pandemonium of the advertising world. *She's got a good eye for trends, that Cathy Voorhees. She'll work hard for her paycheck, too.* I'd taken the hint and conceived myself as the industry's famed girl native guide, leading hapless Lewises and Clarks toward rich and prosperous territory. For five years I'd been a rising star in a company with more glass ceilings than a Coney Island funhouse maze. At long last I saw myself as minutes away from the one thing I'd desired more than anything: an electronic swipe card to a new office in the executive suite.

For all the good it did me, I should have exchanged that eye for trends and gotten myself an eye for the bloody obvious.

"There's extra wine." Thuy Phan's head popped up from behind the buffet where she crouched, her hands brandishing two bottles of merlot. The ends of her short hair, apparently trimmed with a laser level, were in perfect parallel with the table. "Let's get hammered and celebrate!"

After my triumphant product pitch I felt too jubilant for a mere girls' night out. Fireworks. My name in lights! A ticker-tape parade, whatever ticker tape was! I wanted to revel in the moment, but I couldn't until I'd received one final phone call. "You know I can't leave."

"So we won't go out on the town! We'll hit your place. Us and the wine. We can invite the mysterious new guy across your hall." Thuy added two more bottles to the table. "Seen him yet? Is he cute? Single? Gay? Single? Employed? Single?"

We were discussing my neighbor why, exactly? "All I know about the guy is that he plays his music too loud, and he listens to more oldies radio than should be allowable by law. How you've convinced yourself my reclusive new neighbor is your last shot at a relationship is beyond me."

"You aren't in the least bit curious? Come on." Trust Thuy to have already dismissed the campaign we'd finished promoting not fifteen minutes earlier. For her, it had been just another long day at work. For me, though, the pitch had been my make-or-break moment. I felt like Mary Tyler Moore, throwing her hat high into the air—happy, independent, and free. I wanted somehow to commemorate the evening, but I could see it would have to be in my own quiet way. "Fine. But you'll have to meet him tonight when you pick up the flowers I sent."

My giddy feeling vanished. It was as if Mary's hat had plopped into the gutter. "Excuse me?"

Thuy tried to hide her impish expression by tidying

the messy remains on the buffet table. "Yes, I got you flowers. For the congratulations you know you richly deserve. You're welcome. Martha Stewart says that when her executives close a deal, she . . ."

Martha Stewart was, for some mysterious reason, Thuy's business idol. I really didn't care if the woman's philosophy of congratulations was a Good Thing or not. "You left them with *Kurt?*"

"Sure. I suggested he might stash them with the mysterious gentleman in 440 so you could pick them up when you got home. Clever, right?" Kurt, my building's doorman, would have allowed the Manson family to move into my apartment for a two-dollar bribe. "I'll want all the details tomorrow, naturally."

"Mmmm." There was one FTD bouquet I'd never pick-me-up. No worries, though. I was still on top of the world. Or, if you want to get technical about it, forty-four stories up, leaning back in the chair at the head of the long conference table, the kitten heels of my Ferragamos resting on the solid cherry table as I gazed out on the twinkling lights of the nighttime skyline. Our decorators had painted on the room's walls great quotations appropriate for the advertising world, presumably to buck us up when inspiration flagged. *Discovery consists of seeing what everybody has seen and thinking what nobody has thought,* read one epigram from Szent-Gyorgyi—whoever the heck he might have been. My eyes flickered to the copper-lettered saying to its right. I read it aloud. "*Those who cannot learn from history are doomed to repeat it.* You know, Santayana didn't have a clue. Tonight's a little slice of history I wouldn't mind reliving again and again." I sighed, contented.

"You know what Santayana would have said?" I

raised my eyebrows and waited for Thuy to finish the thought. "He would've said, *She who does not hit a club in Williamsburg with her best girlfriend is doomed to regret it.*" Thuy made one last attempt to rally me into action. "You'll enjoy it. We'll do a little dance, drink a little drink, flirt outrageously. You know you want to," she wheedled, when I started laughing at her disco pantomime. "Oh, come *on*. Don't make me wait until tomorrow night. Thursday's the new Friday!"

"I love you to bits, but I've got to wait for this phone call."

"Yes, the all-important phone call that will change life as you know it. Fine. Just trying to think bigger, like you're always telling me. But I," she announced, grabbing a merlot, "am taking one of these darling little leftover bottles, heading home, kicking my shoes off, and getting blind, stinking . . ."

The glass door from the executive suite slid open, its almost-silent whoosh barely giving me time to drag my feet from the table. In stepped no less than John Peter Turnbull—Old Man Turnbull himself, a relic from a past when hip, hot Motive had been known as the Turnbull, Spiller, and Reine Agency, a respectable and stodgy advertising mainstay of minor banks, lesser car dealers, and department stores on the brink of bankruptcy. "Cathy." He nodded and lowered his lanky form into the Aeron chair closest to mine.

"Sir!" Oh, crap. Though I'd been quick to come to attention, he had to have seen me in my Joan Collins–plotting-to-take-control-of-ColbyCo pose. I cleared my throat. "Mr. Turnbull."

"Ohmygod!" I heard at my side in a faint echo. Behind her back, Thuy was concealing the purloined merlot, awed as Oliver Twist caught with a hand in the porridge pot. She looked from me to our CEO and back again, panic playing ping-pong with her eyes. "I'll . . ." She backed toward the door. "Have a nice . . ." She gulped, groping for the latch from behind. "See you tomorrow," she whispered before disappearing.

"Enjoy the wine," our superior called after her, one eyebrow raised. To me, as I hastily smoothed down the slacks of my suit and pretended I hadn't been occupying his rightful place at the table as if it were my own, he added, "The girl seems nervous."

I could certainly understand the reaction. An appearance from John Peter Turnbull was like getting an intelligent sentence from Paris Hilton—rare enough to be momentous. I'd seen the Motive patriarch before from a distance, walking down the hallway in suits tailored to accent his trim build, or smiling with paternal authority from the inside front page of our annual report. But a personal audience? Never had one, not even with my high-flying track record. "So. How do you think things went tonight?" he asked, once we were alone. He clasped his fingers in exactly the same gesture my analyst used when it was nearly time to tell me my fifty minutes were up.

This was the man who, after Spiller and Reine had sold out their portions of the company, sailed around Cape Horn on his own at the age of sixty, and whose favorite sports were still rock climbing and snorkeling. No use in being bashful. "Superbly," I said, relaxing to let him know that, grandfather of the agency or not, I could talk to him like a normal old fart. Er, geezer. I meant, normal old-guy type person. "I felt totally on top of this one, sir. Tip-top. Right there at the summit." Turnbull's expression hadn't changed. "You know the Himalayas? Well, I felt like a Sherpa."

He remained motionless. "Right there at the top of the . . . mountain. At the summit. On the peak." I finished with a zooming motion of my hand and a cluck of the tongue I instantly regretted. Why wasn't he saying anything?

Finally, the old man smiled and nodded, releasing me from the rack of uncertainty. "King of the hill, you mean?" His voice was pleasant, like I'd always imagined it might be. Friendly, even. "Or queen, I should perhaps say."

"You flatter me." No coyness there. The simple fact was that I wasn't quite queen of the hill by that point. Not yet. But I'd made damned sure the agency had noticed me climbing. Alpine Taco's three-year-long television campaign, the one with the guy in lederhosen yodeling *"Taco-lay-hee-hoooooo!"* at the top of his voice in front of baffled teens? My first campaign, thank you very much. The *Who's Your Daddy?* promotion reinventing a long-forgotten cinnamon gum from dentist's favorite into a punishing blast of flavor? Those tongue-in-cheek ads had been mine, all mine. I'd been the come-to girl for improbable products like organic frozen pizzas, or Internet groceries, or slick toys based on Japanese cartoon characters. My career was still riding the tsunami crest of last year's hugely successful *Power Up!* campaign, which had moved masses of joystick-hugging Peter Pans made pale and flabby from too many *Everquest* nights into the weight rooms of a nationwide gymnasium chain. And which had garnered Motive an industry award in the process, I might add.

I'd been the natural pick for Maxwell's Freezer Classics. For years I'd been trampling beneath Motive's glass ceiling, neck cramped from staring up at the big boys' scuffed leather wingtipped soles. For this multimillion-dollar account product pitch I'd gone all out so I could look them in the eye at last. "One. The Maxwell people *loved* the presentation. They laughed through the whole thing." I gestured behind me, where there still sat a working mid-century turquoise stove and refrigerator we'd hired from a cinematic prop company at a not-inconsiderable price. Though we'd cooked only a single demonstration meal in the oven, the conference room trash cans were packed with the shiny aluminum remnants of the Freezer Classics dinners the catering crew had wafted in from the hallway, and the refrigerator held a number of left-over dinners still in their cardboard boxes.

"Two. They laughed at the slogan. You should've heard them." A ten-foot-high cardboard cutout of the campaign's proposed mascot loomed behind me—a bulldog-faced old woman with a hair net and a ciga-rette hanging from the side of her mouth, plain and wrinkled as the housedress hanging from her shoul-ders. Though she had been photographed in black and white, the frozen TV dinner in her hands had been re-produced in the paint-box colors of its retro, 1950s packaging, the crone contrasting the pert and smiling Freezer Classics mom. Their lady on the package could have stepped straight out of *Leave It to Beaver*; the mascot we'd dreamed up for the campaign could have been Hell's cafeteria lady. Across her middle ran our slogan, right above her age-spotted hands holding out the colorful package: JUST LIKE MOM USED TO FAKE. "Hearing them gasp when we unveiled this little lady? I'm not going to lie to you, sir. It was one of the high points of my life."

Old Turnbull nodded. I had the fogey hooked. Any

minute now he'd be telling me the good news that come Monday, I could call that empty corner office in the executive suite my own. "Gratifying," was the one word he said.

"I'm sure you know the feeling, sir." Wait until the others heard how I'd had Turnbull—John Peter Turnbull himself—eating from the palm of my hand! "Third, and most importantly, the top Maxwell dog guaranteed we'd hear his answer shortly. Very shortly. As in, any minute now. I was waiting for his call." And enjoying a spectacular view of midtown Manhattan's twinkling lights that would very soon be like my own. Glass ceiling be damned!

"Cathy, you remind me of a young lady I once knew quite early in my career." Turnbull at last leaned forward from his contemplative pose and rested his hand on the mighty table. "Smart. Energetic. Entirely focused on her career." So far, so good. This crony of his sounded like someone of whom I'd approve. "She was, in a word, remarkable."

"Thank you, sir."

"But . . ."

Wait a sec. There was a *but*? A gear-shifting, tire-squealing, skid-mark-leaving *but*? My mind screeched into overdrive while I careened around the sudden obstacle he'd lobbed. No, I couldn't panic. He was merely going to say, "*But she didn't have a fraction of your determination and drive.*"

It didn't come out that way. "What she had in talent, she lacked in sympathy, I fear. Many of her ideas, though interesting, weren't right for their time. They often weren't well received. Which brings me to my point. Some of the partners feel that your campaigns, while appealing to a certain demographic, have as their hallmark a certain, well, *cynicism* that fails to connect with a broader . . ."

He continued speaking, but his words ceased making sense. All I heard was noise over the prickling sensation of my own shock. I wasn't on top of the world, I realized through my stunned astonishment. I was being chastised. As if from a great distance, I heard my shaken voice interrupting his steady flow of verbiage. "What demographic?"

"Beg pardon?" He blinked at me. I'd thrown him off whatever canned script he'd prepared behind his frosted-glass office doors.

He hadn't attended that evening's presentation. Was he actually suggesting I hadn't connected with the Maxwell reps? They'd loved me. They'd laughed at both my mascot and my slogan. What the hell did this past-his-prime coot know about connecting? He was barely ever in the building, what with his sailing and kayaking and constant world travels. My reply came out as a growl. "I said, what demographic?"

Vaguely uncomfortable, he let his hand stray to the knot of his tie as he cleared his throat. "A certain urban, educated, one might almost say 'hipster' demographic that at most is . . ."

"That's why I was hired!" *An eye for trends.* If he didn't remember, I surely did, and I jabbed my finger to make sure he got it. In my cold anger, I inhaled a mouthful of my blond hair. Long and layered was this year's corporate-approved fad. Though the length softened the roundness of my face, it got in the way at the worst times.

". . . a fairly limited number," he gently concluded.

"It's been discussed that while you were indeed taken on for your insights, as it were, into a world view that I, let us say, could never reproduce . . ."

The man's circumlocutions could have dizzied a whirling dervish. "Let's cut to the point," I suggested, tossing back my damp hair with a no-nonsense flip. "You didn't like the campaign."

I watched his eyes dart to the scowling larger-than-life cutout with the hair net and moles, to the retina-melting colors of the appliances, to the uncorked wine bottles Thuy had discovered. After what seemed an eternity, he shook his head. "If it were for a fledgling company . . . an untested product . . . or for a specialty market . . ."

The old dolt! No vision, no humor! And to think the other senior partners still let the antithesis of hip have a say in what was supposed to be one of the most progressive ad agencies in Manhattan! The man was so obviously out of touch that I felt a stab of pity for him. "Times have changed," I told the guy, feeling both indulgent and contentious in equal measure. "This is exactly the kind of thing they're eating up these days. You see it as cynical. I see it as appealing to the savvy intelligence of the post-boomer consumer. Both a celebration of and a sly wink at the heritage of advertising itself. You know what, Turnbull? Mr. Turnbull?" I hastily amended. My sentences were flowing so smoothly that, drunk on my own words, I couldn't feel too badly about one little error in address. When I had this account sewn up in a few minutes, he and I would be on a first-name basis. Closed-door meetings. Golf. Tasteful present exchanges around the holidays. "Welcome to the future."

"My dear." Turnbull had tolerated my pep talk with

the vaguest of smiles. Where was the apology I deserved, though? He'd called his most talented up-and-comer an adolescent smart-ass. Where was the bow of the head, the gracious nod, the concession? All I saw in his face, in the long pause that followed, was pity. The same pity I'd been feeling for him mere moments before. "It's your future here we should discuss."

Advertising's self-proclaimed girl guide should've been canoeing downstream away from disaster as fast as her little paddle would take her, at this point. Yet I hadn't seen this coming. Not the faintest shadow. "You've heard already." Moments before, my mood had been light and forgiving. The icy realization of what was really happening chilled my marrow. Turnbull's eyes, so baby blue for such an elderly man, regarded me sadly. "The Maxwell reps, I mean. They've called you." He didn't need to reply. I knew the answer. "They didn't like the campaign," I said for him.

"They have decided to go with a more traditional approach."

"Who?" I demanded to know. Which of our competitors had been sneaking around behind our backs, wooing my clients? "DDB? Performance?"

"Deutsch."

"Fine." Ugh. Only one of our biggest adversaries. "There are other fish in the sea."

Turnbull shook his head. "Maxwell's a catch those of us in the executive suite particularly wanted."

"You're right. Not fine. They want traditional? I can give them traditional." I'd made a misstep with my lack of aggression, but I'd make up for it. Turnbull had never seen me thinking on my feet before. Well, I was a one-woman tropical brainstorm when I had to be. He'd see. "I can have a whole new approach for them by to-

morrow morning before they've inked any contracts
with Deutsch. Amber fields of grain. Purple mountains
majesty. Support the troops. As stodgy as they want.
Twelve hours, Mr. Turnbull. That's all I need. Twelve
hours. By then I can have a fresh concept, rough images
for a new campaign, a new slogan . . . I don't need the
sleep. Any of my friends can tell you that." I hoped my
words might arrest the gentle shaking of his head. "Ten
hours. Six. Six hours, Mr. Turnbull! Or give me 'til
midnight. You'll be impressed with what I can do in
four hours. I'll give you rough mock-ups. We can have
final product in place for print and TV in a month. No,
three weeks. Two—!"

"Cathy." As I'd feared, Mr. Turnbull was as im-
placable as ever. "I'm afraid not."

"I'm fired, then? Is that it? Leave the Wang building
immediately?" None of this could be happening. Ten
minutes before, I'd thought myself the hottest young
thing in the ad game. Now I felt as if I were being
given the Walt Disney cryogenics treatment, long before my personal appointment with the Grim Reaper.
On second thought, I didn't know how much grimmer
things actually could get. "I'm finished? On the unem-
ployment line? Washed up? You're throwing out one
of your best idea people over a little cynicism? That's
pretty cynical itself, isn't it?"

"Cathy." I *knew* my name. I didn't need to hear it
over and over when I was waiting for something more
important to my heart and my future. Like a retrac-
tion. "Don't think of it as a step backward. It's an opportunity. Take time to reassess what's important in
your life. Reconnect with your priorities. Enjoy time
with a gentleman friend. Relax some."

Oh. This was rich. The bastard firing me was giving

me tips on my social life. "I don't have a boyfriend. I have a job. A career. A calling. Or at least, I did."

"That," he clucked, "is a pity. Every young woman should have a gentleman friend."

"For all you know about me, I could bat for the other team!" At some point I'd risen to my feet, much to my surprise. My voice quivered with righteous indignation. "I could be a lesbian. I could. I'm not. But I could have been the most lesbianic, les-gigantic-est, lesbian-lovin' lesbian around who's not actually from the island. Of Lesbos. Which is in Greece." I was rapidly getting off-track. "My point is your presumption. My personal life is none of your concern. A gentleman friend! Exactly what year do you think it *is?*"

During my Greek tourism rant, Turnbull had pushed back his chair. Once I fell silent, he rose, looking very much like the too-tanned, over-pampered and indulged figurehead I now knew him to be. "Ms. Caldwell is staying until nine, if you need help in clearing your desk," he said gently. When he walked in the direction of the exit, his footsteps barely made a sound.

"Mr. Turnbull!"

"Good-bye, Cathy."

The doors shut behind him. My own pale reflection in the glass confronted me. Over-pale. Overweight. Just plain . . . *over.*

Twelve hours. I could have created a kick-ass campaign in that amount of time. Part of me toyed briefly with the idea of disregarding the old man and coming up with something brilliant, something so outrageously good that when I left it on my empty desk, they'd find it tomorrow morning and instantly recognize what they'd lost. "*How I misjudged Cathy Voorhees!*" Turnbull would cry out, shaking his head.

"Quick! Somebody! Get her on the phone! We must have her back!" Only, of course, by then I'd be off for some quick therapeutic seaweed treatments at La brecque, prior to my interview-*cum*-lunch with Donny Deutsch. The kicker being that it would be *I* who would be interviewing *Donny's* agency.

For about forty seconds, while I stared at my pale reflection in the glass's greenish cast, it was a hell of a dream. It reminded me of the too-frequent fantasy I used to have as a kid of languishing in a hospital bed, beautiful, young, and doomed, surrounded by all the people who'd ever wronged me begging my forgiveness as I gasped out my final, barely audible dying words: *"I told you you'd be sorry."*

"Screw this," I said to myself, shaking the blond hair framing my face. I wasn't a kid any longer. Martyrdom had lost its appeal. "Screw *you*," I said to Turnbull, presumably still somewhere within the cool depths of the partners' suites. And to that timid mouse of a personal assistant of his, too, with her cringing postures and her scuttle of a walk. "Screw Motive," I said with more confidence, turning my back on the suite. "I'm better than all of you!"

If Motive wanted me out so badly, in fact, they could damn well clean up after me. There was precious little in my office I wanted to keep. Five years of my life flushed down the toilet for these arrogant, sexist asses, and what would I have to show for it? A couple of plaques, a few cartoons from the Net, and drawers and drawers of folders and paper, none of which I'd want, even if Turnbull's tame Chihuahua let me remove anything client-related from the premises. No, my stuff could rot in the file cabinets for all I cared.

I Went to Vassar for This?

* * *

Precisely forty-two minutes later, I stumbled through the allegedly secure front door of my Upper West Side apartment building, clutching an open Boise copy paper box containing:

1) Three bottles of merlot left over from one spectacularly miscalculated campaign pitch
2) Thirteen Maxwell Freezer Classics retro frozen dinners (the entree, judging from the illustration of the foil container on the front: roast beef with gravy, accompanied by buttered whipped potatoes, mixed vegetables, and chocolate-flavored brownie)
3) One Swingline stapler. Simply because I'd never had one of my own.

Kurt, the former public access 3 A.M. talk show host who sucked up money from the building association by masquerading as a doorman, grunted at me inside the lobby. His jacket uniform hung open, revealing the stretched-out T-shirt beneath; his hands were grubbing a copy of *Maxim*. As always, his slovenliness irritated me. Yet mindful of the way FedExed responses to the resumes I'd be sending out could always "accidentally" be lost, I kept my trap shut. He peered into my box. "Havin' a party, Ms. Voorhees?" he said, leering in a way that managed to imply he could provide the hookers, the blow, and the police payoffs for the sort of party involving mass quantities of cheap wine and TV dinners.

Amazing that of the eight candidates interviewed, Kurt had been the only one to pass the background check. "Office leftovers," I explained, praying he'd stop talking to me. Even in the best of moods, I hated our conversations. At the moment, the best of moods and I didn't have even a speaking acquaintance. "I'll get my mail . . ." I said, fumbling with the paper box so I could get my keys.

I've heard rumors that in buildings like mine where the rent is much the same and the views much better, there are doormen who might say something like, "*Hey, let me help you!*" and take a heavy box from a girl, or who might even have opened the bank of mailboxes and retrieved my letters for me. No such luck with Kurt. "Sure. Whatever," he said agreeably, before returning to his magazine's photos. No matter. Having to fumble with the tiny key and the rusty old mailboxes only to discover that not even the most paltry sweepstakes solicitation or coupon book waited within reinforced my new place in the universe as a naught. A nothing. A big, broad-hipped zero.

"Later," said Kurt, once I'd hitched up my boozy cargo and stumbled away. I figured the unexpected farewell to be the full extent of his attempt at weaseling a good Christmas bonus from me in another six weeks. "Oh yeah," he added, after watching me grope blindly for the elevator button for a full thirty seconds without offering to help. "Some hot chick left a delivery for you. She said it would be okay if I sent it up to four . . . something."

"How about 440?" I asked, wanting to bean him.

"Yeah. Amazon package, I think."

"Or flowers, maybe?"

For a long, hard moment, I could almost hear the little gerbil jogging around the wheel that powered his brain. He shrugged. "Could be. She was hot, though. She single? Or need a little extramarital lovin'?"

Of course, I thought to myself on the ride up, the advantage of perhaps having to downsize in the future might mean I could move to a cozy flat in Jersey City where the only immovable fixture at the front door would be the local crack dealer.

Why hadn't I laid down the law back in the office? Instead of being assertive, I'd flinched. "*I don't need sleep—my friends will tell you that!*" God, I'd actually said those words. If my lips had been planted any more deeply in old Turnbull's rear, they could've checked his colon for polyps. What a lie, anyway! The one thing I wanted right then was to crawl into bed for three days solid, covers over my head. Oblivion, or at least unconsciousness, would take the edge off my mortification. No, I needed something to eat first. I'd not chowed down with the other Motive and Maxwell execs when we'd wined and dined them during my presentation. Screw my diet. I'd taken nearly two weeks' worth of roast beef and chocolate brownies, so dinner for the next few days would be on Motive. For a girl who knows nothing about cooking and hates to do it, that's a godsend.

But no, I had to do something about Thuy's flowers before anything else. Sweet of her, as always, to have sent them. Stupid of me to dread seeing the damned things. Loath as I was to confront the freaky neighbor guy who'd moved in the previous month, it had to be done. Or else when Thuy descended on me tomorrow, oozing sympathy, and didn't find the flowers, she'd crow bloody murder. Besides, this would be the last bouquet I'd be getting for some time. Maybe until my funeral. If I could be so lucky.

Tempting as it was to simply make a left and hole up in my place, I sighed and faced the right-hand oak doorway opposite my own. From inside I could hear the sound of a Buddy Holly CD playing at top volume. Stupid ass, always playing his classic rock so loudly! I rapped at the wood with the hand I wasn't using to cradle my work booty. Almost immediately, the music stopped. I waited for someone to come to the door. No one did.

"Hello?" I called, rapping again. "I *heard* you, you know. Oh, come on," I growled, when the thin sliver of light from beneath the door vanished. The bastard had turned his lights off! "I know you're there. This is 430, across the hall from you." My pounding got no response. "You've got something for me. A delivery. Kurt told me. Some flowers? You—come *on* already."

Fine. Or, in the words of Kurt the Doorman, *whatever*. That quotation wouldn't be joining Motive's pantheon of great thinkers anytime soon. Mr. 440 could keep the damned things for all I cared. Thuy could annoy the freak herself, next time she visited. My arms were tiring anyway.

I'd just gotten open my own apartment's three locks and set down my box on the chair inside when out in the hallway, I heard the sound of a door opening. A scraping noise followed. I turned. Mr. 440's door was cracked open wide enough that his unseen foot could shove through a triangular cone wrapped in thick green paper. And I knew it was his foot doing the moving, because in the hallway's light I caught a glimpse of a hand on the doorknob and the brief silhouette of a masculine profile at eye level. Another shove from the darkness, and the package was in the hall. The door slammed shut. "Thank you!" I called for politeness's sake. Then, to myself, I added, "New Yorkers!"

Until I could get changed, the flowers would have to wait on the kitchen counter. I'd never cooked a Retro Freezer Classic for myself, but my Lean Cuisines usually nuked for six and a half minutes, so I popped a roast beef dinner out of the box and into the microwave over my stove, at the last moment remembering to peel back the foil from the brownie. Just like the picture on the box.

I pushed the start button and schlepped into my bedroom. Off came my shoes, my jacket, my pants, my top, and the rest of the corporate drag in which I'd slaved day in and day out for the last five years. I left them in a pile on the floor. Tomorrow I could pick them up. If I felt like it. My comfy terrycloth robe, which I'd bought a decade ago, before my first semester of college, folded around my shoulders like the arms of an old friend. With the microwave's fan as my background noise, I tried a brave whistle. Somehow it made me feel better. I'd be okay. I was the kind of person who eventually landed on her feet. Bad as things were now, I'd feel better once I had some wine, a few bites to eat, and a good night's sleep.

To start the cheer-up process, I picked up my flowers. "How pretty!" Behind me, the microwave made a sputtering noise, as if agreeing. *I'm congratulating you before the actual presentation,* Thuy had written on the card. *So sue me. XO, TP.* With her typical good taste, she'd picked out a selection of flowers in festive autumn colors that, although they didn't exactly cheer me, didn't make me want to do a Sylvia Plath with my head in the gas oven. Not that I knew how. I'd used the thing maybe twice. "Now, about a vase . . ." Perhaps an old Absolut bottle would do.

Once again the microwave let out a popping noise I'd

not heard from it before. This wasn't the percussive forgot-to-vent-the-plastic-wrapping-on-the-Lean-Cuisine burst, or the nuked-the-bacon-too-long crackle. This was a strange, ominous fizzing noise, accompanied by an earthquakelike shaking of the appliance. Yet when I looked around at the rest of the kitchen, nothing else was moving. The microwave's death-rattle intensified. Inside, white sparks began to fly.

What—? Was it—? Had I—? The flowers fell onto the kitchen tile as I groped for the Freezer Classics box. Its smiling Donna Reed mascot grinned inanely at me from both sides of the box as I flipped it over. "*Do not place metal containers or aluminum foil in the microwave*," it read. "*For traditional or convection ovens only*." Crap! Why hadn't anyone told me? Everything could be nuked in a microwave, couldn't it? I'd seen whole turkeys cooked in one! Oven mitts. I needed oven . . .

The last thing I remembered, as I turned back to the microwave with a dish towel in my hands, was a flash of light and a sound like thunder when, in slow motion, the little oven's door exploded from its hinges and winged its way toward my head. Then there was nothing but whiteness, where a familiar face with even whiter teeth smiled maternally at me.

Go toward the light! urged the Freezer Classics dinner woman, her apron's ruffles not a bit mussed. *Go toward the light!*

"*Aw, shut up*," I growled at the wench. Then the lights went out.

Chapter Two

At first the eyes staring into mine seemed immense, like the river of rich, warm chocolate from *Willy Wonka & the Chocolate Factory* into which I'd always wanted to dive as a kid. With every passing second, those vast pools seemed to recede, twirling away in a dizzying spiral until almost nothing of them was left. Machinery had been pounding away somewhere near me, but its sounds faded as well.

No. I was merely dizzy. The factory noises had been my own heartbeat and the blood coursing through my veins. The eyes were, well, eye-sized. After blinking a few times, I realized I was sitting on something soft and that a strange man was hovering over me. "Miss Voight?" The light baritone voice was so loud at first that I twitched, but my ears adjusted quickly. "Are you all right? Miss Voight?"

Oh, right, I thought to myself. *The voice belongs to the eyes. That makes sense.* Were there other parts, too? Any woozy notion I might have had about having ended up in a hellish afterlife inspired by Hieronymus Bosch, where giant noses ran around on tiny legs while knives protruded from between disembodied ears, was quickly disabused when the eyes' owner stood upright. The first thing I noticed about him was the old-fashioned crew cut he sported, so coarse that every short, straight hair seemed to defy gravity. Then I focused on the cleft in his chin. I've always been a sucker for those. Thick horn-rimmed glasses sat on the bridge of his nose, and . . . oh dear, what a deal-killer. The dark red plaid of the geek shirt that hung from his broad shoulders was spotted with little white flakes. If he'd only paid attention to my campaign for Zincsational!, the all-herbal shampoo for problem scalps, little Mr. Retro Hipster could have sudsed, sudsed, sudsed his way to dandruff-free hair irre-sistible to the opposite sex. Or the same sex, if that's what he was into.

I was babbling. My mouth wasn't moving, but, jolted to life once more, my brain was zipping along at a hundred miles a minute. "Miss Voight?" said the guy. His lips didn't seem to be moving quite in synch with the noises he made, but that was okay. I remem-bered something had hit my head. Obviously I was still a little woozy.

Who was this Miss Voight he kept talking about? Prompted by some weird worry that I'd lost it when . . . well, when something had happened, I reached up to make sure my face was still on tight. Touching my head sent a dull, hangover-quality pain throbbing through my brain.

"Miss Voight?" Again with the *Miss Voight!* Who-ever the hell Voight was, I wished she'd speak up al-ready so I'd stop having to hear her name. Mr. Brown

Eyes kept staring steadily in my direction. "Cathy?" he asked.

The word had been so soft and tentative on his lips that for a long moment I didn't even recognize it as my name. "That's me," I finally murmured. I'd suffered massive hangovers before, believe me—after a particularly bad one involving too many Lemon Drops, a friend's bachelorette party, and a stripper dressed like a lumberjack, I hadn't been able to look at citrus for six weeks. Luckily, speaking aloud didn't trigger the massive headaches I usually experienced from too-close encounters of the hooch kind. "I'm alive, right?"

"Why, sure you are. Can I get you something? Ice? Water? A Coca-Cola?"

Knowing my habits, my refrigerator contained nothing more than leftover Thai takeout, a jar of pepper rings, and the mostly-empty supersack of miniature Halloween Milky Ways I'd bought two weeks ago, knowing full well that precious few kiddies tricked or treated in my building. "Coffee," I mumbled. Things were so much better with my eyes closed. They'd improve more with caffeine.

"Your electric percolator's on the fritz, remember? From what I could tell, you must have gotten a shock from the frayed wire. How about I get you some tea?" His footsteps were soft on the floor as he backed away.

Tea? I had some in my cupboards, I knew—a few packets of herbal crap that had come in one of the thank-you gift baskets clients were always sending me. In fact, the only stuff occupying my cupboards had come from gift baskets. Gourmet mustards in tiny jars. Wee samples of exotic, seedy jams. Pasta in novelty shapes. I let the guy fumble around in the other room while I rested my eyes.

I might have nodded off for a minute, or else a nice concussion could have been kicking in, because the next thing I knew, Flaky Pete the Electronics Whiz was back, pressing a cup and saucer into my hands. Who knew I had a saucer? Gratefully I accepted them, and while I peeled open my eyes once again, I took a sip. "Oh my God!" I exclaimed, genuinely surprised. "Real tea. I mean, *real* tea from real tea leaves. I thought I was going to have to drink that homeopathic, Celestial-seasoned lawn squeezings shit."

Ol' Geek Chic stared at me like he'd never heard a girl swear before, but he couldn't have been as wide-eyed as I. The hot liquid had given me focus for the first time in several minutes, and the first thing I focused on was the sofa on which the guy sat. It was low. It consisted of swooping brass and some rectangular salmon-colored leatherette cushions—salmon cushions!—and though it could have come from my grandmother's dentist's waiting room in Schenectady, it was definitely, most definitely, not mine. Nor were the squat wooden coffee table with metallic accents, the rag rug underneath it, the Formica dinette beyond, the wall clock with long space-agey spikes where the numbers should have been, the ginormous table lamp with a plaster base in the shape of a matador, and *especially* not the metallic wall hanging bristling with cutout ginsu-edged leaves and wandering branches. None of it was mine! "Where am I?" I whispered, putting the willowware coffee cup on the table. The sofa on which I sat was armless and upholstered in a dull gray fabric with tiny metallic threads glistening within. Someone was really going for flea-market ambiance, here. The whole tiny apartment was a vintage store's trash-day wet dream. "This isn't my apartment. Where the hell am I? And can you do something about that dandruff? It's driving me crazy."

Suddenly self-conscious, Mr. Plaid Fad sprang up and batted at his shoulders. He seemed mortified. "Miss Voight . . ."

That name again! "Why do you keep calling me that? My name is Voorhe . . ." My name was halfway out before I thought better of sharing it with this guy. "Oh God! Are you a stalker? You are! Are you the bastard who keeps stealing the perfume inserts out of my *Vogue* subscription? Sick!"

"No! I—!" My Prada Purloiner tried to circle around the coffee table to get to me, his hands outstretched. The freak probably wanted to cop a feel! I felt dirty all over. What if he'd tried something while I'd been out like a light? "I'm from . . ."

"I don't care what electrical . . . repair . . . ! Whatever! How did you get me here, you, you . . . *Jeffrey Dahmer?*" I demanded. "Were we at some bar? Did you slip me a roofie?"

"Jeffrey who? Rufus who?"

"Oh-ho-ho, nice!" I laughed coldly, edging my way to the door. He was slick, Mr. Innocent was. I didn't remember having been to a bar that night, but I had a vague memory of something bad happening. "Was it one of those Houston Street lounges? I'll *kill* Thuy."

"You—you're not making any sense." He nervously pushed his glasses up his nose. "Why don't you sit down and drink your . . ."

I recoiled from the cup in the same way Socrates must have when they brought him his hemlock Cosmo. "Shit! You laced the tea with a roofie, too!" I clutched at my throat with both hands. "GHB! PCP! SOS!" I was blacking out. The drug was taking effect. Another ten minutes and he'd be having his filthy, filthy way with my unconscious body. And it was really a pity he was such a depraved bastard, because under normal circumstances I might actually have found him adorable, in an alternative-band-lead-singer sort of way.

No, wait. I wasn't blacking out. The spots in front of my eyes had appeared because I'd gotten off the sofa too fast. And let's face it: Full-figured girls like me have more to haul off sofas. "Are you all right?" my ravisher asked.

I reached down and, because it was hampering my movement, clutched at my skirt as I replied, "Of *course* I'm not all right, what with being stalked and molested and . . ."

Hold up a second. My *skirt*?

One look down was enough to propel me to a mirror surrounded by what looked like the most rococo frame from the Met's Renaissance collection. A ravishing blond creature stared back at me from the glass. Oh, it was definitely me. Someone, however, had stuffed my ample form into an old-fashioned, billowing A-line dress of deep blue covered with white polka dots. Polka dots! Me! Impending violation meant nothing in the face of those polka dots. Somehow the dress gave me an hourglass figure my loose work suits never had. "Wait a minute," I snapped, narrowing my eyes. "Wait one Goddamned minute. Did you—?"

"I haven't done—*whoa!*" When I hauled up my skirts to see what was underneath, he flinched away and held his hands in front of his face. Funny kind of thing for a date rapist to do. "Do you have to show your . . . ? Aw, jeez! I should . . ."

"Oh my God!" What had this deviant done to me? "I've got on some kind of petticoat!" Isn't that what this slippy-type thing was? "And *granny panties!*" They were enormous. They were baggy. They were white. I dropped my skirts back down again. "And my hair! You've, you've . . ." My helmet of rigid, short curls made me look like a young and platinumed Liz Taylor; I had such a round face that the style wasn't something I necessarily would have tried on my own, but danged if it wasn't actually pretty cute. Still, I had bigger fish to fry. "You've *set* it!"

"I didn't!" my would-be hairdresser stammered out. Now he was the one backing away, fear in his eyes.

"Don't look at me like that!" I yelled, alarmed beyond all measure. Obviously my commotion was making him nervous. Good. Score one for victims who stood up for themselves. "What's with putting me in June Cleaver drag? Oh, you sick freak! Were you planning to *video* this? What are you running, some kind of deranged necrophiliac goth . . . *fetish* video ring? And you're the perfume-sniffing hairdresser ringleader?" In my upset I'd clutched my throat. Alarmed at what I found there, I whirled around to the mirror again. "Pearls?" I gasped.

"I think they're Bakelite," said Chester the Molestor. "*I don't care what they are!*"

He flinched twice, once at my screech, and a second time when the door behind him opened. I caught a quick glimpse of a battered antique stairwell beyond, and then in walked two dames. Friends of my Bakelite-lovin' buddy, no doubt. "Oh, thank God," he murmured, scampering over.

I wasn't worried. There might have been three of them to one of me, but the smaller of the women—a short-haired blonde with the tiniest wasp waist I'd ever seen—couldn't have been more than five-three. I could've snapped her like a Saltine. The other was one of those elegant numbers with a deep red mane straight out of the Miss Clairol box, curled at the ends in a Bettie Page style. She was obviously the higher-rent model of the two. Both of them wore the same type of costume I'd been stripped and stuffed into— the short girl in a plaid skirt, wide like my own, and the tall one in an off-the-shoulder emerald number that could have come from the racks of *Butterfield 8*. They both wore long, elbow-length white gloves, I noticed with a wary eye. All the better to leave no fingerprints with. "Say, what's going on?" asked the tall chick. As if I bought her phony alarm!

"Your friends are here now." The pornographer's tone of voice might have reassured a kid afraid of thunderstorms, but not this girl. His accomplices weren't *my* friends. "Can we talk? In the hallway?" he murmured to them. Then, in the same bland way, he added to me, "They'll be right back to take *good* care of you."

"Oh, I'm *so* not doing *that* kind of video!" I shouted at the closed door. "I'm not like that! I don't care what Melissa Lawson from Vassar might have told you! We were drunk freshmen playing truth or dare and there wasn't even any tongue!" I needed a phone. I could call the cops with a phone. As wildly as I raced around the room, though, I couldn't find so much as a single empty cell phone holster. Tricky, planning it so well.

Fine, then. I'd take a good look at my surroundings

28

so I could describe them to the cops after my escape. Judging by the narrow confines of the apartment and the original fireplace and mirror, my jail was one of those run-down converted Victorian townhouses with a dine-in kitchenette and mile-thick walls. I could probably scream for days without being heard. The street outside the heavy window was too dark to see anything more than a distant streetlight glinting from the hoods of the parked cars. Great. So not only was I in some unknown part of the city, but I was going to have to walk through some really crummy neighborhoods before I got back to civilization.

I'd decided that the smart thing to do would be to grab some kind of sharp weapon from the kitchen, when the door opened again and the two women returned. I backed against the mantel, wary. "Where am I?" I demanded. "Don't come any closer. I know Tae Kwon Do." I'd once dated a guy who did Tai Chi in Central Park, anyway.

"Cath, honey." The shorter woman's voice was tupelo honey to the ear; her Southern drawl made every vile word sound perfectly harmless, damn her! She stood with her hands on her hips for a moment, staring at me. "Don't you recognize us?"

"He was right," said the other in her deep alto. "That shock must have hit her pretty hard."

"How do you know my name?" What they were selling, I wasn't buying. "Forget it. You can tell that kidnapper friend of yours—"

The tall woman gave the munchkin a look of significance, then started removing her gloves while she walked in my direction. I backed away. "He wasn't a kidnapper. He came to help after you called for him. Anyway, he's gone, dear."

29

Meanwhile, Short 'n' Southern hopped up and down in what resembled genuine anxiety. "Cath, don't you remember me, Tilly? And Miranda? Your flatmates?"

"You are not . . ." I stopped, putting a hand to my head. These women were far too polished for what you'd expect from necrophiliac goth Donna Reed girl-on-girl porn actors.

"You're in your apartment at 125 East 63rd," said the tall one. Miranda, if I could believe a word of what Tilly had to say. "Everything's all right. You took an electrical shock from the percolator and it gave you—what's-it-called?—temporary gymnasia."

"Amnesia," Tilly murmured from her perch on the sofa's arm.

"That's what I meant. Darling." In one fell swoop, Miranda sidled up beside me to lay a hand on my shoulder. I was so stunned that I didn't move. Her voice throbbed with emotion. "You're very dear to us. We couldn't bear to think that while we were gadding about, you were here . . . hurt. No, injured!"

"That was swell!" Tilly's applause was reduced to a patter by her gloves.

Miranda turned and performed a coy little bow. "Wasn't it?"

"I don't know *why* you didn't get that role in the radio serial," said Tilly. "You're awfully talented." Off she sailed behind us down the little hallway, pulling off her gloves one by one.

"*Quelle* disappointment, I assure you." Miranda sniffed. "It's tragic that talent such as mine has to prostitute itself for wages in retail."

When the redhead laid the back of a hand on my

forehead, I flinched away. She clucked with disappointment when I snapped, "I *beg* your pardon!"

"Ah, that's more like the Cathy I know," she said, obviously pleased. "Didn't Tilly tell you not to use that coffeepot?"

"I did!" A thickly accented voice drifted from the back of the apartment. "I warned her this morning."

"Are you sure?" Miranda bellowed. They seemed to have an easy kind of familiarity; they'd probably worked this routine together before. Or maybe this really was their apartment, when they weren't renting it out for Doris Day fan club meetings.

"Of course I'm sure!"

"So *you* live here." I won an approving nod. "And your *friend* lives here."

"And *you* live here too," Miranda said, encouraging me. She crossed into the kitchen and opened the little refrigerator, drawing out a pitcher of orange juice and pouring it into a little glass she took from one of the shelves.

"And you're actors."

"Oh, heavens!" I heard Tilly padding down the hallway toward us. "I'm no actor, honey! That's all Miranda. And she can have it, with the wolves she has to endure." Miranda raised her glass in a citrusy toast. "You and I work together. Do you really not remember? Come on to bed, honey. You'll feel much better after a good night's sleep. And if you don't, we'll call the doctor to visit." When Tilly reappeared, it wasn't in a leather dominatrix's uniform, much to my relief, but in a fuzzy blue robe with matching fuzzy blue slippers that looked like dust mops.

"That's right." Miranda's voice was so soothing

that I wanted to believe her, too. "Why don't you look at some of your photographs? That might help you remember." So smoothly did she and Tilly take my arms and guide me in the direction of the little narrow hallway that it wasn't until we were halfway down it that I realized they could be leading me to the handcuff or bondage room. "It's okay," Miranda said when I resisted. "We're here."

The bedroom into which they led me was perfectly ordinary, though. Maybe even too ordinary. The twin bed inside had been made with tight hospital corners. Ball fringe hung from the chenille bedspread. A tiny desk sat in front of a window at the room's far end, while a dresser hugged the wall inside the door. With all three of us in there, it was more than a little cramped. "See?" Tilly guided my attention to the dresser, atop which, among the oversized perfume bottles in unfamiliar shapes, sat a number of small silver frames. "There you are. Your graduation photo. Aren't you a dream?"

"Mmm, I like the one of all of us," said Miranda, picking up the largest of the frames and showing it first to me and then to Tilly. "Remember that day? Connecticut was swell."

"And the poodle!" Tilly laughed. "Whatever happened to that boy with the poodle, anyway? Did you ever see him again?"

"Too many fingers," said Miranda darkly. Tilly tsked. "And none of them would wear a ring. Here are your parents," she said, putting down the Connecticut photo and picking up another. "And your brother . . . and this one's of your little niece . . ."

"Cathy, remember? Don't you remember, honey?"

No, I didn't. I was torn. These women were so hell-bent on assuring me that I lived in this strange apartment that half of me was convinced they were straight from the funny farm or had something malicious in mind. Their concern, though, was so genuine that it was impossible to think anything bad about them. And then there was something else—the evidence in front of my eyes. Those black-and-white photos weren't of my parents. I'd never been to that field in Connecticut. I didn't have a brother or a niece. Yet that was *me* in most of those pictures. My smiling face. My eyes. My mouth, my figure. Not my hairstyle or my clothes or people or places I knew. But definitely me. Maybe I'd stumbled into a simple case of mistaken identity that would account for why these women were acting more like concerned chums than malevolent accomplices? Then how could I account for my curls, my dress, my granny panties?

That's when my eye caught a rectangle of cardboard hanging above the dresser. It was an advertising calendar for a funeral home on 60th, the name of which I didn't recognize; only a few slips of paper remained at the bottom to count off the months. OCTOBER 1959, it read.

Everything about that evening came flooding back at that point—my presentation, my firing, the flowers, the exploding microwave—all the incidents that I'd blocked out in the few minutes after the accident. "Oh my God," I said aloud. Had I really . . . ? Was it even possible . . . ? It couldn't be. "I do remember."

Tilly and Miranda were plainly relieved at the news; they didn't want to be stuck with an amnesiac roommate any more than I would. "Oh, good!" said Tilly. "Welcome back, you poor, poor thing!"

"Maybe some aspirin," Miranda suggested. "And a cognac."

"No," I told her. "Nothing to drink. My head . . ."

Miranda chuckled before sailing off. "The cognac's for me, darling. Good night. Get some rest. Everything will be better in the morning."

Once I was alone with her, I asked Tilly, "Is that . . . right?" I pointed to the calendar.

The little blonde blinked, then laughed. "Oh, no! That's not right at all!"

I heaved a sigh of relief. For a minute there, I had actually thought I'd been flung back in time nearly fifty years, thanks to a freak accident with a microwave oven! Oh sweet Jesus. I really was overtired, if I'd let myself become *that* gullible.

"You must have forgotten to change it this month," she said, reaching up and tearing off one of the paper slips, then bounced away with a smile. "I'll be right back with the aspirin. And maybe, just this once, one of my special little purple pills."

November 1959. Forget the aspirin. I needed something much, much stronger.

Chapter Three

"Oh, *honey!*" Tilly's face the next morning was a bouillabaisse of emotion. Everything was in the mix. Shock, horror, pity, despair, bewilderment, a soupçon of amusement, and a jigger of awe. "Did you sleep on your *hair?*"

From the dinette table where they breakfasted, Miranda struggled to her feet and froze, afraid to come any closer. "*Quelle* train wreck!"

The two girls looked perfect. At seven in the freaking morning they were both fully clothed—Tilly in a pretty blue dress with a skirt that stretched from the redwood forests on one side to the gulf stream waters on the other, Miranda in a hip-hugging black wool skirt, a striped turtleneck, and a jaunty beret. Both of them wore shoes. I, on the other hand, was barefoot and, judging by how sick to my stomach everything was making me, quite possibly hungover. "Yeah, I slept on my hair. It's attached to my head, which lies on the pillow, which is on my bed. Which I sleep in. What—?" Without a word, Tilly stood up from what

35

looked like one of those massive buffets of foodstuffs from a TV ad (I half expected to hear an announcer murmur, "Frosted Flakes is part of this complete and nutritious breakfast!") and marched me over to the mantel mirror.

I recoiled immediately from the Medusa therein and screamed, "Holy shit!" From Miranda I heard a gasp. When I wheeled around, she'd clasped a hand over her mouth. Next to me, Tilly cocked her head to the side, lips parted. "Oh. Oops. Sorry." I'd trespassed on forbidden 1950s territory, or broken some social code or something. "Fudge, I meant. Or how about, golly gee, I look like shi . . . poopy-doodles?"

"I heard what you said," Tilly announced in a no-nonsense tone. "I'm just surprised to hear *you* say it. Finally!" She burst into a wild, hyenalike bark of laughter.

This was a joke? The last word caught me off guard. Finally? Miranda sat back down to her eggs, bacon, cereal, muffin, coffee, and orange juice. In her smoky voice she said, "Dr. Freud, I think we have a breakthrough."

"What do you mean?" Tilly was too busy standing on tippy-toe and swatting at my mop of snakes to reply. "I don't curse or something?"

"Hah! Never!" said Miranda, lighting a cigarette. It was all I could do to keep from waving my hands wildly around to keep the as-yet imaginary smoke from my nostrils. "Don't you remember lecturing me, week before last? *Now, Miranda. Men won't kiss lips that say the brown word!* 'The brown word,' no less. And look at you now!"

The way she spoke was obviously a parody of my own voice. The real Cathy Voight's voice, anyway. Interesting. "I'm stretched pretty tight sometimes, huh?"

"Hah!" That word again. "Like a bongo!"

"Cathy, I heard you moving around your bedroom earlier. I can't believe you've been up for so long and you're still not in the least dressed and ready for work!" Tilly tsked. "You've got plenty to do today, too!"

"Huh?" Work? Seriously? I'd been fired less than twelve hours before, and now I had to go to work the next morning? In a different decade? There really was no justice.

"Yes, work, you big silly." She grabbed me by the arm and marched me back in the direction of my room. "Honestly, Cath. I don't know what we're to do with you. You're a completely different person today."

Oh, if she only knew.

My first morning in the year 1959 had begun two hours before at 4:57 A.M., the moment Tilly's special pill wore off. Oh, it had done its purple little magic all right, reducing my burning anxiety to a tiny birthday candle flame that extinguished at roughly the same time that my two new flatmates left me alone in the bedroom. The lovely, contented feeling even lingered a while in the dark, when I lay there convinced that indigestion from the Freezer Classics dinner had prompted me to dream the whole, nightmarish evening. Then I awoke and saw not the cheerful luminous green of my Dream Machine radio/CD with built-in mp3 player, but the twin phosphorescent hands of Cathy Voight's alarm clock, and what had been dampened to the merest flicker instantly combusted into a volcano of panic.

What else is there to do in your prison of ball fringe and blond furniture than distract yourself by rummaging through a perfect stranger's belongings? Sadly, it wasn't as exciting as it sounds, unless your idea of fun is discovering that the woman whose life you've apparently taken over owns an entire drawer—an entire drawer!—full of gloves. White gloves in all lengths. Gloves of gray and of cream and dun. Crazy, absolutely crazy.

Despite having the nagging sensation that at any moment the real Cathy Voight would fling open the bedroom door and demand to know why I was pawing through her stuff, I kept looking. If I had to occupy this time for a while, I had to know what I was in for. Cathy's clothes didn't really tell me much about her save for the fact that she certainly did like her dry cleaning and that she shopped a lot at some place called Peck and Peck, and that she liked her foundation garments in a virginal white. All of them would fit me fine, I noticed— strange that the two of us should be exactly the same size. Only, of course, it wasn't strange at all, since I was obviously caught in some kind of delusion triggered by my untimely firing the night before. Right?

In the other Cathy's desk I found several boxes of stationery engraved in a formal script with her name and address. It was on one of these, at 5:22, that I proceeded to make a little list in order to calm myself down.

I Went to Vassar for This?

<u>This Situation Is B-a-n-a-n-a-s:</u>
<u>A Comprehensive Checklist</u>

<u>Pros</u>	<u>Cons</u>
1. Maybe I'm really not in 1959. Maybe I'm still back in my own time wearing a straitjacket in a nice rubber cell someplace.	1. That's a <u>pro</u>?
2. It could be. Because then someone else is going to have to worry about subletting my apartment. Probably my sister.	2. Your sister let her Tamagotchi starve when she was fourteen, and that was only nine years ago. What makes you think she can manage a grown-up thing like an apartment?
3. Okay, fine. Regardless of whether or not it's actually happening, I'm still getting a nice little all-expenses paid vacation, right? Isn't that what Turnbull suggested I needed?	3. That <u>bastard!</u>
4. Think of the cost of living! Cathy Voight has $25 in her purse and doesn't a steak dinner with like, all the fixings only cost a shiny quarter in 1959?	4. Don't working women in 1959 make only about a buck-fifty a week?

5. Oh my God! I am _so_ going to do _all the fun things_. Like the Beatles! I can be in the audience when they appear on The Ed Sullivan Show! Remember how they talked about that on that VH-1 special?

5. Wait a minute. When were the Beatles? Aren't they like, ten years in the future? Do you really want to stick around that long?

6. _Woodstock!_

6. Whaddaya talk? Woodstock? You don't even like mud masks.

7. Stop being such a spoilsport. Think of the fun we can have!

7. Avoidance much? Listen to you. You don't even know when the hell Woodstock was!

8. All right. So history was my worst subject in high school and the one semester of Ancient Greek Life & Culture I took to fulfill my college humanities requirement isn't really going to do me any good here. So what? I can fake my way through if I have to.

8. So the minute you get out there and you start babbling about things that haven't happened yet, they're going to lock you away here too, that's what. Everything you know about history you learned from VH-1! You don't know jack about 1959!

9. Do too.

9. Okay then, smartypants. Who's President?

10. Truman. No, wait. He   10. Hah! Told you so!
was earlier. Or later.
It's . . . crap.

11. Shut up!   11. <u>You</u> shut up!

I quietly folded the paper in half. Obviously I was schizo, but neither of my roommates had to witness it.

Midway through dressing for work, something occurred to me: If I were delusional and suffering from a nervous breakdown, how much better could it get than this? I had some nifty retro clothes to dress up in. The girls sharing my apartment seemed fairly decent. Why not simply relax and enjoy my psychosis? The thought invigorated me enough to make myself as pretty as possible while I tried to heed Tilly's repeated urgings to hurry. When finally I sailed out of my bedroom, coat on, purse in hand, I looked even more period than the woman on the Freezer Classics box. Yay, me!

If I were telling myself little stories about 1959 in my head in some psychiatric hospital, though, would I really be so thorough about it? Wouldn't my imaginary home have looked like something I'd seen before from television, like Ricky and Lucy's New York apartment, rather than the mix of 1900s limestone townhouse shabby chic and midcentury modern knockoffs? Why didn't I invent a retro version of my own morning routine—lethargy, coffee, energy bar, rue, and a last-minute dash for the shower and subway—instead of one in which the *dramatis personae* wore full period costume? And shoes? Good God, what kind of creatures wore shoes in their own home? I couldn't conceive of such madness on my own!

Another thing that really, really bugged me: If I

were making all this up, where was I getting the *detail?* The massive cars in the street—some new and shiny and finned, some older and bulbous and boat-like, some made by companies I'd never heard of, like a DeSoto that resembled the Batmobile. The men and women in their winter coats. The way nearly everybody wore hats. The near-total lack of any faces in the crowds darker than mine. How could I have made up the Manhattan that in many ways was so like my own, but in countless others so different? At the gaping absences of familiar skyscrapers on the horizon to the gentle familiarity of those that remained, I couldn't stop gawking. Tilly noticed. "Sugar, will you come *on?* We're already going to be late!" she kept saying as she dragged me in the direction of the Lexington Avenue local.

It wasn't simply the big things. On the small scale, everywhere I looked was utterly, breathtakingly convincing, without any of the fudging of my usual dreams. I'm all for the notion that the brain's a sponge that stores away details the conscious mind doesn't notice, but whose brain could pack away so many millions of alien trivialities? Besides that Ken Jennings guy from *Jeopardy!*, anyway. Who could have picked up the notion of cigarette advertisements on the trains? Or of smiling Italians opening up their fruit markets on the corners where Starbucks should be? My own dreams never had smells, but that morning reeked of them—the body odor of men in the subway mingled with the perfumes of the women. Everyone carried the faint sour-and-sweet stench of tobacco. Aboveground, food scents warred with the odors of car fumes and baking bread and of frying bacon from a greasy spoon.

Everything was too overwhelming to take in, especially all at once. Not until we were nearly at our destination did I even notice we were on Third Avenue and 48th Street, the same intersection to which I'd trundled daily. "I know this place!" I cried, stopping dead in my tracks. "I work here!"

"Of course you do, sugar-pie." Tilly patted my gloved hand with her own. "We both do. Come on, now."

Bang went all my theories about this being for real. Wouldn't it be totally typical for a psych ward patient to create fantasies in the past about familiar places in the present? "Where's the Wang?" My volume must have been considerable; several people in the vicinity turned their heads. "The Wang should be here!"

One man grinned and tipped his hat at me. Another, a burly taxi driver in a gray uniform stepping around his car, let out a low whistle. "Cathy." Tilly was a patient soul to put up with me. "I know those tranquilizers have a tiny aftereffect, but can you keep your voice down?"

Oops. "Sorry," I said, chastised. "I just expected the Wang, that's all."

"Honey, at our age, all us girls expect the wang. Honestly, I don't know what's gotten into you! One little shock and suddenly you're Miss Potty Mouth 1959! Now, let's go!" She grabbed my hand and walked us into the building that wasn't the Wang, smiling at the people we passed, as if to reassure them that no, I wasn't a threat to their health and safety. Not at all.

I couldn't have been gladder than to have Tilly guiding me past the reception desk to the cantankerous service elevator in the not-the-Wang building.

Without her cheerful disregard that something dreadful had happened to her flatmate the night before that left me as her sorry substitute, I'd be totally lost. Oh, I had a plan of sorts in place. Namely, I planned to fake it all the way. How many dinners at fancy restaurants had I been to at the start of my career where the only way I'd learned which fork went with which course was to observe how my clients behaved? A little small talk, a little laughter to smooth over the bumpy spots, and I'd be fine. Right? Abso*lute*ly, I told myself.

A woman waited outside the doors of our little moving canary cage for her five-story trip down. The blue cape around her shoulders gave the impression that she was a flight attendant. No, what did they used to call them that we weren't allowed to say anymore? Stewardess. Then again, *everyone* I encountered looked like a retro stewardess or cocktail hostess or jaunty businessman or some other *Nick at Nite* stereotype. "Morning, Agnes!" Tilly said to the woman as our substantial heels clicked down the tiled hall.

"Agnes," I said, nodding.

"Hold!" A boy shot around the corner and raced in the direction of the elevator. "*Hold!*" He frantically waved a wooden clipboard.

"And a typical good morning to you, J.P." Tilly sounded more ironic than cheerful, with this greeting.

"Morning, Miss Sanguinetti," he said, skidding to a halt. The kid looked fresh out of high school, tops, and thoroughly out of place in his argyle vest and an overcoat a little too large for him.

"J.P.," I repeated. The boy adjusted a skinny tie around his skinny neck.

For my efforts I won my second smile of the day. See? I could win friends and influence 1959ers. With-

44

out warning, the kid's hand shot out and landed on the wall beside me. He leaned in and leered. "Hiya, gorgeous." That horrible, intimate tone of voice implied volumes. Volumes co-written by Erica Jong and Henry Miller, that is. Comprehension began to dawn. I hadn't . . . ! The other Cathy couldn't have . . . ! Surely neither of us would . . . !

"Um, hi?" I said.

"Mama looks good this morning." Ick. The kid was half my size; I could knee him in the goolies with a simple twist of my hips. I twisted and got ready to strike.

"J.P., I'm letting this door close in precisely three seconds. One . . ." Good old Agnes, in the elevator. I always knew I liked her. "Two . . ." After a final, intimate curl of his upper lip, he was off and running, testicles intact, a mere cloud of dust and a *mneep-mneep!* away from being a human Road Runner.

"Ew," was my only comment.

Tilly had watched the proceedings with a grimace. "Fresh!" she said, resuming our trot around the corner and down the hallway. "You really should tell Mr. Richmond what a nuisance he is. I don't know if he'd let you fire his own nephew, but . . . Marcia! Good morning."

"Hi, Marcia," I said to a woman in plaid who had stepped out of a double doorway. RICHMOND BETTER HOME PUBLICATIONS, read its brass sign.

"But I think if he got enough complaints . . ." Tilly swung open the door into a massive office area filled with people—mostly women. It took a moment for me to identify the percussive noise assaulting my ears. Rain on the windows? Automatic rifle fire? No, it was the hum and rat-a-tat of several dozen electric typewriters arranged in columns and rows in a large, open space beyond the receptionist's desk where Tilly had

45

paused. Everything—the desks, the walls, the cabinets and work tables—was the same shade of dark oak. It probably was all very modern and slick, but my wide eyes looked at the scene like it was an antique postcard. Specifically, a reproduction of Alcatraz's lowest dungeon. I was a *typist?* In a—what did they call them in days of yore? In a *typing pool?* "Lois, I love that scarf," I heard Tilly say, as if from a distance.

"Nice scarf, Lois," I echoed without enthusiasm. I couldn't type on a typewriter! On a computer I was fine, given a lot of freedom to backspace, but typewriters had like, paper! And ribbons! And oh my God. What if someone needed me for dictation?

"Synin," I heard Tilly say.

The word brought me back to consciousness. I smiled at the pretty girl with the lacquered hair who sat behind the desk. "Yo, Synin," I said to her. Weird name. Maybe she was Swedish or something? "Wassup?"

A silence followed, during which both the receptionist and Tilly stared at me blankly. I was too absorbed contemplating the auto-da-fe of typewriter ribbon before me to realize for a moment how awkward the silence actually was. "Miss Voight?" the receptionist finally said. "Won't you *sign in?*"

"Miss Voight's never late, are you, Miss Voight?" boomed a voice from behind me while a masculine hand pushed away the time sheet the receptionist proffered. Good thing, too, because the flames reddening my face could have incinerated a whole payday's worth of records. "How are we today, Miss Sanguinetti?"

Tilly made a fine little dip with her knees as she giggled. "Just fine, Mr. Richmond."

"Jus' fiiiine?" He exaggerated Tilly's slight accent

into a thick drawl. So this was Richmond of Richmond Better Home Publications, was it? While my face cooled, I turned and gave him the ol' once-over. "Well, well, well. Chowmin' li'l Suthin'—belle, ain't she?" Much to my surprise, Tilly didn't kick him in the groin, as I would've. She merely smiled while he patted together his fingertips in delight, like a French waiter given an unusually *bon* gratuity. Physically, the guy was shaped like a cartoon penguin—round and smooth on top and rotund in the middle; he led with his belly when he turned. "And you, Miss Voight! Let a gentleman help you with your co . . . yes, there we go," he said, tugging at my overcoat. "We don't want you overheating and . . . well, my, don't we look . . . !" The man's pencil mustache bristled at the sight of me.

For a satisfying five seconds I thought I'd done a great job dressing myself with Cathy's Barbie doll classic wardrobe. Until I saw Tilly's face, anyway. Though she goggled at me in exactly the same manner as Richmond, I doubted they had the same thought in mind. "This old thing?" Hey, it worked in old sitcoms. Tilly rolled her eyes dramatically heavenward.

Mr. Richmond cleared his throat. "Indeed. Are you attending the opera after work? The ballet? Dinner at Passy? Oh-ho-ho, Miss Voight, don't tell me you've an interview with one of my rivals today!" I judged it best to mirror his coy laugh, the wink, and the waggled finger he gave me, as if I were in on the joke. It seemed to be working, thank God. We both winked, waggled, and giggled until I worried for our sanities. "Now, you go to your desk and work hard, Miss Voight," he said at last, when his final wink developed into a twitch. He tossed my coat to Tilly. "I expect *great* things from you later this week!"

"Oh, you'll *get* them!" I said in the same sugary-sweet, baby-talk cadences.

"I certainly *hope* so!"

"Don't you *worry!*"

"I surely *won't!*"

I'd had enough. "Well, I'll get to my—*yowwch!*" Many's the time as a kid I had beach trips ruined by crabs nipping at my toes in the surf. What I felt when I turned away from Mr. Richmond was exactly like that, only on my rear end. Holy cats, had my pervert boss *pinched* me?

I couldn't protest; Tilly was already dragging me past the receptionist's desk into the depths of the typing pool and beyond. Pretty head after pretty head turned as I passed; all typing ceased in my wake, replaced by whispering and the crackle of massive hairspray gravitational fields colliding. "That man *pinched* me!" I hissed.

"You should know better than to turn your back on Ol' Grabby Hands," Tilly said, sounding annoyed. "Cath, what has gotten into you?"

Someone else! I wanted to tell her. "He's a molester! Sexual harassment! Hey, why is everyone looking at me?"

We turned down a hallway past the secretarial pool. "Oh, I don't know. Maybe because *you wore your best evening dress to the office?*" Tilly halted and put her hands on her hips, looking mighty commanding for a mere munchkin. "Honestly! Black brocade? For work? Why not wear the furs that go with it, too?"

"I have furs?" I asked, intrigued. Painful memories of Ol' Grabby vanished for a moment. "Really?" Never mind that I didn't like fur. Wasn't it a big status symbol in this decade? And I had some?

Tilly marched on until we stepped into what at first

48

I thought was some kind of kind of school science lab. My heart sank. Maybe I was a lady nuclear physicist, of all the rotten luck! Then I realized that despite the young women running around the banks of soapstone counters in white coats and heels, I wasn't in a 007-type sexperimental laboratory. I was in a kitchen. The biggest kitchen I'd ever seen, in fact, with five identical rows of counters, each with its own cooktops, ovens, prep areas, and sinks. Several refrigerators stood at the room's end.

My spirits sank to depths oceanographers blanched at exploring. I was some kind of mid-century Rachael Ray! I would have been much more at home handling raw uranium.

"Really, Cathy!" With a tiny huff, Tilly handed back my coat and started removing her own. She didn't seem too angry. Her mood was a bit like watching a Chihuahua trying to growl down a pit bull. "If you didn't feel well enough to come in today, you should have said so!" She exchanged her coat for a wee lab coat from a hook near the door. "Coming in to work in a Dimanche Soeurs formal. You couldn't have . . . ?" Suddenly she cleared her throat and busied herself with her buttons. "On'tday ooklay ehindbay ouyay. It'sway Esterchay."

"Huh?"

I wasn't up on my Pork Latin or whatever, though I'd caught the nod in the direction over my shoulder easily enough. Naturally, I turned, only to hear Tilly let out an anguished groan at my stupidity. "Ladies! Lovely ladies!" A titan in white zoomed our way. "Miss Matilda. Don't you look . . . *zut alors!* Words cannot suffice!"

Remember *Bewitched*? That show with the blond simp who could wiggle her nose and *poof!* There'd be a thirty-course banquet and hunky catering squad, yet for some reason she wanted to scrub the toilets of her whiny-ass husband? Well, this guy bore an uncanny resemblance to Dr. Bombay, down to the stocky build and the mustache bristling like cat whiskers atop his lip. His mannerisms, though? One hundred percent, bona fide Uncle Arthur.

I watched with fascination as he glided past me on light feet, seized Tilly's hand, and raised it to his mouth as if he planned to suck in the fingers like so much spaghetti. Was there something romantic going on here? No, judging from Tilly's flushed expression, I was guessing schoolgirl crush. "Oh, Mr. Hamilton." She giggled.

Standing there in my Disomething-or-other Sewers finery, I felt something of a third wheel. "Well," I announced when the hand slobbering had gone on for quite some time. "I'll mosey on along to . . ." Oh, hell. I didn't have a clue where to mosey. Did I have a lab coat? Should I hover around in the background? None of the young women bustling around seemed to want to take Tilly's place as guide.

Luckily, right as I was considering taking my chances with The Pincher, Esterchay took pity. "Allow me, Miss Voight," he said, striding a few doors down the room's perimeter where, in bold letters, read the words:

MISS CATHY VOIGHT
RICHMOND SIGNATURE LINE

I threw a little fiesta in my head, complete with frozen margaritas and mariachi band. I wasn't in the typing pool! I had my own office! I was a Richmond Signature Line, whatever that was. It could be the thin blue line or even the Rock Island line for all I cared. Because I had an office! I escaped into it gratefully, but not before I heard Tilly's swain call out, "Miss Matilda, I have a proposition for you, if you're not busy tonight." I shut the door and let the lovebirds coo.

Maybe Tilly had been right about my selection of daywear. It wasn't exactly work-comfortable, good as it made Mama look, especially with my suddenly terrific figure busting out all over. Same old me—completely new pizzazz! You wouldn't catch Nancy Drew sleuthing in brocade, though. Not that there really was much to snoop for. Cathy Voight's office was even more stripped of anything truly personal than her room had been. No toys on her desk, no correspondence on her shelves, no trinkets on her wall, no packets of mustard in her drawers. Did they even have packets of mustard back then? Now? Either way, I didn't have a clue.

Weird. Definitely weird. What kind of person had such a barren office that if she disappeared, her successor wouldn't be able to tell a thing about her?

It was after a moment's thought and a memory of the nearly empty box I'd carted home from Motive the night before that I came up with the answer. Me. That's what kind of person.

Still, there had to be something. I went back to my investigations and over the course of the next few minutes, began an inventory of a life, finding:

1. Five pads of paper, one small tin of paper clips, seventeen pencils, and three pens with some kind of weird claw tip I'd never seen before.
2. One handkerchief that came in handy for mopping up the inevitable accidental weird claw tip ink pen spill.

3. One pocket calendar, utterly void of any entries, though someone had taken great care to X out the days that had already passed.

I heard the sound of my latch on the far wall. A man walked in. He waited for the door to swing shut before he spoke. "Well?"

Okay. I was on my own here. The guy had caught me at the desk, feeling the undersides of drawers to check for any secret taped packets of papers I ought to know about—because frankly, for someone with as much home and business stationery as Cathy Voight, she surely wasn't keeping any of the mail she received. I gave the guy a quick once-over. Mid-thirtyish. Nice suit. Clean-cut, in a dark and glowering kind of way. The monobrow was kind of off-putting, as were the bristly ear-hairs, but his eyes were large and the lids heavy, if you liked that kind of thing. "Hello," I said carefully, trying to sound cool and businesslike.

"Hello?" he echoed, shaking his head. "That's dandy, Cathy. Hello."

"Good morning?" The guy was confusing me. Maybe he was one of those abrupt types with no social skills.

"And you had to wear *that*?" He held out his hand in my direction. "Why, Cathy? Why?"

I gave my dress a quick once-over. "It's an original."

"It's an or—" Okay, whatever I said seemed to get him miffed, somehow. He swore quietly to himself. "*You're* an original, Cathy. That's what you are. A pure, unadulterated, Goddamned original."

Again, I had nothing. "Thanks!" I said at last. Perhaps it was my delivery, but the word made the guy freeze, then spin on the heels of his polished wing tips and dash out of my office. Hmmm. Friend? Foe? Secret cross-dresser with a thing for brocade? No clue. I went back to my investigations.

4. On the bookshelf was an entire row of titles devoted to cookery. The highlights: <u>Fast, Fun, Fondue!</u>, <u>Casserole Cooking with Campbell's</u>, <u>The Hungry Hungarian</u>, <u>Late-Night Supper Soirees</u>, and <u>Bachelors Are Eaters, Too.</u>

5. One Roget's thesaurus.

6. One covered typewriter on its own table. Covered with a thin layer of dust, that is. And it would continue to be so if I had anything to say about it.

7. One folder containing a typed recipe for Polynesian Pork Chops that began with the ominous words, <u>In a large baking pan, arrange sixteen pork chops and cover with three cans of canned apricots, three cans of fruit cocktail, one cup of sweet pickle juice, and one bottle of maraschino cherries</u>, and an accompanying handwritten note that read, <u>Miss Voight, please let me know if you have any changes. M.</u>

The door opened again, revealing a box with legs. "Where do these go, Miss?" asked a gruff, masculine voice.

I struggled to my feet, trying to identify the person who surely had to be hidden behind the enormous bulk of brown cardboard. "Hold on a sec!" I heard from a higher and reedier throat. A youth darted through the doorway and squeezed his slender frame by and underneath the guy hefting the box, straightening up so he could lead the guy over to the far corner.

"Put her down over there," the kid instructed. He turned to me with a wink that left me feeling oily all over. "Don't worry, Mama. Your loverboy's got it all under control."

"J.P.," I said, dredging up the kid's name. Did sexual harassment count for nothing in this decade? Less than an hour and a half on the job, and I'd been mama-ed and drooled over enough for a lifetime from this twerp, and his uncle's pinch had probably left marks. I was going to have to teach these Richmond boys a lesson or two. "About you calling me 'mama.'"

"Don't worry, beautiful. You can call me your baby boy. Spank me if you wanna." My little vision in woolen argyle accompanied his words with a demonstration on himself, slapping his freckly hand against the flattest butt I've ever seen on a guy. "Oh yeah!" He ran past the second deliveryman entering my office with another box, disappeared for a moment, and returned bearing a cardboard cup. "Coffee, doll. Three sugars and cream, the way you like it." I suppressed a shudder. Sugar in coffee was sacrilege . . . but we were talking about a woman who had a recipe for pork chops so sweet they would rot the teeth of a marble statue. "Keep bringing 'em in, boys," he instructed the men with the boxes. "Hope you enjoy," he said with a toothy grin. "I'll be back to see if you need anything later. And I do mean, *anything.*"

"What—?" A third and fourth container joined the other two, and the deliverymen exited with J.P. to retrieve even more. "I'm sorry, I don't . . . This isn't . . . Hello!"

"Oh, hi!" Thank God. Tilly's familiar face made the invasion of the deliverymen a little more bearable. "Guess what?" She bounced on her miniature tiptoes.

"Lindsay Lohan finally ate a sandwich?" She stared at me blankly. "What, Tilly?" I asked, defeated.

She beckoned me to lean closer as another pair of boxes made their way into the room. "He asked me out!" she trilled. "Chester! Finally! Tomorrow night! Oh, I'm so excited! You'll have to help me pick out something to . . ." She took another gander at my evening dress and hastily amended, "I don't know what I'll wear!"

Theoretically delighted as I was for my flatmate, I was still overwhelmed by boxes. "Guys, how many more of these *are* there?" I asked the deliverymen.

"We're going to a movie—well, an old movie, *A Star Is Born*, but I never saw it—and he says after he'll take me to a funny little hole in the wall in the Village."

"That's the last of them," said the first deliveryman, nodding as he exited. Panicked, I stared at the ten, eleven . . . twelve boxes now in a hulking stack nearby.

"But what *are* they?" I still wanted to know.

"Why, they're the Tiny Minnie Snack Cakes delivery, silly." I stared at Tilly, not comprehending what she'd said. Tiny Minnies? The delicious golden snack cake injected with strawberry filling that reputedly had a shelf life of seventy-two years and that had proved a veritable comfort food staple of my college days? And I had an office full of them? Had I gone to heaven? Tilly, in the meantime, was again growing exasperated with my thickheadedness. "For your new cookbook!" she exclaimed, gesturing toward my bookcase.

Oh, no. Oh, hell no! Like a jigsaw puzzle assembled by a hundred invisible hands, all the pieces fell into place. I ran over to the built-in shelf by my desk, grabbed *Late-Night Supper Soirees,* and flipped to the first page, where I read:

> How many times have <u>you</u> had night owl chums arrive to your high-rise flat at the decadent hour of eleven P.M., hungry for both food and perhaps a gay late-night round of pinochle? If you're a young modern and want the quickest, the tastiest, and the choicest recipes . . .

My eyes flipped to the credits page. *Another fine cookbook of Richmond Better Homes Publications Signature Line.* My heart sank. *Matilda Sanguinetti, Head Kitchen Assistant,* it said halfway down, among a number of other names. And there, right at the top beneath a luridly photographed saucepan of what looked like plum flambé surrounded by canned apricots, was the evidence I'd sought earlier: *Cathy Voight, Author and Recipes Creator.*

I wasn't a Rachael Ray. I was this year's freakin' Martha Stewart. And a trailer-trash Martha Stewart at that. Wouldn't Thuy have been proud?

"Isn't it divoon?" Tilly asked. "About my date, I mean."

"Yeah," I agreed, head reeling. "Absolutely divoon."

Chapter Four

<u>Cathy's To-Do List:</u>
<u>There's No Place Like Home (So Please, Let Me Figure
Out How to Get There)</u>

1. Okay. In <u>Back to the
Future</u>, Michael J. Fox
heads to the fifties and
gets his parents together
and then manages to get
back to his girlfriend in
time for the prom or whatever.

1. Your parents are hap-
pily married and at this
moment your dad is, like,
a toddler in Kalamazoo
and your mom isn't even
a zygote. Besides, you
don't have a boyfriend
to get back to, nor do you
have a well-timed bolt of
lightning and a DeLorean
to propel you decades
forward.

2. Okay.   Remember
<u>Peggy Sue Got Married</u>?
She went back to high

2. You didn't get sent
back to high school. If
you'd been sent back

school and once she fixed all her problems, poof! Back home again.

to high school, your biggest problem would have been whether to take Alanis Morrisette or the Hootie and the Blowfish T-shirt to summer camp. You got sent back to 1959. What in the world can you fix in 1959? You don't even know who's president. Anyway, Kathleen Turner ended up with Nicholas Cage wearing a prosthetic honker. Like his real one isn't horrifying enough. You want that happening to you, seriously?

3. Okay, in 12 Monkeys . . .

3. Ooooh. Don't start on 12 Monkeys. It made our head hurt, remember? And Brad Pitt totally never took off his shirt.

4. But my point is that in all these movies the people end up back in time so they can fix things that have gone wrong. Maybe that's why I'm here.

4. Bruce Willis died in 12 Monkeys. Now, in Kate and Leopold . . .

5. Oh my God, Hugh Jackman.

5. I know! That's what I'm talking about!

6. Although not <u>van Helsing</u> so much.

6. If you're going to cast Brad Pitt in a film, you should make him take off his shirt. Am I right?

The problem with my roommates, I decided, was that they constantly made me feel underdressed. Or even undressed. I mean, I was accustomed to flinging myself through my front door in the evenings and leaving behind a trail of future dry cleaning as I rocketed my way toward the comfy sweats I kept folded at the foot of my bed. These dames, though! Even at their sloppiest, they looked like freakin' *Mademoiselle* models, swanning their wasp-waisted selves down a linoleum catwalk. On this particular night they were holding a hushed conversation in the kitchenette, both dressed to the nines for their dates—Tilly in a smart little gray number with a black patent leather belt cinching a waist roughly the size of my wrist, and Miranda looking absolutely dreamy in jade. "*You* remember him! He asked me out over the summer, during that month in the Catskills I spent singing at Grossinger's."

"No, I swear I don't." Tilly nervously checked her face in the back of a serving spoon.

"The amnesia seems to be spreading. Or else you've been hanging around our psychiatric case too much." Miranda said the words with the conspiratorial hush of a KGB agent whispering, "*The cock crows at midnight, comrade.*"

"Miranda Rosenberg, you're awful."

"Speaking of Cathy, how is . . . ?"

Maybe I started a little at the sound of my name, or perhaps Tilly simply happened to look up right then and see me standing in the kitchen door, wearing the fuzzy white monogrammed bathrobe I'd found in the bathroom, complete with matching slippers. Either way, they both stepped away from the clandestine huddle and covered their faces with forced cheer. "There you are!" Tilly sounded like a mom trying to pretend her four-year-old hadn't caught her playing Santa on Christmas Eve. She gazed at my casual attire. "All relaxed? Did you take another purple pill, honey?"

Miranda, abashed, made a show of tidying her hair and plumping her blond sable. Her tiny blond sable, I noticed. More of a furry maxi pad, if you asked me, or a sewer rat pelt. I'd had a chance to discover the black mink wrap in Cathy's tiny closet—carelessly thrown in, by the looks of it—and with an expert eye, I could tell that my fur was much, much more lavish. Mine was big, for one thing. A girl could really snuggle in it on a cold night, or wrap it around her shoulders and roll around on the bed and pretend that she was Grace Kelly. Not that I had done such a thing. More than twice, anyway. The third time, I guiltily thought of clubbed baby seals, decided I was the bastard offspring of Cruella de Vil and Veruca Salt, and decided that rolling around on a twin mattress would only lead to disaster in the end, anyway. "I thought I'd stay in tonight, curl up with the TiVo, maybe a glass of wine. I mean, not the TiVo. You don't have TiVo. Nobody does, nowadays." Both girls stared at me without expression. "Did I say TiVo? I meant, I'll probably watch some Beaver on the TV. Oh." Eep. Even in these pre–public access days, that didn't come out sounding so good. "Watch something on the TV, anyway. Don't worry about me. Go on. You guys have fun!"

"As I was saying . . ." Miranda shook her head and gave Tilly yet another mystified stare. I'd seen plenty of those during the past two and a half days. "*My* date is the guy I met over the summer. Harold. A banker. Stable as hell but bo-ring!" Miranda scooped up the mangy little sable and draped it over her shoulders. One side slid right off. Amateur! "He's taking me to one of the last previews of a show about singing nuns, of all things. Singing nuns! *Quelle* trash. It opens Monday. And it'll close by Friday, I'll lay you twenty."

"If they can have singing Gypsy Rose Lee, they can have singing nuns, I suppose," said Tilly. "What's the name of this thing?"

"Oh, I don't know. Something about music."

I had to break in. "*The Sound of Music*?" I asked. "How do you solve a problem like Maria? Silver white winters that melt into springs? So long, farewell, *auf wiedersehen*, good night? Me, a name I call myself?" They were gawking at me again, but I didn't care. When you grow up with repeats of Julie Andrews and Christopher Plummer on the TV all the time, you tend to think of a movie as kind of an institution. Being someplace where it was an unknown quantity—where the original show hadn't even yet opened!—made me feel very, very off-kilter. "High on the hill lived a lonely goatherd? Edelweiss?" I finished lamely. "I mean, I hear it's good. A classic, even."

"Hmmm." Miranda looked at me like I was a slab of pork bristling with trichinosis, and changed subjects. "Doubtful. Tilly's man sounds much more interesting. Didn't I always say you'd meet someone at work?"

While I slumped down onto the sofa, idly looking around for the remote control, the girls followed me through the swinging door into the living room. Tilly pulled on her own pretty wool evening coat. "Oh, I hope I don't do anything to ruin the evening. Chester is so worldly." At Miranda's encouraging noises as she inspected her face in the mirror, Tilly continued. "Do you know he and Jason from the art department call each other 'Gladys'?"

"Tilly," I said from the sofa, not really wanting to look her in the face. "None of this rings any warning bells for you?"

"What kind of warning bells? It's just a little game! He says all his friends do it, downtown. And they're very artistic. Why, one of his friend's friends designs gowns for Jacqueline Bouvier, and some people say she's going to be the next First Lady!"

"Okay, finally a topic where I have some expertise." I cleared my throat and prepared to explain. Poor Tilly. I'd had plenty of girlfriends who had done the gay boyfriend routine over and over again. I mean, heck. Even I had dated Oliver Wendt in college and afterwards he'd come out of the closet flamier than every male cast member and very special guest star on *Will and Grace,* multiplied by the spirit of Waylon Flowers and Madame. And then there had been Chaz Martin. Why hadn't I seen through his act? Or Ricky Lee Vogelstein? Or Adam . . . what was his name? But this was Tilly's mistake we were talking about, not mine. "With the boys it always starts off with nice little dinners and nights at the theater. Then it's them and you hitting Marie's Crisis three nights a week, and it's all fun and laughs, true. Believe you me, though, it's a short step in pink pumps from listening to too many renditions of 'Don't Rain On My Parade' to being reduced to utter irrelevance as the only girl sitting on the sidelines at the Big Cup while the boys ogle each other on Tight T-shirt night, which if memory serves me correctly was every night, thank you very much, *Adam Lucas*." I remembered the schmuck's name now. "You don't want that, do you?"

"N-no, I don't think so." Tilly gulped, backing away, fingers searching for her purse on the mantel. "What is she talking about?" she hissed in a panic at Miranda.

"Hold up," I said, pausing. She'd said something to arrest my attention. "Jacqueline Bouvier? Jackie O? Who is president, exactly?"

Uh-oh, said my flatmate's exchanged glances. *Here she goes again.* "It's Mr. Eisenhower, honey." Eisenhower! He'd been the one I'd tried to remember. Honest! Though Tilly had been ready to leave, both she and Miranda paused by the door, gloves neatly lying across the palms of their hands, hats pinned on snugly. "You voted for him, remember?"

"But Kennedy's running the next time around? When is that, exactly? Sometime soon?" I asked, reaching back to the dim recesses of my high school American Government classes. "Excellent," I whispered, happy to wedge myself a little more firmly in the course of human events.

"Funny you should say *that*." Miranda raised a single eyebrow. I envied people who could pull off that particular move. "Since just last week you were trying to get us to save our votes for Nixon."

"I'm a *Nixon supporter?*" I groaned and flopped down onto my back. What worse final blow could a time-traveling girl ask for? "Oh, the indignity!" He was the one behind that scandal, right? The Watercress thing? I'd thought that was later on.

"Yes. Well." Miranda opened the door to the stairwell, adjusted the eentsy-weentsy scrap of hamster fur that I'd been itching to tug back onto her shoulder, and swept through the doorway. "Think about that next year when it comes time to vote again. You could make a difference."

Tilly scampered out without a word. They both seemed anxious to leave, as if I might be contagious, though what in the world they could catch from me other than verbal diarrhea I had no idea. I set my lips, concentrated on the television with its mighty eight-inch screen, and listened to the old stairs pop and creak beneath my flatmates' weight as they descended. By the time I'd lunged from the sofa to yell down after them, "There's no remote!" followed by the plaintive postscript of "And there's only *three channels!*", they were already gone.

It was with a thoroughly grumpy attitude that I stomped back to my bedroom. What was I supposed to *do*, all by myself on a wintry evening in 1959? I couldn't cozy up with a DVD or even an old VHS tape, because neither had yet been invented. I couldn't call Thuy and yammer at her on my cell phone for the same reason, plus the whole thing about her not being born for another twenty-something years. As I'd realized the day before at work, I couldn't Google online recipes for Tiny Minnie snack cakes to adapt as my own. And though I was absolutely starving and hadn't had anything to eat all day save for a roast beef sandwich and more Tiny Minnies than I cared to admit, I was too nervous about subjecting myself to another attempt at cuisine and catapulting myself back to the middle of the St. Valentine's Day Massacre or right smack dab in the middle of the Black Plague.

No, I didn't know what century the latter was in.

"I can't make a bit of difference," I grumped to the teddy bear that Tilly kept on her bed. She and Miranda shared a room; their twin beds stretched out perpendicular to each other. A nightstand with a lamp occupied the corner where their pillows lay. Unlike Cathy Voight's sterile ball-fringed cell, their abode was cheerful and even slightly messy. Pairs of shoes peeked out from beneath the white bedclothes, and Miranda's makeup table was cluttered with jewelry and old playbills. "What can I do?" Mr. Teddy didn't have any answers for me.

Then it hit me. With my vast knowledge of the future, I should be able to do *something*. I could prevent disasters! *Oh, of course, it really was nothing, Mr. President*, I'd say. *Anyone who makes a study of current trends could have predicted it. Oh, no, a medal's really not necessary!* I could become an expert on disasters like . . . um. Like . . . well. Miniskirts on women over fifty. Ooh, and feathered hair. And Yoko! I could so totally stop Yoko. Yet no one gave out presidential medals for keeping Japanese performance artists away from the Beatles, did they? No, I didn't think so. Man! Everything I knew was so scattershot—a handful of cultural references here, a bucket of trivia there. Here I was, careening toward thirty, and although I had a mind full of tiny factoids that had served me well enough in the advertising world for years, I lacked the slightest context for most of them. Why hadn't I picked up anything important, all these years? Names. Birth dates. Death dates. *Something*.

Oh wait. Death dates. Maybe there was something I could do that might change a life! Oh my gosh, what if what I'd been sent back to do wasn't to find my Nicholas Cage or get my parents to fall in love with each other (come 1974, a Kappa Alpha frat party and a couple of bongs would take care of that handily enough), but actually to set right a historical wrong?

My idea sounded better the more I thought it over. Besides, all that engraved stationery in Cathy's drawer would go to waste if I was left to correspond with people I actually knew, right? It only took me a moment to settle myself at the shallow white wood desk and start a letter:

Dear Mr. Kenne

Crap! Didn't Cathy believe in ballpoints? Somehow I'd managed to splotch ink all over the page. Cathy's preference for these weird pens was going to be the death of me. One crumpled ball of paper later, I gave it another go.

Dear Mr. Kennedy,
    My name is Cathy ~~Voor~~ Voight

Because, you know, that's the kind of person a future president listens to. One who doesn't even know her last name.

Dear Mr. Kennedy,
    My name is Cathy Voight and strange as it may sound, I would like to warn you about something that will happen to you in Dallas.

Much better. Once I got on a roll, I really knew how to keep it going. Sure, a couple of my details might have been on the questionable side. Back home

66

at Motive, we had fact checkers to deal with the trivia. Here, I had to wing it a little, but pretty soon, I'd filled up several of the smooth, ivory sheets with my own painfully out-of-practice script. It still looked like I'd long held some undisclosed grudge against my stationery and decided to carve it up with a butcher's knife, but for the most part, I was absorbed enough in the task that I actually found myself enjoying this new noble calling.

So engrossed was I in the task at hand that I didn't notice the rapping sound in the distance, faint but insistent as a woodpecker with a single-minded mission. For a moment I thought it might be the instant messaging program that Thuy and I gossiped across, some nights when neither of us felt like going out on the town. Then my mind drifted back to the present (whichever present I happened to be in) and I jumped to my feet. "Coming!" I yelled to whomever was bruising his knuckles against our door.

Weird that these girls didn't have much in the way of security for their apartment—a lock in the knob and one of those old-fashioned chains was all that stood between me and any hatchet-wielding Jack Nicholson types who might happen to wander into the townhouse. I mean, not even a peephole! It was with a little trepidation that finally I cracked open the door. "Hello?"

A pair of eyes regarded me from the dim hallway. "Miss Voight?" I heard. There was something definitely familiar about the voice.

"Yes?" I asked. I knew that the '50s were when people allegedly left their doors on the latch, even at night, never locked their car doors, and baked cakes for each other at the drop of a hat—from scratch—but

I was a dyed-in-the-wool twenty-first-century New York and knew better. When the man on the other side didn't immediately answer, fear dropped my voice by a menacing half-octave. "If you want your testicles to remain intact, you'd better get the hell out of here. I've got a Rottweiler. And pepper spray."

My intruder sounded more amused than intimidated. "Do you really have a Rottweiler?"

I knew that voice! "Oh," I said, swinging open the door. "It's you!" Kind of pathetic that I was excited to see Flaky Pete, the repairman who'd been the first person I'd met here, but I was a gal all on her own on a Friday night in a strange decade, and he was male, broad-shouldered, and had that cute little chin dimple. What're you gonna do? "Come on in!" I said, reasonably sure that if he hadn't jumped me the last time when I'd been dressed up and pretty, my mile-thick fuzzy robe certainly wasn't going to incite him to ravishment.

He edged into the room. "Because I'm pretty sure that dogs aren't allowed on your lease." My Friday-night garb must have caught his eye, because he paused. "Say, you look . . ."

"I think *casual* is the word we can safely use," I said, leading him in the direction of the kitchenette. "You're lucky you got here before Curler Torture Time. That's when I take curlers—wire curlers, mind you, not the spongy kind that probably aren't much better but at least look softer—and wrap my hair around them until my scalp screams bloody murder and tears run from my eyes, all so I don't dare set my head on a pillow when I sleep. It's in here. You probably know that." I gestured in the direction of the far wall.

"I have a theoretical knowledge of curlers, thanks," he said, pushing by me. Poor guy; a little cowlick ruined the perfection of his crew cut, right at the crown of his head. Through his glasses he peered around the tiny crawl space of a kitchen as if searching for something. "Where is it?"

"Right there." Poor Guy Part Two: Electric Boogaloo. Was he so myopic that he couldn't see the percolator where it sat on the counter's edge? "In front of you."

"The Rottweiler?"

For a moment we stared at each other in such confusion that when I burst out laughing, blank relief washed over his face. "Sorry," I said. "I don't really have a Rottweiler. I like dogs. I'm a dog person. But if I had one, I'd have to walk it. And I don't do, you know, weather. Anyway. There it is," I said, gesturing at the defunct fount of all things caffeinated and wiggling my fingers. "All yours. Work your percolator voodoo, repairman."

Part of me was aware I sounded like I was babbling. Maybe I was; part of me was so overwhelmed at having been alone that I was filling up silence with noise. He stared at me patiently during my nervous outburst, finally saying in a tone most grave, "You think I'm a repairman?"

"You're not?" His question caught me off guard. Why else was he here? Hadn't he said he was a repairman, the first time we'd met? Maybe not. In fact, he hadn't said much of anything during those times I hadn't been ranting at him for being a necrophiliac fetish goth video ringmaster or for stealing my perfume inserts.

"Miss Voight, I live here." He raised his eyebrows,

as if puzzled he had to remind me. "Downstairs. Tilly and Miranda asked me to look in on you."

"Oh, I know," I said loftily, lying through my teeth. What a simp I was! Neither time had the guy seemed to carry a toolbox or wear a uniform that might make him look like the lonely Maytag repair guy. Then again, you hear a guy talk about having been in your kitchen taking a look at wires and things, and you kind of assume that he's there for an official purpose, especially after you've been hit in the head by a microwave oven and shot back four and a half decades in time. Am I right? "I thought you were . . . handy," I finished vaguely, uncertain how to proceed. Then something struck me as odd about the way he'd addressed me a moment before. "You keep calling me *Miss Voight*. You call my flatmates by their names, though. First names. What's up with that?"

"You really have an unusual way of talking." The guy's eyes glanced at me, then slid away.

I knew awkwardness when I saw it. "You're evading."

He was, too. He leaned against the counter and looked up at the ceiling. "I guess I call your friends by their names because they asked me to."

"And I didn't," I concluded for him. He didn't deny it. The sympathetic assent on his face told me everything I needed to know. Oh, Cathy. What in the world have you been doing with your life? "I'm kind of a chilly bitch sometimes."

That got his attention. The guy was chivalry itself, leaping to protect me even when I wouldn't defend myself. "No, I wasn't saying that. You've never told me I *had* to call you Miss Voight."

"But you did. Come on," I urged him. "What else

do I do? Snub you when I pass by in the vestibule? Not recognize you out in the street? Sprinkle you with my wet umbrella when it's raining? Not remember your name?"

He folded his arms. For a guy who looked like he'd moments earlier stepped out of a pocket protector print ad, he had a nice square jaw that he could jut to good effect. The defensiveness of his stance told me that I wasn't far from the mark. "It's Hank. Cabot?"

"Hank Cabot. I knew that," I said smoothly, then followed it up with a less-than-ept, "Hank? Really?" Who was named Hank? "I mean, I always thought it was Henry. Hank's a nice name. There are a lot of nice people named Hank. Hank Aaron, the guy with the home runs. Um, Hank Williams, Jr."

"Hank Ketcham," he said, not uncrossing his arms. When I shook my head, he added, "He draws Dennis the Menace."

"Oh! You have Dennis the Menace? I know who that is. Dumb comic. Only Family Circus out-lames it." Whoops. Back on topic, girl. "Tom Hanks! No, never mind. You wouldn't have him yet. Listen, Hank," I said impulsively. The guy had suffered at my alter ego's hands long enough. "About the rudeness. I used to do all those things, but I'm a different woman now. Ever since the other night—yes, that's exactly it! Ever since the other night I've been seeing things in an entirely different perspective. So, yeah. I think you'll find me a more approachable Cathy from now on. Cathy. Not Miss Voight. Okay?"

He inspected me closely, as if trying to decide whether or not I might be mocking him. Poor guy. His height and broad-shouldered build far outweighed any of the negatives—the cowlick, the glasses, the memory of the dandruff that he seemed to have been very careful to remove, tonight. I felt sorry for the poor guy. *Cathy Voight*, I thought to myself, *you've got a lot to answer for.* "Have you eaten?" he asked unexpectedly. I shook my head. "I was making myself dinner. Spaghetti and wine. If I asked you downstairs . . . ?"

I wasn't going to give him a chance to change his mind. "I'll never shake my umbrella on you again, I swear. Hey." In my excitement, I'd forgotten the papers in my hand. "You wouldn't happen to know how much postage is for a letter, would you?"

I knew that expression by now, the tread-lightly-there's-a-woman-on-the-verge-of-a-nervous-break-down glazed-over countenance. Almost everyone I'd encountered in the past forty-eight hours had worn it at one time or another. But hey, I couldn't remember how much postage was in my own time, so I didn't feel too badly. "Four cents," he said at last.

Wow. Cheap. No wonder people wrote so many letters back then. "Fantastic. Exactly what I thought." He cocked his head, raised his eyebrows, and then nodded for me to follow. Before he could get away, though, I called out, "Um. Do you have any stamps I could borrow?"

"Sure," he said over his shoulder.

"And envelopes?"

"Why not?"

By now I was padding after him in my fluffy slippers like a live-action remake of *Make Way for Duck-lings*. "And then can you tell me where the nearest mailbox is?"

I Went to Vassar for This?

I didn't know much about algebra. I'd sucked at it in high school, and had been so bad at trigonometry that Ms. Bibby had to call my parents and gently suggest a tutor. One simple equation I did know, however, and that was *Me x My Mouth = Pathetic*.

What I'm usually good at, though, is picking up clues about people from their surroundings. It's all part of the advertising bug. Ordinary people in a crowd see simply a mass of unconnected bodies, while those of us stricken with marketing sickness are busily making little lists and classifying everyone according to their demographics. I could tell several things right off the bat about Hank, once we'd entered his place through the big door off the downstairs hallway:

1. This was a man who was used to living by himself. Papers were scattered all over. Paperback novels piled perilously on the coffee and end tables, despite the empty gaps in the glass-fronted bookcases. Albums—actual vinyl LPs— overflowed from a metal stand holding a record player one horn short from being a Victrola. The place wasn't a mess, exactly, but it certainly showed all the signs of being lived in by a single man who didn't notice a little bit of muddle.

2. Something about the apartment really wasn't Hank. I barely knew the guy, but if I'd had to go out shopping on a charity spree after a freak tornado struck his place, I would've picked out tables and chairs from the closest IKEA— not the fussy Victorian stuff his place sported. Was he renting the space furnished? It looked like atop a big fancy loaf of marble-topped ta-

bles and dainty-legged seats was a peanut-butter smear of practical, goofy Hank. I would have guessed that either he'd not been here long, or that he didn't plan to stay forever.

3. The guy had a thing for comic book women. Specifically, long-legged Wonder Woman–type babes in brightly colored bustiers, superhero boots, and a fascinating assortment of space-age headgear. No less than five illustration boards of them graced his fireplace mantel, all in feisty poses, mammaries amplified to eye-popping, Pamela Anderson–sized magnitude.

I couldn't help wondering whether he was a little bit of a fetish perv after all, with those *things* hovering right over the dining table, waiting as he futzed around in a kitchenette even smaller than the one we had upstairs. "So if you were John F. Kennedy," I called out, trying to ignore the busty bombshell in red and yellow tights levitating closest to where I sat toying with the envelopes and stamps I'd duped out of him, "where do you think you'd be living right about now?"

His head poked around the corner, glasses slightly fogged from the vapor. "You wrote John F. Kennedy a letter?" he asked.

I wasn't at all put off by the mildly bewildered tone to his voice. After a couple of days in this place, it was beginning to sound homey. "Well sure," I said. "He's going to be the next president, right?"

My buddy had disappeared again. I heard the sound of pots scraping across the elements on the stove. "He could. I don't know if it's definite or anything. He hasn't announced that he's running yet."

"Oh, he's going to."

Maybe I sounded too confident. Hank stepped out of the kitchen with his arms crossed. "I thought you had some kind of job writing cookbooks," he said, cocking his head. "You know something I don't?" When I startled, he added, "About politics?"

For a second, he'd nearly made me jump out of my skin. "Just because I write enormous cookbooks about fifty recipes made better by cooking in tinfoil baskets doesn't mean that I don't know a thing or two about politics, mister."

"Great!" Good. I'd won his respect. I might have to come up with recipes involving Twinkie lookalikes, but that didn't make me one of them. "What do you think about DiSalle's chances, then?"

"Um." Uh-oh. I gulped, bit my lip, and at last managed a wan smile. "It's a very good university?"

"The one in Philadelphia?" I nodded, grateful that he knew what I was talking about. "That's *La Salle*. I meant Michael Vincent DiSalle. From Ohio?"

I cleared my throat, mortified. "So how about that address, Mr. Smarty-Pants Telephone Directory for the Greater New York Tri-State Area?"

He laughed. I stared at him in astonishment. Hank didn't have one of those gruff, manly-man laughs that guys with his deep bass typically have, nor did he let out a rough bark of amusement. Instead, he snarfed. He sucked in a huge draft of air through his nostrils in a sudden burst, then doubled over in silent, belly-shaking chuckles. It was such a little-boy's laugh that I couldn't help but grin. "Good one," he said, still shaking slightly as he walked back into the kitchen. "La Salle!" I was grumbling to myself and wondering how rude it might be simply to disappear back upstairs when he called out, "You could try the U.S. Capitol. But when I wrote Kennedy . . ."

"What?" I couldn't believe my ears. "What'd you write him about?"

"It was after *Profiles in Courage* came out, but before it got the Pulitzer. I read it after I got out of the army. It was probably a silly letter, in retrospect, but . . ."

"Did you write him to say Texans weren't noted for their hospitality?" The fates would be smiling on me too much to send me a fellow time-traveler.

It took him a moment to answer. "What? No, it was kind of a fan letter. I loved that book. It really changed my life. Anyway, I sent it to his publisher. Harper and Brothers. Got a letter back, too. Probably a form letter, but it made my day."

"Harper . . . and . . . Brothers," I said, laboriously writing it on the front of the envelope. "How about a zip code?"

"A what?" he called out.

"Zip—? Never mind," I added. Apparently I'd landed BZ—Before Zip-coding. "I don't suppose you've ever heard of Martin Luther King, Jr., huh?"

"Well, sure. You're writing to him, too?"

The incredulousness in his voice made me slightly haughty. "I keep telling you, I'm a new Cathy. A political Cathy who wants to reach out to the future leaders of your time."

"My time?"

"Our time," I hastily corrected.

"Try, *Reverend Martin Luther King, Dexter Avenue Baptist Church, Montgomery, Alabama.*"

His voice sounded confident enough, so I wrote it down. "No street address?"

"How many Dexter Avenues could there be in Montgomery? I'll be right back." He reappeared with what at first I thought were several baskets in his hands, but then I saw that they seemed to be some kind of wicker-wrapped dark bottles with stubby candles jutting from their necks. "Don't be alarmed. I never get to use these." He set the decorations on the table and, from seemingly nowhere, whipped out a safety match that sputtered to life as he struck it on the side of its box. "By alarmed, I meant, don't assume that with the candlelight and the wine that I'm trying to seduce you."

"Oh, I wasn't." Was I mistaken, or did my flat and unhesitating denial draw from him a disappointed twitch of the lips? Poor guy, wanting to be Superman when really he was more of a Clark Kent. "What wine?" I asked. So charged was my voice with hope that it probably could have registered on a Geiger counter. *Clunk.* A third wicker-wrapped bottle joined the other two, this one without the candles. "Perfect," I said, trying not to lick my chops like Wile E. Coyote at the sight of the Road Runner.

"It's probably not that great a vintage."

As if the cheesy bottle hadn't clued me in? "Is it red? Is it wet? Does it fit in a glass?"

"Well . . ."

"Gimme." In my haste for something to take away the edge, I spilled some of the deep purple wine onto my robe. "Don't bother," I said, when Hank made vague noises about running to get something. "This is the one piece of clothing I can feel free to mess. Everything else is so dressy-uppy! Honestly, haven't you people ever heard of sweats?"

Perhaps not surprisingly, Hank looked perfectly blank as he asked, "Sweats? Like the DTs?" I shook my head. Talking to people in the '50s? It's like trying to explain relativity to a classroom of kindergarteners, sometimes. "And what do you mean by *you people?*"

Whoopsie. "I mean, you people from New York." Careful now. If I was going to invent an imaginary back-story, I wanted it to be simple and untangled, so I wouldn't trip over it later. "You probably didn't know, but my family's from down South." Newark, anyway, though I left the implication hanging that Daddy owned a plantation in Savannah. "Anyway, God forbid I mess up a precious dress by putting a greasy fingerprint on it."

Hank gave me a curious look as he walked back into the kitchen. After a great clanging of the oven door, he returned with a heavy old black iron skillet. A mess of spaghetti tossed in a tomato sauce sizzled away on one side of it, while on the other were four slices of what looked like toasted Wonder Bread that had been slathered with butter and seasonings. Everything had been covered with cheese (judging by the holes, I was guessing Swiss) and broiled until scalding. "Hot, hot," he warned me as he maneuvered the hissing pan in my direction. Once it had found a home on an oven mitt in the table's center, he finally sat down in what looked like the kind of chair in which you'd have expected Edgar Allan Poe to have met the Raven. "You always seem to take great care with your clothes," he said. "That is, you always look pretty. I mean, your clothes and your hair and your shoes and . . . everything." He had buried the last of his thoughts behind a slice of his makeshift Italian bread. "Don't you think you look good?"

"Are you kidding? I look *gorgeous!* Speaking of looking good, I'm indulging." I took the bacon tongs and helped myself to more than my fair share of the spaghetti. "I mean, the Food Network wouldn't give it a ten for presentation, unless you count cheese as a garnish. *I* would. But I could eat a cloned cow right now. Anyway." After I made certain I'd left a few bites for him, I handed over the tongs and got to work. "I look fabulous. Everyone looks fabulous here. But the gender inequities alone! You should be ashamed!"

From there I launched into a small tirade about all the little discontents I'd built up over the past few days. While we dove in, I covered the cinched waists, the uncomfortable girdles, the gloves that made me feel like Howard Hughes on one of his Kleenex-box-footwear days. Midway through the meal I was on to crippling high-heeled shoes, which I somehow managed to link to the ancient Japanese art of foot-binding, and the wired brassieres that surely had been invented for the Spanish Inquisition. By the time the skillet was empty, I was comparing June Cleaver's neat little pearls to a dog's choke chain. I had no clue where any of it was coming from, but it sounded really good. "You know," said Hank, when I paused for a moment to throw back the remnants of the fourth glass of wine that had left me feeling mighty good. He had been sitting there, staring at me with his arms crossed, while I gabbled away. "I'm coming to find I don't understand a thing you say."

"I know! Me neither!" I enthused, as if it were the happiest coincidence in the world. We stared at each other. Maybe I'd gone too far. But no, he burst into laughter. "Sorry. My friends accuse me of oral multitasking—I can eat and talk like nobody's business. It's a pain."

"No, no, it's great. I like it. I like it a . . ." Hank was a hard guy to figure out. He'd start a perfectly innocuous sentence and then snuff it into a mumble. Was he really as shy as he seemed? "I like it a lot," he finally finished.

I was enjoying this evening. Amiable as Tilly and Miranda were, I constantly felt on edge in their presence, knowing how likely I was to get expressions that made me feel like the oddball I was. Hank and Cathy had never really spoken before, though. He didn't have expectations. I could be the real me with him. Even the whoosis went right over his head. What was that word? The one that described things that were conspicuously out of their time? Ana-something. Anaconda. Anacrusis. Whatever. "Time for me to shut up," I suggested. "Tell me about you. Tell me about these Amazons."

When I gestured in the direction of America's Next Topless Models, he flushed slightly. "No, no, we were fine talking about . . . how Ward never letting June Cleaver handle the checkbook reinforced the idea that women should expect gender inequity as their due?"

He'd stumbled over the words as if they were foreign, but he'd been listening, all right. "We'll make a civilized metrosexual out of you yet," I said, patting his hand. The gesture made him jerk away. Oh, shit. He didn't have a clue what that meant. "It's not bad. I swear. So, these girls? Friends of yours from the stripper bar? Tilly's sisters? Your sisters? Wonder Woman's sisters?"

That perked him up. "Oh, you know Wonder Woman?" He seemed genuinely excited.

"Not *personally*, mind you. But sure. In her satin tights! Fighting for our rights! And the old red, white, and blue. Right?" I'm not the greatest singer. Thuy and I did the karaoke thing from time to time, but even she'd admit that they only let me on stage in order to assure a surge in sales of hard liquor. I had dropped the melody

I'd started and cleared my throat when I realized he was gawking at me again. "Comic book character."

"Yes! That's what I do." Now it was my turn to stare. Do what? Fight off Nazi bullets with his magic bracelets? "Draw comic books," he finally explained when he realized I wasn't getting it.

"Oh. Ohhhhh! Light dawneth and all that. Sorry. Duh. Okay! You draw comic books! Great! Great! Really . . . great!"

Why in the world was I grinning and nodding like an idiot? It wasn't like he'd told me he made a living solely by visiting the local sperm banks to donate his man-goo. He might have been picking up on my skepticism, because he warily said, "I like it."

"Of course you do!" Lord. People had used the same tone of voice when they informed Jimmy Stewart that they could see that giant bunny of his. Harvey, wasn't it? I dropped the patronizing voice and tried to sound sincere. "No, really, it's interesting. You've obviously got the artistic talent. I've seen people in my graphics department, degreed up to their Lasik scars, who can spend hours in Photoshop and not even crap out anything half as great as . . ." Oh, poop. More anaconda-thingies on top of each other. "I mean, you've obviously studied."

The sincerity of my praise obviously pleased him. "Thank you. I try to stick to the basics. Streamlined images, bright colors. Here. Look at this." Hank leapt to his feet and dashed from the table to one of the stacks decorating his coffee table, where he rooted around until he found what he wanted. "This is a classic," he said, returning to the table brandishing a comic book. ACTION COMICS, read the title on the cover. "It's arresting, isn't it?"

"I'll say." Eye-abrading was more like it. If I'd been shipwrecked on a desert island with that comic book cover, the colors alone could have signaled planes thirty-five thousand feet up.

"But look at the power of the images. A picture's worth a thousand words, right? Well, here we have the best of both worlds. Illustrations combined with the starkest of storytelling. Okay, sure, some of the characters can be juvenile, but—"

"Oh, I'm so glad you said that." I sighed with relief. "Because when we were kids my brother used to collect comics about the Mighty Morphin Power Range—" Maybe I'd be better off with my mouth shut. "Sorry. Does it pay well? This little . . . comic book thing?"

For a split second it seemed as if I'd thrown him. "I'm not published yet."

"Oh, I see."

"But I will be."

"Well, sure!"

"I mean, that's why I'm in a perfect position right now with the other job, because I can spend a lot of time perfecting my art."

"Ah," I said knowingly, pretending to follow. "Your other job. Yes."

Hank studied me, his chocolate-colored eyes taking in my crossed arms, my nodding head, my lips that were sucked in so I wouldn't say anything stupid. "You remember what my other job is, right?"

"Of course!" I said, nodding vigorously. Hadn't a clue. What would a comic book fanatic do for money? Run a lemonade stand? Maybe he had a paper route of his very own? "Your, you know. Other job."

"Which is . . . ?"

Good God. Was the man quizzing me? "Which is, which is . . ." I stammered. "You know. Your other job. Which is . . ."

"As . . . ?"

"Yes, which is as . . . ?

After a moment of silence, he sighed. "As your landlord."

"Of course," I said flatly, as if I'd known all along. "Wait, did you want *me* to tell *you* that you're my landlord?" I squeezed out astonishment. "You know what your other job is, silly! It's being landlord! Of . . . this!" I mime something intended to represent the entire townhouse. "What a great position to be in. For your art."

Vermont doesn't get that much of a snow job, even at the height of ski season. My effusiveness seemed to be working, however. He relaxed enough to get up from the table once more and grab a few more illustration boards from an old rolltop desk at the back of the living space. "You might like this, with all your interest in equal rights. I don't know if you remember the history of Wonder Woman, but it's totally contradictory. She came from a utopian society where women rule, but what happens when she comes to this country? She has to *hide*. She's supposed to be almost invincible and smarter than everyone else . . ."

"Oh, totally!" I interrupted. "She's kick-ass! But then she puts on those Coke-bottle glasses and she's all, '*Oh, Steve Trevor, you must never know my true identity.*'" I hoped the old Lynda Carter DVDs had the same basic plotline as the comics. "Like some lug with a mug from the *Carol Burnett Show* is good enough for a princess from Paradise Island? I know, right? I don't like women who are helpless."

Blink. Blink. "Ye-es," he said at last. "Right. Why should she be expected to hide because she's female? It's like you were saying. Culturally, we expect women to be weak, that's why. But what if there were a group of women who didn't hide their superiority? Who stood up for what's right?" He held up one of the illustration boards, which showed all five of the buxom goddesses having some kind of roundtable meeting while they leaned over what was obviously a to-scale model of Washington, D.C. The scenario was a little like the Cuban Missile Crisis, only this time the weapons aimed at our nation's capital came in a 36 triple-D. "What if they lived among us as leaders? Guides? Teachers?"

"I love it." I settled my chin down on my wrist to have a nice, long listen. Isn't zeal an amazing thing? Some people get enthused about gardening, others about reality TV. Some people are into the really obscure, like collecting old Rice Krispies boxes or cultivating blue-billed budgies. Once you find out what makes a person tick, though? Suddenly he'll drop the ol' reserve and become the Energizer Bunny. Hank's transformation from slightly geeky '50s dude to comic book maven (which, let's face it, is still pretty geeky) was really a pleasure to watch.

I let him talk on about his proposed fictional milieu—which sounded a lot like the plot of the X-Men movie I'd caught a few years back, but I was willing to give Hank the credit for thinking of it first—while I relaxed and listened to the sound of his voice. He had a nice voice. A deep resonant rumble that lulled me not to sleep, but gave me the same pleasant feeling of wellness that I'd come to associate with Tilly's purple pills. Some 1950s chick was going to end up hearing that voice every night before she fell asleep before too long, I knew. Lucky bitch. I blinked. The wine must have been getting to me. "This kind of science fiction is the wave of the future! So I thought, what if all through history there'd been a council of these women educating mankind. Actually *civilizing* us through the centuries. Throughout the entire recorded chronology of human events . . ."

Chronology. "*Anachronism!*" The room rang loud with my sudden outburst. "Sorry," I mumbled, not liking his shocked look. "Did I say that aloud? Go on. About your . . . council of education."

What? What did I say to make him sit back in his chair like that? I looked around. Nobody else was in the room. "You know," he finally said after a very long and uncomfortable silence, "maybe we'd better call it a night."

"Why? What'd I say? What'd I say?" He shook his head, rose, and threw the plates into the skillet with a clatter. "What'd I do? What'd I say?" I was on my feet now as well, following behind him like a helpless kitten. "What'd I say? What'd I do?"

"It's been very nice," he said, lowering the remnants of our dinner into his sink. "But maybe my first impression of you was always correct."

"What? What was your first impression?" He shook his head. From Energizer Bunny to Mr. Tight Lips in three seconds flat, I tell you. "Oh, tell me. You can't insult me like that and not give an explanation. Tell me!"

It was very obvious he didn't want to say, but I made him sputter, "I insulted *you?* Tell me about your council of education! Tell me about your *little comic book thing!*" Ouch. I had said that. While I was down and bruised, he ticked off his fingers one by one. "I don't think you remembered I was your land-lord. You seemed to think I was some kind of refrigerator repairman."

"No! Coffeepot rep—!" I slapped a hand over my treacherous mouth.

His eyes narrowed as he slapped another finger. "Cathy, you didn't even know my *name*. With all the talk about the new Cathy, you're as self-absorbed as ever. I thought you might . . . I thought you and I . . . stupid." Well, God! Calling me self-absorbed was bad enough! He didn't have to get abusive! Oh no, that was for himself. "Stupid, stupid, Hank." With his hands on the counter, he kept his back to me as he cursed at himself. "Just go. Please."

"Fine," I snarled with sudden decision. "If you're going to be all *polite* about it!"

It was with a satisfying *thwack* that I slammed the door to the comic-book-lovin', didn't-know-the-difference-between-mozzarella-and-Swiss stupid bas-tard's glum little badly furnished too-dark and probably whatever-passed-in-the-fifties-for-porn-filled flat. "Serves you right if it falls off the hinges, *land-lord-boy*," I growled in his general direction.

Ten seconds later, after a long and painful hesitation, I knocked again. His face was surly when he opened the door. "What?"

"My letters, please?" My tone implied that, left to his own devices with my expensive stationery, he might do something dirty and disgusting with it.

He was already prepared for me. "Here," he said, drawing them from behind his back and slapping them into my outstretched hand.

"Thank you."

"Have a good night."

"Oh, you *wish*," I snapped, stalking away. This time the door was his to slam.

Five seconds later I was back. "What?" he asked, yanking it open.

Looking into his eyes was too difficult. I addressed the dingy ceiling instead. "You promised me stamps," I muttered. "And if you have the address to that publisher lying around." He stared at me, arms crossed, obviously hostile. Well, what did he want me to do? Pull it out of my girdle? "And if you could tell me where the nearest mailbox is, after that."

"Anything else, your majesty?"

I gulped and swallowed what precious little pride I had left. "Maybe you could look over the addresses too, to see if you did them right. You people don't seem to do them the way I'm used to."

"Down South, you mean?"

I could match venom for venom, buddy-boy. "Yes, down South."

"Why don't I mail them for you?" he said brusquely, holding out his hand.

I called his bluff. "Why *don't* you?" I slapped the envelopes into his hand.

He looked at them in surprise, and then turned. As the door shut behind him, I heard him growling out a number of words, of which I caught only, ". . . stuck up . . ."

"Oh!" I cried as the door shut. I heard the sound of a chain rattling on the other side. "Stuck up, am I? Well, let me tell *you* something, Comic Book Boy! You cuddle up to your council of boobage because you're *scared* of a real woman. And those breasts you like so much? They're way too big! I mean, not even Chesty

87

LaRue could handle a rack like you've given those poor dames! How're they going to educate and civilize with all the lower back pain they're going to suffer? What're they going to do, grab mankind's faces, pull them right into their cleavage and give them a motorboat?" I shook my chest at the door and made a noise. *Bubbata-bubbata-bubbata*, if you really must know.

"Cathy? Honey?" Oh, crud. Slowly I turned to find both Miranda and Tilly behind me in their pretty evening coats, standing shocked and still at my performance, shiny handbags dangling from the tips of their gloved fingers. "Are you okay?"

Miranda had her eyebrows raised. "Why in the world are you yelling at a door about breasts?"

I looked from one to the other. It would make sense if I could explain it to them. "I . . ." No. I couldn't start there. "I . . . hey. How was the play?"

"Unless you really like warbling nuns, stupid. It'll close in a week. Now, why are you yelling about breasts . . ."

". . . at a door. Yes, I know the question. Well, you see." Tilly shifted her weight, all ears. I bit my lower lip, thinking. Several times I came up with semiplausible fictions, only to discard them. At long last, I caved. "I've got nothing," I shrugged.

"Darling, I think it would do you good if . . ."

"Yeah, yeah," I heaved a sigh. "I've got the routine down by now. Little purple pill. Best Friday night date a girl could have. Let's go, girls," I called to my flatmates. They watched me ascend the stairs, speechless. The show was over. Nothing left to see, save the pathetic remnants of what was supposed to be a highflying and fabulous life. Everybody move along, please.

Chapter Five

What was my biggest constant surprise about the 1950s? That it was in color.

Okay, there was another difference between this time and my own that I discovered over the long, solitary weekend. Despite the cars honking and the sounds of people talking and the police sirens and the hustle and bustle of modern life that could have been New York City in any decade, 1959 was so much *quieter* than I had expected. It took me a while to figure out exactly why. There simply wasn't any music. I mean, there was *music*. I hadn't slipped into some alternate universe where Elvis hadn't shocked a nation of mothers and moralists, and where everyone discreetly shook their groove thang to the delicate song of the turtledove. I was so used to hearing the sounds of piped-in strings and orchestral arrangements of pop classics and the light rock of Lionel Ritchie and friends everywhere I went—whether the lobby at work or at the supermarket or in the malls—that now in a place where background music wasn't so ubiquitous,

Grant's tomb sounded like an underground rave to my Muzak-addled ears. The only place I'd actually heard the radio had been at O'Malley's, the little bar around the corner. Not pub. Bar. Pub would be too classy a word for that grimy little joint, where I'd spent most of the weekend huddled over beers so that I wouldn't have to endure the horrified stares of anyone living at 125 East 63rd.

You know what was music to my ears, though? It started with the tuneful sound of coins sliding into a slot, followed by the melodic clunks of a knob turning and the sweet release of a lever as a little glass-fronted door flipped up, followed by the coda of a plate sliding through and onto my tray. Yes, I had discovered Horn and Hardart—automated cafeteria bliss. Come lunchtime, there was no worrying about weird-tasting crap or eating with chopsticks or having to pretend you liked sushi simply because your boss was big on the tuna rolls. At Horn and Hardart, all a girl had to do was peer through the window, make her selection from the salads and hot entrees and side dishes, pop in her pennies, and boom! Instant gratification. The lemon meringue pie of which I was having a second slice? One quarter! One freakin' quarter! I knew deep down that a quarter was worth more with the trans-timelantic exchange rate, but at bargain-basement prices like these, I felt compelled to take advantage.

If only they could come up with a similar dispensomatic of men for the single gal. Horny and Hardart, maybe. I could go for some of that.

I was halfway through the tart, tangy slice of pie that was giving me the pleasure I so sadly lacked in my life when a tiny woman in a trench coat suddenly plopped down opposite me with a tray. "Don't worry," she whispered. "I wasn't followed."

There are a couple of ways one can react to that kind of thing. Running away at top speed is probably the one I should have taken, but big dummy that I am, I went with the other. "That's good?"

The woman knew how to make herself at home, that's for sure. Without asking, she picked up my abundance of plates and began to stack them back onto my tray, leaving only my last few bites of lemon meringue because I forcefully kept my hands on the plate's rim. "I brought the you-know-what," she said in a dead hush. "I'll have more later this week, but I spent all weekend formulating these."

Need it be said I hadn't the foggiest? "Great." Every decade had its crazies from the street, right? I looked her over while I stuffed the next-to-last bite of pie into my mouth, preparing to make my getaway. Damn it, this loon was going to force me to head back to the Richmond House of Horrors on time. The Natasha to my Boris was shorter than I by about a head; her dark, curly hair bore a few traces of gray. She had to be at least in her mid-forties. Something about her furtiveness told me that she'd practiced the cloak-and-dagger routine before, probably with other unsuspecting citizens trying to finish their lovely Horn and Hardart lunches. "If you'll excuse me . . ."

"Wait! Don't you want to hear about the new formulas?" Without warning, Mata Hammy began unbuckling her cold weather coat and settling in. Almost immediately I froze. Beneath the trench, she wore one of the white lab coats so popular and mandatory among the Richmond kitchen laboratory girls. Like

Tilly's, it bore her name in red stitching next to her left lapel: MARIE LEMLEY. "It's not *my* fault I was late. That Mr. Hamilton is such a slave-driver around us girls! There ought to be some kind of law! He's only the photographer, but because he's a *man*, he seems to think he has the perfect right to come and go when he pleases, whether or not it pleases *us*." As she had talked, my apparent acquaintance Marie had pulled from the inside of her purse a sheaf of papers in a small manila envelope, which she proceeded to push across the table to me with a gray-gloved hand. "He's *horrible*, Miss Voight."

I hadn't seen enough of the Richmond Better Homes Publications food photographer to pretend to be an expert on the guy, but there's a certain instinct one feels in situations like these to actually kind of participate in the conversation. "I think Chester's on the down-low. Like on Oprah," I said, immediately regretting it. Instincts suck.

She glossed right over anachronism number three hundred and forty-seven to drop from the lemon custard–laced lips of Cathy 'The Mouth' Voorhees. "A down-low dirty snake. Not that I want you to leave, Miss Voight, but when you do and I get your job . . ."

"You get my what?" I asked, suddenly alert.

"Your job!" She stared at me for a moment and shook her finger. "Don't think me impatient. I'm not. Like you've said time and time again, it's all about politics in this company. Don't think I haven't seen that around the office, oh-ho-ho! The way Mr. Hamilton treats Miss Sanguinetti! It's the talk of the office! She's a sharp one, all right. But you'll see to it she's not promoted before me, right? That was our agreement."

"Hey!" I didn't care who this Marie chick was. "Tilly's my friend!"

"Oh, right." Marie craned her neck around as if expecting to find the KGB skulking in one of the next booths. She gave me a long and exaggerated wink. "Of *course* she's your friend."

What the hell? Something about the way the little kitchen lady had treated the topic so offhandedly made me want to slap her, though deep down inside what worried me even more was the notion that Marie was parroting back things Cathy had told her at one point or another. How could anyone not adore Tilly, the purveyor of little purple pills? She was sweet. She was obviously innocent as hell. And I wouldn't be living with her if we weren't friends, right?

Marie, however, didn't seem to notice that I wasn't the same old Cathy she was used to. Nor did she pick up the multiple hints that I'd rather be on my own. She patted the manila envelope and kept talking. "Now, the first in here is the best. I think you'll find it part-ti-cu-lar-ly suitable for your needs. The others I've arranged by category. I've formulated a dozen so far, now. I should have another batch in the next few days, or at least by the weekend, and after that, of course, I'll have to see how much I can do during Thanksgiving week. . . . Miss Voight? Is something the matter? Miss Voight?"

"I'm fine," I said, warring between emotions. So unnerved was I by where this conversation had gone that every good bone in my body—and I hoped there were more of those than a couple of joints in the little toe—urged me to take the mysterious envelope that lay within reach and throw it into the nearest waste

93

receptacle. But curiosity, the thing that always killed the Cathy, made me want to know what was inside. I mean, what in the world could '50s-Cathy be trafficking in? Was she using the test kitchens as some kind of drug lab? What illicit substances did they have here, anyway? Never mind. With the way that people in this decade popped tranquilizers like Tic Tacs, there was no telling what they were snorting. Something had to account for poodle skirts and saddle shoes, right? Or was she giving me government codes? War secrets? Was there even a war?

Oh God. What to do? I could simply walk away. But what was in the envelope? What was the mysterious secret that could shed some light onto Cathy's life? It lay right there at my fingertips, quite literally. Curiosity won out, though I quieted its gloating by reminding myself that every little bit of information I collected would help me—though how, I wasn't sure. A speed-racer's trip down Broadway in a DeLorean with a lightning rod attached to 1 Times Square was beginning to look like the only way I might get home again.

"Swell," I said, imitating Tilly. "That's swell. And now I'm back to work." Cathy's little diamond-chip watch said that I still had another ten minutes before I had to leave the automated heaven of Horn and Hardart, but I slipped on my gloves and slipped the envelope into my purse, glad for the layer of cloth between it and my skin. The envelope already made me feel dirty enough.

"Don't you want to look?" Marie appeared disappointed.

I pretended not to hear. "Have the Bee Cake," I suggested. "It has this gooey top and this custardy filling. . . ."

"I know. You included a Bee Cake recipe in *Cakes, Pies, and Flans with Famous Brand Flour*. Is something wrong?" Best not to answer that question. During my confused gathering of my wool coat and the hat I was going to have to clutch all the way down the wind tunnel that was Eighth Avenue, because I basically hadn't yet figured out the trick of making it stick with pins atop my poofy curls, a young black girl in an automat uniform swept by to clear what was left of my tray. CHERRY, said the embroidered name below her collar. "Oh no," I told her. "I'll take it."

Her voice was crisp and efficient. "Miss, I—"

Why was it that the only faces of color I'd seen in this city had belonged to custodians and garbage collectors, milkmen or dishwashers? This wasn't at all the New York I knew and loved. "Nonsense," I said briskly, standing up in my coat and clutching the tray firmly. If she'd been born thirty years later, she'd be one of the girls in my agency, popping out beautiful graphic designs or handling entire campaigns on her own, like me. But here she was in this sorry era, reduced to cleaning up after sloppy white folks for a dismal living wage. "No need to demean yourself for me."

I'd intended to be helpful, but the girl reacted like I'd slapped her across the face. "Demean myself? For you?" she asked, with a clear subtext of, *as if*.

She made another feint for the tray, but I gripped it tightly, struck by a bright idea. This poor girl didn't have a clue how exploited she was. Maybe someone with a little twenty-first-century perspective could help show her the way to a new and enlightened future, one tray at a time. Now that I'd committed to my crusade, minor as it was, I wasn't going to give up in front of a co-worker. "Don't worry!" I said, hoping a bright smile could take the edge off whatever insult I'd inadvertently dished out. "I'll take care of it. Just this once."

The attendant crossed her arms and tilted her head so that her little art deco cap pointed at an angle toward the ceiling, her stance plainly saying, *Okay, crazy white lady, go on ahead and do whatever.* Marie, in the meantime, goggled as if someone had done a Harry Potter on me and frogs were dropping from my mouth. Fine. I shut my lips into an imitation of that burnished, impersonal glow that the women of this time seemed to emanate without effort, and trotted across the room in the direction of the door, tray held proudly before me. Wherever it was that empty trays went after they'd surrendered their Hardarty goodness, I couldn't tell for the life of me. If you swung up little bank-vault-like doors to get the food out, perhaps there was a larger door where you could return everything back to the faceless automat depths? But no. Either I was blind, or fate wasn't cooperating.

In my heels, I nearly stumbled. Wouldn't that have been a sight? Me, Miss Trying To Do The Right Thing, in a spectacular pratfall right in the middle of the bustling lunchtime crowd? Luckily, a gentleman seized my arm right when it looked as if gravity might take over completely. "Allow me," I heard him say.

"I'm fine. Seriously, I'm fine," I said, setting my foot on firmer ground and balancing my tray. Unable to spit out the rich profanities I preferred, I settled for a half-hearted, "Whoopsie daisy."

"Is there a problem with Cherry?"

Now that I had my equilibrium again, I took a good look at the man, a bald bulldog of an average joe with long hairs growing from his nostrils. His old-fashioned suit wasn't as well-made as Mr. Richmond's, or any of the men I'd seen milling about in the higher-rent business streets, but his shoulders-back, neck-erect stance seemed to say, *I'm in charge here.* I considered my words carefully before proceeding. "Not at all," I told him, reminding myself I was a re-strained lady of the fifties, not the normal person I usually was. "I merely wanted to return my own tray."

"But Cherry is supposed to do that."

"Oh, I don't mind."

Were the McCarthy trials over? The guy looked at me like I was plotting some kind of Communist in-surrection right there near the glass bank of cold sal-ads. He narrowed his eyes. "Did Cherry refuse to do her job?"

"No! Not at all!" The uniformed attendant stood a few yards behind her supervisor, obviously angry yet trying to stay under control. I suddenly understood the stakes; if there was a problem with Cherry, then for a nice, white-skinned customer like me, this guy would be more than glad to get rid of her. "I mean, really, no! Cherry's fantastic. Cherry's great. Cherry is snappy. Her service is snappy—not her tongue! I like Cherry. I wish there were a hundred Cherrys. I only wanted to . . ."

Apparently tiring of my babble, the man turned his head and snapped his fingers. Her jaw set, Cherry in-stantly sprinted forward. "Take this young lady's tray, please, Cherry. Good day." The latter was for me, two words coached in exactly the right tone to imply that he didn't want to speak to me again.

Cherry stepped forward with a raised eyebrow and tightly drawn lips, and took the tray by its far edges. So many eyes were on us that I felt like the center of some elaborate piece of public performance art. "Thank you, ma'am," she said in the flat, diplomatic tone of service personnel across the world. She tugged. I resisted at first, but on her second and more determined yank, I let go. I wasn't serving any purpose with my mini crusade. Hope as I might that some miniscule, Kathleen-Turner-as-Peggy-Sue gesture might land me back in my own noisy time and my own outrageously priced apartment, it simply wasn't going to happen. Not this time. Not by being condescending. "It's my job to help," said Cherry quite pleasantly, but in a growled undertone she quickly added, "If I still *have* a job after this afternoon. Thanks a *lot*." Tray finally in hand, she stomped off, but not before she cast one final dirty look over her shoulder.

Ah, growled threats delivered in a saccharine tone. *That* was the New York I knew and loved. I slunk off, feeling miserable.

I always entered the building-that-wasn't-the-Wang with my stomach in turmoil. Back in my Motive days, I'd always suspected myself of working up to a nice big ulcer, but it was a gradual sort of approach and I'd hoped we wouldn't really have a barfing acquaintance until I'd hit my late thirties. The sheer amount of tension my little masquerade was causing, though, made me taste my perforated stomach lining more and more every day. I now knew exactly all the little rituals I was supposed to perform before I could make my way to the inner temple of the test kitchens. From the genuflections to Lois at the front desk, to the invocation of the hundred secretaries' names as I wound my way around the typing pool, to the slight bob and curtsy as I maneuvered around Mr. Richmond's office with my posterior sheltered from scrutiny—it was all as complicated as the Stations of the Cross and ten times as unnecessary for my already blackened soul.

Make that my blackened behind. I'd scarcely stepped through the door of the kitchens when I felt an unexpected pressure on my backside, followed by the inevitable sharp pinch. "Who's been eating my porridge?" I heard someone say.

I didn't have to turn to identify the voice's source. The slick and oily scent I'd come to recognize as belonging to some kind of hair goop called Vitalis, combined with a piney aftershave, meant one thing. "J.P.," I growled.

"Mmmm, Mama Bear, come to Papa!"

"Jesus H. Christ." The little intern didn't even back off when I turned around to face him. Throw in my purely stubborn refusal to step away, and there was more invasion of personal space going on by the coat rack than there had been on the shores of Normandy. "You know, if I were back home right now, I'd slap you with a sexual harassment lawsuit so fast, you'd be bald from the backdraft."

All I got for my threat was the kid's freckles rearranging themselves into a toothy leer. "What was that about your ass?"

Oh, good lord. If I had to be cursed with cheap smut puns, why couldn't I have been sent back in time to the era of my second serious boyfriend, Brady, the one who thought that Benny Hill was the absolute apex of western civilization's wit and wisdom? At least then I could've made myself comfortable with his extensive Lenny Kravitz remix CDs and freezer empty of anything save his homemade Jell-O shots. Though he was taller, I grabbed the Richmond nephew's collar by the spindly tie and pulled him closer. "Let me put it to you this way," I said, lowering my voice somewhat, though not enough that I would be drowned out by the hubbub of noise from the room's opposite end. "Lay a hand on my hindquarters again, and I will haul off and knee you with such ferocity . . ."

Again with the leer. "Maybe I like it rough."

". . . that you will have to hire a team of archaeologists with some heavy-duty tools in order to excavate your testicles from your ribcage," I finished. The one good thing about being a plus-sized girl? It gives you enough heft to shake around a little twerp like J.P. like a rag doll. "The industrial kind of tools. With diamond tips. And claws."

"Aw, come on, doll. Nobody likes a hard dame."

That wasn't quite the apology I expected or deserved. "Well, this dame doesn't mind being hard, if it means . . ."

"Hey," he interrupted, goofy grin on his face. "You want to know what else is hard?"

"*Quelle* ick," I muttered in imitation of Miranda, pushing him away. The kid lost a full two inches of height when I let him off his tiptoes. One nice thing about my time? I might have had to start each morning by pruning perverted spam messages from my e-mail junk folder, and we might have had celebrities running around in next to nothing on cable, and sure, pornographic magazines stand on the newsstands next to *People* and the *New Yorker*, but we'd managed to tame our city men enough that they didn't feel the need to fill every idle moment of workday chatter with filthy come-ons. Or, for that matter, post cartoons of their busty wet dreams on their mantels. I had a sneaking suspicion that men had been pigs throughout history, but at least in my millennium and my office, most of them confined it to the screens of their little laptops. "Just back off. Got it?"

There must have been an edge to my voice that warned him how serious I was. Maybe the girly-girl dress and pumps I was wearing made my physical assertion even more surprising for the kid. "Fine, fine," he said, brushing off his nubbly jacket and skinny, shiny tie. "But one of these days, when I'm boss around here and you need my say-so . . ."

"Right," I drawled. "I know when you're talking about. That fine afternoon when meteorologists receive the notification on their Doppler radar that Hell has indeed developed a sudden and pervasive case of frost."

He coughed. "I don't know what you just said. But it sounded pretty fresh to me."

"Right back at ya, my callow young friend," I said over my shoulder. This interview was done, as far as I was concerned. I wanted to see what the rest of the troops were up to. "See ya; wouldn't want to be ya."

I didn't care that the last thing I heard from him was subdued mutterings. J.P. might be able to maul the goody-goody gals in this office at will, but I was no creampuff; things were going to have to change around here for the better if I was going to take an extended furlough in Pleasantville.

All the girls were crowded around one of the flat soapstone surfaces near the bank of refrigerators, a veritable glacier of white clustered around a—well, I didn't exactly know what it was. At first glance I thought it was a wedding cake, thanks to the multi-leveled extravaganza that seemed to be the object of everyone's focus. Yet was it a cake? The outside edges of each tier looked as if they'd been liberally spread with vanilla frosting, but the tops were an odd, glossy pink that made me think more of a gelatin mold, perhaps of salmon. And what kind of cake did you decorate with sprigs of parsley and wedges of lemon, as well as an abundance of green olives? What was that strange, breakfasty smell? It definitely wasn't fishy. Why would anyone make pastry from Canadian bacon?

I drew closer. Apparently my flatmate was in charge of this gala spectacular, staged on a sterling silver tray that had to have been made by the same fussy artisans who'd fashioned the mirrored eyesores in 125 East 63rd. While the girls stood with their rigid charm school postures around the counter, hands at their sides, and while Chester Hamilton hovered over her shoulder, beaming like a proud papa at the birth of his firstborn, Tilly stood on tippy-toe as she reached up and placed what looked like number-two pencils and an eyeball on the topmost layer of what looked and smelled like the most inedible culinary opus ever conceived. "Jeepers!" she said, after the tricky operation was done and she looked up and noticed me for the first time. "Where were you? We were looking all over. Here she is, gang!"

Tilly's smile was one hundred-percent genuine, but for the life of me I couldn't fathom why in the world the rest of the kitchen staff should break out into the enthusiastic applause with which I was suddenly lauded. Was it my birthday? I wasn't actually going to have to *eat* a slice of that horrible, olive-trimmed, botched cuisine? Good God, why hadn't that microwave outright *killed* me? "That's right," boomed Chester. "Let's hear it for the brains behind this scrumptious, sinfully delicious masterpiece!"

I saw a late-night movie years ago in which Jane Fonda woke up one morning after a drinking binge with absolutely no memory of how the man lying next to her in bed had gotten there. Or how the knife sticking out of his chest got there, either. This revelation was much the same, but instead of recoiling in horror, I cleared my throat, stumbled a little, and feigned delight. "Oh, golly gee," I said, substituting a tame phrase for the rich obscenity I wanted to utter. "Is that really mine?"

Perhaps my reaction wasn't as bubbly as it should have been. Tilly's delicate eyebrows furrowed. "Is it okay?" she asked. "I mean, I followed your every direction so it would be perfect."

"Richmond Publishing is going to have its most popular cookbook ever, with this on the cover," said Chester, his hands on Tilly's shoulders as he beamed broadly at me. "It's your best work ever, in this lowly photographer's humble opinion. Your magnum opus. Your pièce de résistance. Your *Boheme*!"

Lord. "No, it's beautiful," I assured Tilly, happy to see relief flood her face. "I really love how you've brought to fruition my . . . my . . ." I took a deep breath of air and stared at her. "You know."

It took her a moment to recognize the plea for help for what it was. Either she assumed I was having a purple pill brain fart, or she was now used to my little "memory lapses." "Your Deluxe Festive Buffet Three-Tiered Party Treat Loaf!"

"That's right," I said, grateful she'd come to my rescue once again. If Tilly ever visited me in the twenty-first century, there'd be a place for her on my staff. "My Festive . . . Deluxe Party Buffet Three-Tiered Party . . ."

"Treat Loaf," she repeated. "For the pamphlet, *Treats by Treat*."

"Right. Treat Loaf. And what a treat it is!" Everyone assembled let out a polite little laugh. I inhaled deeply, grateful to have glossed over that little pickle. The bacon-y aroma was a lot stronger now that I was closer to my putative brainchild. When I once more looked at the glistening mottled pink surface atop each tier and remembered the somewhat inept cookbook title, my brain made a rare leap of intelligence. "Oh, sweet Jesus. You don't mean *treat* as in a special indulgence. You mean *Treet*, the processed pork product that's a knockoff of Spam. Spam, as in Monty Python. Spam!" I said in my best Graham Chapman voice. The act wasn't going over too well. I cleared my throat once more. "Of course, that kind of Treet. A Festive Party Deluxe Three-Tiered Buffet Treet Deluxe . . . for *Treats by Treet* . . . I love how you got the . . . so smooth."

Tilly watched where I traced my finger over the white frosting. "Mayonnaise cream cheese," she supplied.

"Oh yeah, that's exactly what it had to be, right? Beautiful!" Our little celebration had attracted the attention of some of the typing pool. While many of them crowded around the far door, a few of them had ventured halfway across the room and leaned on the counters in their prim little working-girl dresses. "And look at that trim on top! It's a hard-boiled egg slice! Not an eyeball, folks." I announced, picking it up and turning in a semicircle for everyone in the room to see. "Not an eyeball. Egg. In case you wondered. And these aren't pencils. Carrots, everybody. Beautiful." Tilly, who had been grabbing for my hands, succeeded in wresting her garnish away from me. While she checked it for possible damage, my mouth kept flapping away. "And to think I thought it all up. Wow," I said, clapping my hands together. "Just . . . wow. I am a genius." It was a statement that only was true if by "genius" I meant *candidate for public stoning and pillorying.* "But let's give Tilly a big hand, everyone, for the final execution!" Execution, as in, please, won't someone chop off my head already?

No one could have beamed more proudly at Tilly than I. Except perhaps Chester. The tips of his smile had gone adventuring into the rain-forest depths of his mustache. "Yes, let's give Miss Sanguinetti and Miss Voight all the credit they so richly deserve." He rolled the R of *rrrichly*, so that it rrrresonated throughout the room.

Tilly was plainly unused to so much attention. Her fair skin had turned a lovely shade of plum, and she tried to wave away all the plaudits. "It was mostly Miss Voight. And Mr. Hamilton thought up the garnishes. Especially the bed of Cheez-It crackers for the bottom layer and the cunning little olive penguins."

Now, why did that not surprise me in the least? I led the group in yet another round of applause for everyone who made this glorious mess possible. Generations of artery-clogged heart-attack victims who'd ingested my Deluxe Festive Buffet Three-Tiered Party Treet Loaf were going to curse my name on their deathbeds, I felt sure, but that was no reason not to relish the moment. My advertising background came roaring back into life. "Hurrah for Treet, the Versatile Meat!"

I didn't know whether the kitchen assistants and the typists were laughing at me or with me as they shouted out a lusty cheer, but it didn't matter. They enjoyed themselves, either way. Everyone's morale had soared during the midday break, but it was pretty plain that everyone felt it was over. The typists began drifting back to their pool, and the tight cluster of white lab coats around the Tower O' Treet first became a little less cohesive, then quickly dissipated. Only Chester and Tilly and I remained, and I felt so uncomfortable with the doe eyes they were making at each other that I felt compelled to excuse myself. "I'll be back in my office," I announced, not feeling the need to add that I'd probably spend the afternoon pawing for inspiration through the pulpy paperback copy of *The Time Machine* that I'd picked up from a drugstore for a dime.

Tilly started from her daydreaming to ask, "Aren't you going to supervise the shoot?"

"Am I?" All week there'd been plenty of photography going on in the versatile corner of the room that could be dressed up to resemble a suburban kitchen, or arranged with furniture to resemble a buffet or dining table. Was I supposed to have been there to supervise? Oh crap. It was funny how although I felt no real sense of ownership over this job, the notion that I might not have been doing my duties sent me into a tizzy. Disconnected as I was from it, I didn't plan to lose it. When the other Cathy came back, I wanted her to find things as they had been, and maybe a little better. "I mean, I didn't know. . . ."

Tilly didn't seem to notice my mortification. "Oh,

but you always stay for the cover shot, sugar! It wouldn't be the same if you didn't!" She freed herself from Chester's feather-light touch and began to trot around the counter, concern in her eyes. "I know you haven't been feeling well this week." Hah! Understatement of the Year Award, 1959! "But at least watch Chester photograph your masterpiece."

If my life's masterpiece was a two-foot-high slab of spiced processed pig parts beneath a counterpane of mayonnaise and cream cheese . . . well, words couldn't describe my despair at the thought. Is that really all women wanted during this decade? The ability to whip up pointless pseudo-gourmet dishes for festive buffets? Because if that was the case, it was depressing. I mean, hell. In my decade I could dial up a good caterer and kick back with my shoes off and with a Mike's Hard Lemonade to wait for the delivery. Tilly's little pout was so pretty, though, that I couldn't resist. "Oh, you know I'll stay," I told her. Instantly I was rewarded with her almost imperceptible jump into the air, a balletic spring of happiness. "I mean, heck. You did all the work."

"Only the handiwork!" she exclaimed. "The recipe was all yours." Already she was busily racing to the wall to retrieve a pushcart that she propelled next to the counter where the Treet loaf stood. I watched as she and Chester expertly slid the silver tray onto its surface, and trundled it in the direction of the little corner kitchen setup. Tilly and the other kitchen assistants had labored for who knew how long on an assortment of dishes for this one photograph, all of which lay spread out on the cheery tiled counter as if for an actual buffet. Among the many gastronomical oddities I saw were: a casserole dish of what looked like Treet and spinach with a handful of dried monkey brains sprinkled on top for crunch; a heaping bowlful of Treetballs in a cream sauce that looked alarmingly like sputum; links of Treet sausages garnished with orange slices; and what appeared to be some kind of green gelatin salad filled with radishes and, of course, the inevitable Treet. The Monty Python guys would have had a field day with this one, all right. Then again, maybe they'd had *Treats by Treet* in hand when they wrote that Spam skit.

The whole thing had been made up to look as if invisible party guests had been lightly nibbling at the pork-laden goodies; all the casseroles had a neat little square removed and gaily colored spoons decorating the void, while a ladle protruded from a fancy crystal punch bowl half filled with a red (and, hoped, Treet-free) liquid. A perfect slice of the quivering gelatin salad sat on a dessert plate of turquoise blue, as if set down by a party guest. To be honest, I would've abandoned it, too. Two of the girls in lab coats hovered close by my Treet high-rise, assisting when it was time to transfer it to its place of prominence. While Tilly wheeled away the cart, they both began to inspect the piece for any imperfections, adjusting a Cheez-It here and there, and using a watercolor brush to remove whatever dust their eyes could see that mine couldn't. It was all very impressive. Since no one seemed to require my immediate assistance, I simply stepped aside and watched them work.

I'd attended photo shoots in my own time, of course, and had always found them long affairs in which inert products were modeled by living commodities styled to perfection, where the photographers fussed endlessly with their cameras and lenses and the displays of their iMac G5s and a squadron of other crew fretted over the lights and the makeup and whatever else made it look like they deserved to have a job. Here, though? For a cookbook that I doubted anyone would ever seriously read? I thought it would be a simple matter of pointing the camera, pushing the button, and then dumping forty pounds of Treet down the disposal.

But no, these people took their tasks just as seriously as the people in my time. Maybe even more so. At my photo shoots, the product was sometimes pretty much an afterthought. A jeans ad might only feature out-of-focus denim in a pile behind some nude and writhing models, or I might be selling a high-tech watch that was barely visible among one really hot babe and a hundred ass-kicking ninjas. These guys, though, were really proud of what they'd accomplished. It showed in every little gleaming, colorful, Treet-scented detail.

When I felt the gentle pressure of a hand on my ass, I yanked myself out of my trance and whipped around, ready to rip J.P. a new one. "Listen, you little—! Oh-ho-ho, Mr. Richmond!"

"Cathy, Cathy, Cathy!" said the company's owner while I tried to sidle away. Apparently in this decade, a lady's backside was a free-for-all zone for any passing man's hands. They didn't get so liberal with the front. "What an asset you are to the company!"

With my bullet bra now shooting invisible projectiles in his direction, it was pretty clear what assets Mr. Richmond had in mind. He stared at both of them quite plainly. "Well, thank you, sir," I said humbly. "But it's really the work of the fine staff here that . . . Mr. Richmond? I'm up here, Mr. Richmond." Once I had his eyes looking at my face instead of at my other, pointier regions, I continued. "It's the staff here that really does most of the work."

Flicker. His eyes immediately snapped back down to chest level. "Oh, don't be so modest," he said, his pencil mustache twitching in a way that made me feel as if I'd crawled, sweaty and panting, out of one of the orgy scenes in *Eyes Wide Shut*. "It amazes me how a dumpling like you can come up with so many versatile recipe ideas. I honestly don't know how you do it."

"Oh, I don't know how, either." My mouth snapped shut at the sentence's conclusion. I'd intended it to be harmless self-effacement, but even as I spoke the words, I knew them to be a bald-faced lie. I did know how the dumpling did it—or I suspected I did, anyway. Despite the warm stuffiness of the test kitchens, I felt chilled to the bone.

"Whatever your secret is, you keep right at it!" My boss wrinkled his nose at me and poked an index finger in the general direction of my boobs. Only with a last-second squeeze play past Chester's tripod did I manage to avoid the impending molestation. "You hear me, little lady?"

"Yes, sir. Um, just a moment." Say what you would about the guy, but no one could ever accuse Mr. Richmond of slacking off in the condescension department. I skipped away backwards, keeping my posterior out of reach of his nimble little fingers. He watched me go with a mixture of speculation and disappointment, his hands running over the lapels of his light gray worsted suit. At the same time, I'd begun blindly digging into my purse, fingers running over the lipsticks and compacts and newspaper clippings the other Cathy seemed to find so essential to lug around everywhere, until I found the envelope clandestinely entrusted to me less than an hour before. When I was away from the busy corner, I ripped open its sealed flap, certain of what I'd find within. I wasn't disappointed, either; no fewer than two dozen three-by-five index cards spilled out, their lined surfaces covered with printing that was miniscule, yet tidy. I flipped through them.

TINY MINNIE DESSERT TRIFLE

In a crystal dessert bowl, arrange 12-15 Tiny Minnie Snack Cakes for the bottom layer of the trifle, radiating them lengthwise from center of bowl in a bicycle-spoke formation. Atop the snack cakes, smooth one can of Ry-Del Brand Butterscotch Pudding until smooth, and top with Ry-Del Orchard Fresh Brand Strawberry or Huckleberry Jam. For the next layer, repeat spoke formation with more Tiny Minnie Snack cakes. . . .

Gagging to myself, I rifled through the others. TINY MINNIE INDIAN CANOES, read one, with detailed instructions on how to split Tiny Minnies lengthwise, line them with cut-open Clark Bars along the outside, and make cunning native rowers from toothpicks, grapes, and tissue paper. *Great for the kids!*, it raved. There were Tiny Minnie S'mores, Deep-Fried Tiny Minnies, German Chocolate Tiny Minnie Cake, and something called a Tiny Minnie Mock Martini that I couldn't bring myself to read. All this time, while posing as some kind of recipe expert, I'd been taking ideas from Marie and pretending they were my own.

Or the other Cathy had. I hardly knew who was

whom anymore. And what was Marie getting out of it? "Mr. Richmond?" I called out. If I'd allegedly been plumping Marie's name to the big boss, he'd know. Or would he? Still clutching my caloric recipes, I eased back over to the plump man's side, where he was watching Chester focus on the Tower O' Treet. The photographer murmured encouragement to the lard-fest as if it were a finalist on *America's Next Top Model*. "You know I wouldn't be able to do any of this without my staff," I said smoothly. "All of them are wonderful, really."

"You do a fine job in selecting your girls. Admirable."

The slick little bugger made a move to position himself within reaching distance. I dodged. "Do I?" I didn't realize I hired. That was news. "I mean, I didn't know you thought so."

"Of course I do! I've mentioned it many times. Are you fishing for compliments, my dear?" Even a chuck under the chin was too touchy-feely for my taste. I developed a sudden interest in discovering what was around the corner of the counter we stood near. "I was wondering when you were going to bring on a replacement for little Maggie May, now that she's gone and married Mr. Burkens from the warehouse."

An idea that had been forming in my mind sprang into full flower. I instantly saw a way to make some amends for the wrong I'd committed earlier that afternoon. "I have someone in mind, but I need to see if she's available," I said, delighted with my cleverness. "But about my existing staff. Marie, for example."

"Yes?" By the way his mustache twitched, I could tell that his eyes were busy again, climbing Twin Peaks.

It was all I could do to keep talking to him without

crossing my arms over my chest. "I'm sure I've told you about Marie? Who's given me so much help?"

"Marie?" he asked abstractedly. One of the younger kitchen assistants had moved into view, distracting him momentarily. "I don't believe so."

"Marie Lemley," I said, enunciating the name. "I'm sure I have."

"No, I don't believe so." Before I could describe her, he added, "Now, Miss Sanguinetti! You've told me lots about her! What a fine girl she is, too. Make some lucky man a good little wife someday, won't she?" He leaned in close and lowered his voice. "Between you and me, Cathy, I wouldn't be surprised if the lucky man were our own Mr. Hamilton. Hm-mmm? She's a very pretty girl indeed."

I knew it! While relieved that Cathy Voight wasn't badmouthing her flatmate to the boss while pretending to be friends, she was a sneaky snake for promising Marie a break, taking her recipes, and welching on her end of the deal. I mean, jeez! What kind of thoughtless, cynical Machiavelli treated her co-workers like that?

Well, some things were going to change around this place, if I had anything to say about it. I'd start with the basics—credit to anyone on the staff who wanted to come up with a recipe. Maybe small incentives for those who created batches of good stuff. None of these clandestine meetings, or promises that never were kept.

And then, I thought, maybe Richmond Publishing could start creating some cookbooks that didn't make the arteries clog merely to look at them. Something with real food, the kind of food that I was used to eating, where the primary ingredients didn't have to be jiggled out of a can or shucked out of their cellophane wrappers. Good-tasting, fresh food. *Nutritious* meals that weren't laden with saturated fats or reliant upon gimmicks. Oh yeah, I could see it now. The ol' eye for trends was back! I was going to . . . "*Ow!* Holy frickin'—!" I stopped my yelping before I said something that would get me fired.

Damn me for not paying attention! Mr. Richmond had slunk to my side during my abstraction and had helped himself to a pretty substantial pinch. I was going to have another bruise the size of a silver dollar by tomorrow. "Oh yes," he murmured while I rubbed the aching welt. "She's a very pretty girl indeed."

Chapter Six

<u>Cathy's To-Do, Part II:</u>
<u>In 1959, No One Can Hear You Scream</u>

1. The sucky thing about <u>The Time Machine</u>? The guy actually had a time machine to get around in. Where am I going to pick up one of those in this decade?

1. I still can't believe you spent an entire dime on that book.

2. Oh wait. What was that movie where a dad in the 1950s talked to his son in the modern days over a ham radio?

2. <u>Frequency</u> with Dennis Quaid. Honestly, considering the way your mind works sometimes, it's a wonder you made it out of high school. Though you know when Dennis Quaid looked

mighty tasty? In _The Big Easy_, that's when.

3. Back on topic, if you please. _Kate and Leopold_, again. I loved that movie.

3. Back to Hugh Jackman! Remember how hot he was as Wolverine?

4. You've noticed I'm totally ignoring you, right?

4. He can sing, too.

5. Oh! _Somewhere in Time_! How could I forget that?

5. Oh my God. Where are the Kleenex?

6. "Come back to me!"

6. No! Don't! I'll turn on the waterworks! Honest! You know, Christopher Reeve looked mighty good in his day.

A _Somewhere in Time_ Exercise in Self-Hypnosis

Noises: The sounds of computers chiming as they booted. Door buzzers. The gentle beeping of security checkpoints and the hum of the metal detectors. Satellites in the sky—no, wait, you couldn't hear satellites. The throbbing boom of electronica on someone's satellite radio. There we go.

Smells: Falafel on every corner. Gyros, resplendent with onion. Street urine, too, and the musty smell of steam from the subway gratings. No, I needed to concentrate on strictly modern smells: The plastic-and-ink scent of a freshly opened CD. Exotic teas from my favorite little store in Chelsea. The strange, stale, piped-in air of skyscraper lobbies.

Sights: Gleaming skyscrapers in the afternoon sun. The gaping maw left on the horizon after 2001. Starbucks signs, green and white, so inescapable that they'd practically become invisible. SUVs the color of candy. Gas prices in the triple digits. Blackberries, white iPod earphones, cell phones in everyone's . . .

"Should I ask what you're doing?" I heard a deep, masculine voice say. No! I couldn't let anyone interrupt my meditation! Laptop cases, Bluetooth earpieces, laser pointers, television advertising in Times Square . . . "Or is it some beatnik yoga thing?"

I couldn't help myself. My eyes popped open to find Hank standing before me, a paper grocery bag in his arms, studying my position on the townhouse's stairs. I suppose I had assumed something of a modified lotus posture during my exercise. "You have yoga in 1959?" His eyebrows slowly rose in the direction of the sooty glass chandelier that cast a dim light in the foyer. The words had flown out of my big, stupid mouth without thinking, but I'd honestly made the assumption that yoga had arrived on American soil only in my last decade, prepackaged with the shiny mats and the laminate flooring. I scrambled to cover up. "I mean, it's 1959. Don't you think everyone should be doing yoga?"

I couldn't quite decide if he was buying it. I'm not sure I would have been particularly receptive if I'd caught my least-favorite tenant spread all over the building's one staircase, legs akimbo, in an eye-popping, waist-cinching dress of red and white diagonal stripes. His mouth opened, certain to say something snappy, but then it shut again and he shook his head. "You dropped your paper," he said at last, bending down to get it.

"No, I'll—!" I bent down, too, reaching for the sheet of Cathy's engraved stationery that had fallen from my fingers during my trance.

Only at the last minute when Hank, more attentive than I, reared back, did we avoid conking our noggins. We stared at each other for a second, wary. Finally he grinned. "Close one."

"Mmmm." I wasn't committing to this conversation. After our last encounter? Not at all. "Pardon me." I reached again for the paper lying on the bottom step.

"I'll get it."

Then, of course, we knocked our heads together for real. Luckily, we'd been so close that neither of us could work up a serious velocity, but I still saw stars. "What'd you have to do *that* for?" I snarled after a dizzy moment, clutching my cranium. "It seriously *hurt.*"

"I was trying to be polite." He seemed to be in no less pain than I, which at least was a small consolation. For a second I thought he'd do himself another injury when he tried to sit back on the floor, seeming to forget that he was on the stairs. But when I reached out to grab him, he managed to right himself. "That's what people do. They try to be polite. And helpful."

Hank held my list between his fingers. I snatched it away before he could study it more closely and discover my Christopher Reeve–inspired scheme. "Normal people, you mean? *Nice* people? Oh wait, according to you, that would exclude me, right?" He bit his lip. Good. That had stung. I folded my paper and tucked it in my . . . well, none of Cathy's dresses had anything practical like actual pockets that weren't decorative and could hold anything bigger than a safety pin, because God forbid that any woman of the 1950s be able to walk around unhampered and carry things that might help them be functioning members of the workplace. And there was no way I planned to stick the thing down my cleavage, like my grandmother and her glasses, tissues, and mad money. Instead, I stuffed it under my patent leather belt as I stood. "Ever so sorry to clutter your stairs."

"Don't be . . ." My raised eyebrows interrupted whatever insult he was about to throw my way. "Imperious. And don't give me that blank stare, Cathy. You're a smart girl. I know you know what it means."

"What is it with men calling me 'girl'? Am I less threatening to you when reduced to a diminutive? Is a 'woman' too much for you to handle? Because if that's the case, let us know. I'm pretty sure I could find squadrons of women who would be more than glad to give up the cooking and cleaning and low-paying menial domestic tasks that none of you have bothered to learn, so you can see how you all would do on your own without us. Oh yeah. We could secede, you know. We could form our own union and while you men are floundering around trying to figure out how to work the dials on the oven and the washing machine, we could have our society up and running pretty damned smoothly. So you want to know what I know, Mr. Bull-Headed Cabot? What I know," I groused from between clenched incisors, "is that if one more man condescendingly calls me a 'girl' in this decade, I'll rip his balls off. With my teeth." For good measure, I added a snap of my jaw and a vague canine sound somewhere in the mastiff-to-Doberman range.

I'd intended the remark as a challenge. So he thought I was imperious? Maybe I was, with the added height a few extra stairs granted me. I stared down at him, arms crossed. Was he going to let me have the last word? Fine!

I'd turned and was prepared to stalk upstairs when over my shoulder I heard Hank snarf laughter through his nose. The bastard was actually doubled up in glee! And clapping! "Classic!" he declared, pounding his palms a few final times. "Are you sure you don't want to be a heroine in one of my comics?" While my jaw trembled too strongly for me to say anything, he shook his head. "Oh, stop. I know you think I'm out of line with practically everything I say. I'm bull-headed. You're imperious." He shrugged. "Doesn't mean we can't get along."

"I don't want any more remarks about me being stuck up!"

"I didn't make any!" he protested.

"Not tonight!"

My interruption arrived at the same time he added, as an afterthought, "Tonight." We stared at each other for a moment. His jaw and lips twitched, probably still amused at my expense. "Okay, listen," he said, rubbing the cleft in his stubbly chin before stuffing his hands into his dungarees. "I'm sorry I called you a girl. You're very clearly a woman." I couldn't help but notice his eyes roam down the landing stripes that covered my body. Considering I'd spent a good week and a half at Richmond Publishing with my boss and his nephew undressing me optically at every opportunity, it should have made me feel dirty all over again. It didn't. For some reason, I didn't mind at all. "I'm sorry I called you stuck up. If I'm honest with myself, it was because I had hoped . . ." There were a hundred paths that sentence could lead, but he stopped short. "Never mind what I hoped. But it was ungentlemanly of me. Impolite, even."

I nodded, but I wasn't ready to forgive him completely with open arms. Not yet. "Okay."

"It's very plain that you're not the same Cathy who used to saunter by without saying hello. You're not the same Cathy I'd pass down the street who didn't even seem to realize I lived in her building. At least you have some consciousness that I'm here."

He said the last words in a joking manner. I unset my jaw and conceded, "You're kind of hard to miss. You know—with the jaw and the big hands and the height and all. And the chin dimple." I still couldn't look him squarely in the face.

"It was unfair of me to invite you into my apartment and then proceed to clout you around, the way I did." He cleared his throat and shuffled. Ouch. The apology was nice. I was grateful for it, really I was. I'd meant to make him uncomfortable, but not so much that it was bleeding over and making *me* ill-at-ease. "So if you could accept my apology . . ."

"Oh, shut up already," I mumbled, feeling badly. "I shouldn't have mentioned it."

". . . And not bite off my testicles, I'd appreciate it."

I looked at him squarely then. "Consider them unchewed. Let's draw a line, step over it, and forget what's behind." We nodded at each other. I mean, okay, he'd been a bit of a prick, but I could concede I hadn't aspired to be Little Mary Sunshine, either. I wasn't exactly in a position to pick and choose my allies, here. And besides, how often was I going to run across a comic-book-lovin', fast-drawin', science-fiction-adorin' lug of a guy? Outside of a modern-day *Star Trek* convention, anyway? "Hey, wait a second," I said, struck by a thought. "Have you ever read H. G. Wells?"

"Sure. What book? *The Island of Dr. Moreau? War of the Worlds?*"

"He wrote flicks for Marlon Brando and Tom Cruise?" I asked, amazed.

His lips parted in a grin. "Again, when you talk, I recognize half the words. Brando's good, for example. But the rest . . ."

"Never mind. I meant *The Time Machine.* Recognize it?" He nodded. Of course he had. He probably could talk more concretely about time travel than all my lists put together. "Have you had dinner yet?"

"Now there's a sentence I understand. And the answer is no. Can I rustle up something for us?"

That settled it. "Nuh-uh. Put on your shiny shoes, Hank, and meet me upstairs in five. Dinner at my place this time. I owe you."

If there were any lingering doubts about the pact of forgiveness we'd made moments before, my invitation erased them. "Swell!" he said, wearing one of the biggest and most genuine smiles I'd ever seen on a guy my own age who wasn't trying to sell me electronics at Best Buy. "I'll be right up."

Here's one for the record books: the total elapsed time between my invitation and subsequent giddiness to tearing my hair out in utter despair? Approximately thirty-seven seconds. That's how long it took me to sprint back upstairs in high heels, nearly knock over and then save the matador lamp, catch a quick look at myself in the mirror, and discover that the refrigerator was full of food utterly unsuitable for consumption. That is, there was plenty of milk in bottles and butter and eggs and iceberg lettuce and salad dressing and tomatoes and cucumbers and carrots and beef and chicken fresh from the butcher. In the cupboards were cans of spaghetti sauce and oils and spices. Pots and pans and knives of all sorts lay in various drawers and cubbyholes. In other words, the kitchenette was chock full of raw ingredients that certainly could have been combined into some sort of wholesome and nutritious gold if one were a culinary alchemist, not the queen of Thai takeout.

From the hallway, where our pretty princess-line phone sat in an alcove, I could hear Miranda talking to one of her friends. "Oh, it was divine," I heard her say. "*Quelle* delish. So lucky to have seen it during previews! Of course, before we went I was saying to Harold, 'Harold, mark my words, this *Sound of Music* will be a smash hit!' I've got an instinct for these sorts of things." I tiptoed quietly away.

Hank had already changed into a sports jacket and a narrow tie that showed off the stretch of his (thankfully, again dandruff-free) shoulders when I clattered back down the grand old staircase. "Change of plans," I announced. "About-face! Ten . . . hut!"

"Ma'am! Yes, ma'am!" he barked, executing a salute and a swivel so mechanical that he had to have learned it in the service. Hank was a bit of a smartass. Since I also dabbled in the art, I figured he could run with me and have no problems.

One of the things I most loved about my Manhattan was the sheer diversity of it. You could walk through the most innocuous neighborhoods and always find something remarkable: a tiny, funky costume shop tucked away under a stodgy brownstone. A restaurant you'd never notice save for the tendrils of mouth-watering aroma beckoning to you. Romantic getaways in old industrial areas. Shops that specialized in something you'd never expect anyone to have an interest in, like porcelain doll heads, that seemed to stay in business forever. I'd been worried that this Manhattan might be different—that instead of being the city that never sleeps, it might be the city that decided to take a disco nap for a couple of decades while waiting for the 1970s. After all, from what I'd seen around the corner, Lexington Avenue seemed once to have been Truss Store Central.

Not at all encouraging, when I wasn't one hundred percent certain what a truss was and didn't really want to explore the definition. Hank, however, seemed to know exactly where we should go. We ended up ducking between a truss shop and what looked like a deserted bakery into a place called The Flanders, where the men were burly and wore enormous, shapeless flannel coats and the women—well, there weren't any women, save me. And don't think that didn't cause a stir, when I shucked my coat and revealed my eye-popping stripes.

"Good thing I put on my shiny shoes," Hank said, looking down uncertainly at a pair of penny loafers that could almost be used as toe mirrors. "And gosh, I'm glad I brought a jacket. I'd hate to be out of dress code and forced to wear the house coat."

"I bet it would smell like urine." Speaking of which, I examined the surface of the ancient booth leather, just in case. "And you're attracting nowhere near as much attention as me. Now I know how the chum feels when it's been tossed into the shark tank. I'm the only person in here with breasts."

"Nope." Hank nodded in the direction of the pool table, where two bald-headed brutes at the pool table had stripped down to their wife-beaters, exposing more hair on their shoulders and back than the average grizzly. "They've *definitely* got 'em."

My nervous giggles were so loud that everyone in The Flanders turned to peer through the gloom to see, pool players and barflies and groups at the tables nearby and mean-looking bartender alike. One fellow at the bar's far end scowled at me longer than the others, his gaze lingering on our table with such loathing that although I couldn't see his face, I knew that I was going to feel better having an ex-serviceman escorting me back home in the dark. "This doesn't really seem *you*," I confessed.

He shrugged. "It'll do. I thought you liked it."

"You thought *I* liked it? Al Qaeda meets here, right?" He squinted at me, shaking his head. "Okay. That's a back-home thing. Forget I said it. But why in the world would you think I liked it here?"

Our argument was fresh enough that he hastened to reassure me. "Didn't mean it as an insult. But haven't I seen you coming out of here before?" When I only stared at him, he cleared his throat. "I have, a couple of nights. Six months ago was the last time, maybe. Sorry if I was mistaken."

On the radio over the bar, a woman's voice crooned as though trying to console the lost souls nearby. I recognized the voice as Patsy Cline's, but not the song.

"Maybe I did," I said carefully. With my bad luck, I probably moonlighted as a barmaid in this joint. "Once or twice, tops."

Right at that moment appeared a guy in a tattletale gray shirt wearing a filthy, stained apron flung over his shoulder, and, a towel that had apparently been recently used to degrease all the moving parts of a steam locomotive. Like everyone else in this little dive save Hank and I, a cigarette dangled from the corner of his mouth. "Brought your favorite, Cath," he announced, sliding two bowls and two beers across the ring-stained table. He looked straight at me.

"Thanks," I said in as wry a voice as possible. The Flanders was the last place I pictured Cathy Voight habituating. I'd sooner imagine her running a secret whorehouse. "I don't come here often enough to have a favorite," I assured Hank, talking to him as though the oily little chef weren't two paces away, staring at us both.

"It's lamb stew," he said, obviously unhappy at my declaration. "You love my lamb stew, Cath. You said to me, 'Cappy, I love your lamb stew.'" I smiled at the guy, while trying through eye-rolling and an amused tilt of my head to convey to Hank that Cappy was obviously in need of a Xanax or two and maybe a short stay at Bellevue. I think I came off as spastic. "She used to say she loved my lamb stew," Cappy said to Hank, and then to the four truckers/longshoremen/murderers at the next table, "Loved it."

"I'm sure she does," Hank said without a note of condescension. "She'd probably remember if she tasted it." He smiled blandly in my direction. Cappy crossed his arms and nodded in agreement, waiting.

Oh my God. He wasn't serious. I had to *eat* the

stuff? Again, it seemed as if everyone in the bar was looking in my direction. The malevolent presence in the far corner, who apparently kept a nodding acquaintance with the meaning of *schadenfreude*, if not the word itself, shook his head and let out a laugh loud enough for me to hear. It was the laugh that decided me. How many times had I watched the casts of *Survivor* chow down on rotting fish slices and embryonic chicks and scoffed that I could do better? Prepared for the worst, I grabbed my utensil, steeled my nerves, and spooned in a mouthful of the coffee-colored solution, complete with a chunk of meat that in my too-vivid imagination might have belonged to a living, barking creature. "Mmmmm," I said, eyes watering as my tongue and mouth's top scalded. "Oh jeez. It *is* good."

I wasn't lying. Marlboro ashes and cuts of meat from Sweeney Todd's barbershop might have been the guy's secret ingredients, but the stew was really, really tasty. Perfect for a November evening, in fact. Once my mouth stopped feeling like I'd sucked down a molten lava bubble tea, I'd probably wolf down the rest. "Ish fantashic," I raved, fanning my face. Ever the gentleman, Hank held out his beer. I grabbed it and cooled off with a swig.

At least my loyalty mollified Cappy. "I knew you said you loved it," he said, proud as a new father. As he waddled back to the dark depths of the kitchen, he crowed to the murderers/teamsters/grandfathers of the Sopranos, "See? She loves it!"

Not until he was finally out of earshot did Hank burst out into muffled sniggers again. "Okay," I said, trying to keep a shred of my dignity. "I might have been here three or four times."

We had both been eating the hearty, surprisingly spicy stew with some gusto for a couple of minutes when Hank couldn't restrain himself any longer. "Here's what I don't understand. You write cookbooks." I nodded, admitting that much. "But you can't cook?"

"I can cook!" I howled in protest, ignoring the fact that in my own time, preparing for an intimate dinner party primarily involved sliding the contents of plastic takeaway containers into pretty bowls or plates I'd borrowed from the nice lady in 440 before she'd moved away.

He studied me closely. "That's not how it sounded when you were raving about carrots and cucumbers and saying 'The horror! The horror!' on the way over."

I ripped in half one of the hunks of bread that Cappy had brought out to accompany the stew. "I can cook. I'm a fantastic cook. I'm a trained, magnificent . . . no, you're right, I'm terrible," I admitted, dropping the pretense. "But I still owe you a dinner! Homemade! And I'm going to keep to it. You watch."

He still appeared mystified. "Don't you have to know how to cook well to write cookbooks?"

"Ah." I had him there. I jabbed the crust in his direction. "You haven't seen the cookbooks!"

Though I had to completely block from my mind the idea of Cappy as The Flanders' resident chef, I hadn't been lying. The stew was excellent. The bread was fresh, and there was plenty of it. By the time we had both finished our second bowls and second beers, we'd covered a number of topics, from his stint in the military (Him: "I was stationed in Okinawa during the Korean War." Me: "Is that the one *M*A*S*H* was

128

set in?" Him: "Huh?"), my background (Me: "After college I thought about taking my LSATs, but ended up putting myself through an MBA while working at an Internet startup company. Did I say 'Internet'? I meant 'international.'" Him: "Huh?"), and his family (Him: "I don't talk about them much." Me: "Huh.").

It wasn't until Cappy returned and rewarded our gluttony with a plate of cream-colored hard cheeses, a bowl of apples, and a grin so wide you could see his missing molars, that Hank cleared his throat and asked, "So what's all this about H. G. Wells?"

I could have kissed him. I'd been trying to think of some way to broach the subject, whether by directing the conversation back to books or simply flat out changing the topic, but this was the most graceful entry that could have been mustered. I cleared my throat and tried to sound casual. "Well, I picked up this paperback, *The Time Machine*, at the drugstore. Something silly to read on my lunch break. And you know, it was kind of interesting once I got into it, but I was thinking about whether time travel was possible, and then I thought, hmmm, who best to ask that question to than my old buddy Hank who likes comic books and fantastic worlds?" My explanation, lame as it was, came out in a rush. I suspect it had something to do with both my embarrassment and the fact this was the first alcohol I'd had since the last time we'd dined. Onto a small plate, I accepted several of the slices of cheese he'd cut with a wooden-handled knife. "So. Any insights?"

He saved the remainder of the cheese as his own portion. "Insights into what, time travel? Do you mean whether or not it's possible?" While he removed a clean handkerchief from his pocket to clean the topmost apple, I nodded. "Of course it's possible. Time-travel's quite real. You're time-traveling right now. Do you like the peel or not?"

"What?" I squawked. He had stunned me with his pronouncement. How in the world did he *know*? Being able to talk about my situation with someone would have been the greatest relief in the world, but oddly, hearing him say those words only made me sick to my stomach. How had I given myself away? I mean, other than the bazillion verbal gaffes, and that I had to present myself to Tilly in the mornings for clothes inspection, and the fact that I stuck out like a sore thumb wherever I went? When he indicated the apple and began to repeat his question, I brushed it aside. "Peel's fine. Why did you say I'm a time-traveler?"

From his trousers he had withdrawn a pocketknife. I was actually in a decade in which men carried around pocketknives on a regular basis, never once expecting them to be confiscated at some security checkpoint. He studied it for a moment, pried out the largest blade, and began slicing the apple down its center. "Because you are," he said, too intent upon his task to look at me. "We both are." His voice was utterly devoid of emotion or concern. My spleen, in the meantime, was doing cartwheels in my mouth. "I saw you on the stairs, what? An hour ago? And here we are now. We've both traveled an hour forward in time from then until now. There you go, for starters." He presented to me half an apple, sliced into neat sections with the core removed.

I'd been so startled that I couldn't trust myself to speak right away. Immediately I stuffed one of the sections in my mouth and chomped away, while tears prickled at the backs of my eyes. "I see what you mean," I managed to say by the time he'd finished coring his half of the fruit.

"This is not bad," he said, indicating the cheese. "Kind of like Swiss, but not exactly. No, what most people mean by that question is whether or not it's possible to travel backward and forward in time."

"Yes!" I worried that I'd replied too loudly. "Like in the book. Or do you think it's impossible?"

"Impossible to what, build a machine that would move a person in time? I don't know about that. It's dangerous to say what's possible and what's not. Sixty-five years ago, there was a guy, Lord Kelvin of the Royal Society, who declared on public record that a heavier-than-air flying machine could never be built. Look at what we've got zooming through the air now. People scoffed at the idea of telephones and computing machines and of that thing." He pointed in the direction of the bar. For a moment I thought he meant the guy sitting at its end, who kept turning his head every now and then to look at us; after a moment I realized he was talking about the radio. "So maybe sometime in the future, someone could build a Wellsian time machine. It would be fun to see, anyway. Don't you think?"

"Oh yeah. Fun by the mile." I bit my tongue before I really launched into sarcasm.

He hadn't noticed. "There are so many paradoxes to time traveling. For example, what if there was an event in history where it was recorded that only a certain number of people were present? Like, say, the Last Supper. Jesus and his twelve disciples. Thirteen people. How could you take a time machine back to that event to see it and be in the same room? Would the history books reflect fourteen people when you got back? Or would you find yourself in the room next door, unable to get in? I think if you were sent into a different time, it would have to be somewhere where you couldn't affect anything."

"So if I went back fifty years in history," I said slowly, trying to comprehend, "I wouldn't be able to change anything important. I couldn't stop a president from being assassinated or anything."

"You shouldn't be." Well, damn. There went my escape route, leaving me with only mixed emotions. On the one hand, knowing I couldn't mess things up was a relief. Realizing that nothing I did would have any effect whatsoever, though, kind of bit the big one. What was the *point?* "But." He took a bite of apple and cheese together, then sucked the stickiness from his thumb, deep in thought. I waited breathlessly. "There's one theory that says if you did, it would form an alternate universe. A universe like ours, but on a completely different timeline. Who was assassinated fifty years ago? McKinley? Okay, if you went back to the McKinley assassination in nineteen-oh-something and stopped it and he shook your hand and said thank you, that timeline would split away from this one."

"And if I went back to the future again?"

"There'd be two Cathys." This was already so close to the truth that I stopped eating altogether. "One Cathy in the regular old timeline where McKinley was assassinated, and one Cathy who was a hero in the other. But of course, neither of them would be aware of the other. The one Cathy would return to a future where everything was the same, but because the other Cathy's timeline has been irrevocably altered, she might find things very different." I had a sudden vision of hopping back into the future and finding it all

Planet of the Apes. The Tim Burton version. Freaking fantastic. "Of course, it's all pretty moot, unless you've got a time machine in your pocket."

"Hah-hah-hah-hah-hah!" Talk about hysterical laughter. It came spewing out of me like pea soup from Linda Blair in *The Exorcist*. "I don't. It would be funny if I did. But I don't. Nope."

God, I sounded like a fool, but Hank didn't seem to notice. His eyes were narrowed and a half-eaten slice of apple rested between his fingers. "I think it would be amazing to get a glimpse of the future. I mean, in the year 2000 I'd be what, seventy and surrounded by kids and grandkids and great-grandkids? Hard to imagine."

Not really. I could easily imagine what he'd look like as an old man, his thatch of hair gone threadbare, the rugged features still visible beneath an overlay of wrinkles. Hank was one of those guys who had a full life ahead of him. Maybe if I got back—when I got back—I could try finding him again, see if he lived in the area or had retired down in Florida. Maybe I could find out if he'd lived the life he'd wanted, and whether any of those comic books of his were in the hands of modern-day collectors. Yet why did that thought make my heart hurt so much? "So long as they looked like you," I joked.

He grinned. "Did you go to the '39 World's Fair? No? I did." He had to be kidding. That World's Fair was one of those cultural touchstones so remote that it seemed impossible that real, living people might have attended. "I was a kid, all of nine. It was all about the future. What it looked like, how we'd live. I think it was at the fair that I realized what I wanted to do with my life. Not that I wanted to be a comic book illustrator—my parents didn't let me read that kind of thing. Oh, no. But I knew that I wanted to have those kinds of visions of the future, some way or somehow. I wanted to be the guy who designed picture telephones or zeppelins or breakfast pills . . ."

He had such a wry grin on his face that I couldn't help but laugh. "Breakfast pills! I thought dreams of those went out with the Edsel."

"What do you mean?"

"I mean, who wants to eat pills instead of good food, for one thing?" Then I saw what he meant. I'd made another anachronism. Whoops. "Oh, the Edsel. It's a car, where I came from. A disaster of a car. Don't sweat it."

"Why was it a disaster?"

"We studied all about it in one of my MBA classes," I said, automatically warming to a subject I could actually address. "They had a terrible marketing campaign and it ended up being abruptly discontinued after only about two years. Anyway, I'd rather have a good omelet and hash browns and bacon any day, than pop a pill. You can take that from a cookbook expert."

Hank, however, wouldn't let the topic go. "I know what an Edsel is," he said with good humor. "My older brother has an Edsel Pacer. He likes it."

Like a dry sponge dropped into water, the following second of immensely uncomfortable silence ballooned into a moment, and then into an all-out awkward pause. "You know," I said at last, improvising, "Did I say Edsel? I don't know why I said Edsel. I meant some other car. Yeah, I think I saw an Edsel earlier and it kind of stuck in my brain. You know how that goes sometimes? It was some other car I studied. From another country. My bad." I developed a sudden absorbing interest in the last of my cheese.

"I thought maybe it was something like that." He grinned at me in a way that made me feel slightly better, but not enough to make me completely stop ruing the moments I lost control of my brain and opened my mouth. "Oh, my. Don't look now, but here comes trouble."

"What do you mean?"

He nodded to the side, where moments earlier I'd heard a loud percussive noise. Everyone's favorite patron had banged his shot glass onto the shiny bar surface and walked a few paces away into the room's middle, where he stood on unsteady feet, glaring in our direction. I watched as he wiped his mouth and jaw on his shirtsleeve. "Great."

"Don't worry. If he bothers us, I'll . . ."

The man lurched forward, cutting him off midsentence. I didn't get to hear what Hank might do, but I wasn't too worried. He had a Swiss Army knife, after all. "Wait a minute," I whispered. There was something about the guy. Unlike most of the other bar patrons in their plaid flannel and dark trousers, now that he was in a less shadowy section of the murk, I could see he wore business pants and a shirt. Probably a tie at one point, too, though he'd loosened his collar and removed it. He carried a remarkably wrinkled jacket over one arm. Nothing on his person, however, was as messy as his hair. He looked as if he'd been dragged through a hedge. "I've seen him before."

Hank raised an eyebrow and turned to see the man more clearly. "Yeah, I know."

"How do—?"

Before I could ask anything more, the man reached

our table. His eyes were large against his face, though alcohol had given his lids a heavy appearance. He struggled to keep them open as he faced us. His mouth opened. "Cathy . . ."

I did know him. Monobrow. The guy from my office, who'd popped in my first day to represent the Unwelcome Wagon. I hadn't seen him since then. In fact, I'd forgotten he existed. What in the world was he doing here? "All right, Merv." Cappy, wiping his hands on the already impossibly dirty towel that clung to his shoulder, moved up and took the man by the arm. "Let's leave them alone, okay?" He employed that special voice people use for drunks and the slow of understanding, mixing compassion with firmness.

Merv, if that was his name, shrugged off Cappy's hand. Still staring at me, he attempted to smooth down his shirt and then reached to tighten a necktie that wasn't there. Hank rose to his feet, revealing himself to be a good head higher than the interloper. In his neat clothing, he looked twice as broad-shouldered and nimble. "We're not looking for any trouble," he said in a manner that was friendly, but just as unyielding.

"Hear that? They're not looking for any trouble, Merv. Maybe you should let me coffee you up some."

Was the guy too drunk to talk? His face screwed up with irritation in the same way a toddler's might, right before a tantrum. He was too uncoordinated to strike out, though, so when Cappy grabbed his arm and started to lead him away, he couldn't resist. Back into the shadows they went, with the man casting only a few more glances back over his shoulder before they were gone. "Problem solved." Hank sat back down and pretended to dust off his hands.

"My hero." Dry as I sounded, I really was grateful and more than a little touched at the knight-in-shining-armor routine. It's not as if I got much of that white-glove treatment at home. "But what do you mean, *I know?*" He stared at me. "When I said I'd seen him before, you said, 'I know.'"

"Oh."

Maybe I'd touched on an embarrassing topic. He certainly didn't seem anxious to explain himself. "Well?" I said at last.

He shrugged. "The times I saw you coming from here? That's the guy you were with. That's all."

When finally I looked into his eyes, though, I could tell he was playing the gentleman yet again. That wasn't all. Not by any measure.

Chapter Seven

For me to give a tour in a kitchen facility? I might as well have been asked to conduct an annotated expedition around the Vatican. Yet I gave it a valiant effort. "Here's a sink," I said. "We here at Richmond Publication Kitchens adhere to a, uh, high level of sanitation. Wash, wash, wash!" I sounded like someone's Home Ec teacher. Problem was, if I didn't get my act together at work, I probably *would* end up as someone's Home Ec teacher. "Here we have a stove top, for cooking. And here's another stove top, for more cooking, and . . ." Out of desperation I began opening cabinets at random. "Pots, pans, weird scrubby things, lots of weird scrubby things. Costco must have had a sale. Cookie sheets. Lots of cookie sheets. Sinks. Refrigerator, refrigerator, refrigerator."

Tilly followed behind, shutting every drawer and door I left ajar and tutting at the way in which I sloppily glossed over state-of-the-art features. "Our refrigerators are Frigidaires with separate freezer compartments on the bottom. The sinks are stainless steel, so they reduce germs and are a dream to clean!" Fabulous as that might have been for her, I was less than impressed. I'd come from a future where fridges had flat-panel TVs installed next to the ice maker and juice dispenser. Cable-ready.

"I see. So you hired me to do your cleaning." Our one visitor, arms crossed over her little white purse, didn't sound any too pleased. From the time I'd walked her through the front door and escorted her through the outer offices and typing pool, my charge had been regarding the premises with wary eyes that darted from face to face, silently absorbing every detail. Only rarely had she glanced back at the gaggle of white-coated kitchen assistants who followed at a distance behind us. They were making me nervous, too.

"Oh, no," I assured her. "No, no. Not at all. Absolutely not. That is, beyond the usual . . . Tilly? Do your assistants clean their own dirty dishes?"

"Usually the junior staff do the dishes." Tilly sounded apologetic. "But we all pitch in! And our modern dishwashing equipment makes the job a dream!" Like one of Bob Barker's *The Price Is Right* dames, she waved her hand in a practiced motion over what looked like a hose hanging from the ceiling and a flat, shallow sink.

"Great," I said with enthusiasm, trying not to think about my two-drawer dishwasher at home with its whisper-quiet operation that I used maybe twice a month to rinse out wineglasses and coffee cups.

"And don't forget our Thermador ovens!" Tilly gushed, gesturing to the double panels set into the wall. "No more stooping to check on meals or breaking your back to pull out heavy dishes! And they cook like . . ."

"Let me guess," I interrupted. "A dream?"

". . . A dream!" She appeared slightly annoyed with me. "Well, they do."

Oy. But what was the newest member of my staff thinking of it all? I couldn't really tell. If any of the gleaming technology impressed her, she was doing a mighty fine job of not letting it show. Her face was polite and interested, but guarded. She reminded me of a dog brought from the rescue society into a new house for the first time, uncertain whether the destination might become home. I decided to check in. "Is it too overwhelming for you?"

Cherry Bradford's Sunday best might not have been from Peck and Peck, like mine. Her black hat and veil were more practical than pretty. Her gloves might not have extended much beyond the ball of her thumb, and her purse might have been small and somewhat shabby compared with those the other girls carried. Yet it would have been wrong to judge her state of mind by her clothing alone. "Overwhelming?" She sounded as if the idea was ridiculous. "I *know* my way around a kitchen."

Cherry flustered me. "Sometimes things are in different places, though, different shelves, different equipment. . . ." My phony rationalization withered under the intensity of her gaze. She pitied me, she really did. It's like my mom always used to tell me, over and over—a gal only gets one chance to make a first impression. I could tell by the mingled tilt of her nose and the slight sneer on her lip that my one shot at not treading on her goodwill had been spent the day before yesterday. "I'm only trying to be nice," I said to her in a low voice not intended for the ears of anyone else, my teeth bared in a grin.

"Oh, so I'm supposed to feel *grateful* that some white lady made me lose a job I'd had for almost two years." Contrasted against her dark brown skin, Cherry's teeth seemed ten times whiter than mine and definitely straighter. And I'd had braces in my youth.

"I don't expect *gratitude*." That was a lie. I could have used a little gratitude for having spent a good half hour and bribe of ten dollars, which could have bought six months' worth of Horn and Hardart Bee Cakes, extracting Cherry's name and address from her prick of a supervisor. I'd taken a cab to Harlem on my own after dark to beg her to consider working for me at a salary that was more than three times what she was making at the automat. I suspected that integrating on my own the lily-white offices of Richmond Publishing was not exactly written in my job description. But I'd done it, and though I'd done it out of remorse and shame for having been the cause of a whole day's distress and anger for her and the mother and father who had glared at me from the front door as she and I had talked on the stoop, a little thank-you might have been nice. It wasn't as if I was asking for a muffin basket. Yet liberal guilt would never let me admit what I really felt. "But you know, if you wouldn't badmouth me in front of my staff. . . ."

"Oh, yas'm! No'm! I won't be sassin' the boss lady, lawdy no!" Considering that she and I were still wearing the broad grins of two very polite hyenas with their foreheads almost butting over a carcass in the desert, it was amazing how much sarcasm she managed to force through her incisors. "Is that better, *ma'am?*"

"You told me yesterday you have a college degree. You know perfectly well it's not."

"Um, are you two okay?" Tilly wanted to know from her safe distance.

As if we'd discussed it beforehand, we both wheeled around to face her with bright and sunny smiles, pretending for all the world as if absolutely nothing was the matter. "Why, sure!" I even put my arm around Cherry's waist as if she and I were the best of chums.

You could almost hear the magical *ping!* of a sound effect to accompany the sparkle in Cherry's eye. "I can't wait to use the fancy ovens!" she enthused in the whitest voice I'd ever heard. "I bet they're a *dream!*"

No one would have faulted me if I'd given the girl a savage pinch right then, but mindful of all the pinches I'd received recently, I refrained. Truth be told, what did she have to lose by striking out in my direction? She probably thought she'd be let go within the week anyway, if not by the end of the day. Maybe, shocker of shockers, she really didn't like me. Whatever the punishment, as long as she did her work, I decided I'd suck it up. "Yes?" I said automatically, when one of the kitchen assistants nearby raised her hand.

"So we're going to be working with a colored girl?" she said.

Cherry hadn't been in the offices a half hour, and already the ugly underbelly of the 1950s was . . . well, whatever underbellies do. Begging to be rubbed, probably. The young woman who'd spoken wasn't one I really recognized yet. I made a note of her dubious expression and pursed lips while Tilly, bless her helpful little heart, frowned and said, "Negro."

"Black." Cherry crossed her arms and smiled as pleasantly as she could at Bigoted Betty.

"Afro-American. I mean, African-American," I said, then in confusion added, "or person of color."

The woman narrowed her eyes and shook her head. "That's what I said. Colored girl."

I didn't care what Hank thought about time travel. In about ten seconds of conversation we'd catapulted through five decades of politically correct vocabulary changes and had somehow come full circle. "I am adopting a new non-discrimination policy," I said loftily, "in which I will not consider race, creed, national origin, disability, or sexual orientation in our hiring decisions. We will simply hire the best-qualified people for the job. Miss Bradford holds a degree from Virginia Union College, and has an extensive background in food preparation and service gained at one of the highest-turnover restaurants in the New York metropolitan area. Anyone who feels she can't work with her in an open and supportive environment may feel free to seek employment elsewhere. Am I clear?"

You can take the girl out of the new millennium, but you can't take the new millennium out of the girl, I'm guessing. So cowed were most of my employees that I didn't hear even a rustle of skirts or the scrape of a lab coat. For a moment I felt more than a little smug. Then the applause began in the background. One pair of hands clapping, a solo ovation. "You tell 'em, mama!" I heard at the other end of the room, from a lanky figure sitting on a counter.

In the daily funnies, characters often have balloons over their heads in which appear a bunch of typewriter symbols in lieu of swearing. At that moment I was cooking up the biggest brew of dollar signs, asterisks, and ampersands the world had ever seen.

"Tilly?" I said, trying to keep my composure. "Would you see to it that Cherry is made comfortable?" I spared a smile for Cherry before I took long strides across the room in the other direction. The expression she returned was forced and false, but I was relieved that when Tilly started charming her with that sweet little Southern accent, my new charge seemed to soften a little. After all, who could resist Tilly? "You. J.P." I barked, snapping my fingers at the little twerp. "Get your rear end off my clean counters and into my office."

Oddly, it wasn't until he'd obediently slithered down that he found his confidence and voice again. "So we're going to consummate our passion right now?"

"Yeah, something like that." At least the little scene was taking focus off Cherry for a few moments.

"You sure you don't want to go to the Plaza or someplace special like that?" J.P. leered in a way that exposed as much gum line as teeth. What girl can resist that? "I got my uncle's Diner's Club."

"Get in there," I growled, shoving him through my door. Once through, I slammed it behind me. "Sit down."

Instead of listening, he wandered into the corner of my office, where I still had more Tiny Minnies than I knew what to do with, and pried off the top of one of the cases. "Hey!" he yelled when I grabbed him by the ear and pulled him away. "Our love makes me hungry, baby!"

"I am *not—!*" Before another collective of carats and ampersands and pound signs started forming, I tried to calm myself down. Kids like this got off on getting a reaction from someone. Becoming angry would play right into his agenda. I needed to stop my blood pressure from soaring, remember to stay unperturbed, and pretend that he was an adult human instead of a hairy primate whose knuckles still scraped the ground. Easy enough, right? "I'm sorry," I said soothingly. "Maybe a Tiny Minnie would do us both good. Would you like one? Two? I'm going to have two."

"Yeah, that sounds good." He watched while I fetched us both a couple of snack cakes and caught his adeptly when I tossed it to him on my way back to the other side of my desk. With his teeth, he ripped open the cellophane. "You eat up, my vision of loveliness. I like a babe with an appetite, you know."

Oh, those are words that every big girl longs to hear and so rarely does. J.P. did not know how close I was to ditching the hostility and settling for his hand in marriage, right then. I cleared my throat and assumed a friendly, almost motherly smile. "J.P."

"Yeah, doll?" He leaned into the desk, matching me pose for pose with his inclined frame and intertwined fingers.

"Did your mother ever tell you not to shout indoors?"

He wrinkled his brow. "I wasn't shouting."

"No, no, of course you weren't," I said with a warm and reassuring smile. "I mean, some mothers tell their children not to use their outdoor voice when they should be using their indoor voice."

He leered. "I can show you my bedroom voice."

Again, oy. This was going to take longer than I'd hoped. "I'm trying to be serious, kiddo. How about it? You and me, talking like adults. Serious adults. Think it's a possibility?"

J.P. cleared his throat, seeming to understand. His head drooped a little. "Yeah. We can do that. But so you know . . . I don't have a mother."

Oh, man. The poor kid. He'd been a prick, sure, but I couldn't help letting the soft and squishy side of my heart feel for him. No wonder he was such a junior yahoo, without a mother's influence to keep him courteous. Not that I'm the kind of girl who thinks that men can't be civilized—I simply hadn't seen much evidence to support the theory in this particular decade. The era of daddies who wore baby backpacks and were adept at the art of diapering was well in the future. "I'm sorry." It explained so much. It didn't explain his skinny ties, but I'm not sure anything would. "That must have been rough."

He shrugged. "It was okay. You don't have to feel sorry for me or anything."

"But I do." We were getting slightly off track here. Maybe there was a way I could bring it around. Gently, I told him, "See, I think if you'd had a mother, she would have taught you about appropriate work behavior. Just like there's an outdoor voice, there's a kind of friendly, fun, flirtatious behavior that you can enjoy *outside* the office with your friends and the people you know well. Really, really well," I added for emphasis. He nodded. If I didn't make it as a Tiny Minnie magnate, I could very well have a career in school counseling in my future. "You know. Like joking around and pretending you're in love with someone."

"I am in love with you!"

That I doubted, despite his apparent sincerity. The kid actually seemed borderline angry that I suspected his motives. "Oh, J.P. Maybe it's easier for you to flirt with me because I'm—let's face it—not quite as pretty as the skinny young things who work for me." That was no biggie to admit. I'd faced it all my life. Guys preferred bony little things to cuddling up to a cush-

146

iony blonde. Facing it might deflate this illusion of a crush he believed he had.

"You don't get it at all." J.P. hunched forward, resting his elbows on his knees. "And don't go telling me you're not pretty. You are."

"J.P. . . ."

"You're like Marilyn Monroe!"

The comparison was so flattering that I couldn't help but blush a little. There *may* have been a few similarities between the greatest sex bomb of all time and myself. And now that I thought about it, Cathy's curly 'do might have had the intention of drawing attention to the vague, *zaftig* likeness. But me, Marilyn? Of course I had to set him straight with a flat denial. I regret to confess that what came flying from my mouth was instead, "Do you really think so?"

"Well, sure!" Was that a little glimmer of sincerity I saw deep inside there? He smiled at me shyly. "I think so. Hey, this is a gas, being able to talk to you this way."

"I think it's a gas, too." I was going solely on context that we meant something good that wasn't flatulence.

We sat quietly for a moment while I watched his face grow long and grave. "Hey, can I tell you something?" Was I actually cracking through that bluff post-adolescent shell and to a feeling being within? "Something personal?"

By George, I thought I'd got it. I was about to get a one-hundred-percent genuine, actual insight into what made this boy tick beyond the hormones. Perhaps even the first vision of the nascent adult lurking within that anyone had ever before seen! "Sure, J.P. Go ahead."

There was a long moment in which I feared that he might reveal something really on the high end of the

T.M.I. scale. A case of juvenile gonorrhea, perhaps, or something embarrassingly personal like not being to able to cast the ol' bait and tackle, if you know what I mean. Finally the kid's Adam's apple bobbed up and down as he gulped and said in a hurry, "I know that I come off as kind of a goof. I know people get frosted about it. You too, I guess." He shot me a quick look. "I guess this is kind of . . . it's hard for me to say."

"No, go on." He shook his head, refusing. But we had been doing so well! I was going to have to give something before he would. "Listen. I know it's hard to open up to people when you're keeping your true self inside. I have that problem myself, sometimes. I spend a lot of time—a *lot* of time—trying to make people think I'm someone I'm not."

"Yeah?"

"Yeah. I guess before I reveal more of myself, I want to know that it's going to be safe. That no one's going to laugh or point fingers or make judgments or any of that crap." Now he nodded. I figured he might understand that one. "We all have these false fronts that somehow get in the way of people knowing the real us. But you know, kiddo, the friends who get to see the *real* you are the ones who are going to stick around when things get rough."

Hope filled his glistening eyes. "You mean . . . if I was more . . . I don't know . . . you'd want to get to know the real me?"

Oh my gosh, was he about to cry? It surely looked it; aside from the shining eyes, his lower lip was wobbling dangerously. Had I made a real breakthrough here? A real connection for the first time since my arrival? Maybe I was wiser than I thought. Showing the real me had gotten through the boy's tough exterior.

"Of course, J.P.! Not romantically, of course. There's a little age difference there, and your uncle's my boss, and it's all very complicated. But yes! Absolutely!"

"Because you're the first . . . first . . ." He was crying. His shoulders convulsed, and he buried his face in his hands. "You're the first person to say that to me. Ever."

J.P.'s breakdown called for immediate reaction. I grabbed a box of Kleenex that dwelled in my lowermost drawer and raced around my desk until I sat in front of him on its edge. "Hey, it's okay!" I brandished a few tissues while I reassured him.

"Don't tell anyone!" he said in a gargle.

"No, of course I won't!"

I could barely be heard over the sound of his nose-blowing. He still held one hand over his eyes so that I couldn't see his tears. "When I was in high school . . . all the girls . . . thought I was a nerd," he said between hiccups. "And the guys . . . pounded me . . . it was awful. Awful!"

I'd asked him to open up. Who knew I would get more than I'd bargained for? He was practically curled up in a fetal position in the chair. "It's okay," I murmured. "You're better than that. You are." I rubbed his shoulder with a hand. "Sssssh."

I was surprised when he reached up and grabbed my hand, fumbling to intertwine my fingers with his. We had a real connection now, J.P. and I, a common shared misery, something rich and fine and thoroughly human. "I should go." His words were barely audible. "I can't face a woman like this. Not . . . not you."

"Hey." He was already bent forward. It was simplicity itself to help him to his feet and wrap my arms around him in a big, comforting hug. He automati-

149

cally laid his head on my chest and his hands on my shoulders, like a hurt little boy. "It's okay. Everything's going to be all right."

"No, it won't!"

"You've got to believe it will. You've really got to believe that everything you've been through is all for the best," I said, stroking his hair.

I mean, it was true, wasn't it? Wasn't it Werner Klemperer who said that what doesn't kill us makes us stronger? No, not him. He was in *Hogan's Heroes*. Some other German guy. Didn't I have to believe that thought myself, though? I hated to think that I'd taken this mighty jump backwards if I wasn't going to gain something from it. Even if it was as simple as a life lesson, corny and sitcommy as it sounded. Every morning for the last week and a half I'd woken beneath that chenille bedspread with a first thought of, *I'm still here*. It was impossible not to wonder why. I had to believe it would lead to something. Maybe I couldn't be the fourteenth wheel at the Last Supper, but surely I could help someone change a little. Couldn't I?

"Really," I said in barely more than a whisper. "It's for the best."

"I know." His words vibrated through the fabric of my prim little cotton blouse, lower on my torso than before. "It's for the best." For someone who'd been weeping and wailing only a few moments before, he was suddenly strangely calm.

An awkward pause followed in which I removed my hands from his hair, peered down at him, and narrowed my eyes. "J.P.?" Because my neck was constricted, my voice came out funny.

"Hmmmm?" he murmured, not letting go.

"Is your face between my breasts?"

I Went to Vassar for This?

"Yes?"

"I see," I said calmly, trying to decide how best to extricate myself from his amorous clutch. "Is your mother really dead?"

"My dad says she's dead in the sack."

"Was all this . . . *hey!*" He had copped a squeeze. I'd walked blindly into the kid's ambush. Damn it! With both hands, I shoved his shoulders. "You little shit!"

J.P.'s freckled complexion was slightly red from all the hand-rubbing he'd done over his face, but they were totally free of any tear tracks. His broad mouth parted in a toothy grin. "Aw, come on! You loved it."

"Oh, I *so* did not!" Honestly, I was more in awe of the kid's chutzpah than I was outraged by anything he'd done. I mean, sweet mother of Jesus, with the ability to lie like that, he could grow up to be President of the United States or even a television executive!

He rolled his eyes in the universal adolescent signal for utter disbelief. "Whatever you say, ma'am."

"No," I warned him, shaking my index finger. "Don't be doing that thing, that juvenile *thing*. I know that *thing*. I did that *thing* to my mother until I was twenty-five and I still trot it out at the holidays so I can give it an airing. I did *not* enjoy you feeding me a whole song and dance about your pathetic, sex-starved pubescence simply so you could get your face between my bubbies."

J.P. apparently found great interest in the ceiling, from the way he studied it. "Whatever you say."

"Do not . . . do . . . that *thing!*" I warned him, ire rising.

His head rolled to the side. "Besides, I didn't just get my face in your bubbies. I got a good handful, too."

151

"That's it!" I didn't care if they could hear me outside the office, the way I screamed. I didn't care if they could hear me in Dallas, Texas, if it meant I got my point across. "You and I are poison, J.P. Richmond! Poison! Finished! Kaput!" When I stalked closer, he darted away. "I don't want you around unless you address me in a respectful, businesslike manner. I don't want you coming near my staff and bothering them with your masturbatory fantasies. I *especially* don't want you scaring off the new girl. Do you hear?"

He dodged around the rear of my desk when I dashed toward him. "Why would I?"

"You know why!"

"Because of her skin color?" he said, sounding incredulous. "That doesn't make no never mind to me! I'm all for integration!"

"Don't try to suck up to me, you pimply freak." Ow. I banged my knee against my desk chair, but it didn't stop me from my pursuit.

"I am! It's my uncle you got to look out for there." He yelped as he tried to make a dash across the room, misjudged his position, and barreled into a stack of Tiny Minnies. "Anyway, I like sweet, blond vanilla better than chocolate. Hey!"

He clawed at the doorknob to my office as I caught his shirt by the neck. I could feel seams give as I tried to tug him back, but I was really no match for a determined teenaged boy. He slid to the floor only to land flat on his ass, fumbled around for a foothold, then finally scooted as hard as he could across the linoleum until I let go of his collar. "And don't come back, you little *perv!*" I yelled at the top of my lungs.

Only after he'd run to the safe haven of the typing pool did I observe that the entire test kitchen staff had stopped dead in their tracks to observe my tantrum. Ovens stood open, pots boiled unattended, and no one moved a muscle when an egg timer went off with the resonance of a fire alarm. One of the girls stood with a running electric hand mixer aimed at the ceiling, not even noticing she was splattering cake batter everywhere.

"Well, he is a perv," I announced, trying to pretend a dignity I didn't feel. I turned. Tilly and Cherry stood only a few feet away, a pair of marble statues turned rigid by my gorgonlike powers. Tilly had frozen in the middle of helping Cherry don one of the work coats hanging on the rack nearby, so that they had inadvertently been the closest eyewitnesses to the grand event. "And he won't be treating me like that again," I said, feigning confidence.

All I wanted to do was slink back inside my office, close the door, and bang my head on the desk. As I turned, before I locked myself in for the afternoon, I heard Cherry ask quite loudly, "Is she crazy? Because I am not working for a crazy woman."

"Only lately!" Tilly said, managing to make the statement sound optimistic.

I didn't wait for the rest of what she might say.

Men! Overgrown adolescents! If they weren't letting their hands run amok over a girl in a wild attempt to get to second base, they were drinking too much and lurching in her direction, or pinching her fanny, or indulging in any of the thousand humiliating ways to demean her. While I trudged home from the Lexington Avenue local that evening, the greasy film left by too many Tiny Minnies making the roof of my mouth slick and sour, I took special notice of the opposite sex. Weren't guys supposed to be thinking about sex every eight seconds? Fog and gray mist had descended upon the city, causing all the men to pull up the collars of their overcoats as they hurried through the damp, cold street in the direction of their homes and dates. The law of averages dictated that one out of every eight of those rushed steps was devoted to nasty thoughts. *Cold work home food cold Thanksgiving food BOOBS. Fear cold worry hurry rain mom Sunday SEX.*

The steps to my townhouse were slippery. Almost icy, in fact. From outside I could see Hank's tall and familiar silhouette through the glass. He stepped aside when I pushed open the door. "Hey," I said without preamble, whipping off my hat. "When I say *now*, tell me in one word what you're thinking. It can be anything. I want to test a theory. Don't worry about shocking me. Okay? *Now.*"

"Cathy." Hank's face was a little pale. I took it as a symptom of standing in the chilly foyer.

"*Now*," I said after a second's lapse.

"Cathy."

"*Now.*"

"Cathy."

"You're not playing!" I shook droplets of rain from my coat onto the floor as I unbuttoned it and began slipping it from my shoulders. I half-expected Hank to help, but he still stood before me with an unreadable expression. No doubt I was confusing him. "Sorry," I apologized. "I had a theory about men."

He shook his head. "What are you?"

Oh, we were being frisky, were we? His expression didn't seem to say so, but I could play along. "Me woman. You man!" I said, digging a finger into his chest.

154

I Went to Vassar for This?

Hank simply looked at me as if I were crazy. "No," he repeated. "What *are* you?" I still didn't understand. "Do you know what this is?"

I looked at the floppy, folded item he brandished in his left hand and ventured the obvious. "It's called a newspaper. They're printed every day."

"Read the front page." He thrust it into my gloved hands.

"Hey, ink smudges lambskin." A mere couple of weeks in the '50s, and I'd gone all girly-girly. Was Hank mad at me or something? What in the world had I done? At his insistence, I started reciting from the top. "Thursday, November 19, 1959."

He jabbed at a headline farther down. "There."

"Fine, Mr. Pushy. Eisenhower said . . . *okay*," I grumbled, when he kept jabbing away. I started to read in a drone. "Ford Announces Discontinuation of Edsel. Detroit-based Ford cites poor sales and customer disinterest as the primary reason for . . ."

I looked up, my voice trailing away. Hank stared at me full-on, his eyes boring into mine. "This is today's paper, Cathy," he said. "They announced this *today*. In what marketing class did you study the Edsel, Cathy? Where was it? Where *was* it?"

I opened my mouth to speak, but the voice that came out wasn't mine. "I hoped I'd find you two!" Tilly, clad in a comfortable sweater set and plaid wool skirt, clattered down the stairs. "One of Chester's friends is a waiter and he's gotten us a table for six at a new Italian joint that's opening tomorrow."

"Italian?" I said, glad for any interruption. Hank and I still stared at each other with locked expressions, though.

"They're doing a practice run tonight. The food's

155

free, but we have to pay for the wine. Miranda's bringing Harold. And you two will be the third couple. Perfect! Come upstairs and get ready!" she added for my benefit. "We need to be there by seven-thirty."

"Perfect," I echoed, so faintly it was inaudible. Hank didn't say anything. The question he'd asked me hung in the air between us. For one of the first times in my life, I realized I didn't have a ready answer.

Chapter Eight

"To Tony!" roared Harold Silverstein, hefting up his glass so high and with such vigor that it threatened to shower the table with red wine. "Whoever the hell he is."

"To Tony!" echoed Chester, joining in on the toast. Harold had been loud, but Tilly's ostensible beau had such a thunderous voice that half the restaurant turned around, grinned, and shouted out their own paeans over the music a little jazz trio played in a corner. TONY LUPONE'S, had read the neon letters above the little corner restaurant's entrance outside. DINE—DANCE.

"Oh, Chester. You're so full of life!" giggled Tilly. Her cheeks were flushed. Everyone's cheeks were flushed, actually. The food was free. The wine had been flowing liberally from the time we'd sat down, through the appetizers and salad, until they'd delivered our meals. The restaurant was overheated. And the booths and tablecloths were all red and reflected from our shiny faces. I was surprised we weren't all the color of pickled beets.

This kind of spontaneous night out was exactly the sort of thing that Thuy and I would have done on a dull and chilly evening at home. As everyone else in Tony Lupone's joined in the loud revelry, I figured I might as well attempt a little fun myself. My undergrad days weren't so very far away that the prospect of cheap eats didn't still rouse me, and besides, there was already one person at the table who'd spent the entire meal staring sullenly. I didn't want people to think I was ripping off his act. "To Tony!" I called.

Mid-chug, Hank ladled out more of the questions with which he'd been assaulting me all evening. "Do you work for Ford?"

"No," I said, trying to pretend he wasn't there.

"Do you know anyone who works for Ford?"

I waved away the offer of a cigarette from Chester, and was appalled to see that Tilly had actually accepted one. At the very least, she smoked it inexpertly, and nearly let it drop from between her fingers a couple of times. "No," I said, politely, but firmly.

"Do you have any sources who might know someone who works at Ford who could have told you about the Edsel being discontinued?"

Pretending that this conversation wasn't happening wasn't succeeding. My big, fat mouth had caught up to me, and good. The panic in my stomach wouldn't subside, no matter how much I went through the motions of enjoying my meal. Minus the freezing water, the iceberg, and Leonardo DiCaprio, I knew what Kate Winslet felt like when the *Titanic* was going down for the last time. "Listen," I said to him, leaning in close so he wouldn't miss a word. "You're making a mountain out of a molehill."

"Am I?" He, too, had moved in, his arm resting

atop the booth's back behind me. For all his serious-
ness, I'd never seen him look more animated. He was
onto something—more than he suspected, probably—
and wasn't about to let go.

Why couldn't I tell Hank everything? Why not un-
burden? Hadn't I been dying, absolutely dying, to
have a confidante since the moment I'd gotten here?
Hank was smart; Hank was a nice guy. Hank was
handsome, too, more so every time I saw him. It was
as if he'd been making an effort to clean up for me after my comment on his dandruff, the first night I'd
seen him. Although both Chester and Harold had chosen a more conservative approach with their coats and
ties, Hank was more than holding his own with a dark
burgundy turtleneck and a cardigan with diamonds
running down the side panels. I tore my gaze away
from his physique and looked into the serious eyes on
the other side of his thick glasses. "Yeah, you are. My
tongue slipped. I told you I made a mistake. That's all
there is to it, my friend." I tried playing it cool with a
sip of wine, but my hand trembled so much that I
didn't dare lift the glass very high.

"There's something you're not telling me," he insisted.

I shrugged, smiling. My gaze flickered over to
Harold and Miranda. They were both looking our way,
speculation in their eyes. They quickly swiveled their
heads when they saw I'd noticed, but not before they
exchanged a significant glance. When I turned my head
to Tilly and Chester, I caught them looking at us, as
well. They also reacted with the same embarrassment.

Suddenly I became uncomfortable. They were totally trying to figure us out, as if they suspected we
were a couple or something. Why in the world would

they think that? My eyes took in how close together Hank and I sat, with his arm around my shoulders. I remembered as well the coy little cat-and-mouse smiles we'd been tossing back and forth ever since we'd been wedged in on either side by the other couples. Oh. That's why. I've always noticed the tyranny of couples; a girl can be as single as she likes as long as her friends are all unattached as well, but let one of them become partnered, and suddenly she'll be trying to fix up all the less-fortunates. It was contagious; coupling had spread like wildfire through my groups of friends. Save me, anyway, the seemingly immune. Why couldn't it infect me, damn it? Not that I could afford to start anything with Hank. I was fifty years older than he was! Or the other way around.

Plus, it was simply unwise. What if I were yanked back to my own time unexpectedly? I couldn't easily tuck him in my pocket and take him along for the ride. Why get my hopes up for something good when it would only be taken away from me? Maybe some of my discomfort showed, because Tilly gave me a pitying look and grabbed Chester's hand. "Let's go dance, honey," she suggested, pulling him from the booth.

Hank didn't notice their departure. He had eyes for no one but me. Ordinarily I'd be complimented and a little abashed. Considering that I was still the object of his little inquisition, though, it wasn't so great. "The way I see it, there are three options," he said to me. "One. You know someone who works for the company and got some inside information that way. Two. You're psychic. What number am I thinking of?"

"Hank?"

"Tell me. You should know."

Okay, fun's fun, but he was making me decidedly ill

at ease. "Maybe, just maybe, I was telling the truth and my tongue slipped and I meant some other car. Or how about this? I'm a smart woman. I read the papers. I see that Edsel isn't selling well. It's not exactly a secret, right? Then I make an intuitive leap and, from a purely business perspective, guess that the line can't survive long." It was so convincing that I half believed it myself, save for the fact that in her own century, Miss Eye For Trends rarely read any news beyond the Arts and Leisure section and a few gossipy blogs online. "How about that, hmmm?"

He leaned in still closer. "See, Cathy, here's the thing. You don't pick a story and stick to it. One minute, you're confident as hell about what you're saying. I know confidence. I grew up around confident people. Then you're pretending to be a dizzy blonde and saying that your tongue slipped."

I gasped in outrage. "Pretending! I don't have to pretend to be a dizzy blonde!"

"Don't fake with me," he continued smoothly. "And then, you try to hand me some cockamamie story about predicting it all because of some business intuition. Don't get me wrong. You're obviously a smart woman. But which story is it?"

"Every time we're together, you haul out your worst adjectives for me, don't you?" I'd tried to calm myself with wine, but I was too nervous to drink. I'd tried to finish what was left of my steak, but I had no appetite left. "Now I'm a fake? If I'm such a horrible person, why do you even care why I say what I say, Mr. Cabot?"

Though I'd been forcing the words through my teeth, I must have grown shrill during my angry speech. Both Miranda and her date stared at us, stunned. For a moment, it seemed as if we'd never achieve any kind of conversational equilibrium ever again, but at least everyone relaxed when I suddenly laughed and tried to smooth things over. "Politics," I explained. "Apparently I voted for Nixon, you know."

"You did?" Hank seemed surprised.

I shrugged. "That's what they tell me."

"Cabot?" Harold and Hank had met under the red neon at the restaurant's front door, but in the confusion and urgency to get inside out of the cold, he might not have caught Hank's details. "That's quite a name in some circles." I didn't know Harold well, or at all save through the things I'd heard Miranda say about him, but he struck me as the kind of guy whose intentions were better and bigger than his ability to read others. He didn't seem to pick up, for example, the way in which Hank crossed his arms over his chest at that statement, or the bald hostility leveled in his direction. "Cabot, as in Philander Cabot? Funny thing about that. Philander Cabot is one of the accounts at the Maritime Bank—where I work, don'tcha know— well, he's *the* account at the bank, and he was the one who bought a block of tickets for us at Maritime to see *The Sound of Music* last week, at one of the last previews before it opened."

Miranda, the big show-off, snuggled her shoulders more deeply into her sable. "You have *got* to see it," she told us both, waving her hands over the breadsticks. "*Quelle* divoon. The critics agree with me. I felt so uplifted afterwards. Didn't I, Hal?" The banker smiled at her, nodding. "We were so *lucky* to be able to see it before the masses. It's like I told Hal when we

162

sat down with our playbills. Some things you have an intuition about. Don't you agree, Hank?"

"Oh, yes." I didn't dare look to the left of me, because I knew the landlord would be staring my way. "I am in full agreement about intuition."

"And my intuition told me that little play would be a classic. An absolute classic!"

You know, if I'd had time to drag *my* fur from the closet for this shindig, I could have made hers look like the scrap of rat pelt it really was. Luckily for Miranda, I was staunchly against the wearing of expensive furs in public. And I'd only had time to grab my wool coat, damn it. I felt like grinding my teeth. Instead, I muttered, "Funny. I think I've heard someone say that before."

"Philander Cabot. Quite the capitalist. I don't suppose . . . ?"

Hank didn't flinch at showing his resentment at the question. "I think the phrase you're searching for, Mr. Silverstein, is *stinking rich.*" He uncrossed his arms and slugged back what remained in the bottom of his wine goblet, then helped himself to some more. "And yes, I'm acquainted with Philander Cabot. I'm the last of his six grandchildren."

Talk about being thrown for a loop. For a second I completely forgot about my own dilemma. "What?" I said, looking from Hank to Harold to Miranda. "You're fabulously wealthy or something?" It was as if I'd suddenly and loudly been flatulent without acknowledgment or apology. Hank stared at me without answer. Harold pretended to find the next table over more interesting than our own. My flatmate seemed slightly embarrassed by the entire conversation.

Slowly, comprehension dawned. "Oh, am I not supposed to talk about money?"

Miranda reached across the table past the rose in the white porcelain vase and patted the back of my hand. "*Quelle* vulgar," she murmured.

Oh really? I couldn't help but flare up with irritation at being patronized. As if her little dips into French weren't stagy and affected? Back at my job—the job I'd lost, anyway—I used to talk about money all the time. Primarily about how to help my clients part with it. My whole culture was frank about money: who had it, who wanted it, who showed it off, who squandered it. "Oh, I didn't mean to be rude," I said, trying to keep my voice light despite the fact that I *did* intend just that. "It seems funny to me that in this decade . . . I mean, in this day and age . . . it's *vulgar* to talk about money. It's like Lucy not being able to tell Ricky she was pregnant, or married couples on TV sleeping in twin beds. Where do people think those babies are coming from, the stork? Money's the same way. We like to pretend we have it, don't we? I mean, Miranda, honestly, look at you and me. An out-of-work actress and a cookbook writer living in a tiny townhouse apartment so we can afford our nice dresses and our big fur coats and our hair dye and our gay little nights out."

"I *beg* your pardon." Miranda's eyes flashed. "I am a *natural* redhead."

I'd meant to lash out for a bit of revenge, but I'd gone too far with the hair dye comment, maybe. "I'm the 'Does she or doesn't she?' girl in our little trio," I fibbed, for Harold's benefit as much as Miranda's. Her hands had flown to her head the moment I'd brought up the topic. Risking Tilly's disapproval, I grabbed a handful of my own curls. "There's no way this blond mess could be real. But my point is that no matter how much you—we—pretend we're not interested in money, we really are, aren't we? Isn't it a bit hypocritical to pretend we're indifferent when we're really lovin' the bling?"

Okay, so it was no speech of Shakespearean magnitude, but I thought I had a good point. And though I regretted embarrassing Miranda about her cinnamon-candy hair, part of me was a wee bit happy to spout off after an enforced diet of French interjections. She looked vaguely embarrassed, though, as if a certain odor still lingered in my vicinity. I made a mental note to myself: *Don't poke cultural sore points.*

"Bling?" asked Harold. At least he didn't look at me as if I smelled. Only as if I had measles. When she thought I wasn't observing, Miranda shook her head with dismissal, her standard response to what she thought of as Cathy's recent eccentricities. Harold went back to observing the dancers, nodding his head in time with the music, and looking amiably dim.

Hank spoke up for the first time since the new topic had been brought up. "As a matter of fact, Cathy, I can't really say that I inherited the Cabot family tendency to either make or hoard money." His tone was matter-of-fact, which after my speech I appreciated. He inclined his head in my direction. "I'm not wealthy at all."

"Oh, that's not true." Miranda was still distinctly uncomfortable with this entire conversation. She laughed lightly. "Your grandfather owns practically our entire block. You manage all those townhouses! You're practically a land magnate."

"That toehold to respectability is my one concession to the family." Was it my imagination, or was Hank speaking primarily to me? "I earn enough collecting rent and seeing to repairs to let me do my work. The family leaves me alone, mostly. It's a civilized arrangement. But I'm not wealthy."

"But you could be," I said, wondering how he'd react.

When was I going to learn that people were not my science project? I could practically see the defenses fly up as I watched his face. "But I'm not."

"But you *could* be. If you buckled down and did what? Wore the family crest? Spoke through your nose when addressing the hoi polloi?" I said in my best Miss Jane Hathaway.

His shoulders deflated slightly in a sigh I couldn't hear. "But I'm not. And I don't."

"Thank Boca!" I think we had, for a few moments, completely forgotten that Harold was at the table. His exclamation was so unexpected that all three of us stared at him in wonder. "Hank Cabot," he said at last, as if that explained everything.

"Harold loves anagrams," said Miranda, touching her date's elbow. Her tone was more in line with a statement like, "*Harold has hemorrhoids*."

He beamed. "That's right. Thank Boca. Hank Cabot. See? It's like Cathy Voight. Ah. . . . wait for it." His face contorted in a frown.

We waited. Oh, how we waited. Miranda attempted to put a brave face on the situation, smiling at Harold as if he were the brightest little boy in grade three, while Hank and I fidgeted on the booth's leather seat. We waited while Harold licked his lips, and while he leaned back with his fingers to his temples, and while he moved his lips in thought. We waited while everyone else politely applauded for the conclusion of the jazz trio's song. I was about to stop waiting and call for another bottle of red when Miranda said, by way of prolonging the suspense, "He's marvelous at this, really."

That was all the inspiration Harold needed to get the job done. "Itchy vat hog!" he yelled at the top of his lungs.

"Fabulous." How I managed to keep my voice level, I didn't know. "Thank you for that."

"Let's dance, darling," Miranda tactfully suggested as Tilly and Chester returned from their foxtrot.

"Great!"

Tilly's face was flushed with pleasure, I noted. The way she looked at Chester—well, it was the look of a woman falling in love. I was going to have to speak to her frankly, one of these days, before it got too late. For now, though, I was grateful to have her at the table so that I wouldn't have to be alone with Hank. I reached out and grabbed her hand. "Having fun?"

"Oh, it's a swell night!" she gushed, plopping beside me. "What did I miss?"

"I'm an itchy vat hog."

"Oh really?" I was surprised that Tilly took it all in stride, but she turned to Chester and said, "Miranda's date is fond of anagrams."

"Hmmm?" Although he'd been guiding the darned near prettiest girl in all of Tony Lupone's around the floor for the past ten minutes, Chester's eyes were dancing over the slim waist and V-shaped torso of a passing waiter. Poor, poor Tilly. "Auntie who?"

He got a swat for that one. "Anagrams, you big silly! Where you rearrange the letters of words to make them spell something else. He did it for me the other night, when I was talking to him on the phone. I'm a sunlit gentility. Isn't that nice?"

You'd think that with the ample buffet of stresses laid before me that evening, I'd choose anything else to get upset over. But no. "*A sunlit gentility?*" I said with a gasp. "How in the world did you get a sunlit gentility and I got stuck with big vast hog?"

"Itchy vat hog."

Oh, so *now* Hank was being helpful? I spared him a quick evil eye. "Foul! Foul, I cry!"

Tilly thought I was being humorous. "Oh, Cathy. It's so good to see you having fun again."

"I'm not—!"

I heard a rustle beside me. Hank was sliding out of the booth. "Let's dance," he said to me.

No, that was the last thing I wanted. "I'm not . . ."

"Oh, go on!" Tilly was den mother now, playfully pushing me along. "You two dance!" Didn't she see the appeal in my eyes? I really didn't want to! Apparently not. "Shoo!" she urged. "Shoo, now!"

One last time I tried to beg off. "I can't."

"Cathy." Hank was standing by the table now, tall and commanding. He held out his hand. "Dance with me."

Was the decade getting to me? Had wearing a girdle for days on end stifled the flow of blood to my brain, or was having to pretend to be a good little girl actually getting to me? In my own time, if some guy in the bars had tried pulling the alpha male act with me, I would have laughed in his face, told him where to get off, and then spent the rest of the evening making loud derogatory comments to Thuy about the probable size of his genitalia. But this was Hank. What could I do but agree?

I Went to Vassar for This?

Oh, I cursed every inch of that trip along the U-shaped booth bench, and cursed myself for standing up and smiling as if I were thrilled to comply. I cursed Tilly for beaming at us like a yenta delighted to have knitted together another happy couple. Mostly, though, I cursed Hank and his insatiable curiosity. Why couldn't I have spent 1959 shut in my bedroom with my supply of Tiny Minnies and a stack of old True Romances?

The band was playing a slow, jazzy number that I recognized as a Sinatra standard, though I couldn't quite remember the words. It was with a sure grasp that Hank pulled me close to him, his left hand holding my fingers, his right arm poised at the arch of my back. He smelled of English Leather and hair cream and the slightest odor of mothballs that I attributed to the sweater. I hadn't been this close to a man since . . . well, I couldn't remember when had been the last time. Why was I so terrified? I had to say something to ease the tension. "I hope I'm not too much of a pauper to dance with."

"Never use wealth against me," he said, close to my ear. I'd heard Hank's voice startled and on guard, my first night here. I'd heard him peeved, the night we'd had dinner. And I'd heard him laughing on the evening we'd made up. Never before, though, had I heard his voice low and intimate and so close. His breath tickled my neck, raising goose bumps. "That's a weapon I know how to dodge."

"Sorry," I said immediately, marveling at myself again. What was making me so compliant around the guy? All my life I'd been breaking down every conventional barrier that had stood in my way, and here I was acting like some kind of . . . some kind of . . . gee, his eyes were awfully brown, like big melted pools of Bently Brand Toffee Bits, the little bitty chew with the great big taste. Wait a minute. What was I thinking about? I'd forgotten.

"Do you remember the night you came down to my apartment?" he murmured.

Why, the big old softy. Was he thinking about that, too? "Oh, yes."

"Hmmm." He laughed slightly, barely more than a rumble of amusement at the memory. "Remember how you told me that Kennedy would be the next president?"

"Mmmm-hmmmm." The guy was a pretty smooth dancer. Much better than my granddad, who'd taught me. Over Hank's shoulder I could see Harold clutching at Miranda as if she were a bundle of fishes wrapped in a green silk gown.

"You knew that because you're some kind of mentalist, didn't you?"

Zzzzzzip. That was the sound of the needle skipping right across the record, thank you very much—a metaphor that made much more sense in this particular era than in my own. Everything I'd been fearing about being alone with Hank came rushing back into my brain after the momentary amnesia induced by his spicy scent. "You are insane," I told him, trying to jerk away. "*Insane.*"

"There's got to be an explanation." If he was going to be so bullheaded, I'd simply head back to the table. Yet though I attempted to break away, he had too good a grip. "Why were you asking about time machines?"

"I was trying to discuss literature with you," I growled at him, then yanked my hand away from his. "If you're going to dance, dance nicely."

"Did you build one?"

"Yes, with my trusty little toolbox, a nail file, and a transistor radio."

"Really?" He sounded impressed.

"No!"

"Did you find one? Did one of your friends at Ford build one?"

If I were honest, I'd have to admit I wished he'd come out and guess what was really happening. What a relief that scenario would have been! How unlikely was it, though? He'd seen Cathy Voight for months and months before I'd arrived on the scene. Coming up with *"Did you get hit in the head when a microwave oven exploded, time travel half a century, and take over my tenant's body?"* was going to be a bit of stretch even for someone with a big imagination. "Yes, that's it," I responded as flatly as possible. "Actually, I ordered a time machine kit from the back of one of the comic books you love so dearly." Drollery wasn't all that easy when dancing; I nearly tripped over myself as we turned in a slow circle near the jazz trio. Luckily Hank was still clutching me firmly around the waist to help me regain my balance. I thought about what I'd said. "You can't do that, can you?"

"I'm not going to tell anyone," he said, in much the same way that the other men on the dance floor were whispering sweet nothings into their lovers' ears. "I won't turn you in to the government or to scientists at Johns Hopkins."

"Oh, so *sweet!*" I exclaimed. "Keep up that kind of talk and who knows, I might be tempted to let you have your wicked way with me."

"If you've been to the future, tell me who's president in twenty years. And who wins the space race.

And maybe what stocks I ought to be buying." When I didn't answer, or do anything other than stare over his shoulder in an impassive way, he added, "I thought we were friends now, Cathy. If you've got something to tell me, tell me."

"This is the way you treat your friends?" I asked, so frustrated that it hurt. I wanted to tell him. I really did. Yet deep at heart I knew this was all some kind of game. He didn't really believe in my biggest secret. Nor would he be able to handle the truth about me if I burdened him with it. "Seems to me that you've got a lot of family members who'd be glad to help you out with stock tips if you were interested."

"I told you not to use that against me."

I returned the undertone of warning in his voice with a certain snappishness of my own. "So don't you be using my big fat misspeaking mouth against me. Are we dancing here, or wrestling? Can't we just, you know, enjoy the moment?" Not that I was sure I'd enjoy it again, myself.

"I'm sorry," he said after a moment.

"I don't know why one of us always needs to be haranguing the other," I said, not yet able to let go.

"I said I was sorry." He spoke directly into my ear. "You probably think I'm crazy. It was an insane idea, like you said. You're right. I've been a meatball all evening." I wasn't about to deny the admission, but neither did I want to agree with it. We danced to the soft music for a moment more, while beyond the dance floor I caught glimpses of Tilly at our table, speaking animatedly to Chester while he smoked a cigarette. The wine was catching up with me, I realized. All this weaving and turning from side to side was making me dizzy. Right then, Hank's chest heaved slightly. He was laughing to himself. "Itchy vat hog."

I let go of his shoulder and swatted him on the ass. "Shut up." I replaced my hand on his shoulder.

"Are you?"

"No, I'm not an itchy vat—!"

"No," he interrupted. "Are *you* enjoying the moment?"

"Of course. Wait." I owed him better than an automatic politeness. I considered the question for a moment. My shoulders and neck betrayed signs of a slight ache from the clenching I'd done during his interrogation; I'd forgotten how tense he'd made me. I was still a little upset at not having been able to tell him who I really was. But on the whole? I felt wonderful. The wine was relaxing me more and more every moment. Here I was, dancing in a strange new place in a beautiful dress I wouldn't normally wear, surrounded by glamorous, laughing people. I was dancing cheek to cheek— actually dancing as a couple and not thrashing about to a persistent techno club thump—with a guy who knew how to lead. And it all seemed more natural than anything I'd done in years. For the first time, 1959 seemed more like a vacation spot than a pop quiz.

Hank seemed a little mystified at how long I considered the question. "Well?"

"Yes," I told him at last, looking up into his eyes. "I'm having a wonderful time."

His face lit up. Instead of responding, his arm slipped farther around my waist and, with a fluid motion that startled me, dipped me backwards. I yelped a little in surprise, not knowing whether my body would actually bend that way. When I came up again, though, I was laughing. "Sorry," he said. "It's been a while since I've had a pretty lady on the dance floor."

"No, no!" I protested, getting a handhold on his shoulder again. "My bad. I've never been dipped."

"You haven't?" he asked, a mischievous grin playing over his face.

"My granddad was too arthritic to—whoa!" At least this time, when I felt his body's center of gravity change, I was ready for him. Together we swooped in a more or less graceful arc down to the floor, and then back up again. I even managed to refrain from whooping, though laughter bubbled from my chest. I wasn't exactly sure that I was ready for a guest shot on *Dancing with the Stars*, but I wasn't doing too badly for myself, either. "Oh, man oh man," I said, using my free hand to wipe tears from my eyes after a moment. "I haven't had fun like this in years!"

"Really?" Some of the other couples on the dance floor had seen our acrobatics and were now attempting their own. I liked to fancy that we'd been the best of the lot. "You know," he said thoughtfully, "we could have more."

"What do you mean?" I was still laughing.

"See more of each other." Before I could react, he cleared his throat. "Look, Cathy. I'm not going to beat around the bush. I've had eyes for you for a long time. A long, long time. Don't—don't say anything," he ordered. "Let me finish." I nodded mutely. "I never really thought that we'd connect enough that we'd do anything like this. Dinner. Dancing. You and me. Hell, I never thought we'd connect at all. So if you're interested, I am. If you're not . . . I hope we can still be friends. I'd hate to go back to the way we were before."

Now seemed a good time to speak. "You mean, when I didn't even know who you were."

"Yeah," he said, voice thick. "Like then."

Poor, poor Hank. He had a thing for Cathy, and had it bad. How long had he been itching for her from afar, without her even knowing he lived in the same building? It was sweet. To whom was he making this confession, though? To me? Or to her? God, everything was so confusing. "I'm not the same person I was a couple of weeks ago," I said, telling him more truth than I thought I might.

"I can tell." Another dip brought another smile to my face. The sheer joy of it, oddly, made me feel all the more hopeless. Was Hank fond of the idea of being with Cathy, or was he actually getting to like *me?* Every time I thought I was getting the hang of this damned decade, it got harder. "That's the only reason I'm telling you any of this."

"Why didn't you say hello earlier?" I wanted to know. "A lot of us don't like that faint-heart-ne'er-won-a-lady-fair crap. We like our guys to be guys. You should've said something."

"I did. Twice." Whoops. I should've kept my mouth shut. "You don't remember?"

"Hank, I . . ."

"Once I tried talking to you outside on the street, to see if you'd like to have a cup of coffee. You stared at me, then walked inside. The second time, I didn't even get out that much." Oh, Cathy. What a bitch you were! How in the world could anyone turn down Hank? I felt suddenly protective of him. "No, it's okay. Like you said, you're different now."

"I am," I apologized, relaxing into him. The music

175

was slowing now. I could tell it would soon come to an end. "I really, really am. Hank . . ."

"Sssssh."

We were barely moving now, our motion reduced to the slightest of swaying. He looked into my eyes, and I realized he was going to make a move. Hadn't I hoped he might? Fear kept me paralyzed, so that as he leaned in, head tilting, I couldn't break away. I wasn't even sure if I wanted to. What it if wasn't me he really desired? What if his kiss was for the old Cathy's lips? Wouldn't I be doing them both a disservice by letting him get his hopes up? Around me I heard applause; the music had ended and our fellow dancers were drifting back to their tables. "Hank," I whispered, my words flying mere inches from my lips to his. "I don't think . . ."

"Then don't think," he commanded, meeting my mouth with his. We kissed, my lips parting as his mouth enveloped my own. We stood there alone on the dance floor in our embrace, watched by who knew how many others. I didn't care. The other Cathy? Forget her. Hank's kiss was meant for me and only me, I could tell. I greedily accepted it as my own, and returned it with a ferocity that seemed to spring from nowhere. I would have given anything to him at that moment. "Wasn't I right?" he murmured, when after what seemed like long minutes we withdrew. "Isn't not thinking a lot nicer?"

"Thank Boca!" I murmured, enjoying the moment. He pressed his lips against mine once more, kissing me more insistently until at long last, yet too soon, our mouths separated again. "Ronald Reagan," I breathed, my head lolling. "The U.S., when Lance

Armstrong walks on the moon. And IBM, though I'd sell it all for Microsoft in twenty years."

"Hmmm? What was that?"

I'd had too much to drink, and the kiss-induced haze only added to the sense of unreality. Words came tumbling out of my mouth. "I'm from almost fifty years into the future. You were right. You were so, so ri—"

His arms dropped from around me and he stumbled backwards, astonishment filling those deep brown eyes. Or was it fear? "What did you say?"

I'd gone too far this time. Now there was no turning back. "Probably too late for a do-over, right?" I asked, biting my lip.

I was seriously going to have to rethink the not-thinking thing.

•

Chapter Nine

"We like to think of ourselves as being in the here and now, as it were. A leader, not a follower. Innovation, not complacency." If Mr. Richmond was going to fire me, I wished he'd get around to doing it, because every one of his inspirational words was like a bludgeon to my head. I was swearing off cheap Italian red wine, from then on. "We set the trends, rather than follow them. And what's our motive? Get this down, J.P."

Over near the doorway of my office, hovering close to the ever-diminishing stock of Tiny Minnies, Mr. Richmond's nephew suddenly came to life. Though he didn't stop chewing the wad of gum keeping his jaw busy, he pulled out a small pad of paper from his back pocket, grabbed the pen tucked over his ear, and started scribbling. "What's that?"

"Our motive?" he asked, an innovative, trendsetting, leader-type gleam illuminating the gaze he fixed on an invisible horizon. "Why, it's the simple desire to give the modern woman what she wants. Freedom! There's a whole world of convenience products out there, and it's our mission . . . no, Miss Voight. Not our mission." He slammed his hand down onto my desk so hard that I thought my pounding head might explode. "It is our *duty* to promote them and to see that they make their way into every kitchen across this great land! Read that back, J.P."

His nephew stared at his notepad and recited, "Simp. des. give mod. wom. what want."

"Precisely. Precisely! Working at Richmond Better Home Publications is not a simple matter of 'another day, another dollar,' is it, Miss Voight?" He was being damned literal, judging from the pay envelope I'd received that morning. "Indeed not! It's a sacred trust put into our hands by no less than the Modern American Woman!"

If the trumpets and pipe organ started in with "My Country 'Tis of Thee," Richmond Better Home Publications was going to have the sacred trust of cleaning up my hemorrhaging brain from my office walls. It was a struggle to keep my eyes open when all I wanted to do was moan softly and lay my head on the desk, but I managed to maintain an attentive expression, painful as it was. Oh. He wanted me to say something. "Hip-hip, hooray?" I mustered.

Mr. Richmond beamed so broadly that the pencil mustache hovering above his lip formed a straight line. "That's the spirit!"

He'd been lauding God, motherhood, and apple pie for a good five minutes now without really giving me any indication of why he'd invaded my office. I thought I might at least try to get a hint. "Is there a particular reason you wanted to see me, sir?" I said, clutching a throbbing temple in what I hoped resembled a thoughtful pose.

"Yes, I was coming to that." No matter how buddy-buddy they tried to be with their staff, there was always a world of difference between bosses and employees. They got to be the ones who talked on and on, the ones who could be big bores with license, the ones who told the bad jokes that everyone else had to laugh at. This boss, as well as my last, had been the lecturing type, promulgating tedium in the name of some grand point. "Of course, vanguard though we may be, we cannot violate the mission entrusted to us. We cannot, for example, be so far ahead of the curve that America cannot catch up to us. Let moderation be your guide, Miss Voight! Always let moderation be your guide. That is Cicero, I believe."

I wanted to wipe that smile of smug self-satisfaction off his pompous little face. This was all about Cherry, wasn't it? The bastard wanted to have it both ways—pretend he was liberal and forward-thinking while in reality he kept the halls of his provincial little business lily-white. "Mr. Richmond," I said, "I really do feel that all the decisions I've made recently, while perhaps not universally popular, are for the best at your firm. I . . ."

"Tut-tut!" You know, that's one of those phrases you read in books, but until you've traveled back to the '50s and heard a rotund man say it while waggling a finger at you, you've really never been *tut-tutted*. "Now, Miss Voight. I would *hate* for you to think that I'd come in here with criticism on my mind. Nothing would distress me further."

"Okay . . ." I said, both hands now clutching the sides of my head to keep it from lolling off my neck altogether. There had to be an awfully big *but* coming. I waited for it. And waited. Both of us stared at each other across the table in silence, waiting for the other to say something. Then it occurred to me: The man was going to make me *suggest* that the problem was with Cherry, wasn't he? That way he wouldn't have to come off as the bad guy? Oh-ho-ho! He could simply wait forever, then. In the background, J.P. tapped his pad impatiently. That and the quiet smack of his mastication were the only sounds. "Mr. Richmond . . ."

"Unless, of course, there's something you want to tell me?" he prompted. Here it was. All the bigotry would come gushing out now. "About your, shall we say, future marital status?"

Talk about the last thing I expected to hear. "My *what?*" Oooch. No, Cathy, more quietly, I reminded myself. "What in hel . . . gloriosky are you talking about?" I spluttered in my shock.

"J.P.?" Mr. Richmond nodded at the door, and without a word, his nephew exited. If only I had such luck with the kid. I was glad for the privacy, though. He smiled. "I've been informed that due to certain *events*, we expect a change in your, shall we say, domestic situation, in the near future."

Oh my God. Who in the world had told him about last night? Tilly? I'd only kissed the guy! "We only had one date," I said carefully.

"It's often enough, my dear. Don't worry. It has happened to women throughout the ages."

"It wasn't even an entire date," I babbled. "I mean, we weren't even talking through most of it."

He nodded with sympathy. "I should imagine not. But Cathy. Cast your mind back to last year, when Miss Olivander found herself in a similar situation. Weren't we all sympathetic? Why should you expect anything less?" Since I had no clue who Miss Olivander might be or how many dates she had had before she donned an engagement ring, I limited my response to a nod. "We expect you young women to stay with us only a year or two before finding nice husbands and settling down. Why should I mind when one of my girls has to do it a little more quickly than another?"

"But I'm not leaving!" Did he have spies at Tony Lupone's, the night before? Had I jumped through time again and bypassed all the stuff about, you know, dating and falling in love, and gone straight to picking out china patterns? "Who told you I was?" Damn Tilly!

"Why, Merv, of course." I'd say I felt as if he'd beat me over the head with a cement bat, but my head already ached twice enough for that. "Don't you worry," he added, laying a finger beside his nose. "Your secret's safe with me. You're doing a sterling job, as always, Cathy. We're going to miss you, when the day comes. No, don't bother to get up. Especially not now. I'll see myself out."

"But I'm *not leaving!*" I yelled to the closing door. Then, clutching my forehead, I abandoned any pretense of keeping it together. My limbs went limp. "Ohhhhhhh," I groaned. When my door creaked open slowly, I didn't even bother to see who it was. "Go away."

"Is he gone?" Even Tilly's soft Southern voice was too much for me to bear. "I brought you something, honey."

"No more purple pills," I whimpered. "I feel like I've stumbled into *Valley of the Dolls*."

"Don't be silly." Her tiny feet padded across the room. Over the scent of my own impending unconsciousness I could smell something familiar and sweet. "It's warm milk with honey and salt. Daddy used to swear by it when he'd had a little too much the night before. Drink up," she urged, pushing a cup into my hand.

Obediently, I slurped up a mouthful. Only half of it I actually swallowed; the rest went either straight down my windpipe or got spat across my desk. For a full minute I tried to clear my pipes. "Daddy used to swear *at* it, you mean. The man must have been a freakin' *masochist!* Pour this crap down the drain! And don't *tsk* at me! Wait," I said. Even my foul temper couldn't drive away Tilly forever, but it was obvious from her smirk that she was going to indulge me by leaving me to myself. "Two questions. One. Do I know someone named Merv?"

Despite my still-throbbing headache, I watched my flatmate's reaction carefully. "Merv from accounting?" she asked without hesitation. If Merv and Cathy had some kind of past, it seemed from the blandness of her reaction that Tilly knew nothing about it. But then she made a face. "Has he been bothering you again?"

"Was he bothering me before?" I asked, trying to sound casual.

"He was always down here to talk about your budgets. Honestly, you would have thought the production costs were coming out of his own pocket, the way he kept an eye on them! I assumed you'd finally worked it out with him."

Oh, good cover story, Cathy. The ol' looking-over-the-budgets alibi worked every single time . . . when you were *seeing someone on the sly*. The notion that Cathy and my stalker might have been canoodling? A whole world of *ick* was not enough to expression my disgust. "Where is his office? Why don't I ever see him around here?"

Tilly's brow furrowed. "He's in the business offices on the next floor up, honey. You know that."

"I meant, I haven't seen him up there when I've been," I lied, semi-smoothly. "Next question. Do you remember Miss Olivander?"

"Who? Oh! Jane!" Tilly crossed her arms and shook her head. "Did you hear from her? Did she ever find a husband to take care of her and the dear baby?"

"She was . . . ?"

"I know you and I disagreed when she was let go, but maybe you were right," Tilly was saying. "An unwed mother might have been a bad example for the other girls. Still, she was one of our best. Did she telephone? Oh, I wish she'd stopped in with the baby. Wasn't it a boy?"

I let Tilly prattle on while I mulled over the news. An unwed mother? In this decade? In this office? Didn't they stone single mothers back then? And why in the world would Mr. Richmond say that she and I were in similar . . . ? "Arrrrrgh!" I yelled. The burr of sound was a red-hot poker to the brain, but I didn't care. I wanted something to blunt the horrible realization that my monobrow-sporting stalker had informed my booty-grabbing boss that I was with child. What kind of freakish, deranged personality did that kind of thing? Just like Charlie Brown in his wordless frustration, I bared my teeth and growled, hard. *"Arrrgh!"*

"Are you okay, sugar?"

"Just . . . go away! Just go!" So angry and mortified was I at the memory of my conversation with ol' Richmond that I struck out with my arms, flailing until I swiped a stack of papers onto the floor. Childish as I knew it was, it felt good. Really good. I picked up my copy of *Late-Night Supper Soirees* and threw it down so that it hit the floor with a thud. Stupid young moderns and their stupid choicest, crappiest reci-brown-word-pes. "I can't take this anymore!" Tilly, startled, tiptoed out as I started searching for other books to add to the pile in my frenzy of anger.

I was trapped. Trapped! Here I was in a strange place and time, surrounded by strangers who all thought they knew me. I wasn't simply out of my depth. Malevolent forces had brought together a legendary perfect storm of confusions, and I was drowning. Every time I tried to assert myself a little, I found myself overwhelmed by another wave of things out of my control. Admittedly, some of it was my fault—I was still regretting the impulse that had led me to confess my secret to Hank the night before, and then, in a panic of regret, to spend the rest of the evening sticking so close to either Miranda or Tilly that most of the other patrons probably thought I was some sort of morose Siamese twin. Not that Hank would have talked to me, after the way he'd run away at the conclusion of our kiss. But this pregnancy thing? Nuh-uh. That was all the original Cathy Voight and this Merv guy, not me.

I'd gone from mere fuming and growling to a sort of frantic pacing around my linoleum-lined cage when I heard the door open again. "I told you to go away!" I yelled, regretting it instantly when I realized it had been almost loud enough to make my eyeballs bleed. "Christ." Even in my wildness I knew how lucky I was to have a good friend like Tilly to put up with me. The thing was, however, that when I looked up, it wasn't Tilly who stood leaning against the door with her arms crossed and a smirk on her face. Cherry surveyed me from my miserable head to my cinched waist to my high-heeled toes. "What?" I asked, sinking back into my chair. It was one thing misbehaving for someone like Tilly, whom I trusted. Acting out in front of the biggest mistake of my visit—though how could I narrow it down so easily?—was another.

Cherry pushed herself upright with her shoulders, shuffled by the pyramid of Tiny Minnies, raised an eyebrow at the stack of cookbooks that was one match away from being a bonfire, pushed my cup of pencils back from the desk's edge where I'd pushed them, and then perched there. She crossed her arms once again. "Word on the street is that someone's got a hangover."

"Yeah, well, word on the street is—crap." My forehead was clammy and cold now. I shouldn't have exerted myself. I felt like I might pass out. I sighed and rested my elbows on the desk so they could support my head once more. "What are you doing here, anyway? Quitting?" Wouldn't that be the maraschino on the stinking pile of manure served up to me as dessert?

"Why, you going to lose me this job, too?" she asked. I wasn't in the mood. I waved her away, but she continued talking. "For your information, Miss Voight, I think I could grow to like this position. I like all the pretty white uniforms . . . the pretty white countertops . . . all the pretty white people. . . ."

"Subtlety's not your strong point, Cherry." I abandoned all pretense of having vertebrae and laid my head down on the desk. "As my dad always says, either you're part of the problem or you're part of the solution, and right now you're not part of the solution, so would you exit my office with the absolutely softest tread that you can muster and barricade the door behind you, please?"

"Wise daddy you've got." Again, she didn't go, and I wasn't strong enough to make her. "My daddy knew one sure remedy for a hangover."

"Oh, God. Everyone's daddy seems to have a hangover remedy. It couldn't be half as bad as what Tilly's dipso father dreamed up, could it? Or is it something awful like the blood of a bat mixed with Alka-Seltzer?"

"Do you want to hear, or not?" She wasn't at all amused.

From the way she spoke, I knew she was going to make me ask. "Fine. What is this fine remedy of your father's?"

"Here goes: Don't be drinking." To that weak witticism I raised my head, mimed fake laughter, then gently laid it back on my forearms. "And I don't like the way you treat Miss Sanguinetti, sometimes. She's your friend. You ought to respect her more." I wasn't at all sure if twirling my index finger in the universal sign for *big whoop* would translate to the 1950s, but I gave it a shot. It must have communicated its message, because Cherry defended her argument with new vigor. "You should have seen the way she scurried out of here, tail between her legs. With you shouting and throwing things at her like she was some kind of so-and-so!"

"I wasn't shouting and throwing things at her," I said, pained. "I was shouting. And throwing things."

"Well, I've got this to say about that. I like Miss Sanguinetti. For all that she's from Alabama, she's a lot nicer to me than most of you white folks around here. So until she proves different, I'm sticking up for her."

"Fine," I murmured. "Fine. You're right. Miss Sanguinetti is a fine person. I love Miss Sanguinetti." My voice made a hollow echo against the wood of my desk. "But could you stick up for her somewhere else? And quietly?"

Boy, I really knew how to drive people away. Hank had nearly tripped over his feet in his haste to get away from me, the evening before. I'd thrown things to vanquish Tilly. And now I could hear Cherry sliding from atop the desk and walking toward the door without a sound. That was fine, though. Maybe I was one of those people better off alone. Alone and unloved. Alone and unloved and stranded far from home. Alone and unloved and stranded far from home without a friendly face to . . . no, I had to stop. My melancholy was too rapidly turning into one of those kid's memory games where the old lady went to town and returned with an apple, a bat, a cookie, a diamond, and so on, all the way up the alphabet to zebra.

Maybe my headache was casting too much of a pall over things, but I couldn't see a way out of any of this.

The door opened again. What was my office, I wondered with irritation? Grand Central Station? "All right, Miss High and Mighty," I heard Cherry say, accompanied by the tinkling of something striking glass. "Drink up."

She proffered something vile-looking right before my nose. "I thought your daddy's hangover recipe involved dry wit and a twist of homespun wisdom."

"And what's in this glass," she noted, "is my mama's. Drink up."

Though I hesitated, I really had no choice but to obey. Not when the alternative was spending the rest of the day regretting every nerve in my body. I took a deep breath, pretended I was going for the grand prize in *Fear Factor*, and took a giant swig.

The sounds I made probably cannot be described. There was a healthy helping of choking and gasping, followed by a few wheezes, some gagging, and a moderate amount of howling. There would have been swearing, too, but some ingredient in the brew had rendered my tongue temporarily unable to form consonants. "The *hell!*" I finally managed to spit out. I looked at the slimy mess that was left. "What *was* that?"

"Raw egg, Tabasco, salt and pepper, and the juice from a can of sardines. Drink all this down without stopping," she said, taking back the glass that had held liquid death and giving me another full of water. She snapped her fingers. "Now." While watching me chug away, Cherry shook her head. "I thought this job was going to be different, but here I am picking up after white folks all over again. Don't you dare stop," she commanded, when I nearly protested. While I finished filling my gullet with water, she took the chair opposite mine. "What really gets me wondering is how someone who's got it all can find time to throw a tantrum like my sister's three-year-old. You're pretty, you've got pull, you've got the world at your feet. At least my sister's kid knows she'll get smacked if she threw something."

"I was provoked!" I protested, my head spinning. Maybe the water was doing me some good, though. My headache wasn't clearing yet, but at least the combination of proteins and heat in my stomach and a little hydration were making it easier to sit up.

"What, did Macy's run out of your favorite face

powder?" Cherry's arms were crossed again, and I could tell she wasn't buying a gram of what I was trying to sell. "Did your cashmere sweater shrink at the dry cleaner's?"

"No. Are you done?" I could give just as much attitude, thank you very much, and then some. "You want to take more digs at me? Bring it." She shook her head. "Then please leave me alone."

"The only thing I'm trying to figure out is what justifies hangovers and hissy fits in your little ivory tower of a world when the view is so nice looking in from the outside."

"You don't know anything about me." I sniffed, though I was determined I wouldn't cry. "I really sympathize with what you've got to be going through in this decade. I mean . . . never mind what I mean. Resent me all you want for the color of my skin or how much money you think I make or where I live or my socioeconomic whatever. That's fair game. But you haven't got the market cornered on woe, you know."

"Man troubles, hmmm?" At my astonished reaction, she shrugged. "What's left?"

"I don't have man troubles. To have man troubles you have to *have* a man. What I have is a stalker." Did they even have stalkers here? "Right here at Richmond Publications. And apparently he told Mr. Richmond that I was pregnant, and now Richmond thinks I'm leaving."

Cherry gave my midsection an appraising look and let out a low whistle. "You're knocked up? You *do* have problems."

"I'm not pregnant!" I shouted, perhaps a little too loudly. "I mean, I don't think I am! I'd know, wouldn't I?" The only thing more horrible than being stuck in someone else's body would be if that body was carrying a child I hadn't even screwed around to create. Fantastic. Now I had a whole set of newly minted fears to worry about in addition to those I'd already been carrying. "What I am is pissed off!"

"What you are is slandered." Cherry's comment made me sit upright. Yeah! I was, come to think! The worst kind of slander, too—it hit me right in the wallet. "The guy sounds like a real heel. So what are you going to do about it?"

"Well, I'm totally going to ignore the guy next time I see him, that's for sure." Not the right answer? Cherry cocked her head and raised a single, graceful eyebrow. "Maybe a strongly worded letter?"

"I don't think so! If you could do anything to that man right now, what would it be?"

"Anything?" I echoed faintly. I could think of a lot of things I might want to do to Merv if I saw him right then, but none of them were exactly civilized. "I don't know."

"Oh, you know all right. You don't want to say. You folks think you're living in some kind of pretty magazine picture, where if you keep a smile on your face and look good, everything's going to be fine." I knew she was talking about the women of 1959, but damn if she didn't have me nailed as well. "You're bright. I can see that. You've always got something smart to say, but so far I haven't heard anything real come out of that mouth of yours. Oh yes," she went on, nodding at my astonishment. "I said what I said. If *you* said what was really on your mind instead of trying to be that picture-perfect *Look* magazine ad, you wouldn't have to be drinking too much and regretting it the next day. So tell me." She leaned forward and rested her arms on the desk. "What would you do to him if he were here right now? Come on, what would you do?"

"Yell at him. Smack him." She nodded. "Smack the hell out of him. Kick him. Right in the nuts!" I grinned. Her therapy was crude, but effective. "What I'd really like to do is get something big and heavy, like a cast-iron skillet, take it up there, heft it over my shoulder, and let him have it. *Pow!* Right on that monobrow."

"All right, lady!" That seemed to get her approval at last. She stood up and beckoned to me. Thinking she was going to exit the office, I automatically stood and walked with her in the direction of the door. "He's here in the building?"

"Upstairs, supp . . . hey." I instantly grew wary; if hackles are those hairs on the back of the neck that prickle at danger, mine had sprung into action. "Hey! What do you think you're doing? Hey! I'm not going to bean him with a skillet!"

Her hand firmly on my back, Cherry hesitated from opening the door fully. "You did me a favor. Of course, you *owed* me a favor after you got me fired, but you did me one anyway, and that's something that most people like you wouldn't have done, so I'm doing you one back. You're going to see that rat and you're going to tell him what for, and when you're done you'll feel like you *did* something instead of bending over and taking it where it don't fit."

This time, my hand was keeping the door shut. "I don't bend over!"

"Of course you don't, honey." Suddenly Cherry's voice was kind and sugary. "You're your very own person. Sure, you let that fat Mr. Richmond come in and tell you you're knocked up and you let him walk away without correcting him. . . ."

"Okay, I get the point."

". . . And you let him and that nasty little runt of a nephew of his pinch your behind black and blue day in and day out. I mean, *I* wouldn't let anyone do that to me and if they did, I'd probably slap them 'cross their ugly white faces, knowing that I'd probably be fired on the spot because of the color of my skin, but *shoooot*, you know what you're doing."

"Cherry Bradford, you are sheer evil." We studied each other frankly. "I like that."

She smirked.

The Richmond Better Home Publications business offices on the sixth floor were in an smaller suite than what we occupied on the story below. After barging past a bewildered receptionist, Cherry and I tramped through hallways arranged in a labyrinth that would have set the Minotaur's head spinning, sticking our heads through every doorway into small, often windowless offices cluttered with index card files and piles of paper and manned (or womaned) by uniformly pasty staff. A few of them seemed to recognize me, but seemed puzzled to see Cherry at my side. Others simply stared. Without apologies or explanations we moved swiftly from room to room, my hands growing increasingly clammier with suspense and anxiety.

Not until we were somewhere deep in the heart of the maze did I hear a familiar voice nearby. "Yeah yeah, *you're* the one holding up the distribution, pal. You're the one holding it up; that's right, you heard me."

I had a quick flashback to my first morning here, when the voice's owner had burst into my office. "*You're an original, Cathy,*" he'd told me. "*That's*

193

what you are. A pure, unadulterated, God-damned original." He'd been right on more levels than one. This was the office, all right. MERVIN POWERS, read the sign outside. With Cherry giving me a nod of reassurance, a stern look, and then finally a push, I stepped into the office doorway. It was him, all right. A cigarette that was little more than ash hung from the corner of his mouth. His hair was slicked back so that he looked like some kind of sleazy lounge lizard, not at all like the mussed mop he'd sported at The Flanders. "Well, well, well," I said with what I hoped passed for confidence. "If it isn't Merv."

"Cathy!" I'd startled him so severely that his cigarette fell from his lips, landing on his lap. He jumped up with a yelp, wildly brushing at his pants and finally stamping out the embers. If it's true that you can tell a lot about a person by the way he keeps his office, this Merv guy was a total mess. His workspace looked like the 'after' photo of a magnitude nine earthquake. Fountains of files cascaded from open drawers and cabinets. An overflowing ashtray in the desk's center acted as the only paperweight, and there were so many empty vending machine wrappers that I suspected his entire diet consisted of Planter's Peanuts and Lance Toastchee crackers. Was he living here like some kind of homeless person? "What—?"

"Oh," I heard from beside me. Cherry was peering over my shoulder. "Mono, meaning one. Brow, meaning . . ." She drew a strip across her forehead. "Boy, that *is* something. Don't let him hit you," she said in an undertone, as she pulled shut the door and left me alone with him.

I hated hearing that door close. Maybe she was right, though. Maybe a confrontation would be a lot better for me than a thorough snubbing. Besides, I had a bit of an upper hand, with him frantically scrambling to make his pigsty of an office habitable for someone other than himself. "Well, well, well!" I said again, when the latch clicked. "Well, well!!" I seemed to be stuck in the same groove.

Thank goodness he started out. "I didn't expect— that is, I didn't think—God, Cathy. You look fantastic. I kept hoping you'd . . . I knew you'd realize the mistake you made."

That was a better opening than most. "The mistake I made, apparently, was ever associating with you." I mean, honestly. What could Cathy have seen in this guy? His squinting, ingratiating photo could have appeared in the dictionary next to the word *sleazeball*. A woman could never trust a word that this kind of guy spoke; she'd have to clean out her ears from the oil it carried. No wonder Cathy didn't keep any letters or personal mementos from their romance. She was probably embarrassed as hell about it. Enough to have ended the relationship between them anyway.

He got to his feet and ran a hand through his hair. Ah, there was the mop emerging. His hands shook nervously as we talked. "I told Betsy about us. She wasn't happy. She's leaving me." At my blank stare, he snapped, "My wife, Cathy. Don't pretend you don't remember her name."

I needed a bath, I felt so dirty. Maybe he had been living in his office, after all. Then again, this wasn't my affair. I hadn't been the one involved in any of it, and the least I could do was extricate poor Cathy as best I could. "I broke up with you," I said, more as a test balloon than anything else.

"You didn't mean it."

"You know, desperate isn't a color that looks good on you, Merv," I said, my confidence galloping and dragging me along behind. He really was a pathetic little creature, relying on booze and revenge to get him through the lonely nights. "I must have meant it. So if all this moping and cringing you're doing is over me, get over it."

"I can't." Once again he ran his hands through his hair. "I can't."

"Get over it," I repeated. "And if you tell Richmond any more of your pathetic, sick fantasies about me being pregnant . . ."

"I didn't say that!" he interrupted urgently. "We were in his office having a drink and a cigarette. I told him that I was planning to marry you as quickly as possible. It slipped out, Cathy! He drew his own conclusions."

"Conclusions that you apparently didn't deny!" I said, more than a little upset with the schmuck. I felt protective of Cathy now. She was a mess, but she was my mess to clear up. "What kind of freak talks about that shit with his boss, anyway? If there were any loose strings before, leading you to think there might have been a chance between you and me, they're cut now. Hoo, boy, are they ever."

"You said you loved me! You sure didn't object when I bought you tokens of our love!"

I was rolling with my tirade now. "It's a simple little mantra, mister. Three words. *Get. Over. It.* Move on. Go back to your wife, if she'll have you. But don't bother me anymore. Got it?" Poor guy. It had been a little too easy, dressing him down. He sat there behind the chaos of his desk, in that room that smelled of stale cigarettes, with the wind completely taken out of him. Good. I didn't know the guy at all, but nothing about him exactly recommended him to me. Time for my grand exit. "Goodbye forever, Merv," I said, grabbing the knob and pulling hard.

It didn't oblige. Or rather, it opened a couple of inches, and then was yanked shut again as if restrained by strong elastic bands. I tried again. Same thing, only this time I didn't even pry it as far open as the first. "What are you doing?" a sullen Merv wanted to know, as I planted my feet on the floor and, with all my weight, tried heaving the damned thing open.

"Shut up," I growled over my shoulder. Cherry was on the other side of the door playing doorknob tug-of-war with me. "I'm done in here!" I yelled through the crack.

"Not until . . ." She temporarily got the better of me, so that I didn't catch the rest of what she had to say.

"What?" I gave up and pressed my ear to the opening. "I can't hear you." Still more mumbling.

"Cathy?" My married swain whimpered behind me. "I'll always love you. You'll see."

One palm shot outward in a talk-to-the-hand pose, while I used my other to pound on the wood. "Cherry, I can't hear a damned thing you're . . ."

With a shudder, the door suddenly opened. "You are useless," Cherry said, scowling at me. "You!" she added to Merv, her index finger pointing to heaven as she moved it from side to side. "What *you* are going to do to make things *right* is to march yourself downstairs to Mr. Richmond and tell him in no uncertain terms that no rabbits died because of anything you might have done with Miss Voight here. Nuh-uh," she added, when it seemed he might contradict her. "You're going to do it, and you're going to do it right now." She clapped her hands together, treating Mr. Monobrow like a kid late for school. "*Now!*"

Before I could even wonder what rabbits had to do with anything, Merv jumped from his chair as if Cherry had rammed an electric cattle prod to his manbits, and ran past us out of the stinking office. We watched as he disappeared down the hall and around the corner, presumably to obey. "Were you listening through the door or something?" I asked. Cherry gave me a look that very plainly said, *oh please*. "I can't believe you talk like that to the people here. I mean, it's not like you have to be docile because of . . . you know . . . but aren't you afraid of making waves?"

"*Nice* doesn't get a girl anywhere." Cherry made a face at the state of Merv's office, then pushed me gently out and shut the door behind us. "Besides, I figure the way things are in the world, I'll get fired out of here any day now, but the money I'll take home will still be more than I got at the automat."

Just as I'd suspected, then. "I don't intend to fire you, you know. You can count on that."

"No offense, Miss Voight? But I don't count on what I can't hold in my own two arms." Still, Cherry regarded me with something resembling appreciation. "In the meantime, while it lasts, I'll speak my mind. You should try it. There's no freedom like what you've got when there's nothing to lose. But that's something you might not understand."

"No, I do," I said, nodding slowly. After all, I'd left a whole lifetime behind, somewhere in the future. Who had less to lose than I? "I get it now. I totally do."

Chapter Ten

November 20, 1959

Dear Cathy (Voight),

I've left this letter for you beneath your hair-brushes in case I'm called away suddenly, or you come back from wherever you've been vacationing, or whatever. I'd hate for you to have to figure out on your own what's happened while you've been away.

1. I kind of went all Equal Employment Opportunity Commission on your job. Hope that isn't a problem. Even if you voted for you-know-who.

2. You know your good cashmere sweater set? The cream-colored one with the pearl buttons? I had a bit of an accident with the cardigan and a staple remover. So the 'set' concept is purely theoretical at this point. Sorry. But I saved the buttons in your jewelry box.

3. If you notice that your fur looks like someone's been rolling around in it? Miranda's been looking awfully shifty.

4. I broke up with Merv again. I hope it's what you wanted. Why in the world you'd get involved with a married . . . no, never mind. Not my place to judge, right? Just please don't go running back to him and . . . no, pay no attention to me. Really. Consider my lips zipped.

5. Your doctor and I had a little talk on the phone this afternoon. If you speak to him, he might seem to have the impression you didn't know how babies are made. Ignore him. I think he drinks. Either way, we agreed you're most likely not pregnant.

6. Okay, this is the most important thing. There's a guy downstairs who's your landlord. His name is Hank. He's a nice guy. And if you pass him and he calls you "itchy vat hog," please don't go all ice princess on him. For my sake, if nothing else.

Well, that's it, I think. Don't be too mad at me. I've been doing the best I can.

Sincerely,

Cathy (temporarily Voight)

P.S. About #4. We're way too pretty to let low self-esteem tether us to a guy with rampant ear and nose hair. Trust me. You're way out of his league. There are way better guys who like you a lot. Just trust me on this one, okay?

Chapter Eleven

In my real life—the one back in the new millennium, that is—I'd always wondered what it would be like to live in one of New York City's authentic old townhouses. Admittedly, my fantasies had all been about renovated interiors, Arts and Crafts furniture, a modern kitchen, a panic room like Jodie Foster, the cover of *Architectural Digest*, and winning the Mega Millions jackpot. The people in this era didn't know how lucky they were to live in little slices of the city's history, before they all got bought up and revitalized and priced out of the range of ordinary people.

Of course, none of this was actually running through my head as I stood in front of the tall doorway to Hank's flat, that Friday evening. I wasn't lovingly admiring the crown molding or eyeing the wood floors with an eye to a sleek refinish and buffing. No, the only thing on my mind was what Cherry had said that afternoon. "You've got nothing to lose," I told myself aloud, willing myself to knock.

Yet my fingers wouldn't cooperate. There's a mo-

ment in *The Bride of Frankenstein* when the bride
rises from the slab, all shock-headed and lipsticked to
the gills, and Dr. Frankenstein's Monster stumbles forward, filled with as much glee as a monster's face can
be when he's been stitched together from a dozen
corpses in the throes of rigor mucho mortis. And what
does the bride do? The bitch hisses at him, like she's
some kind of heroin-chic model wannabe in the VIP
area of some Williamsburg club and he's a chubby,
horny computer nerd trying to cross the velvet-rope
barrier. Much as I loved the bride, girlfriend wasn't all
that. Anyway, the night before, I'd felt a deep sympathy for Frankenstein's Monster, after watching Hank
pull away once he saw what I really was. Okay, he
hadn't actually hissed at me. Maybe there was hope.
On the other hand, maybe I was fooling myself.

No, Cherry had been right. Having squat should
make a person bolder, not the opposite. I closed my
eyes, envisioned success, and cleared my throat. "I
have nothing to lose," I said slowly, convincing myself
I meant what I said. I raised my hand to make the fa-
tal knock.

It never met the wood. "Why are you standing in
the hall?" When I opened my eyes again, I found
Hank standing before me in another of his form-
hugging turtlenecks. "Get in!" He grabbed me by the
wrist and shut the door behind me. His apartment was
dimly lit, as if he'd been inside all afternoon and had
forgotten to turn on more than the one lamp near the
sofa after sunset. Books and papers had been strewn
over the coffee table and the floor around it, but they
weren't as out of control as Merv's mess had been.
There was a motive to the madness here.

And madness there had to be, because Hank looked

a little wild. You might think it impossible to make a flattop stand up any straighter, but Hank's did. He seemed galvanized. His eyes were wide, his motions more abrupt and excited than usual, and his voice crackled with electricity. "Hello," I said cautiously, and then broke into my rehearsed speech. "I thought it might be a good idea if I checked in with you to see . . . and, you know, I owe you a home-cooked dinner and I'm planning to take some lessons so that I can actually prepare it, so I was wondering . . ."

"Okay, okay," he said, his hands on my shoulders as he guided me to the room's center. He dived at the sofa at the very last possible second, swept away some of the clutter there, and then sat me down. "I spent most of the morning at the library. I didn't find anything about . . ." He consulted a clipboard that lay on the topmost layer of the coffee table. "Lance Armstrong. You didn't mean Louis Armstrong? No, that's kind of ridiculous," he said, dismissing the notion of Satchmo on the moon. Then, erring on the side of caution, he added, "Right?"

"Right." I kept my voice steady. I hadn't been in his place for more than ten seconds and already he was making me smile. I'd been expecting tears and regret. Damn him for keeping me off balance! Bless him for doing it, though.

"There were a couple of other Armstrongs in the papers. One was a pilot, another was an . . . astrophysicist." He finished consulting his notes, set down the clipboard, and then removed his glasses to rub his tired peepers. I'd never before seen him without the horn-rimmed frames; it was remarkable how handsome he was without them. Not that he was hard on the eyes with them, by any means. "So I figure, hey, at best it's inconclusive. NASA's been around for what, only a little over a year? Maybe he hasn't joined up with them yet."

"Hank?" I asked, trying to interrupt the manic flow of his words.

"Now, IBM."

"Hank?"

"What?"

This was the most difficult question I'd ever had to ask. "Are you trying to say you believe me?"

"I'm getting to that. IBM. International Business Machines. Founded as Computing Tabulating Recording Corporation in 1911, and dealing mostly with punch-card systems for timekeeping and the like. Until after the Second World War, that is, when they started working with the government on aircraft defense systems. I'm on the right track, aren't I?" The way he searched through his sheaf of copious notes bordered on the frantic. "Aircraft . . . computing machines . . . space ships . . . time machines, right? Right? You were telling me to invest in IBM because they're the ones who make the time machines, where you came from!" He peered through his spectacles at a page. "They used to make meat slicers, too."

"Hank." I was chuckling by now. "IBM doesn't make time machines."

His face fell momentarily, but he rallied quickly. "They *make* you say that. Because they don't want the truth to get out."

"No!" So intense was my relief that my chuckles turned into outright laughter. He wasn't going to hiss at me after all. "They don't make time machines, honestly. IBM is the classic story of a company in the right places at the right times throughout the twentieth century. We studied them in marketing."

"In the *future!*" Hank crowed, triumphantly thrusting his finger in my face. He was practically swaggering from having been right. It was a good thing he was so damned cute about it, because otherwise he'd be a terrible, terrible person to lose an argument to. "The Ronald Reagan thing I figured for one of your jokes." I shook my head. "No, really."

"I have spent the last twenty-four hours absolutely terrified you'd never want to speak to me again." I couldn't help myself—I stood up and reached out for his hands. "I worried you thought I was a freak, or crazy, or worse, a liar. . . ."

"Ronald Reagan? *Hellcats of the Navy* Ronald Reagan? Really? Hmmm." He seemed too busy absorbing that one for a moment to address my concerns, but once they'd sunk in, he shook his head. His voice was earnest as he said, "You could still be a freak or crazy."

I flopped back down again. "Oh, gee, thanks for that."

"Admit to me that you knew about the Edsel being discontinued." After a moment, I nodded. "And that you didn't learn about it from someone in Detroit."

"In my time, the Edsel's kind of a joke," I said, marveling at the fact that he didn't flip out when I said things like, "in my time." "A punch line. Something so monumentally *wrong* that it's in the annals of history as a big mistake."

"Hah! My brother is going to *hate* being a punch line." As if realizing it for the first time, Hank added in a quiet voice, "Wait. All this is history for you."

When I didn't deny it, he lowered himself to a sitting position on the coffee table. "I'm a historical figure. I'm ancient history."

"Hank, no!" How could he say such a thing? How could he think I believed it, when he was real and warm and living and sitting so close to me. I reached out and grabbed his hand. "You're not ancient. Or history!"

"I'm a relic." His eyes widened. "I could be your grandfather."

"Unless you plan on changing your name to Sal Voorhees and becoming a hunched-over little man who complains bitterly that the Internet drove travel agencies out of business, you are most definitely not my grandfather."

"What's the Internet?"

"It's this big . . ." My hands flew into the air as if trying to grab from it words to explain. "Thing. It's all these computers that are linked together all around the world to share information. So if you're at home, and you wanted to look up some facts, instead of going to the library," I explained, trying to make it more personal for him, "you'd Google it. That is, you'd go on your computer to this service called Google and look it up, and then boom, it's there in about two seconds. News, weather, sports, all at your fingertips." I sounded like copy for one of my advertisements.

His head had shot forward as I spoke. "You have a computer? At home?" I nodded, timidly biting my lip. Talking about any of this stuff was equally frightening and exciting. "You own one? Do lots of people own one? Do people in the future have really big houses? For the computer machines?"

"What? No. Your computers are really big, aren't

they?" I had a vague memory of old TV shows featuring big, boxy monstrosities with reels of tape whipping around at high speed. "Ours are like . . ." From the stack of books nearby I plucked out one of larger proportions, no bigger than a laptop. "And you open the lid like this, and the screen's here, and then below is a keyboard—like a typewriter—that you type on." He'd gone silent. I wasn't even sure if he believed a word I said. "Lots and lots of people have them. They're pretty common, actually. And there are tiny, tiny computers in lots of things, like cars, and iPods, and . . ."

"What's iPod? Is he your robot servant?"

The poor guy looked so pathetically eager that it was a struggle not to laugh. "I don't have a robot servant."

"You don't approve of robot servants? Or did you spend all your money on your computer?"

"Nobody has robot servants, Hank. My computer only cost about two weeks' worth of salary."

"How much does a flying car cost?"

"There's no such thing as flying cars."

"Flying buses?" I shook my head. "Jet packs?"

"What?" I had no idea what he was talking about, but his questions were so rapid-fire that I felt I was deflecting them like Wonder Woman with her magic bracelets.

"Jet packs. On your back. So you can take off, fly where you want, and land."

"No jet packs."

"Do you have your own plane? Helicopter?" Again, I had to disappoint him. He looked seriously crushed. "Do you live in a giant skyscraper on the two-hundredth floor?"

"Well, I live in Manhattan," I said. "There are a lot

of skyscrapers. But I live on the fourth floor of a building from the sixties."

"You make it sound like your time isn't that much different from this."

"Well, it's really not," I had to admit. "I mean, we still take cars and trains to our jobs. It's a little more progressive, I suppose. But on the whole . . ." He looked so disappointed that I felt I had to throw him a few bones. "Oh, but in the future we get our money out of slots in walls. And everyone has his own tiny little telephone he carries around in his pocket. And they don't have any cords."

That perked him up. "Really?"

"Mmm-hmm! And there are more than a hundred channels on television! Though most of them are crap. But they're in color! And on really, really big screens."

"No robot servants, huh?" I'd never seen him look more like a disappointed little boy. I wanted to pinch his cheeks and give him a great big hug. Instead, I sat back and clutched one of his throw pillows while it all sunk in for him. "I guess the computers are pretty good. And the color television."

"There you go!" I said.

"And the time machines." I shook my head again, knowing it would disappoint. "What do you mean? There have to be time machines. How did you get back here if there aren't any? Golly, how long have you been here? Are you studying us? Is it some experiment? Do you get paid bundles of money? Is that how you can afford your own computer? Does it talk to you?"

"Slow down there, buckaroo." I sighed. This was where it was going to get tricky. I could natter on for hours about all the modern conveniences I missed— and some that I didn't, like global warming and inflation and my inability to find a really good handbag that lasted for more than a month—but now we were heading into uncharted territory, where I couldn't explain much of what had happened. "I've only been here for a little over two weeks, for one thing."

"That's impossible. I've seen you nearly every day since you moved in three years ago."

"Yes," I said slowly. "And no."

All my talk of modern technologies had created an animated spark in his eyes. In the short time it took to explain that I'd suddenly leapt into Cathy Voight's life from my own, I'd managed to dim the glow a little. "So you didn't get here by a time machine. Wow."

"The last thing I remember is my microwave exploding."

His brow crinkled. "Microwave. Micro—little wave? What does it do?"

"It's a—um." Why hadn't I paid more attention in any of my classes other than business? "It's a box for the kitchen. An oven, but it doesn't have any heating elements or gas or anything. When you put the food inside, a magnet-type thing in there produces these little waves of energy that make the food's molecule electron atom things rub against each other, and it warms up."

That sentence alone should have convinced him that I wasn't some kind of brainiac scientist from the future. "Oh," he said. "Kind of like a Radarange?"

"You have microwaves here?" I asked. "I didn't think they were popular until like, the seventies or eighties."

"I saw one on a television show. Big box like a refrigerator?"

"Well. Maybe it shrunk a little by the time I bought my first one," I apologized, approximating the dimensions in the air.

He watched my miming. "It seems like everything in the future is smaller," he said thoughtfully. So serious was his expression that I feared I might have gone too far. Maybe he'd been willing to listen to my tales of the marvels of the new millennium, but my lame story of how I'd landed here had ventured too close to la-la-land. "Computers. Telephones. Ovens."

"Cars get bigger," I said. "SUVs. They're like, trucks that suburban moms drive. And Hummers. Guys like those." He raised an eyebrow, making me blush a little. "It means something else in the twenty-first century. Trust me. Listen, Hank. I know this is all kind of out there. I wouldn't believe it myself, if you were telling it to me." He wasn't confirming my worry that he didn't have faith in a word I said, but neither did he deny it. Bad sign? Or was I worrying too much? "There was a good three days or more when I thought maybe all this was in my head, the deranged fantasy of someone who'd had her brain shaken like a martini. I mean, God. I still wake up in the mornings and see Cathy's flouncy dresses sticking out of the closet and I think maybe it's something I've dreamed up."

"Do you know everything about me?" he asked. The question was so unexpected that I couldn't answer. "I mean, do you know where I grew up, or what I think about, or what my parents' names are, or what I called my first dog? Because as much as it scares me to think that I could be some kind of figment of your imagination that might vanish into thin air the minute you wake up in that hospital bed of yours in the future—do they have hospitals still? Yes? Okay—what scares me more is that I've got a lifetime of memories and feelings and experiences that I thought were my own. It hurts my brain to think that they might all be an illusion."

"No, they're not, Hank. They're yours. Honestly. You're perfectly real. You were the first person I saw when I woke up here, you know. And I'm sorry I thought you were a refrigerator repairman. I honestly didn't know."

Dim as it had been when I'd first entered the apartment, now it was completely dark outside save for the distant streetlight and the occasional flare of headlights from beyond the curtained windows. Hank and I sat within the narrow circle of light cast from the one lamp he'd bothered to light, leaning toward each other, our voices growing softer. He seemed unusually thoughtful. "That was the first . . . ah. And you'd never . . . oh, I see." He sat up, pulling away from me slightly. "So Cathy still hasn't talked to me. The other Cathy. You said your name's Cathy, too?" When I nodded, he seemed relieved. "That's something, anyway. One less name to learn."

"When you were angry with me for not knowing who you were, that night you gave me dinner, I really didn't know your name at all." All those misgivings he'd had about me when that evening had ended so badly—surely now they'd vanish. "I didn't know you were my landlord, or anything. I'd barely been here at all."

He nodded. I could tell he'd been thinking along the same lines. "Okay," he finally said. "I can't fault you for that. Not you, anyway. Cathy, though . . . the other Cathy." He shook his head, struggling with words and emotions both. "I'd thought that she'd changed, but she wasn't the one here. You were."

This could be a really, really tricky moment for the both of us. Intending only to give him comfort, I reached out and took one of his hands with my own. "You had a thing for her."

"If by *thing* you mean an infatuation, yes, I supposed you could say that. Mild at best." His mouth curled up into a wry, downward arc. "Cathy is . . . was . . . remarkable. Even when she would treat me like a peasant, she had a way of walking that made her look like royalty. She sailed. She looked like somebody who knew secrets you didn't."

"Are you kidding?" I tried to keep any trace of bitterness from my voice. Yeah, yeah, yeah, so Cathy had it all. Big whoop. "That dame had more secrets than Victoria."

"Queen Victoria?"

"No. Back home, it's a lingerie . . . never mind." When Hank cocked his head, I was more than willing to elaborate on my earlier theme. "I've found out some things about Cathy that kind of surprised me a little. And made me feel a little badly for her. Oh, like remember Drunky McDrunkerson at The Flanders?" He laughed and nodded. "Totally having an affair with him."

His reaction wasn't quite as taken aback as I'd for some reason hoped. "Really."

"I know, right? Not so regal now, is she, hmmm?"

"Would you look at that!" He reclaimed his hand, sat back, and chortled. "Someone's jealous." At the sight of my dropped jaw, his mild amusement blossomed into outright laughter. "You are! You're jealous!"

"I so totally am not," I sputtered. Sometimes when cats have attempted a leap too long for them and they miss and fall flat on their feline rumps, they stalk away with their necks stiff and looks of disdain on their faces that say, *I meant to do that; if you think otherwise, it's a pity you have such a small and miserable mind.* I felt like one of those cats, right at that moment. "Why in the world would I be jealous of her? I mean, because she's all *remarkable* and everything is no reason to get my nose bent out of joint." Hank immediately put a damper on the frivolity and opened his mouth, presumably to apologize. "I'm confident. I'm secure in myself," I announced. "I have good posture. I can sail."

"I never—"

"I'm sure it's easy for you, Mr. Long 'n' Lanky. Mr. Chin Dimple. Mr. Broad Shoulders. You're *used* to the stuff you wear and it really doesn't change in the next half century. Guys always wear pants and shirts and comfortable loafers. However, in *my* time, we gals aren't accustomed to girdles. Or bullet bras. Or these God-damned mandatory high heels. Some of us, anyway. I could sail if I didn't have to wear these. As a matter of fact." I reached down and, with my index finger loosened the leather around my heel enough to slip it off my foot. Then I used one of my pumps as an audiovisual aid, waving it in his face.

"Cathy?"

I felt a good rant coming on, and I could no more have stopped it than a speeding locomotive. "In modern circles, some see these as a totally barbaric symbol of a society—*yours*—in which women were second-class citizens, denied access to jobs and equal wages for no good reason other than the subjugation of half the human race out of . . . of . . . *pigheadedness!* Oh yes, Mr. Brown Eyes, in *my* century, not only would Ricky let Lucy into his tacky-ass show, but she'd have her *own* revue at the Tropicana!"

I didn't know what had gotten me so upset, but I wasn't at all surprised when a very patient Hank, having listened to me for far longer than anyone should have, said, "Cathy? Shut up."

Still, there was enough orneriness left in me to narrow my eyes and challenge, "Make me."

His hand slipped under my curls to cup the back of my neck, and together we closed the inches between us until our lips connected. He tasted like coffee with cream. I knew I could become addicted to the way he held me. "That's a good method," I murmured, letting him lower me back onto the sofa.

"Yes," he said, not letting go of me for an instant as he changed positions. He stared at me, removed his glasses, and then began leaving a trail of pecks along my jaw. "I like it."

"I like it, too." I laughed. "I sound like an Irish Spring commercial. Oh, don't stop. That feels so good. Don't stop."

"I won't," he promised. Yet he did, moments later, pulling away and peering at me myopically to bring me into focus. "Admit that you were jealous."

"I wasn't. Maybe a little." When he dove for my ear and gave it a playful nuzzle, I groaned. "I totally was."

"I watched Cathy. I watched her for a long time," he murmured, his deep voice no more than a rumble in my ear canal. "But you were the one I danced with. You were the one I sat next to. You were the one . . ." He lifted his head to look me in the eyes. "I kissed."

"You historical figures know all the right things to say to a girl," I whispered.

Then, for a very long time after that, he didn't give me an opportunity to say anything at all.

Chapter Twelve

From the expression Cherry wore as she toured our little kitchenette, one would've thought that some skunk had snuck into the apartment, given itself a quick rinse in sulfur water, dabbed eau de rotten eggs behind its ears, had a good scare, and had promptly died underneath the sink and gone unnoticed for a good couple of weeks. She opened drawers as if expecting tendrils of filth to shoot out and seize her by the wrist. From every newly opened cupboard door she reared away with a sense of drama that I'd never suspected lurked within her blunt heart. At long last, after she'd inspected everything twice, looked at me, back at the kitchen, then at me again, she finally spoke. "That's it?"

Her thumb and forefinger formed an L shape that she propped against her chin and cheek as she spoke. In my time, held against the forehead, it would have been the sign for *loser*. Maybe I was seeing the gesture's first documented historical appearance. "I told you it was a small kitchen!"

She ignored my exasperation. "This isn't a small kitchen. This is a cubbyhole. No, this is what a cubbyhole looks like after it's had all the air let out of it and then some foolish single girl who didn't learn squat from her mama takes it and throws it in the hot wash water and it shrinks." Again with the stare. "How in the world do you expect to cook an entire Thanksgiving dinner in here?"

"I can and I will."

"How in the *world* . . ." she started to repeat.

"Hey. You're the one who went all Mr. Miyagi on me with the advice about overcoming great obstacles when there's nothing to lose." When she didn't comprehend, I did some karate moves. "Wax on! Wax off! Forget it. It's a movie."

To no one in particular, Cherry muttered, "Some crazy movie that only crazy white people saw."

"The point *is* . . ." Did I have a point? Cherry had a way of unnerving me. "I want to serve someone special a home-cooked dinner for Thanksgiving, this is where I have to do it, and frankly, with my utter lack of ability, I haven't got a thing to lose. So let's get cooking!"

Maybe Cherry didn't recognize my perky head-bobbing and the clapping of my hands as meant to indicate my new, can-do attitude. "You expect to cook an entire Thanksgiving dinner using *these* pots and pans?" She opened up the tiny cabinet by the stove to reveal our collection of baking sheets and enameled cookware—more pieces total than I had in my apartment at home, I might add. "And *these* ingredients?" She opened up the cabinets above the sink, which were fully stocked, and then grabbed the locking handle of the refrigerator, unsealed it with a *ker-chunk*, and displayed the unlit contents of our refrigerator. Again, it was more food than had collectively ever graced the interior of my stainless steel side-by-side.

"Uh-huh?"

With one final trademarked look of scorn, Cherry shook her head. "It's a good thing I brought reinforcements." She crossed our little apartment until she reached a bulky piece of luggage she'd left by the door. She hefted it up and dragged it back in the direction of the kitchen. "What's in here's going to be your best friend, come Thursday."

"Is it a robot servant?" Then, in case she interpreted that in the worst possible way, I added, "Joke. Hank's always going on about robot servants." Cherry unzipped her bag and raised her eyebrow in a way that left no doubt that for the sake of our tentative friendship, the less she said about Hank, the better. And that's when she started to place on the counter huge metal objects that had probably seen service under in the Spanish Inquisition. I couldn't keep the panic from my voice. "What in the heck are those?"

She rested her hand on a miniature iron maiden with an ominous dial gracing one end. "A turkey roaster." Next up was a long device featuring a skewer and a turn-handle I was pretty sure I'd seen on *Alias* being used to remove an enemy spy's eyeball. "An apple peeler, for your pie. It'll double for your potatoes, too." She fondled the lethal gizmo as if it had been piercing enemy eyeballs in her family for generations. "And finally, a pressure cooker."

I gawked at the monstrosity she hoisted up with both hands. That was no kitchen implement. That was the kind of blunt device you'd expect to catch a shame-faced Professor Plum trying to stuff behind the conservatory's potted plants while the still-warm corpse of Mr. Boddy lay nearby. "No, seriously."

"Wash your hands," she ordered.

"Maybe I'd better start with something smaller. Do you have Kraft dinners in your supermarkets? Yes? No?" As Cherry advanced on me, I backed away slowly. "Lean Cuisine?"

"I don't know what you're talking about," she said through gritted teeth, "but I'm not going to repeat myself. Wash. Your. Hands."

I'd never heard three more threatening words in my entire life.

I was half a dozen painful, but successful, test potatoes and nearly an hour into my so-called training when heavenly powers took pity on me and granted a diversion in the streamlined shape of Miranda entering the apartment, patent leather bag swinging. "You would *not* believe what a day I've had," she said, instantly launching into a conversation. "There was a terrible matron at the store who *insisted* she was two sizes smaller than her posterior could accommodate." She began unbuttoning her overcoat and walking in our direction. "*Quelle* catastrophe! It seems as if I spent *hours* trying to stuff her ample rolls into sharkskin. Frightening, I know. And then I came home and changed and Harold and I were going to go out to a tony little bistro uptown he'd read about in the *Times*, but when we got there, the publicity had attracted *hordes* of the most gauche . . . oh. Hello." She'd finally noticed Cherry leaning against the kitchenette doorway, overseeing my drudgery.

Save for the fact that Miranda was slightly lighter in hue, they could have been twins, with their heads of upswept hair and their form-fitting casual pants, their crossed arms, and their suspicious exchange of glances. I wasn't going to break the silence. They were big girls. Finally Cherry nodded and said, "Nice coat."

There was no surer way to Miranda's heart. "Oh, thank you!" she cooed, running her hands over the fabric as she finished removing it to reveal the harlequin blouse underneath. "Lord and Taylor. I adore it. Bumpy tweed, but see, it has an alpaca lining so it's reversible. And a darling little oversized uppity collar of black rabbit. I'm Miranda." She held out a hand that Cherry studied for a moment before shaking. "I love your capris."

"110th Street U-Pick," said Cherry. At least it was in a pleasant tone.

Didn't I get a shout-out? "Cherry works with me," I called, struggling with the handle of my torture device.

"Oh, you're *Cherry!*" Miranda, now that she was free of the confines of her outerwear, lounged opposite my cooking instructor and laid a hand on her arm. "Tilly has told me so much about you! She says you're marvelous, really. I can't stop her from raving!"

"Tilly is a very nice woman."

"So you know? I really, really, really admired *Porgy and Bess.*"

"Did you, now?" Cherry's voice, softer at the mention of Tilly, had grown slightly flinty again.

"And Mr. Sidney Poitier, in *The Blackboard Jungle*? Revelatory."

"Mmmm-hmmm. The man is a credit to his face, isn't he?"

I recognized the dangerous tone. Time for me to intervene. I abandoned my station and quickly made my way across the kitchenette. "Cherry is teaching me how to cook. Isn't that great?"

"How odd. I thought you already . . . *darling!*" At the sight of me, Miranda shrieked with dismay. Her glance traveled from my face down to the calico apron that usually hung from a hook next to the refrigerator. I suspected the apron was supposed to be strictly decorative, but boy, had it been used that evening. "What have you been *doing?*"

"Well, I wanted to make Thanksgiving dinner for Hank, you see." That admission won a sharp look of interest from her, but no comment. Instead, she stepped into the kitchenette and, jaw hanging, made a quick inspection. "*Quelle* Hiroshima."

"It's not that bad," I tried to joke, but already Cherry and Miranda were exchanging covert expressions of sympathy.

"You've got something on your . . ." Miranda delicately applied the tip of her pinkie to her cheek. Automatically I reached up and rubbed, eliciting a wince. "No, on your other . . ."

Cherry shook her head when I plucked a quarter-sized slice of potato peel from my face. "It's like trying to toss one life preserver to all the people on a sinking ship."

Miranda giggled. "She is a bit hopeless, isn't she?"

"What?" I demanded to know. "What?"

"Hellooo-hooo!" Again the front door opened with a rattle of its chain. Tilly's accented lilt echoed through the living room. "Is everybody decent? I brought boys!"

It was a bit of a moot question because the most undressed I'd seen either of my flatmates was when Miranda wore her quilted pajamas and matching robe and slippers, or Tilly appeared in her neck-to-ground flannel nightdress. Nonetheless, Miranda shouted, "Cathy's not!" Cherry, apparently Miranda's ally again, giggled for the first time since I'd known her.

I pushed past the smirking pair so I could get a gander at myself in the living room mirror. "I am, too, decent! What's wrong with—oh, Christ!" Now I knew what Miranda had meant with her Hiroshima reference. Over the last hour and a half I'd managed to transform myself from pretty and prim figure of the '50s to some kind of international war refugee with no discernable race or identity. The only clean spot on my face, in fact, had been where the potato had stuck; pulling it away had left a small white patch that, against the grime I'd somehow managed to transfer from my potato to face, looked a little like leprosy. My hair? Well, people with their fingers in electrical sockets had better coiffures.

"Honey! Are you all right? Are you hurt?" Perhaps afraid I might have had another accident with the coffeepot, Tilly didn't even bother to close the apartment door behind her when she rushed in. "Did you give yourself an injury? Do you know who I am? Should I call the doctor?"

"I'm fine," I reassured her. "No amnesia, this time."

Slightly reassured, she undid her coat. "I declare, sometimes these days when I walk through that front door, I never know what I'm going to find you doing. What were you up to this time?"

Miranda, in a spectacular example of being helpful at the wrong time, said, "Cherry was teaching her how to cook."

"Oh, isn't that . . . ?" Tilly's face lit up as she noticed Cherry for the first time, but then her brain caught up. "What do you mean, teaching her how to cook?"

"It's not how it sounds," I said in haste. "She was showing me some new recipes. And some new techniques."

"That's one way of putting it."

Cherry shut her mouth when I glared, daring her to say anything else. "You see, I'm going to implement a new system around the office. I'm trying to think bigger. It's unfair, don't you think, with so many talented women in our kitchens, all of whom have experience in the culinary arts that far exceeds . . . well, don't you think it's unjustified that I'm the only one who comes up with recipes? Think how much better our books could be if all the staff were able to contribute their own ideas, and I screened out the ones that would be best suited for, um, our customer, the modern-day housewife!" It was quite a stirring little speech, and not exactly impromptu; I'd been trying to think of a way to give the Marie Lemleys of the office a little autonomy of their own, so that they didn't have to sneak around and meet me with Tiny Minnie recipes concealed in their body cavities. "What do you think?"

"Why, it's a great idea!" Tilly enthused. "In fact, I liked it the first time I heard it coming out of my own mouth, oh, a year ago!"

There's little worse than a cheery little sarcastic Southern woman. Unless it's the black woman and the redhead sniggering into their hands behind her.

"Knocky-knocky!" I heard a deep voice call through the open door. Tilly had dragged Chester home with her, obviously. "Are you girls decent yet, or should we menfolk come in anyway?"

"Why don't I . . . if you let me slide by I can . . . a little more space and I can . . ." It was with a shiver of horror that I recognized Hank's voice. I didn't have any time to hide before his head poked through the opening. He blinked at the sight of me. "Oh, hi. Wow. Are you okay?"

No matter how willing they were to rag on me when we girls were alone, the moment we confronted The Enemy, my three friends formed a united front, shrieked at the tops of their lungs, and began hustling me out of scrutiny's way. You'd have thought it was one of those campus—what did my granddad used to call them?—panty raids from days of yore, with us as the helpless coed virgins and them as the galumphing young bucks, set on ransacking our frillies. It wasn't until they'd sequestered me in Miranda and Tilly's bedroom, which happened to be closer, did the shrieking and giggling stop, including my own. In my decade, you wouldn't catch anybody above the age of fourteen acting that way. Even in adolescence we liked to think we were far too sophisticated for that kind of silliness. And you know, I kind of thought that was a pity.

"You girls go tend to the guys," Miranda instructed Tilly, setting me down in front of her pink-and-white vanity. With a flip of a switch, what seemed like a hundred little bulbs came on around the mirrors. I'd always been amazed at how much space these gals devoted to their face preparation. Considering I was the queen of juggling a compact and lipstick with one hand and a cell phone in the other while I maintained my balance on the swaying F train every morning, these little tables seemed like a veritable Taj Mahal of narcissism. "I'll fix up the little matchstick girl."

"I don't really care if they see me like this!" My

frank admission elicited a squeak of dismay from Tilly, whom Miranda finally had to push from the room. Cherry shot me a look laden with sympathy before she left.

"You hush your mouth, as Tilly would say." Miranda, the gleam of a perfectionist in her eye and the tip of her tongue wedged in the corner of her lips as she studied me, at last let her fingers dive into a porcelain jar shaped like an antebellum Scarlett O'Hara. "You and I have not had a heart-to-heart in some time," she said, dipping the fluff into a jar of some kind of sweet-smelling cream and then dabbing it on my face.

"Haven't we?" was the best I could do. Tilly and I, after all, saw each other all the time at work. Between auditions and her job and Harold, Miranda and I barely even managed to shout out good-mornings and good-nights to each other on a daily basis.

"Oh, Cathy." Her shoulders fell. "I know we have our disagreements. But do you always have to be so secretive? I know you were upset with me when I wondered if you were seeing someone earlier this year. Maybe I did overstep my bounds. I don't know. But you can't be mad at me forever, can you?"

"No, of course not," I said, feeling a little badly while remembering that none of that had been me at all. I bit my lip while she continued to blot, blot, blot away the grime. "I'm not mad at you at all, Mandy," I said, using the nickname I'd heard Tilly use a few times. "The truth is, you were right. I was seeing someone. He wasn't good for me at all. It's over." In the mirror I caught a smile flickering across her lips for a moment, only to be banished and replaced with concern and sympathy; she'd been so close to crowing about how right she'd been. "It's been over for a while now."

"Well, good. I'm glad it's over. Why, the way you were skulking about, we didn't know what to think. Tilly and I thought it might be something horrible. Like a married man. Or worse."

"What's worse than a married man?" I asked, trying not to gulp too visibly.

"An actor," she said without hesitation, then grinned at me. She put down the last of several cotton balls she'd used on me, and let her hands wander over my hair, tucking and flouncing here and there. "Trust me on that one. I found out the hard way this summer, in the Catskills. Oh, some of the talent who came to Grossinger's were nice enough, but there were *so* many out-of-work actors they hired cheap for the entertainment. Like octopuses, every single one of them. Octopi? Regardless. Not at all stable. You can't say that about Harold, though. They don't come more stable than Harold. So! Tell me about Hank." She went from resigned to intimate in two seconds flat.

"Oh, there's really nothing to tell."

"Hmmm." She looked at me in the mirror. "He's a good man, Cathy. A girl in your position could do far, far worse. He's attractive, fun to talk to. Likes to read, but some girls enjoy that in a guy. Good family— excellent prospects for the future."

"I thought being the super or rent collector or whatever for this strip of flats only got him a place to live from his family, and that whatever income he earned was from freelancing with those illustrations."

I didn't like that knowing expression she wore. It seemed to imply we were in on the same plot together. But I wasn't the one settling for a guy whose most fascinating conversational talent was the ability to make anagrams out of anyone's name. "*Now*, maybe," she said, patting a curl back into place. "Who knows what would happen if he decided to give up his bachelor independence and settle down once and for all? I'm sure a few right words and he'd give up that silly hobby and find something useful to do." When she pulled her lips back into a smile, it was more vulpine than friendly. "Don't you think? Now, stand up, and let's get that filthy apron off so we can join the others."

"You don't think a man should follow a dream?" I stood there numbly while she attended to me like one of her customers, trying not to let my jaw tremble.

"Of course I do, silly. To a point. But when opportunity comes along, a man would be a fool not to take it. And a woman would be more fool not to talk him into it." I don't think I could have pitied her more at that moment. From my vantage point in time I could see the arc of her entire life right then: abandoning her aspirations for the stage to marry someone dull and steady, settling into a comfortable home of her own that would seem more like a prison the moment she'd finished decorating, the drinking and rue and chain-smoking, followed by years of resentment. "Now, don't go near those potatoes again. You look much better."

At the same time, I knew I shouldn't scorn the poor girl. How was she any different from the other women of this era, agreeably marching in lock-step fashion toward suburbia and a lifetime of convenience foods and frozen TV dinners, eternally smiling, smiling, smiling on their long and rugged hike toward obscurity? Why in the world should she think I was any different?

A thought occurred to me as Miranda led me back.

Did I want to be any different? If I were stuck here for the rest of my life, would I avoid that fate? Could I, if I found myself increasingly involved with Hank? Because if I wanted to be with him, I'd have to give up any hope of ever getting back to the future. Gone would be all my career aspirations, my network of friends, my entire resume. By the time I'd catch up again, I'd be pushing eighty. It was a scary thought.

Hank sat on the edge of our sofa, fanning out some playing cards between his fingers. Cherry sat opposite. She drew a card, reviewed what she held, and laid down another. "You're close, aren't you?" she asked.

He selected a card from the deck, sorted it into his hand in some complicated shuffling motion meant to confuse, and played a card onto the upturned discard pile. "A good player never reveals his hand," he said with an air of mystery. To me he added, "All freshened up, sunshine?"

"Yuh-huh." I watched him with mingled affection and fear. Hank was as much a product of his times as I was of mine. Could we ever really find common ground together? Was it even possible?

From the other room I heard a distressed wail. "But my *kitchen!*"

"Oh dear," said Miranda, leaving my side to join Tilly at ground zero. "She saw it."

I could hear Chester murmuring some words in an encouraging tone. "But my *kitchen!*" lamented Tilly once more.

"The girl's been a broken record since she walked in there," Cherry warned me.

"Gin," Hank announced. He laid down his cards with a grin.

"No!" Cherry's jaw shot out. "I never lose at

227

rummy! This boyfriend of yours is an out-and-out cheat, I swear." Like a soap bubble, though, her resentment instantly vanished. She tabulated points with a pencil and then scooped up the cards to deal again.

"Um, we're not . . ." I appealed to Hank for a little help, but he returned the blandest of smiles. "We haven't declared any formal kind of . . . that is . . . we're still . . . we only . . ."

"But my *kitchen!*" I heard.

That was my sign to make like a bandit. "Maybe I should . . . yeah," I concluded before slinking from the living room under their twin scrutiny.

"Now, now, I'm sure she'll clean it up." Chester hugged his arms to himself as if frightened that some of the potato skins the peeler had splattered everywhere might be magnetically attracted to his crimson velveteen sports coat. Tilly, in the meantime, quivered like a Chihuahua in the cold.

"Oh, sure!" I said, trying to sound breezy. "It'll be a snap!"

Tilly didn't seem so sure. I knew that second only to the Richmond test kitchens that were her pride and joy, the little kitchenette was dear to her heart. She kept it spick-and-span, always wiping it down of imaginary grime every night before bedtime. If a cupboard stood ajar, she couldn't rest until she'd closed it. If I left a jar in the tiny fridge, she'd be sure to rotate it until its label was clearly legible to anyone looking in. And here I'd strewn peels and potato water everywhere. "I don't understand what you were doing." Clearly shaken, she stumbled over to the counter and picked up one of my aborted potatoes that I'd somehow managed to trim into a squat bowling-pin shape. "What is this supposed to *be?*"

"It looks like the fertility goddess in my apartment. Har-har-har!" Even while I shuddered at the photographer's forced mirth, I forced down my nightmare vision of what his apartment must look like.

"It's like I said, sweetie. I was trying to pick up a couple of techniques from Cherry. To broaden my range." From nothing to a little something, if we had to get specific about it. "You know I wouldn't perform a hit-and-run on your kitchen without making it up to you. All I wanted was to make a nice Thanksgiving dinner for . . ." I jerked my head in the direction of the living room beyond the swinging door behind me.

That certainly changed things. In an Oscar-worthy quick-change, she careened from the verge of tears to the brink of excitement. "For Hank?" she all but screeched. "Oh, honey! That's wonderful! What a good idea! How sweet of you! Hank, you lucky dog, here's one woman who knows the way to a man's heart!" she called out before I could shush her. Oh, I'd tried. I was waving my arms and shaking my head and no doubt setting loose all the curls that Miranda had painstakingly fixed only minutes before, all in an attempt to keep Tilly from bleating out anything that Hank might construe as an attempt to strong-arm him into a relationship with me. No matter what the century, men were men; none of the good ones wanted to move too quickly from a couple of bursts of physical lust to a domestic situation. Through the door to the living room, Tilly leaned out and shook a finger. "You scamp!"

"Thanksgiving?" I heard him say, followed by the sounds of him peeling himself from the salmon leatherette.

"You scalawag!" I cringed and fruitlessly looked for

someplace to hide. Honestly. There were reasons I lived alone in the future.

"Really, Cathy? Is that what you were planning? Um . . ." Oh God. I steeled myself. Here it came. I knew the indicators of commitment-phobia. First would be the gentle touch of humor. Right on cue, he chuckled. "Funny you should mention that." Next would come damning with faint praise and some filler to pad the eventual crash landing. "Having you cook Thanksgiving dinner for me would be swell, you being a cookbook writer and everything. And I fully intend to take you up on that grub you owe me."

"Swell," I echoed, trying to sound pleasant, but knowing I would be facing disappointment very shortly.

The next and final symptom, of course, would be the demurral. It would sound gentle, but it would sting. He thought I was moving too fast, too far, and neither of my friends had helped any with their too-obvious matchmaking. I steeled myself for what was to come, my stomach queasy. "But . . ." See? I knew there'd be a but. "The one event I'll do with the family all year is Thanksgiving at my granddad's club, the Old Ivy. A gentleman's club. Mahogany, whiskey, boring old men avoiding their boring old wives. Thanksgiving's kind of a big deal, though. It's the one day of the year they allow 'the gentler sex,' as they call you, to step through the front doors. So I was hoping—"

Hah! I knew it. "I understand," I said quietly, before he'd even finished his sentence. I felt more like the pathetic, ignored Little Match Girl now than I had when I'd been a mess. "No, really, it's okay."

I'd already turned to make my way back into the kitchenette when he spoke his unexpected coda. "I was hoping you'd be my date. You know. Gussy up a little, spend the day with a bunch of squares." I must have looked as surprised as I felt, because he nodded. "Why do you look so shocked?"

Everyone seemed to have cleared to the side, leaving a direct and unobstructed path between us. Even Cherry watched quietly from the sofa. I fumbled for words. What was it that girls said to guys in this decade? "I don't have anything to wear," I said weakly. Maybe there was hope for Hank, after all.

Thank God for '50s sitcoms. Everyone recognized the punch line for what it was and broke into enraptured conversation. "Actually," Hank said above the babble, "I think I might be able to swing it so that you guys can all go as my guests. Hell, my granddad practically owns the place, so I don't know why not."

Tilly bounced up and down in place, the catastrophe of the kitchen all but forgotten; Miranda looked a ghastly, excited white, as if she'd heard that all the funds in Harold's accounts consisted solely of Monopoly money. Chester, in the meantime, had assumed the puffed-up chest of a man attempting to make other people believe he was invited to exclusive gentlemen's clubs all the time, if not a member himself. And Cherry was quietly playing solitaire on the coffee table. "Honey, say yes!" Tilly urged. Miranda still had the air of a kid hoping for something so hard that she might accidentally spit up if she opened her mouth. "It'll be fun! Unless you want to go by yourselves, of course. And then we'd understand. Wouldn't we?"

Her appeal to the crowd got no response from either Miranda or Cherry, but Chester nodded. "Oh, it would be delightful. Delightful, to see the Ivy again.

Was there years ago, you know. Friend of mine had me there for drinks. Absolutely delightful."

"Hank?" I asked, stepping forward a few steps. My voice was as shy as the smile on my face when I took both his hands in mine. "On behalf of everyone, I accept."

Amidst the hubbub that followed, his reply was for my ears alone. "I was hoping you might. Listen, though. I found . . ."

"Let's go celebrate!" Tilly's voice cut through whatever Hank had been about to say. "Chester and I had stopped in to see if any of you wanted to go out with us. There's a funny little bar there on Third Avenue near 45th where a woman with a deep voice plays piano and everybody sings. We went last weekend and Chester and I sang—this is funny!—" 'The Rain in Spain.' " You know, from *My Fair Lady*? Only I was Henry Higgins and *Chester* was . . ."

"Isn't it a little late to go traipsing out to bars?" I interrupted.

"Oh, come on, you party pooper!" said Miranda, having gotten back her wind. "It's not even nine o'clock, and it's a Saturday night! Hank, you're going to have to teach her that life can't be all work and no play."

"I had a little of that in mind for tonight," he agreed, winking at me.

"Let me clean up the kitchen some," I grumbled. I heard Tilly call out something about leaving it until the morning, but I was already on my way.

I wasn't at all surprised when Hank joined me. "Hey," he said, while I shoved Cherry's pressure cooker into a cupboard. "What's the matter?" I shrugged, expecting him to go away, but hoping to hell he wouldn't. "Is something wrong? Don't you want to go to the club for Thanksgiving? Say the word and I'll cancel. I'd love an excuse to."

Somehow the peeling machine had gotten itself firmly attached to the counter, and I couldn't for the life of me remember how Cherry had done it. I tugged at it fruitlessly. "No, it's not that. That's lovely. It was really nice of you to offer, and I know it made Miranda's and Tilly's days."

"Are you disappointed about not making a dinner for me?"

"No. Yes! No." Even I didn't know why I was so frustrated. The peeler still wouldn't come unstuck from the counter. "Damned thing."

With expert hands, Hank reached beneath the counter and unfastened the wing nut holding the peeler's vise firm. He removed the defeated-looking potato from its lethal spike, dropped it into the wastebasket, and began rinsing the entire contraption in the porcelain sink. "I would love nothing more than for you to make me a Thanksgiving dinner," he said. "A real, old-fashioned . . . that word probably isn't right for you, is it? A real Thanksgiving dinner from the future. Why don't we do it Friday or Saturday?"

"Friday or Saturday's fine," I said, waiting for him to finish in the sink before I drew closer. I kept my voice low as I spoke. "It's not dinner. I'm going to make dinner for you and it's going to suck royally . . . it's going to be really bad . . . but I'm stubborn that way. It's not the club thing. That could be fun, or not, depending on your family, but either way, it'll be interesting. It's . . ." I prided myself on being good with words, generally, but Hank had a way of making me feel helpless. Or maybe he made me feel safe about appearing helpless in front of him. Either way, it wasn't something I was used to. "Everything's getting to me," I admitted to him. "All of it. Miranda's going to yoke herself to Harold for security. I'm worried that Tilly's going to do the same thing with a gay guy. Sorry, it's the slang thing again. I meant, a ho—"

"I know what the term means, thanks," said Hank. "I was in the army. But who—?" His eyes widened. "You mean, *Chester?* You're kidding me."

I shushed him before anybody else heard. "Oh, please. Nothing against the guy. He's nice. He's very attentive to Tilly, I suppose. And he's a great photographer. I mean, if he can make a Tower of Treet look appealing . . ."

"A who? Is that one of your futuristic references?"

"If only. You know Treet? Like Spam? A whole frickin' Chrysler Building of the stuff. One of Cathy's creations. Don't look at me that way," I warned him. "You're the one who was sweet on her. Not me."

Hank reached up and rested a thumb on my chin, tilting my head so I couldn't help but look in his eyes. "She's not the one I'm sweet on."

I melted, but some hamster in my head had started running on a little wheel, and therefore my jaw kept flapping. "My point is that in my time, there's not quite as much stigma against it as there is now. A lot of gay guys take wives in this time period, and then later on when things are less repressive, they devastate them by leaving. They made a whole Julianne Moore movie set in the '50s about it. The last thing I want for Tilly is to have a husband on the down-low." Crap, another idiom barrier. I barreled on. "I feel so *helpless*, Hank. There's nothing I can do here to help anyone. Look at Cherry. I mean, you met her. In my

234

decade she'd be a close friend, someone I'd go out drinking and dancing with. Here she thinks of me as the enemy. And I *am* the enemy, because of the color of my skin. God, why did I hire her? She's convinced that someone with more power than me at work is going to fire her any day now."

"You hired me because of a misplaced sense of guilt." Hank and I both started. Cherry stood in the swinging doorway, her overcoat draped over her crossed arms, staring at both of us. Instantly I felt guilty. God knows what she'd overheard. With my luck, it would have been the *why did I hire her?* part. I started to apologize, but she silenced me with an upraised hand. "Like a good Democrat, right?"

My shoulders slumped. Even with Hank standing close behind me, I felt defenseless. "Rumor has it I was supporting Nixon in the next election, actually."

She shrugged. "Well, Lincoln was a Republican, and look what he did." After a quick glance over her shoulder at the girls in the other room, Cherry took a few more steps in. "I think I'm going home for the evening."

"Don't you want to go out?" I protested. "I know Tilly would want you to. Me, too." Not that she'd believe the last part. "Really. We'll have fun."

"You have yourself some fun then," she said, beginning to unfurl her coat. Hank instantly leapt to help her into it, a gallantry she acknowledged with a nod. "No offense? But I don't think I'd be popular wherever you're going. And thank *you* for the invitation for Thanksgiving," she added to Hank. "But I spend the day with my own family, and I don't really reckon the old Ivy Club would welcome me with open arms anyway."

"Why?"

I'd meant the question innocently enough, but Cherry leaned heavily against the door frame and scolded me. "Do not say that I am going to have to explain to you the politics of discrimination in this country."

"And that's another reason I tend to stay away from my family," Hank said, his eyes full of apology to us both.

"Oh," I said, embarrassed and ashamed. Cherry was right. It was modern liberal guilt chewing me up from the inside out that had prompted me to hire her. This was exactly what I'd been telling Hank about moments before. What did I really expect to *do*, stranded back here in time? Save the world, one minority member at a time? A single world slipped from my mouth. "Shit. That's not right. Don't go away mad."

Cherry regarded me with raised eyebrows. "Shoot, Miss Potty Mouth. I'm not going away mad, and I'm not going away forever. If anything, you've got to invite me back so I can figure out how this boyfriend of yours is cheating at cards." She gave Hank a tap on the chest. "I know you are, rich boy."

"We'll see you later, Cherry," he said, grinning at her.

She finished buttoning her coat, but before exiting, she took a step past Hank and faced me. "Cathy." The word gave me gooseflesh. It was the first time she'd used anything other than my surname. "Republican or Democrat, at least you did something. You took a stand. That's more than most folk of any color would do. Okay?" She pulled out a pair of woolen gloves from her pockets. "And I'm going to want my stuff back after you fix that dinner. You hear?" On her way out of the kitchen she paused briefly in front of Hank, laid a hand on his, and murmured, "Lord help you."

"Hey!" I protested to her back. She raised a hand and made a dismissive motion with it, before Tilly attacked her with good-byes. Hank moved back across the room to be with me again. I felt vaguely embarrassed by the entire time. Cherry might have been abrupt. Abrasive, even. At the same time, though, she was one of the few women I'd met in this year who spoke exactly what was on her mind. I had to admire her for it. "She didn't need to do that."

Hank didn't care about my self-consciousness. He put one hand on my shoulder and used his other to chuck my chin again. "You feel helpless?" he asked. "Let me help you. I was coming up to see you anyway when I saw Tilly and Chester in the hallway." He paused. "Is he really . . . *that way?*"

"Trust me," I assured him. "And please, don't treat him any differently. Help me what?"

Instead of an answer, he asked, "Do you trust me?"

"Trust you to do what?"

"Do you trust me?" he repeated.

"Well, sure I do. Kind of. Unless it involves padded handcuffs. Or cold things on my skin. Or blindfolds. And I really don't like . . ."

His thumb traveled up to my lips, silencing them. "I spent today asking some questions around town. I think there's someone you should meet."

"Now? But—"

"We can only go at night." Before I could protest further, he repeated what he'd said earlier. "Let me help you. It might not work out. And then again, it might. The worst that can happen is that you'll still owe me a meal next weekend." His eyes traveled around the kitchen. "Speaking of which, did you learn *anything* from Cherry tonight?"

Now it was my turn to punch him in the chest. "Who is this someone?"

"You'll see," he promised. "Tell the girls we'll catch up with them in a couple of hours. And get your coat. You don't happen to have a chicken foot lying around, do you?" he added, his voice bland.

Mine was quite the opposite. "What *for?*"

"Kidding!" He laughed.

To be honest, I wasn't convinced he was.

Chapter Thirteen

"Weird. Déjà vu," I said, grabbing on to Hank's arm. Partly I wanted to steady myself. Mostly, however, I simply enjoyed being able to hold on to him. Nor were we the only other couple strolling closely together; walking down Bleecker Street, we must have passed at least a dozen other pairs huddling tightly for the warmth.

"You mean, you've been here before?" His question made curlicues of frost in the air. "Is all this still here in fifty years?"

"Yes, but it's different." The federal-style buildings were the same, certainly, as were the painted fire escapes decorating their exteriors. If it weren't for the plainer neon signs in the windows, or the vintage cars moving slowly through the streets like the set for some retro movie, I could have almost been back home. "It seems a little more run-down now. A little more *real.*"

"Of course it's real," he said, his arm slipping around my shoulders. "We're both here, aren't we?"

"Yes, but . . ." He was sweet, and very real. How

could I explain to him about gentrification? Or the international chain stores creeping onto every street? Or the skyrocketing real-estate prices that would eventually drive out the artists and bohemians and all the very people who made this end of the city the unique place it was? Would it depress him, change him, corrupt him in some way? Was I changing him too much already and breaking some law of time? "You're right," I said at last, letting him squeeze me close to ease my anxiety. "Where are we going, anyway?"

Again he didn't answer. How many times had I asked that very question and gotten no reply? It made me distinctly nervous.

"Is the San Remo still around in your time?" he asked. I didn't know what he was talking about. "Over there," he said, nodding ahead to the corner. I peered through the naked branches of the trees that lined the street in the direction of a red brick townhouse much like all the others. A number of people stood outside of one, chattering loudly. It looked like any other Village hipster watering spot. "It's kind of notorious. Lots of beatniks. Do you have beatniks?"

I'd seen Audrey Hepburn in *Funny Face*, and with Tilly I'd twice watched Gilligan playing the bongos on something called *Dobie Gillis*. "No, they kind of disappear after the Beatles. You'll see," I said, knowing what he was going to ask. "The Beatles are big. And they're not too far off, if I remember right. Hey," I added, dropping my voice to a whisper. "Would you look at that?"

Across the street, in front of the San Remo, a boy and a girl were busily giving each other tonsil exams. With their tongues, naturally. They were like any young people who'd forgotten the world around them while they were lost in each other. Ordinarily I wouldn't have given it a second thought, but this was no ordinary couple. He was white; she was black. For an entire second I gawked—not because it was so unusual a sight for me, but because it was entirely out of place for *here*. "The San Remo's one of the few places in the city where interracial couples meet without being harassed," he explained. "It's a pretty hip place."

"All right," I said at last, when the boy and girl parted and walked in opposite directions. "I feel a little bit encouraged. Stop staring," I said, swatting at him.

"I'm only getting ideas!" Without warning, he spun me around and, as a passing car's headlights danced across us, lowered his face to mine. How could I resist? By no means was I a virgin to smooching; I'd stolen my first kiss from Joe Something-or-other, the French horn player in my middle-school band, at the tender age of thirteen, and since then I'd had good kissers and terrible kissers cross my path. Sometimes I felt like the Goldilocks of that particular sport. A lot of kisses were too hard, and others too soft and tentative. Some were all tongue, while some guys seemed to think that merely sandpapering my lips with theirs was foreplay enough. A few were so fleeting that I couldn't remember them immediately after, while some lasted so long I nearly passed out from lack of oxygen. Hank, though? Like the baby bear's bed, he was just right.

"Get a room!" called a man's voice from a passing car. I grinned up at Hank, glad to see he was smiling back. When it came to catcalls, at least, some things never changed.

It wasn't until we turned onto McDougal that Hank spoke again, a doleful quality in his voice. "So the race issue—that's been solved in your time?"

Ah, so he was thinking about the future again. That explained the sadness. "Well, no . . . not solved, exactly. But it doesn't always feel as painful as now. I think knowing how much things have changed in fifty years might give people hope, but it's not perfect. Yet."

"It sounds wonderful." He sighed.

"It's . . ." How could I convey what seemed to me something very important? "It's not always wonderful, Hank. I mean, the stuff about tiny computers and big cars and integration probably sounds pretty nifty to you, but there's a lot of stuff I realize I took for granted, stuff that wasn't so good."

"Like?"

"Like worrying about the next time I might wake up and find the country under attack. Or what big diseases might be brewing next. Or worrying about wars I don't agree with, or knowing that all the little places that make a city special—like this one—have become like every other little place in every other city across the country. The future's not faultless, Hank. This decade is screwed up in so many ways, but so is when I live." I was growing a little out of breath, and scarcely noticed where he was leading me. "My job's in advertising, back home. All I do, day after day, is try to persuade people that my clients' products are the quick fix they need. It's superficial. My time is superficial. Want to appear patriotic? we ask people. Here, pay us fifteen dollars and slap this magnet on your car and you're all set. Want to pretend you care about people with an illness? Shell out some cash and wear this little rubber bracelet. It's like the automat. As long as you can stuff in enough coins, you can open a slot and grab whatever you want, fast and easy. Ease your guilt. Express your love. All for quarters." Something occurred to me. "Speaking of rubber bracelets, I'm now thinking it probably wasn't Lance Armstrong who landed on the moon. I'm terrible with names."

"I still believe you," he assured me. A street lamp cast a warm yellow glow above our heads. In an alleyway nearby, we heard the sound of two cats fighting. The noise from the San Remo had vanished as soon as we'd turned the corner. "I think it would be swell to time travel with you."

"Swell. Everyone here says *swell*. No one says *swell* in the future."

"What do they say?"

I thought about it a moment. "We say *totally* a lot. As in, I *totally* like being with you. Or, I *totally* want to make out with you."

"I want to time travel totally with you."

The slang sounded so funny in his mouth that I couldn't help but laugh. "Atta boy. Anyway, according to you, we're time traveling now, aren't we?" If he didn't remember what he'd told me when we'd talked about H. G. Wells, I surely did. "One second at a time." I got a squeeze of the hand for that. Only then did I notice we'd turned down the alley that moments before had been the site of a feline smack-down. "Hey, exactly where are we going?"

"It'll be good for you, totally," he said, trying again to sound more like me. He coaxed me forward. "Don't fret."

I wasn't so sure. I'm not a fan of surprises. "Good for me like a wheatgrass smoothie? Or good for me like a visit to Coney Island?"

"If a wheatgrass . . . what is it? Smoothie? If it's made from real grass, I'm forming an entirely new opinion about the future." To say the alley was a little scary was an understatement. With what little light still crept around the corner from the street lamp, I could see rustic bricks and creeping vines that grew unhindered over the buildings. Ragged old street stones lay underfoot, uneven and, in some spots, missing entirely. Save for the beat-up metal trash cans, I might have thought we'd stepped back another hundred years in time to a younger, darker New York. "You may thank me. How's that?" he asked.

I was reserving judgment. We stopped at a doorway that directly faced the alley, set into a squat building that had probably once been a carriage house. Only the tiniest of windows graced its second story. They glowed with a dim bluish light that was almost malevolent. I shivered. This whole setup didn't agree with me. "Hank?"

"Everything will be okay." He knocked on the door.

In what feeble light trickled from McDougal, I noticed that something had been painted on the door. The artwork was crude at best, even softened by the darkness. An upside-down triangle took up most of the wood, outlined in black. In its middle, chipped away by weather and wear, rested an eye. I thought it was supposed to be one of those ancient Egyptian types of eyes, a stylized outline with an intense, staring pupil. "I really don't like this," I repeated, my anxiety multiplying.

Hank stepped back, looked up at the building's second floor with annoyance, and then returned to the door to knock again. After the third time he rapped away, I was about to suggest we go ahead and go sing songs from *My Fair Lady* at the cute little piano bar—and that's not a sentence I ever thought would be coming from my mouth—when with a creak of a rusty hinge, the door swung inward. I gulped. "Okay," I whispered, holding him back. "You know how in *Scooby Doo*, the gang is always going into haunted houses uninvited and regretting it afterwards?"

"Scooby who?" he asked. In the alley's quiet, his normal voice seemed four times its usual volume. "Come on. I got this woman's name from a perfectly legitimate guy this afternoon."

"A perfectly legitimate guy where?" I wanted to know. "An Italian mob bar?"

"No, a voodoo shop." He ducked his head and pushed his way in.

"A voodoo shop. Great," I muttered. What choice did I have but to follow, when the alternative was standing out in the alley by my lonesome? "Fan-freakin'-tastic, in fact. The one guy I decide to confide in turns out to be an aficionado of voodoo shops. What were you doing in a voodoo shop, anyway?" My voice sounded unnaturally loud in the low hallway.

"Ssssh," he said, stepping through a doorway at the corridor's end.

I had to blink several times once we were inside. In a large open room where decades earlier, a horse and carriage or a Model T might have occupied space, a woman sat at a round, wooden table that was the only furnishing. A painted lightbulb hanging from the ceiling cast an eerie light over the room, seeming to fill it more with shadows than with illumination. In the strange blue luster, the woman's eyes gleamed with uncanny brilliance. Because she wore a high-necked cloak and a turban, it was almost impossible to tell her age—she could have been anywhere between thirty and fifty. "Welcome, strangers from afar," she intoned in a deep, sonorous voice that seemed to vibrate the marrow in my bones. "I have been expecting you."

"Hank," I whispered.

"Thank you," he said, not seeming to hear me.

"Hank." I tugged at his shirt.

"Ssssh," he repeated.

"But I have to pee." I really did. Once the adrenaline kicked in, my bladder followed.

The woman's turban, a tall number I'd really only seen on aging movie stars and Johnny Carson, seemed to be speckled with glowing points of light that lent her an even more supernatural presence. Her hands reached toward the table's center, on which was painted the same insignia I'd seen ever-so-faintly on the door outside. Slowly, she traced the triangle's outline. "The Eye of Zohar sees all," she declaimed. "And I am its most exalted high priestess."

Once she fell silent, I heard another noise that hadn't been quite as apparent before. From somewhere close by came the sound of a television, perfectly audible to my ears. Now that my eyes had adjusted somewhat to the strange light, I could see a sliver of white beneath a closed door at the room's opposite end; it flickered from the set beyond casting a glow on the floor. "*And to start off the proceedings,*" said a genial male voice, "*Mr. Bennett Cerf.*"

"*Thank you, John,*" I heard another man with a reedier throat reply. "*Mrs. Gilliam, in your occupation you provide a service. Is that correct?*"

"*Yes it is,*" said a girl faintly. Somehow the broadcast voices gave me back my perspective; this setup was the silliest thing I'd seen in ages. My bladder began to settle down.

Apparently our turbaned hostess could hear the

television just as clearly. She raised her voice to drown it out. "I am the priestess of the Eye of Zohar!" I thought we'd already gotten that part established, but she cleared her throat and explained, "I, among all beings, have been chosen to penetrate the veil that separates the living and the dead."

"And that's five dollars down and we'll move on to Miss Dorothy Kilgallen," I heard.

"Thank you, John. Now, Mrs. Gilliam, would I be correct in assuming that in your job you deal with ladies as well as gentlemen?"

Once again, the woman attempted to talk over the noise. "I have been expecting you, strangers."

"Didn't she already say that?" I whispered to Hank.

"And Mrs. Gilliam, would I be further correct in assuming that the service you provide is something that I myself might enjoy?" A studio audience burst into laughter.

"*MA!*" I nearly jumped out of my skin when the piercer of the Veil of Whatever slapped her hands down upon the table and screamed over her shoulder in a manner decidedly unbefitting a priestess. "*MA!*" she repeated.

The television went silent for a moment. The priestess shook her shoulders, resumed her regal stance, parted her lips, and managed to get out, "For what purpose do you seek—"

But the silence had only been a lull in the program. *"After careful consideration,"* said the game show announcer, *"Mrs. Gilliam and I have decided, Miss Kilgallen, that yes, if you were to avail yourself of her services, then indeed, you would most likely find yourself in a position afterwards of having enjoyed them."* More audience laughter.

The priestess seemed fed up. "Goddamn it, Ma!" she brayed, hauling herself up from the table. Her normal voice, I was somewhat pleased to note, reminded me of Fran Drescher, only without the sweet, honeyed qualities. What a big, fat charlatan!

"Maybe you should start patronizing a better-quality voodoo shop," I said to Hank.

He didn't seem overly impressed, either. "Um, pardon me . . ."

Turban-head had already cracked open the other door and stuck her head through it. "How many times do I gotta tell ya that when I've got God-damn customers, you need to keep the God-damn TV *down?* Yeah, well, I don't care if you like Arlene Francis. That society bitch's voice gets on my God-damn nerves. Move closer if you can't hear. *I said, move closer if you can't hear.* No, you're not gonna get God-damned cancer from being too God-damned close. They say that about cigarettes and look at Aunt Sue. She's ninety-four and still sucking 'em down like they're going out of God-damned style." She slammed the door shut and turned around, muttering to herself, "Even though she has to hit *me* up for money for smokes, God-damn it." With a tortured sigh, she heaved herself back in the chair, and *poof!* The voice was back again. "Where were we?" she demanded, sounding imperious.

"Are you Annie Spivak?" asked Hank, before she could go into the Zohar routine again. When she didn't answer right away, he reached into his coat pocket, pulled out a slip of paper, and quickly gave up trying to read it in the bad lighting. "A friend of mine told me to ask for Annie Spivak."

"God-*damn* it," said the priestess in her normal

voice. "Why didn't you *say* so? *MA!*" she yelled, using the table to heave herself to her feet again, muttering all the way. "Wasting my time when . . . *MA! You've got some people here to see you!*" Great balls o' fire, but that voice was like an ice pick to the ears! Without any finesse, the priestess yanked open the other door to reveal a den of sorts. Though the only sources of light within were a rickety table lamp and the blue-gray flicker of the television, my hand flew up to my eyes at the sudden brightness. "MA!"

There was one syllable I could gladly go without hearing again, thank you very much. I followed Hank as he stepped around the table, ducked his head under the low door, and looked around the room. "Annie Spivak?" he asked, finally able to double-check the note he'd written to himself.

Seated in a battered old bundle of plaid cloth that seemed to be more slipcover than actual chair, was one of the tiniest old women I'd ever seen. Her aged back was hunched like a question mark, and she stared ahead at the television without seeming to hear Hank's inquiry. She cackled at something on the screen, exposing a line of lower gums totally without teeth. "Look," I muttered. "Norman Bates's mother."

"Who?" Hank whispered. I'd been so sure he'd get that one! Wasn't *Psycho* in black and white?

In the meantime, the priestess had removed her one-piece turban, run a hand through her substantial head of frizzy black hair, and begun to unbutton her long robes. She bent down next to her mother and said, using one of those deliberate tones one uses for the hard of hearing, "These people are here to *see you.*"

The old lady's voice, when she finally parted her lips to speak, sounded like a rusty hinge only one good rainstorm away from crumbling into dust. "I'm watching *What's My Line?*"

"It's a God-damned ad." The priestess marched around and turned down the sound.

"But the mystery guest is about to come on."

Hank decided to counter the complaint with a little of his natural charm. "I really didn't mean to intrude on your evening, Mrs. Spivak, but a friend of yours in a shop on Third told me you might be able to help a friend of mine with a little problem." He smiled at me with reassurance. "She's a little lost, you see."

I didn't know how to feel at that juncture. Flattered, because Hank had apparently spent a good portion of his Saturday prowling the voodoo shops of New York City on the off chance of finding someone adept in time meddling? Absolutely. But also a little embarrassed that he'd put his trust in obvious charlatans. I mean, honestly. The high priestess of Zohar was bending over and showing off her substantial rear end as she retrieved something from a stove so tiny, it made ours look like a mighty Food Network installation. Her mother, the one we'd come to see, could have been licked in a slap fight by the littlest of the *Golden Girls*. And I was supposed to believe this was my one shot at heading back home? "Hank, why don't we let them alone?" I suggested.

He shushed me right as Mrs. Spivak finally turned to peer at him through the thickest glasses I've ever seen in my life. "Who's lost?"

"She is." Hank nodded at me, prompting the old woman to turn in her seat and look me up and down. I smiled politely, wishing we would simply go. Her inspection was making me nervous.

"Waffle?" Junior Spivak was back, bearing a plate

stacked high with breakfast food. She speared one with a fork and held it out in my direction. "They're yummy." As if to prove it, she took a bite, without benefit of syrup.

"Where are you from, child?"

My automatic instinct when it came to the elderly was to be as polite as possible, on the idea that one day when I got to be up there in years, I'd like others to do the same for me. "I'm from here, ma'am. New York."

Something freaky happened right then. Usually when a myopic removed his glasses—Hank, for example—he looked a little defenseless, as if physically affected by the fuzziness of his sight. When Mrs. Spivak reached up and very slowly pulled down her thick lenses, however, something totally freaky happened. Her eyes didn't seem squinty or fuzzy at all. If anything, I got the distinct impression she could see right through me. The way those eyes probed was utterly chilling. I had in my head the thought that maybe she wore those Coke bottles to *prevent* herself from seeing as clearly as she seemed to be. That was crazy, though. I'd only felt impatient up to that point, yet her examination rooted me to the spot. I even stopped noticing the priestess's steady chewing. "What year?" Somehow I felt reprimanded, and without any hesitation whatsoever, I told her. She nodded and moved the wire frames back into place. "I see."

"You can help?" asked Hank.

I had a question of my own. "Has this—has this happened before? To other people?"

On the television screen, a number of well-groomed men and women exchanged smiles and jabbered away silently behind their table. Mrs. Spivak considered them for a moment, then reached for a cane propped against the chair. Hank sped to her side to assist her, but she waved him away. "Have you done what you came to do?" she said, once on her feet. Without waiting for an answer, she started walking toward the rear of the little house.

"I didn't . . . that is, I didn't come deliberately. It was an accident," I babbled, following behind. Our little parade through the cluttered den was a strange one, led by an arthritic psychic, with Hank and I following, and a waffle fiend in Harry Potter drag bringing up the rear. "I mean, it's not like I came back with an agenda."

I nearly ran into Mrs. Spivak when, without warning, she halted and very slowly turned around to stare at me. I prayed she wouldn't remove those glasses of hers again. "Oh?" she asked. Only when she'd re-oriented herself in the direction of an outside door next to a sink old enough to have been Moses's baby bath did she speak again. "Yes, you did."

"No, I didn't." Though I still had on my coat, I recoiled when she flipped a switch and pulled open the door. The cold air outside made me shiver. "Honestly, I didn't. It was a complete accident. I was making myself dinner, you see, and I'm such a goof, I didn't read the instructions on the microwave dinner, and . . . oh, my."

We'd stepped out into a screened enclosure that obviously doubled as the Spivaks' storage shed, illuminated by a weak bulb hanging from the porch roof. And what a weird lot of stuff they had to store. In one corner was a battered and no doubt broken-down coin-operated fortune-telling machine, the likes of which I'd last seen in the movie *Big*. A stuffed monkey sat in a lawn chair, one of his glass eyes missing. A homemade Eye of Zohar banner hung from a nail near the ceiling. Old boxes, a rack of clothes, someone's fishing poles, and a croquet set added to the garage-sale-at-the-big-top feel. "No one travels without an itinerary," said Mrs. Spivak. "Not even on vacation. Hattie, come move this for me."

"Okay, Ma." A waffle still in her clutches, the younger Spivak detoured around us and, with a liberal peppering of *God-damns*, wheeled to the side what looked like a covered Victrola.

"But I don't have—" What unfinished business could I have? Was there anything I would gladly leave behind to get back home? I didn't understand.

Then I turned to the man behind me, and stopped. Did she mean Hank? Was he my unfinished business? The smile he gave me then made something in me snap. Unfinished? We'd hardly even started. I could leave the dresses and the shoes, the hairstyles. I could gladly abandon the hundreds upon hundreds of Tiny Minnies in my office. My new friends—well, they had been taking care of themselves for years before I arrived on the scene, and they could survive without me. My mink, I could do without. Hank, though? More than anything I wanted somehow to wrap him up and put him in my pocket, to keep him with me always. How was I supposed to finish any business between us?

My eyes must have been frantic. "Hey, hey," he said in a soft voice. He reached out and pulled me to him, so that our shadows cast by the porch light merged into one. "Everything will be all right. I wouldn't let anyone hurt you, would I?" I believed him, but I couldn't do anything more than shake my head. My throat had suddenly swelled, leaving me unable to talk. "And if it works, hey. That's good for you, right?"

"Approach," said the old lady from the porch's other end.

That made me find my voice. "Now?" I said, aware of how panicked I sounded. "But I haven't . . . we haven't . . ." I clung tightly to Hank. "I can't."

"Come on," he said, stumbling forward and forcing me with him. "It's for the best, right? Going back where you belong?"

"But how? What has she got, a time machine? This freak-show reject has a time machine that no one else in the entire world knows about? I know you like the comic books, but I can't believe you're buying into this, Hank." Anger felt good; it cauterized the gaping wounds I'd felt opening moments before. He only squeezed me tight again. I was aware that the two women were waiting at the far side of the porch, but I didn't care. "This is it, then? See ya, Cathy! Nice knowing ya!"

"Don't you want to go home? You said this was a screwed-up . . ."

"Yeah, it is," I snapped, cutting him off. I pulled away and stood on my own two feet. "It's a screwed-up place with screwed-up people, and yeah. Maybe you're right. Maybe it's time for me to hightail it out of here." When I wheeled around, I gasped. "Whoa."

Surrounded by so much clutter that it practically had to be excavated stood a wooden cupboard, six and a half feet high. It reminded me of a sarcophagus, for some reason—perhaps the general coffinlike shape and size. Then again, it might have been the intricate painting on the box that triggered the idea. Like some prop from a carnival sideshow, all of its sides had been painted in what once had been bright colors, starting with a green at the bottom that resembled a grassy field spiked with trees, and moving up to an intense blue to represent the sky, to a deep starry black around the top. Astrological characters, graceful and impassive, graced the box's uppermost reaches—the lion, the twins, the water bearer, the fish. Fifty or a hundred years ago, it would been a sight to see. In the darkness, with its patina of time, the box was a hulking menace. In the center of its door was what must have been the original Eye of Zohar, intricate and nimbly executed next to Hattie's crude attempts.

You don't expect to see a relic like that out with the baby carriages and old *Life* magazines. "Whoa," I repeated, impressed, but skeptical. I was supposed to get in that? It was a portal back to my decade? Unlikely. I might have swayed from earlier skepticism to superstition a moment ago, but I was back in the camp that this was all hooey. "Fine, then. Hook me up, bitches!" I told the pair. "Let's get this show on the road!"

Hank must have guessed how angry I was. He stepped forward, hurt. "Cathy . . ."

"Oh, no. I'm glad it's so easy for you to stuff me into a box and go on your merry way. That's what all you guys do here, isn't it? Put your pretty, pretty dolls away in pretty, pretty boxes and never let them see the light of day. I'm glad to know you're not any different." In my fury I barely noticed the old woman licking her thumb and then tracing a triangle on my forehead as she murmured words in a language I didn't understand. "In the end it'll make it easier not to miss you. Though I will. Just not as much. Especially now."

The women had been guiding me backwards to the

box, but right as I reached the open door, I stepped on something and nearly broke my neck. "God-*damn* it, Ma!" Hattie leaned down and picked up something metal that clunked in her hands. "Is *that* where my roller skates went?"

Hank didn't say anything. The bastard. Maybe he *was* enjoying this spectacle. Whatever. When I walked out of that box in a few minutes, after he'd gone drinking or whatever comic book illustrators did after they ditched their girls, he'd have a nasty surprise when he found I'd moved out of his granddaddy's building. Surely I could afford something on my own, away from him. I let the ladies cross my hands over my chest, mummy-style, and stared him down. "See ya," I said as my benediction. "Wouldn't wanna be ya."

Then he had to go and laugh at me. "You are perfectly adorable," he said, stepping forward.

Mrs. Spivak reached out and stopped him from coming too close. "Only the lost may enter," she warned him.

I was happy to see a flash of annoyance cross his face, at that. "If it works, promise you'll Giggle me when you get back, and if I'm still around, pay an old man a visit. Please," he finished quietly.

"Dream on." Mrs. Spivak was closing the coffin's lid now, her daughter reaching across to help. The last I was going to see of Hank, apparently, was him biting his lip. "And it's *Google*, you freak!"

The door thumped shut. Just beyond the thick pine I could hear Mrs. Spivak mumbling something in that strange foreign tongue again. There seemed to be some kind of inclined board at my back to lean against, so I figured I might as well get comfortable. At long last, after some inaudible conversation, I heard Hank's voice again. "No," he said. "I'd prefer to stay a while, if I could." More mumbling. "Please."

There was a long silence. For the first time, I noticed how much the box stunk. And I do mean stunk. It was a little like being shut in the armpit of one of the sweatiest bodybuilders at Crunch.

"God-damn it, Ma," I heard the priestess gripe. "You should have let the guy stay if he wanted. Why do you always have to be God-damn rude to people? It's driving my customers away. All you think about is your stupid television. . . ." Her voice had been fading as she and her mother retraced their path across the messy porch. The slamming of the back door was the last I heard of either of them.

So, how long should I stay in the box, I wondered? Now that I was getting used to the clammy odor, I figured I could endure at least for a little while. The last thing I wanted to do, mad as I was at Hank, was time things badly and run into him on my way home. Five minutes should do. Maybe seven. Ten, if I could take it. One Mississippi. Two Mississippi. Three Mississippi. . . .

Unfinished business! What bull. The only business that Hank and I'd apparently had was to see how quickly he could unload me, in the end. And bringing me here, of all places, to do it! What kind of guy went into voodoo shops to find a most exalted high priestess of Zohar? Who even knew there were voodoo shops in the city, anyway? Well, I supposed they'd always been there. Look at all the new age and occult shops that had sprouted all over Manhattan in my time, selling candles and herbs and aromatherapy oils and spell books. But what would you even say in those places? *Say, this girl I'm seeing needs to be sent back to the future. Any ideas?* Actually, picturing Hank asking such a stupid question with his serious face made me smile. He would have, too, just for the perversity of it.

The darkness hadn't seemed oppressive at first, but it lay so close and thick around me, it almost seemed to have actual weight. Where was I? Four Mississippi . . . shouldn't I be well above that by now? Oh, crap. I had to face up to facts. Even when I'd been throwing my tantrum, I knew why I'd done it. Parting from Hank was bad enough. Having actually to say goodbye would be worse. Wouldn't it be easier on us both, in the end, if I slipped away toward home when he wasn't around? No messy crying. No making him feel bad with promises I couldn't keep. And most important of all, I'd protect myself from the pain that was sure to follow—at least for a little while.

What was I supposed to do, if I ever did get back to my own time? Did he seriously expect me to find him wherever he was and—and what? Pick up where we left off? When was he born? 1930? In my time he'd be in his seventies by now, retired to Long Island or given up our winters to move to Florida. Married or widowed, with dozens of grandkids and great-grandchildren with dimples in their chins, glasses on their noses, and strong, masculine jaws. Which would be a shame for the girls, really. What would he say, even if he recognized me after all that time? Could I bring myself to kiss a geriatric? Would he see the pain in my eyes when I compared his elderly self to the young man I'd known? It was all too distressing to think about. I'd done the right thing, trying to make him mad at me during those last minutes. It would save us both a lot of hurt in the end.

How long had I been in the cabinet, anyway? I'd forgotten to count. I breathed deeply, noticing that the stink seemed to have gone away. In its place was a strange, purply smell—I couldn't describe it any better than that. It was the kind of scent you might imagine lingering in an old alchemist's laboratory, or that a black candle might give off in some kind of pagan rite. Even more oddly, I couldn't feel anything around me. I'd felt enclosed before. Now it felt as if I was floating in empty space. I couldn't even detect the surface on which I leaned.

Oh my God. I couldn't move. Something was happening. I felt a spinning sensation; my forehead burned where the old woman had traced her mark. No matter how big a fake the daughter might have been, the mother was in touch with some old Gypsy magic, surely—maybe this box had been the portal I'd sought since arriving. I was going home again. I might be there already.

And I'd never see Hank again. Not in his youth.

I opened my mouth to speak, but at first the words wouldn't come. I was in the power of a bigger planet's gravity, making dense the featherweight sound of his name. "*Hank*," I finally whispered. The word broke through the invisible shackles seeming to bind me. The next time I spoke, it was louder. "Hank?"

I couldn't leave. Not with business unfinished between us. I hadn't met his family. We hadn't spent Thanksgiving together. As Hattie might say, I hadn't cooked him that God-damned dinner. "Hank!" I yelled, from deep in the darkness. We hadn't done anything that we might have, and he was the one guy I'd known who was worth having—the one man I wanted to stand up and claim. As loudly as I could muster, I yelled, "*Hank!*"

"Ssssh. It's okay, sweetheart." The air around me was suddenly cold again and my nostrils twitched from a reek that had returned without warning, but he was there and that was all that mattered. Through the open door he pulled me out of the painted box, holding me tightly and caressing my hair. "I didn't go far."

"I did," I babbled. "I think I went somewhere. But I didn't want to go."

His voice was husky in my ear. "I didn't want you to go, either."

Opening my eyes was painful; it felt as if I'd slept longer than Rip Van Winkle in there. "You didn't?"

"God, no!" He looked down at me with an intensity I'd never seen before. "It was the hardest thing I've ever done. I didn't know it would be that hard." He pulled me close again, as if afraid of ever letting go again. "They wouldn't let me stay. I climbed back over the wall, in case . . . but I thought you wanted to go."

"I did. I do. But I can't go without . . ."

I trusted he understood where I was going with that sentence, because I couldn't speak anymore. I let out a shuddering sob against the wool of his coat. As I'd hoped, he held me until I felt stronger. "Cathy. You can always count on me."

"I only count on what I can hold in my own two arms," I replied automatically, then wondered where I'd heard it before. "I guess that means you." My laugh that followed was weak. I was embarrassed at the sheer amount of moisture dripping from my nose. "That was the longest five minutes of my life."

"You were in there for nearly an hour." When I looked at his face, I could tell he wasn't joking. "Honestly. I didn't know whether to leave, or try to follow, or . . ."

An hour? I thought of that strange smell, and the sensation of floating, and felt a chill spread from my neck to my limbs. "Get us out of here," I whispered, deathly frightened. "Take me home."

With his arm around my shoulders, he led me off the porch in the direction of a garden gate a dozen feet away. As we sped away, I knew I could never come back here again. I'd given up this opportunity, and there were no second chances here.

Before the gate locked shut behind us, I looked back at the little carriage house. In the kitchen window, I thought I could barely discern the silhouette of a human figure, aged and hunchbacked, watching our flight.

Chapter Fourteen

I wasn't really sure where they had obtained the bowl. I wasn't even aware we had room enough to store the thing. I had to admit, though, that it was the biggest single piece of crystal I'd ever seen in either of my lives—an extra-large punch bowl on the most spindly glass stand ever fashioned. Beneath the photographer's lights on high tripods, every facet of its carved face sparkled while J.P. and two of my assistants very carefully scooted across the linoleum to set it in its place of honor. Once safely on the decorated counter, one of them pulled out a chamois and began buffing away any fingerprints they may have left.

"Okay, ladies, let's work quickly," I called out, clapping my hands together. I'd been through enough of these shoots by now to know how they worked. "It's hot under those lights, and this trifle is a delicate thing. Right, Marie?" The curly-headed woman was practically beet-red with pride. She stood nearby, watching the shoot like a nervous stage mother.

"I'll work quickly, mama." I didn't actually have to

see J.P.'s face to know he was leering. Into my ear he added, "It'll be over so fast, you won't even know I was there."

"Yeah, that's pretty much how I imagined it would play," I snarled. "F.Y.I.? Not something I would brag about."

"Whaddaya mean?" he said, genuinely puzzled.

I didn't have the time. I swept by him on my way to the set. "How are we doing, Chester?" The photographer was too busy to answer, as he adjusted the aperture or the exposure of his shot, or whatever it is that photographers do other than actually push the buttons on their cameras. "Should I get some fans blowing to keep the trifle cool?"

He raised his head where he stood close beside me, then shook his head. "Condensation," was his brusque reply. "If you'll pardon me?" His mustache twitched like the whiskers of a cat none too pleased with the dinner in front of him.

"Oh! Of course." I shut my mouth and watched him fiddle with his camera some more.

After heaving one of the most dramatic and lengthy sighs I've heard outside of one of my teenaged slumber parties where the topic of discussion had been how horrible our mothers could be, the photographer flagged down Tilly, who happened to be fluttering by with a vase of daisies to offset the dessert. "Miss Sanguinetti," he said in his most formal, let's-pretend-we-don't-date-outside-the-workplace voice, "Would you be so kind as to clear the set so that I can shoot in peace?"

Neither Tilly nor I could mistake the pointed look Chester shot in my direction. Since I didn't want her to dither over whether to listen to her boyfriend or to respect her immediate supervisor, I backed off. "I should probably move, too," I said, hoping to smooth things over. Secretly, though, I was more than a little irritated. Never mind that until this week, I'd barely had the courage to venture out of my office unless it was absolutely necessary—I mean, groundhogs made more cold-weather appearances than I had. Now that I had more or less accepted the notion that I actually wanted to be here a while, I'd been throwing myself into my job with a little more vigor. And since Chester was technically supposed to be working for *me*, I could've done without the attitude.

Tilly scampered behind me as I backed off by a dozen paces. "Don't take it personally," she begged. "He's just mad at you."

"That's exactly the kind of thing I take personally," I told her, keeping my voice low. "Why's he mad?"

The chuckles with which she disguised her explanation were meant to soften it. "Oh, the silly. He doesn't understand why you and Hank didn't join us at the Blue Parrot after you said you would, the other night. He had his heart set on doing *My Fair Lady* again for you guys. I know," she added quickly, when I opened my mouth to explain. "You don't have to explain to me. Lovebirds need time alone, I told him." Even behind the chuckles, I could tell how trapped in the middle she felt. "Chester has this idea in his head, ridiculous, I know, that you . . . don't like him."

"Tilly . . ." Oh, crap. The words weren't coming fast enough. She stared at me as I struggled. I'd already tried to warn her once and she hadn't picked up on it. Either I had to spell it out for her, or let it go for good.

"You don't dislike him, do you?" she asked, now worried by my hesitation.

"No, that's not it at all, honey!" I reached out and grabbed her arm. "And I'm sorry about the other night. Hank and I were both whipped after going downtown. I like Chester fine. Really."

"Oh, good." Poor little thing. She straightened up as if I'd taken a terrible burden from her shoulders. "I think he was worried you didn't approve of—well, you know. The two of us."

She stuck a thumb in her mouth and flicked her teeth with the nail, staring at me. Wait a minute. I had a suspicion she wasn't talking about Chester any longer. Was she really asking for my approval? "Why in the world would you think that?" I asked, playing along. When she didn't answer, I said, "There's nothing bad, is there?"

"Well . . ." One of the girls walked by right then, bearing a squirt bottle of glycerin that we sometimes used to make certain foods appear shinier in their photos. Tilly waited until she had passed, and then looked around to make sure we were alone. "There is one thing."

"No, no, *no!*" I turned my head in time to catch the sight of a notebook fluttering through the air at high speed. It hit a refrigerator and fell to the floor. Chester yelled at the top of his voice, "The lights are *all wrong.* Quickly! Quickly!"

I wasn't going over there if he was in a mood for throwing things. "Is it his temper?" I asked, oozing sympathy.

"No. Oh, no! Though I think he might be a little mad at me as well. You see, Saturday night, when you and Hank didn't come, we stayed at the bar until one and then decided we might as well go back home. Only Miranda and Harold went to *his* home, if you know what I mean by that."

"Oh, I think I do." The little redheaded minx!

"So—I hope you don't mind—I asked Chester if he wanted to . . . well . . . I'd had two banana daiquiris and I was feeling a *wee* bit, you know. I didn't think you'd care too much if he came back to the apartment to talk for a little while."

"Oh, not at all," I said, trying not to laugh at how embarrassed she seemed.

Her pitch grew a little higher and her pace faster. "So when we got back home, we saw Hank's lights on and we were in the front hallway wondering whether we should knock at the door and ask where you'd been, when we heard . . . things."

I was stumped. "Things?" Tilly hugged her arms close to her chest, flushing. "Oh," I said, suddenly remembering exactly what Hank and I had done on his sofa once we'd gotten back to the warmth of his apartment. "*Things*," I said sagely.

Tilly was so grateful that she couldn't look at me. "Yes, things." She cleared her throat. "Well, Chester wanted to go home right then. I think he was embarrassed. But we went upstairs and were on the sofa and I . . ." She bit her lip and looked over in Chester's direction, where he was barking out orders to the girls. Cherry stood on a chair, oven mitts on her hands as she attempted to move a light to his liking. "I wanted to do things, too."

"Well, honey, that's understandable!" We were exactly where I hoped we'd go, right to the heart of the matter. "It's all right for a girl to want to do things."

"I know! And that's the problem! He was the one who didn't want to. Why, he gives me kisses goodnight, but when I suggested we try the French kiss, he had a fit." Mmm-hmmm. Not surprising at all. "And why, when I told him I was prepared to go as far as the oral-genital kiss of love, he practically . . ."

"*Whoa!*" I yipped. I would have jumped into the air from shock, but for my heels. "The what?"

"The oral-genital kiss of love. I read how in *Sex Practice in Marriage*. Don't you know what it is? It's when . . ."

"Whoa! Whoa there, Nelly!" I held out my hand. "I know what it is."

"Why, Cathy, don't be so old-fashioned. In *The Sexual Behavior of the Human Female*, Mr. Kinsey said that the oral-genital kiss of love is one of the most common premarital . . ."

"Can you not say that again?" I asked, covering my ears. "That phrase? I know what the oral . . . genital . . . I know what it is. I have nothing against it. I'm all for oral and genitals, separately and together. We've crossed the border into T.M.I., thank you very much." She waited for me to calm down. It was going to take a minute. "Okay," I said at last, trying to be frank without getting back into explicit. "So you were on the sofa and you wanted to do *things* that I'm perfectly okay not hearing the details of, and he said . . ."

In a gruff imitation of Chester's voice, Tilly said, "Dear heart, why don't we do the crossword instead?" I would have giggled if she hadn't seemed so disappointed, and if I hadn't sensed how serious she was. "He thinks I should save myself for marriage."

"Did he ask you to *marry* him?" My nails clawed into the soapstone counter.

"No." Though I'd managed to keep the hysteria from my voice, Tilly could barely keep the bitterness from hers. "He says I'm moving too fast."

"Oh, Tilly. Sweetie." My hands flew out to comfort her. Tilly might have picked up on a few techniques in her sex manual, but she really was a naive thing. "It's natural for two people, when they're attracted to each other and think they might be falling in love, to . . . do things. Even have sex before marriage, if they're both psychologically ready for it and are prepared for the consequences."

"I'm attracted to him," she said. I held my breath and silently hoped she'd come to the next logical conclusion. After a struggle, she admitted, "Maybe he's not right for me. Oh, I hate saying that. He's so handsome and masculine and artistic and does the funniest things that make me laugh!"

"You are an attractive—no, you're a beautiful woman," I said, squeezing her hand. "You are going to have so many men who are going to want to get to know you better. And one of them is going to see how very special you are and ask you to marry him, and you are going to do things that made the stuff Hank and I did in his apartment the other night look like Ed Sullivan's amateur night. Not that you'll be doing it on TV. Strike that. You're going to have one of the happiest lives around. Don't feel you have to settle."

"Okay," she said, obviously unused to so much praise at once.

"Have fun with Chester if you want. But keep your eye out for a handsome, masculine, artistic guy who's interested in all the other stuff you read about in the Kinsey report. Okay?" I smiled at her. "Oh, and don't keep your eye out for Mr. Right at the Blue Parrot, I'm thinking. Or any of the funny little bars down in the Village. Just to be safe."

After furrowing her brows, Tilly impulsively stood on tiptoe and gave me a quick hug. "Gee, Cath, you're really swell to listen to me go on and on. You know you can always do the same with me, right?"

My chin bobbed up and down on her shoulder as I nodded; I felt a little *verklempt*. She was going to be okay after all. "Make sure to tell Chester I don't hate him. And to get over himself."

"To do what?" she asked. Her eyes shifted sideways. "Richmond approaching."

"I'm not surprised. I turned in my ideas for the new books yesterday. He's probably here to . . . where is he?"

"Eleven o'clock. I mean, my eleven o'clock. Your five o'clock. I think."

Too late! "Ah, Cathy. Exactly the lady I wanted to see." Over the past couple of weeks my Richmond radar had been developing at a rapid pace; a set of questing fingers had barely come within a few millimeters of the small of my back when I instinctively arched away and turned around, hands covering my rear. "Something wrong, my dear? You're quite jumpy today."

"Excuse me," said Tilly, bobbing up and down, giving me a barely perceptible wink.

"Lovely girl. Yes, lovely." Mr. Richmond watched her go. "Cathy? Shall we? My office?" He beckoned with a pinky, turned, and led the way.

Well. Now I was getting somewhere. This was the first time I'd ever actually been invited to the old guy's office. I wasn't simply the little apron-wearing cook he visited in the test kitchens, but the trusted colleague, the go-to girl, the one with the eye for trends. I marched with my head high through the secretarial pool. Had Cathy started in this orderly grid of desks, hoping to move up in the world? Or had she simply jumped full-blown into her cookbook career? No clue. If she'd started typing off her manicured fingers, I felt sorry for her, because Mr. Richmond's office, which lay beyond the typing pool at the top of a very short flight of steps, had a panoramic view of the girls' backs. I could imagine him in there for hours at a time, peeping through the blinds and stroking his mustache with the back of his index finger as he appraised every girl's figure and posture. The big perv. Well, so long as he stayed on one side of the desk and I on the other, everything would be fine between us.

Once seated, I decided to take the initiative and show him what this particular Cathy was made of. "I expect you wanted to talk about the new directions I'm taking, sir."

"Ah, yes. Yes, exactly," he said, interlocking his digits and tapping the tips of his index fingers together. "New directions."

"Mr. Richmond, you're not a little man." Whoops. With his portly silhouette, Mr. Richmond was probably the wrong person to say that to. "You don't think little. You don't want to settle for people who are content with the way things are. You need strivers. Achievers. I'm focused on this company's future. A stronger Signature Line. A bigger, better Richmond Better Home Publications."

Tap-tap-tap. "Certainly, Cathy. But . . ."

"What I've done is re-envisioned the future of your kitchens publications. Starting from the bottom up.

The new structure I've given my department, encouraging my kitchen assistants to contribute recipes? It's going to up the quality of your cookbooks considerably. And you know why? Diversity. A dozen creative minds, all focused on the project at hand. Trust me, Mr. Richmond. Diversity's the key."

"Diversity?" he repeated.

"The types of consumables we're advocating now? All the casseroles and church basement one-dish meals? It's on the way out. The future of food is in fresh. The future of food is in ethnic, in diversity. The future is in high-quality, nutritious, healthy portions. I see you've looked over the portfolio I've built for you?"

I nodded at the illustration boards lying on his desk, and took the liberty of spreading them out. Hank had given up his Sunday to help me design them—it had been an all-day job that would have taken only a couple of hours at most if we'd had my trusty computer and layout programs. "You'll see here the direction I'd like to go. A publication devoted entirely to baking." Hank had whipped up some tasty line illustrations of crusty loaves, an assortment of rolls, and muffins that looked fresh-plucked from their pan. "No tasteless instant mixes. No shortcuts. No *faux* gourmet cooking from cans. Just aromatic goodness, hot out of the oven. Sweet breads for breakfasts, sandwich bread for nutritious lunches, and delicious rolls for dinner." I flipped to the next one. "And that's just the first building block in an entire series of similar publications, Mr. Richmond. After breads, we have salads—they're going to be *huge* in the future. Not these Jell-O monstrosities. Chicken Caesar salad. You have *no* idea how popular that's going to be. A craze, practically. Different types of lettuce that aren't iceberg. Romaine.

Boston Bibb. There's another brick in the wall for you. And even more. A book on soups. Another on barbecue. Meats. Chicken. Fish. And then the ethnic foods. Mexican's always popular. Thai. Thai food's going to explode. And sushi. You might not have heard of sushi, but . . ."

I was brandishing the sheet on which Hank had done his best to illustrate tekka rolls and someone rolling up sticky rice in nori wrappers when Mr. Richmond said in a plaintive voice, "But Cathy. I don't understand." By now he had his palms together and tapped all his fingers together. "Why would women want to do any of this?"

"Any of what?" I asked. This wasn't good at all.

"Any of this." He picked up the sushi illustrations and tossed them gently in my direction. "I've never heard of it. And this," he said, flipping the four-panel bread board at me. "And this. All of it." He resumed his finger-tapping, that pencil-thin mustache of his twitching as if he were about to sneeze. "I sat here this morning staring at these and at your proposal, and frankly, Cathy, I'm baffled."

I'd been in this position not so long ago. While I thought, I stared at his hands. *This is the church. These are the people. Open the doors and fire all the people.* "I'm looking to the future, sir."

"Where you're looking, Cathy, most frankly, is the past." There was a wheedling note to Richmond's complaint that I'd never heard before. "That's what I find most worrying. We live in an age—a wonderful age, I thought you agreed—of modern conveniences. Kitchen science is reaching new heights with every passing day, presenting the modern wife and mother with amenities beyond her imagining fifty, forty, or even ten years ago."

I couldn't let myself be bulldozed again. Not in this century. I sat up straight in my chair. "See, Mr. Richmond, this is where I disagree. What the modern woman—the modern *cook*—wants is not a box of Hamburger Helper. What she wants . . ."

"Is convenience, pure and simple. Those tasteless mixes and those gelatin desserts and the cans are the key that have given the modern woman her freedom. They allow her to provide her husband and family with delicious meals that can be prepared without all the labor of days past. They are precisely what have allowed her to leave the kitchen for more congenial climes. The bridge club. The PTA. Golfing. Even the workplace. Now, what is this Hamburger Helper idea of yours?"

"It's not my . . . Hamburger Helper?" Didn't they have that here? "It's a box filled with dried noodles and packaged flavor that you mix with hot water and simmer in a saucepan, with ground beef. And it tastes like . . ."

"Now, *that* is the kind of forward thinking I'd like to see more of! That is why I hired you! Cathy, no woman in her right mind is going to want to spend hours preparing bread like her grandmother, or spend hours making a meal from scratch when she can have a product like this . . . Hamburger Helper, you say?" I tried to formulate a verbal parry, but then he struck the final blow. "Frankly, I find your other ideas reactionary, backward-looking, and old-fashioned."

If I'd been standing, I would have reeled. "Old-fashioned! *Me?*"

"Truthfully, Cathy, lately I've been concerned about you." This couldn't be happening. Not again! "I've noticed in the past several weeks a certain . . . unreceptiveness, as it were. We like team players here at Richmond Better Home Publications, Cathy. People who understand our goals and are sympathetic to the plight of our customers. Not only that, our clients, Cathy. We have manufacturers paying us to produce those cookbooks that the public adores. Where would we be financially if we abandoned them for this . . . fresh food idea? It's ideas like your meal-in-a-box that are pure gold. We could sell that to one of our corporate partners and do away with the drudgery of cooking forever!" He spoke as if homemade meals were an abomination unto the Lord. "These other matters—personnel issues, solicitation of recipes, hiring and dismissals, anything having to do with the girls or the interns or your clerical staff—that's all under your control. But to strike out at the very basis on which the Signature Line is founded? I'm disappointed, my dear. Severely disappointed."

I can't really say that being on the raw end of a boss's tongue-lashing was any easier the second time around. It hurt. If anything, this rejection hurt more than the one I'd gotten from Turnbull, because I knew how right I was. Everything I'd showed him was the future of the food industry, and he was throwing away the opportunity of a lifetime to stick to the old standbys of chocolate pudding mix and canned mushroom soup. And then, insult on insult, to call me old-fashioned! It made me tremble. "You've only had these mock-ups for a day, sir," I said, hearing the strain in my voice. "That's scarcely a basis for weeks-long disappointment."

His face twitched briefly, as if an invisible insect had buzzed close. I didn't care about his irritation. I'd let Turnbull run all over me back in my own time, and that had been a mistake. "It's been confusing, my dear, with this whole odd business with Merv Powers, to whom you seem to have made promises that you couldn't or wouldn't keep. And my nephew tells me that you've been difficult to work with."

"Oh!" I said. "Oh-ho-ho! That's rich! J.P. tells you I'm difficult to work with and suddenly I'm a problem. Listen, Mr. Richmond. With all due respect, your nephew . . ."

"Miss Voight." The old man looked tired, but his words were curt. "Remember your place. As I told you earlier, as an intern, my nephew is yours to deal with. I suggest, if you wish to keep your position, that you find a way." That was it, the blunt dismissal. I wasn't done, but he apparently was. "Now, good day." I was truly cursed. In the twenty-first century I maybe hadn't been aggressive enough. Here, I was more uppity than the rabbit collar of Miranda's coat. I grabbed my illustration boards and stalked out of the room, head held high. Nobody was going to make me slink away this time. Before the door closed, I heard him call out, "Hamburger Helper. No, Cathy, the name's all wrong. Ground Burger Helpmeet! Now *that's* a name. And a pun as well. Help*meet*. Yes, yes . . ."

Both Cherry and Tilly raised their eyebrows when they saw me reenter the test kitchens. Determined as I was to maintain a cool, professional air, all I really wanted to do was—oh, I didn't know. Hit the gym for the first time in years so I could kickbox a punching bag. Or lie on the floor and pummel my feet against the wall to get out some of the anger and replace it with pain. All those movies I'd ever seen in which a furious hero punched a wall or glass window, getting a reaction of *Don't be so stupid!* from me? Now I had a sudden sympathy for the guy. Tilly trotted over, all sympathy and nervous fingers. "Are you okay?"

"I'm fine," I lied through my teeth.

"You don't look so fine," was Cherry's observation.

"I'm fine." I couldn't deal with sympathy now. It would only make me more emotional than I already felt. "Why is Chester still . . . Chester?" I called out, marching over to where he was still making minute adjustments to the Tiny Minnies trifle. "You've been at this for over an hour. Take the damned photo already."

If he had been hostile to me before, my ultimatum didn't endear me any further. "If this is going on the cover of your Tiny Minnie cookbook," he intoned so frostily that his immediate vicinity could have kept dry ice intact for weeks, "I should think that you'd *want* this photograph to be perfect."

"We're talking about a bowl full of tapioca and whipped cream from a can mixed with snack cakes that sit next to beef jerky in gas stations. Not something from the Cordon Bleu." I snapped my fingers. "Push the button and get it over with."

"You heard the lady." J.P. had materialized by my side, trying to appear natty and authoritative as he adjusted his thin tie. "Take the photo."

"Shut up, J.P."

Chester glared at me. "Some minor adjustments with the *garni* are all I require."

"*Garni*, my ass." Aware that everyone in the room was staring at me in my tantrum, I stomped over and grabbed a little glass bowl of mint leaves from the girl who was distributing them at his command. "Look. Even a monkey can do it." I stabbed a few sprigs into the clammy mixture. "Now shoot the thing before it's a puddle of goo."

"Yeah," J.P. echoed. "You heard the lady, Nancy-boy."

I whirled on the kid, incensed. Chester might be acting like a prick, but he didn't deserve that kind of name-calling. "Uncalled-for. Unprofessional. And if I ever hear you say anything like that again . . ."

"Oh, come on, doll." J.P.'s head lolled. God, I hated his cockiness. "Don't tell me you'd pick a limp rag like that over a real man like me."

That was it. With a quickness that amazed me—I felt like the special effects in a Wachowski brothers movie—I reached out and grabbed the little bastard's collar. "Apologize," I said, dangling him in Chester's direction. The photographer had been quaking with unspoken emotion during the last dozen seconds, poor guy. He was probably too terrified to stand up for himself. Fine. Even though I'd chewed him out moments before, I'd stand up for him. "I *said*, apologize."

Spit bubbled on his lips. "You can't make me—!"

"You can't pick and choose what types of people deserve respect, you little moron." Considering how tall he was, the kid weighed surprisingly little, thanks to his sticklike frame. My adrenaline-fueled strength helped me keep him choking. "None of this name-calling. Not to anybody. Not on my watch. *Say you're sorry.*"

"I'm not—!" I shook him again. One of his shirt buttons came unfastened. "Okay, okay! I'm sorry! I'm sorry!"

Chester had at least recalled enough of his innate dignity that he was able to reply, trembling. "Ugliness of all kinds is always inappropriate. Especially in an artistic environment. You should know that, young man." Then, more quietly to me, he added, "Thank you."

When I let the kid back down to the soles of his feet, his face screwed up into an ugly moue. "You can't treat me like that. My uncle . . ."

"Who hired you, J.P.?" I asked, suddenly interested. "Who actually signed the paper that made you an intern? Was it me?"

"Yeah." He attempted to straighten out the clothing I'd rumpled. "Because you *had* to."

I couldn't mistake the smug satisfaction behind those words. "Biggest mistake of my life. In fact, time I undo it. J.P.? Consider yourself fired."

I'd forgotten I had an audience of twenty watching our little performance until they all let out shocked gasps. If I wasn't mistaken, there were a few murmurs of satisfaction as well. "You can't do that!"

"Why, I do believe I can. In fact, your uncle reminded me a few moments ago that personnel decisions in this area were all under my purview. So . . . so long!" He cocked his head, ready to say something else smart. "Farewell!"

"You—"

"*Auf wiedersehen!* Buh-bye!" He couldn't stare me down. There was no way he'd win. Finally, at long last, he started to slouch out in the direction of his uncle's office. I didn't care in the least. There'd been an immense satisfaction at finally being on the firing end of things. "Tilly?" I asked, making sure it was loud enough for him to hear. "Why don't you go in my office and find J.P. Richmond's file so I can tear it into shreds?"

Tilly didn't need me to repeat the orders. She skittered toward my door. "Turnbull?"

I didn't quite understand. The word was familiar, but why had she said it? "What?"

"J.P. Turnbull," she said. "Filed under his last name, right?"

I couldn't breathe. Worse than that. It felt as if I'd been thrust into a vacuum and was being sucked inside-out. "J.P. . . . John . . . Peter . . . Turnbull?" I managed to gasp out.

"Well, sure." Tilly noticed my stupefaction and hesitated. "Do you still want me to get the file?"

I raised a hand, arresting her. The old lady had talked about unfinished business. The position where I was right now couldn't be coincidence. There had to be something to it. This was important, somehow. "J.P.," I called out. "J.P.!"

"What now?" Though his face was sullen, I could now see the resemblance. The snorkeler. The sailor. The gaunt, bald head that fifty years from now would grace the preface to the company's annual report now pouted at me in the flush of adolescence. I'd just fired my boss.

There was some kind of perfect synchronicity to that.

I sounded slightly hysterical as I called out, in a higher pitch than normal, "Know what? Consider yourself hired again." He looked both stunned and suspicious at my announcement. "On *probation*. No more groping, no more *dolls*, no more name-calling. You want to know why?"

"Why?" His jaw jutted out.

"Because decades from now I want you to remember this day. Some day you're going to pick on someone. Maybe she'll deserve it, maybe she won't. Maybe you'll fire her yourself and think you've done the right thing. But that someone's going to deserve a second chance, and you're going to give it to her!"

"Yeah, right." He turned and started to stomp away.

"You damn well *will!*" I yelled. Wasn't this supposed to be a sitcom moment, when everything wrapped up neatly and nicely and the episode came to an end? The little shit was ruining it for me. "You're going to call her up the next morning and tell her she's got her job back! And a raise! And an office in the executive—*arrgh!*" The kid was out of earshot now. I held up my arms and gazed at the plaster ceiling, in the general direction of heaven. "Wasn't that what I was supposed to do?" I wanted to know. "Isn't that what I was sent here for?"

"Should I get the file?" Tilly asked, uncertain what I was going on about.

"Forget it," I growled. "Just . . . do your jobs," I told everyone, trying to get out of the way so I could go back to my office and fume. In my abruptness, my skirt caught on something as I swept by. I gave it a tug, only hearing Chester's cry of alarm at the last moment. "What?" I'd managed to unbalance one of the tall lights on its rickety metal stand. It toppled in Chester's direction while my hands flailed helplessly. All I could envision, in those split seconds, was exploding glass and third-degree burns and concussions. At the last moment, I managed to grab its pole before it had dipped much below a forty-five degree angle. "Got it!"

What I hadn't counted on was the light colliding with another one nearby, and sending it toppling toward the trifle bowl. There wasn't a person in the kitchens who didn't hold his or her breath as the silver metal arced brightly in its descent, all of us certain that within seconds there would be an explosion of fine crystal and Tiny Minnies, and all of us equally unable to do anything about it from where we stood.

Then, *plink!* The tripod on which the light towered hit the edge of the soapstone counter, bounced twice, and then simply lay there. The crystal bowl didn't even tremble. Not a single mint sprig moved from place. Disaster had been averted.

I let out a deep sigh. Chester, too, looked relieved. "Oh my goodness!" one of the girls said, then started to giggle.

Laughter was what we all needed. In fact, our laughter was so loud that none of us heard the joint that held the hot light fixture to the tripod snap—though we did all see the extension cord acting as a pulley to aid the shuttered bulb's dramatic plummet into the depths of the trifle, followed by the volcanic eruption of steam and pudding and Tiny Minnies over the bowl's side.

I glared at the ceiling. Had that been a sign from heaven? Because in the advertising world, we would say the execution had been good, but the overall concept lacked a little in the subtlety department.

Chapter Fifteen

What a difference fifty years makes! In my time, as one of those women genetically doomed to carry a few extra pounds here and there, I found myself practically invisible. Eyes glided past me, landing only on those girls whose general outlines resembled carrot sticks, to whom at home I'd always been tempted to shout, "*Eat a cookie already!*" In 1959, though ... I'll say it again ... I was ripe. I was luscious. I had that thing they call va-va-va-voom. Especially in my Dimanche Soeurs formal black dress with the brocade and the net and everything that made me feel all curves and sex appeal. My hair, like my breasts, was bouncing and behaving. My figure looked fantastic. And despite all the bad things I'd said about Cathy Voight, girlfriend had a massive shoe collection. Whether people were actually looking at me, or the mere fact I stood next to Hank, didn't matter. I was being noticed, and that was enough to give me a glamorous aura I'd never before felt.

Maybe it was the fur. For the first time ever, I'd

worn the mink out in public. I felt dirty with it around my shoulders; a lifetime of anti-fur political correctness had left me about as likely to sling a woven chain of fresh pig fetuses around my neck and swank about town. On the other hand, when you're forbidden something too strongly, it's difficult to resist the taboo allure. Especially when it was soft and sumptuous and made me look like a freakin' movie star. And those little minks had died for someone's fashion sins half a century before, so what could I do about it, right? I'd sworn to myself a hundred times that this would be the only occasion ever, ever, *ever* that I'd actually haul out the darned thing. Except maybe New Year's Eve. So I shifted it around my shoulders so I could feel it sliding against my neck. "Do you want to check that?" Hank wanted to know.

"No!" Couldn't he see I was working it? Actually, I didn't really know what "working it" entailed, but despite the enormous fire crackling in a chimney at one end of the parlor and quite a lot of heat issuing from the creaky pipes near the windows, none of the other women in the Old Ivy had yet removed either their furs or gloves, and I wasn't about to be the first. They made me feel, maybe for the first time in my life, terribly, terribly sophisticated. "Your tie is crooked again," I told him, suppressing an impulse to fix it myself.

He looked down at his bow tie and shrugged. "If I re-tie it, you know it won't stay."

Hank was right, I knew. No matter how dashing and James Bond-y and long and lean he looked in the tuxedo he'd produced from nowhere, Hank simply wasn't a formal kind of guy. His ties would always spring loose of their own accord. Buttonholes would work their way off the cufflinks that fastened them. I half worried his clothes would suddenly shoot off, spring-loaded, and that he'd then spontaneously combust. "Where are Miranda and Harold?" I wondered, looking around the room. A whole mahogany forest had been cut down to appoint that parlor. The stuff was everywhere—paneling, ceilings, furniture, even the enormous teeth of the woman who, like so many others in the brief time we'd been there, seized Hank's hand and pumped it vigorously.

"Henry, my dear!" she said, every vowel resonating deep in her nasal cavities. "Katherine said you'd be here. Don't you look so very much like your grandfather in his younger days! Is this your lady friend? Charming, really. Did you see Frances? Oh, you did? Lovely. Perry!" she squealed at top volume, moving on to her next victim.

"Relative?" I murmured.

"Friend of the family," he said. "I think. She might be a distant cousin. It's sometimes difficult to tell."

I might have run with the big boys back at home, having my share of good lunches and dinners at a few top spots around town, but that didn't make me one of Manhattan's moneyed. "Inbreeding, huh?"

Hank laughed abruptly, looking distinctly uncomfortable as he clutched his whiskey. "If your income is above a certain level, you're permitted to call it *good* breeding."

"Henry Pew Cabot!" said an old man in the requisite tuxedo, who carried a cane. Since I'd watched him stride at a quick pace across the plush Persian carpet unassisted, I wondered if the carved wood was purely ornamental. "Aren't you looking fit. Didn't you get married this year? No? That was your brother? Pity I couldn't come. You don't happen to have any change, do you? Had nothing smaller than a ten and you can't tip the bartender with . . . yes, well. Annabelle Cameron Hughes!" he called to the next person within eyeshot. "Aren't you looking fit!"

"Cousin?"

Hank shook his head. "Friend of the family."

"You know," I said, watching the old man book around two leather sofas, a telephone table, and a chaise lounge before reaching his next mark, "you wealthy folk don't so much hold conversations as send each other messages in Morse code when you sail past."

Hank took a healthy slug of his whiskey. "In my bank account I have exactly seventy-four dollars and thirty-odd cents," he murmured in my ear. "And five of that is going to buy the three of you a new bathroom faucet this week. That is how wealthy I am."

"Oooh," I purred, playful. "Big spender. It makes a girl want to do things."

"Oh?" he said, curling an eyebrow. "Naughty things?"

"Henry." While we'd been preoccupied, a regal-looking woman had navigated through the crowds of New York's best to reach us. She clutched a glass of something dark and alcoholic in her elegant hands; an enormous diamond sparkled on her ring finger as she shook the ice in her drink. Her right hand stretched out to meet Hank's in a formal shake. "You look well. How is the—what is it you're doing?"

Hank's smile was polite, but not especially friendly. "I'm trying to break into comic book illustration."

A couple of passing gray-haired septuagenarians waved at the woman, prompting her to waggle her fingers at them. She really was quite handsome for her years; more than anyone who'd stopped to greet us so far, she seemed to have that rigid, brittle posture I associated with having to shoulder the family burden of enormous sacks of moolah. "Oh yes. How could I forget? You know, my grandson reads Huey, Dewey, and Louie on a regular basis. I don't suppose you draw them, do you? No? Excuse me a moment." With a most gracious bow of her head at the both of us, the woman took a few steps away to speak to the elderly couple.

Hank shook his head. "Annoying."

I took a surreptitious opportunity to enjoy the sensation of fur against my neck again. Cro-Magnon women had it pretty darned good, you know. "I'd be annoyed, too, if anyone suggested I had *anything* to do with Scrooge McDuck's impish identical nephews. They're hellions, all three of them."

Hank took the opportunity to slug back the rest of his whiskey. "It amazes me," he said, chewing on a piece of ice, "that you manage to get through life accumulating that kind of trivia without any effort whatsoever, yet you can't remember the name of the man who landed on the moon."

"Listen," I said in my defense, "I don't know about you, but I grew up expecting history to stay in the past. If I needed to look up the Armstrong guy who went to the moon, I could do it in a hot second back in my time, thus allowing my precious few brain cells to retain things like the complete lyrics of every song by They Might Be Giants and the phone numbers to every noodle shop in a ten-block vicinity, thank you."

"Those who cannot learn from history are doomed to repeat it, you know."

I had a flashback to the Motive conference room. "I know the quotation well. It's probably why I'm here in the first place, thank you," I said, as if he'd only made my point. "And let me guess. Friend of the family?"

"That woman?" he asked, nodding at the *grande dame*'s back. "Nah. My mother."

Blinking rapidly with shock, I could only reply with the immortal words of one of the mighty heroes of my youth, the titular protagonist of that majestic masterpiece of the cinema, *Wayne's World.* "Exsqueeze me?"

"Goodness, Cathy!" Tilly had borrowed a long Estévez black dancing dress for the occasion. Bits of jet cellophane had been sewn into its skirt, so that as she wended her way through the parlor furniture in our direction, it sparkled and glowed. She looked wonderful. "It's *enormous* in here! We walked all over the ground floor and even got to go back into the kitchens when I told them what I did for a living. Have you been yet? The library is *amazing.* And they have a *swell,* real, honest-to-God Tiffany window at the top of the grand staircase!"

Chester seemed subdued and a little out of his element in a rented tux. He'd even trimmed down his mustache from its usual push-broom proportions to something neat and tidy. The only recognizable feature about him, in fact, was his poof of curly hair. "Now, now, Tillykins," he said, his eyes darting around as he indulged in nervous laughter. "I'm sure Hank knows exactly what's in his club. Hah-hah! What, old chap?" We seemed to be friends again after the incident in the office earlier that week.

At that moment I couldn't really focus, either on Tilly's delight at the Old Ivy's architecture, or on the fact that Chester seemed to have developed a sudden mild case of British Accentitis and that I fully expected him to pull a cricket bat from his back pocket at any moment. "Your *mother?*" I whispered to Hank. "That woman with whom you exchanged a handshake is the mother you haven't seen since last *Thanksgiving?*"

"Where?" Tilly wanted to know immediately. She stood on tiptoe and craned her neck to see.

"That's a bit of an exaggeration." Hank laughed. "I saw her at my brother's wedding." I raised my eyebrows to signal I wanted more details. "In March."

"Who?"

"Tillykins," chuckled Chester. "Let's not cause a scene."

Tillykins shot her escort a look of thin tolerance. "Don't call me that."

"Mother?" Hank spoke in a low and civilized tone to the woman we'd spoken to only a few moments before. She turned and, as if spotting an old friend for whom she didn't particular care but to whom she was determined to be civil, she made her way back to us. "I'd like to present my friend Cathy Vo . . . Voight," he said, stumbling over my surname. In the meantime, the woman reached out and squeezed my hand. "And our friends Tilly Sanguinetti and Chester Hamilton." Tilly smiled and tried not to look overawed, while Chester bowed low and murmured over Mrs. Cabot's hand for so long that he gave the impression that he might be trying to appraise the diamond on her ring finger.

"Charming, Henry. So like you, to bring so many people to your father's club. By which I mean, of course, how generous," she said, smiling around at all of us without any real warmth. Noticing how closely her son and I stood together, she reserved the last, lingering look for me. "You never told me you had someone . . . special . . . in your life, my dear. Voight, did you say? Of the Philadelphia Voights?"

"Um." I had no clue. "Probably not. Sorry." Immediately I felt annoyed. Why in the world was I apologizing for who I was? That wasn't right.

"Mother." Hank's voice was as protective as the arm he'd laid around my shoulder. "Let's have a nice holiday."

Mrs. Cabot's immaculately groomed eyebrows shot up in twin arches of mock bewilderment. "I am having a nice holiday, darling. And what is it you do, Miss Voight? Surely a capable young lady such as yourself must have a career."

She sounded perfectly pleasant, but the way she said the word *career* carried about the same sort of sting as if she'd said *extensive history of syphilis*. "I work—that is, Tilly and Chester and I all work for Richmond Better Homes Publications. We produce cookbooks."

"For the modern cook!" Tilly enthused.

Mrs. Cabot looked at both of us with pursed lips. I suspected that at some point later in the evening, after she and her husband had been well-pickled in alcohol, we were going to be the subject of a droll anecdote. "How exciting for you."

"We live in the same townhouse as Hank . . . Henry, I mean," Tilly continued, unaware of the woman's chilliness. "That is, Cathy and Miranda and I do. Chester is a photographer. He lives somewhere else. Oh dear," she said, fanning her hand before her face. "I think I've had a bittle lit too much crème de menthe." She clapped her hand over her mouth.

Chester roared as if the gaffe had been intentional

and Tilly was the next Lucille Ball; after a moment Tilly joined in, surprised at herself. Even Hank grinned and looked at the bottom of his glass, though he obviously wished there were still whiskey inside. Only Mrs. Cabot and I seemed unamused. "Miranda?" she asked, looking around.

"Miranda Rosenberg," Tilly said. "The three of us live together. Oh, I said that already, didn't I? Maybe you'd better take this!" She handed Chester her glass and giggled. "I don't want to make a scene."

"This is your first, and you haven't even had half of it!" he protested, sniffing at the green liquid.

"How many people did you invite, Henry dear?"

"Five. How many did you invite, Mother?"

I could pretty much see why Henry—I mean, Hank—avoided his family like the plague, if his mom was at all representative of the clan. Though their conversation was mannerly enough, the words flying back and forth between them seemed written in an emotional shorthand decipherable only by studying years and years of mutual disappointments on either side. It was distinctly uncomfortable. "Why, I didn't count," she said, smiling dangerously. "And Miss Rosenberg? Does she write cookbooks, too?"

"She's an actress," said Tilly.

"And singer," I supplied loyally.

"Her boyfriend will be coming as well." Hank said, raising his chin in some sort of defiance I didn't understand or recognize. "A Mr. Harold Silverstein."

"How delightful." Mrs. Cabot looked around the room as if hoping someone else might be demanding her attention. "Does Miss Rosenberg sing anywhere your father and I might know?"

"She was in the chorus of *Say Darling* last year."

Tilly said. "I don't know if you saw it. With Vivian Blaine. She had several lines."

"We didn't see it."

Anyone who has the chutzpah to put herself out there and try to make a go of it on Broadway has my support, and I didn't like the way that Mrs. Cabot seemed to dismiss Miranda's accomplishments without even seeing her. "She was booked for an entire month at Grossinger's," I said, rising to Miranda's defense. "In the Catskills."

"The Catskills? My. Isn't that . . . lovely." Mrs. Cabot graced me with another of those genteel expressions that made me suspect Medusa would be a winsome kewpie doll in comparison. "If you'll excuse me."

We all watched her go, her imposing figure making its way out of the room with an innate grace that I knew I could never reproduce, not even in my best Dimanche Soeurs. After that encounter, even my mink felt a little shabby, like squirrel fur scraps I'd duct-taped together. Hank only looked at me. "I warned you."

"I'm sorry." I felt for the poor guy. What must it have been like to grow up in that household? And how had Hank managed to survive without needing five-days-a-week therapy? Chalk it up to the mysteries of the ages, I supposed. "Maybe we should go."

"Hell, no!" He hugged me close to his side. "You wanted the full Cabot experience? You're getting it."

"I hope I didn't say anything too awful." Tilly looked regretfully at the tiny glass Chester held for her. "I've never had crème de menthe before. I only ordered it because I thought the green would look good with my hair, actually. Oh!" She put her fingers over her mouth. "It's still making me say the silliest things!"

I detached myself from Hank and put my arm around her shoulder, so that we looked like conjoined twins in black evening dresses. "Come on, you big silly," I said affectionately. "Show me that Tiffany window."

The amount of money that had gone into the construction of the Old Ivy really was a little frightening. Though it hadn't been built to look ostentatious, the whole thing was an obvious temple to Mammon. We peeped briefly into a smoking room in which some of the oldest club members seemed to be taking refuge from the wives and daughters who for the only time this year were allowed within the august chambers. With Chester and Hank bringing up the rear, we took a good look at the dining room, in which dozens of tables had been made up with gleaming silver and crisp linen, their centerpieces made from real fruit overflowing from cornucopias. Waiters in high livery bustled about, setting place cards and tiny individual menus on every gold-rimmed plate. In the big room's center, an elaborate brass chandelier splayed out in all directions like a giant squid having a good stretch; a number of servants busily entwined the last of a colorful garland of leaves and gourds around its arms. From the kitchens we could smell turkeys roasting. It all bore about as much resemblance to the original Thanksgiving as Trump Tower did to a Mississippi mud hut.

I realized with a pang of guilt that the money spent on the centerpieces alone, fruit that would probably go untouched during the meal and find its way into the garbage pails by the end of the evening, could probably have fed hearty meals to any number of the homeless and poor. But like my mink, there was a certain irresistible appeal to it all. I was in a gentlemen's private club. In another—what? Decade or two?—the Ivy Club and others like it would have vanished, and along with it all the Old Manhattan Money, replaced by real estate moguls and Internet brokers and software developers. What other chance was I going to get to sit down among the Cabots and Pews and Chews and Cadwalladers and the finest of New York Society? I couldn't wait.

"I want to meet these brothers of yours," I murmured to Hank when we'd refreshed our drinks in the crowded bar and wandered back into the parlor. Chester lounged against the fireplace in a jaunty way intended to imply he'd done it many a time, but that really came off more as a Sears catalog menswear model audition. "Stop tugging at your collar. Are they like your mom? Tell me that they'll all be wearing their Ivy League college ties and will talk about nothing else but how hard it is to get good help these days."

"It's their wives who talk about finding help, and very likely Charles is not only wearing his Philips Exeter tie, he's found junior versions for his three sons as well."

He looked so distinctly uncomfortable in his surroundings that I felt sorry for taking so much glee in seeing him in what I'd thought was his natural habitat. "You really hate all this, don't you?" I said, waving my hands around.

"I'd give it all up in a flat sec—"

We were interrupted by the arrival of the Old Ivy doorman—or doorboy, if we had to be honest about it. The kid scarcely looked old enough to be out of high school, and his formal uniform was so big for him that his hands barely protruded past the cuffs when he reached up to tip his hat at us. "Begging your pardon, Mr. Cabot," he said, keeping his voice low. "Could I have a moment? Outside?" he added, after a hasty look around the room.

Hank's lips compressed. He nodded, gave me a quick nod, and followed the kid out into the hallway. I set down my drink and followed. Chester and I might have made amends, but I wasn't so fond of his lord-of-the-manor act that I wanted to stick around for it on my own. More and more people had arrived, now that the dinner hour was approaching; they wandered from the bar across the hall to the parlor, greeting each other and chattering so loudly that I couldn't hear any of the words passing between Hank as he leaned over to hear what the doorman said to him. What I could tell, however, was that he wasn't happy. He spat out an expletive, slugged back the rest of his second whiskey, gave the bewildered doorman the glass, and strode off in the direction of the front doorway at the building's center.

Darned heels! I tried to keep up with him, but nothing about my outfit was designed for speed. Only when I called out his name did he stop in his trajectory to let me catch up. "What's wrong?"

He made a gurgling sound. "My mother," he finally spat.

Twin coats of arms with a dark patina of age greeted us in the front lobby. His leather heels pattered down the wooden stairs. "What about her?" I said, following carefully.

"Once again she's only proven why I'm better off without the Cabot name." I was grateful he wasn't mad at me. I'd never seen his bark before, and the savage way he bit off his words made me hope I wouldn't see it again. More to himself, he added, "God forbid I should ever, *ever* really need them for something."

"But what—?"

Hank's voice was more pleasant when he reached the older doorman inside the entrance. "Phil, what's going on?" he asked. "Tommy said . . ."

I reached the bottom of the broad staircase as the more mature and experienced doorman spoke. "They asked to speak to you," he said in discreet, cultured tones. This was how a doorman was supposed to behave, I noted. Kurt from my building could take a few lessons in posture, decorum, and the advanced art of fastening jacket buttons from this guy. "They wouldn't go away without seeing you, Mr. Cabot, sir."

Simultaneously, Hank and I looked through the open doorway out onto Fifth Avenue. In the afternoon's weakening sunlight stood Miranda and Harold, looking as if they'd been standing in the cold for some time. Immediately I clattered out the door. "Where have you been?" I cried. "We've been wondering! Come in out of the chill already!"

They looked distinctly uncomfortable. Miranda looked sideways at Harold, who refused to look at any of us. His lip was curled into his mouth as if he bit it. "We're going home," she said at last, when it was obvious Harold wasn't going to chime in. "We wanted to let you know before we did, so you wouldn't worry."

"Is something wrong?" I asked. Neither of them looked sick. Upset, maybe, but not unwell enough to need to pass up Thanksgiving dinner.

"Cathy," I heard Hank say.

Harold, his neck rigid to the point of trembling, finally spoke up. "Apparently the club is too exclusive for our blood." He shot a look at Hank, laden with loathing. "You could have let us know."

"Hal, buddy. I didn't know they'd do this for a guest of mine. My dad's on the club board; I thought . . ." He turned to the doorman. "They're on the guest list."

"What is going on?" I asked them. I didn't understand a word of this.

"I know they were, Mr. Cabot, sir, but your mother . . ." Hank cursed some more. "She told me they were Hebes."

They were all talking some other language. "Hebes?" I repeated. Neither Miranda nor Harold would meet my eyes.

"Yids," said the doorman. For a moment, I thought Hank might deck him. Apparently Phil did as well, because he quickly retreated back inside.

"I don't—"

"Oh, for God's sake, Cathy," Miranda snapped. "Why do you have to pretend to be so naive? Hebrews. We can't go in because we're Jewish. Are you happy now?" She fumbled in her purse for something.

"What's going on?" Tilly's voice rang out in the crisp November air from the top of the stairs. "Miranda?"

"Guys." Hank held out his hands. "I sincerely apologize. I didn't think it would be an issue. It's my mother's way of telling me she *loves* me." He sounded bitter.

I reached out and stroked his shoulder, knowing it would be a futile gesture. Yet what else could I do? "No, I'm not happy at all," I told Miranda. "You're not allowed in because you're Jewish?" Of all the days to have an inane prejudice slammed in our faces!

Tilly reached our side, alarmed and dismayed. "They're not? Is this that kind of place? Oh no!" She turned to Chester. "We told Hank's mother about Grossinger's. Stupid!"

Finally Miranda fished out a handkerchief. "Yes, Cathy. Big news, isn't it? Jews put in their place yet again. Say, maybe they won't admit colored people as well. Should we ask them? No, wait, your friend Cherry already figured that one out, didn't she?"

My eyes stung from the unexpected backlash. Hank squeezed my arm, telling me not to respond. "She didn't know. Honestly, she didn't. This is my fault."

"I don't think so, honey." Tilly shook her head. "You're not the one who told the doorman not to let them in. Isn't there any way we can convince him to let them by?" Phil, eavesdropping on the conversation from above, suddenly feigned deafness when we all turned to look his way.

"God!" Hank's sudden expostulation startled several well-dressed arriving guests walking up the avenue. They scurried past as if he might be contagious. "Sometimes I could—!"

My heart ached for him. "Sweetie."

"We'll go," Miranda said. I couldn't stand the downcast expression on her face, either. "It's getting colder by the minute out here."

"Don't move," Hank said, calming down. "We're all getting our coats. We'll find somewhere we can all enjoy Thanksgiving dinner together. Unless anyone has any objections?"

When Hank stared around the group, Chester was the only one to clear his throat. "It seems to me that to pile unpleasantness upon unpleasantness . . ."

"Oh, Chester!" Tilly's eyes flew wide open. "Of all people, *you!*"

Was she finally on to him? Or was it wishful thinking on my part? Either way, I've never seen anyone do a faster one-eighty in my life. The photographer turned beet red and concluded weakly, ". . . but yes, I agree, by all means, let us retrieve our coats and dispatch ourselves with all . . . er, haste."

"I should think so," Tilly grumped, turning to head up the stairs.

"No, wait," I said. I waited as another group of smiling, wealthy guests made their way indoors, all of them ignoring Phil's dutiful greeting. "This is your solution?" I asked Hank. "Running away?"

"That harridan has pulled my strings for the last time. We're going."

"Did it ever occur to you that maybe she wants you to go? And you're simply going to roll over on her command?" I had him now. This felt right. "Stand up for yourself. Stand up for your friends, at least."

"I'm not going in there to make a fuss." He crossed his arms with uncertainty, looked up at the Old Ivy's leaded glass windows, and shook his head. "I won't stoop to that level. But you might be right."

Miranda twitched with impatience. "Let's find some other restaurant. Horn and Hardart, if nothing else. Don't make a stink on my account."

My mind had been working furiously during this whole debacle. How was I supposed to know that Miranda and Harold were both Jewish? Fine, maybe there'd been clues I might have picked up on if I'd been attentive. Yet it's not as if they'd set out a Seder in front of me. Knowing that friends of mine had had this day ruined, of all days, made me want to do something. It was like Cherry had told me—taking a stand made a difference. While the others disagreed about what to do next, I opened my mouth and said with authority, "Rosa . . ." They all shut up and blinked at me while I tried to dredge up the last name. I needed to get this one right. Green fields. Trees. "Rosa Parks," I said at last, certain I had it right for a change. Apparently it was a bit of a non sequitur. Everyone stared at me, waiting. "You've heard of her?"

Miranda's eyebrows knit together. "Of course we've heard of her. She's famous."

Whew. If I'd come up with another anachronism, I was going to pack it up and head back to the Refrigerator Box of Zohar. "Well then. Observe."

With all my friends in a circle around me, I spread out my hands to give myself room. It was a pretty little pirouette; my skirt flounced out nicely as I twirled. Slowly, gracefully, my feet crossed at the ankles, I lowered myself until I was sitting on the sidewalk below the lowermost step. "Catherine Voight," Miranda said, somehow managing to channel the voice of my mother. "You are sitting on the pavement of Fifth Avenue in a Dimanche Soeurs formal that will be difficult and expensive, if not impossible, to clean."

"Be careful with your mink," said Tilly, looking as if she wanted to take it away from me if I couldn't tend to it myself.

"What do you think you're doing, anyway?" Miranda continued, lowering her voice as an old couple tottered by on their way in, staring at me with odd expressions. "You're attracting attention."

I raised my eyebrows. "That's the idea. This is a sit-in." Maybe they'd not heard of those. "Civil protest. It's going to be all the rage soon."

"Sit in what?" Miranda wanted to know. "Dirt and chewing gum?"

"Thorn hand radar." When we all stared at him, Harold looked at his watch. "Horn and Hardart," he said, seeming to blush a little.

"Hank?" I looked up to where he towered above me. "I'll get up if you tell me to. Only if you tell me to, though."

For a long second, he hesitated. When he began lowering those long limbs of his to the ground, though, my heart sang. He crossed his legs and rested his knees on his patent leather shoes. The both of us looked mighty silly in our evening wear, splayed out on the sidewalk, but nobody could ever say we'd tried to blend in. "Sweetheart," he said once we were at face level, "I think you might be better at this decade than I am, sometimes."

We locked our lips together in a quick kiss while Miranda continued to squawk. "Rosa Parks was arrested, you know. She was arrested and convicted for disorderly conduct. Are you ready for that? Because frankly, Cathy, you're so pampered that I don't think you could stand the lockup."

Tilly cleared her throat. "Chester, be a dear and fetch my coat, would you? Knowing Cathy, we may be here a while." After a few impotent protests, Tilly's escort finally turned tail and ran back inside.

"Oh, Tilly Sanguinetti, you're *not*."

"I am." Tilly didn't have as far to go as the rest of us to reach the ground, but somehow it seemed to take her longer—probably because she actually cared about keeping her knees together all the way down. "I can call you by both your names as easily as you can mine, Miranda Rosenberg. Don't give me that look.

Cathy's right." She adjusted her skirts so that they covered her legs. This was going to be the prettiest sit-in ever. "It's a shame you can't go in, and it's not right. We all know it. So why pretend otherwise?"

Her arms crossed across her chest, Miranda looked as if she wanted to be anywhere else in the world than with two girls in black formals and a leggy guy in a tux sitting in forty-degree weather on the cold sidewalk. "Can't we just go home?" she pleaded.

Chester returned with not only Tilly's wrap, but both his and Hank's long overcoats as well. Hank accepted his gratefully and slung it around his shoulders. His teeth had started to chatter. Without a word, Chester donned his own, capelike, and sat down next to Tilly, spreading his coat's hem over her legs. She smiled at him in gratitude. Harold, in the meantime, barely seemed to know what was going on. He pretended to be interested and attentive, but somehow managed to give an air of being too embarrassed to ask what it was all about. "Do you want to go home, darling?" he asked, sounding more than a little hopeful.

Apparently she wanted more resolve from him. She turned to us again. "This is all our fault. I'm sorry. Can't we forget about it and leave?" she pleaded.

"Miranda." I kept my voice firm. She wasn't going to make me give in. "Nobody should ever make you feel sorry for who or what you are." I caught Chester's eye right then. "Nobody." He nodded slightly, thinking to himself, then turned his head from me.

In any movie starring a dog, there always seems to be a climactic scene in which two people claiming ownership of the loveable mutt both call out its name, begging it to love them best. Neither Harold nor the rest of us were actually whistling or making clicky noises to attract Miranda's attention, but it was plain she was wavering between two sides. Finally, and without warning, she held on to her skirts and sank to the ground. "Oh, God," she murmured to herself, an anguish on her face that wasn't in the least staged. Tilly reached over Chester to pat her on the knee. "I hope no one important sees me."

"I thought we were going out to dinner?"

"Darling?" Miranda's voice was more of a growl than anything else. "Shut up and sit down."

As Harold mutely obeyed, Hank grinned at me. "This ought to get interesting." And interesting it got, fairly quickly. Both Phil the doorman and his little assistant for the day came out on the front steps to look at us, finally gathering up the courage to ask outright what we thought we were doing. "I'm proving a point," Hank called to them.

"To whom?" Phil said. His loud voice must have attracted attention indoors, because two middle-aged club members in tuxes poked their heads around the door, stared at us, and then eased outside to get a better gander.

"To my mother," Hank called out. He chuckled. "To the whole damned family. To the club! And to her." He pointed at me. I slapped his finger away, joining in his laughter. "Happy Thanksgiving, Phil!"

"Happy Thanksgiving, Mr. Cabot." Phil shook his head as he wandered back to his post. The two club members immediately began to question him.

"This is insane," Miranda muttered to herself. She rummaged in her purse once more, and finally produced a yellow pack of gum. "Juicy Fruit?" Harold

302

accepted a piece. The rest of us shook our heads and waited.

What were we waiting for, exactly? I'm not sure any of us knew. Somehow it seemed right to be sitting there on that cold, hard pavement strewn with the last of the fallen leaves. None of us was exactly comfortable, or full, or at all warm, but there was some unspoken understanding between us that as long as that dinner went on inside the hallowed halls of the Old Ivy, we would be there, sitting quietly, unwanted outcasts on a day of family and of inclusion. Hank's hand was warm around mine, that much I knew; every few minutes we'd smile at each other. We didn't need to speak to know we were both proud of what the other was doing, even if it happened to go unnoticed by anyone else.

That wasn't the case, though. The two gentlemen who'd seen our conversation with Phil had carried news of our civil disobedience back into the clubhouse. Small groups of dinner-goers would step outside, shiver, and stare at us, mingled bemusement and disdain writ plainly on their faces. After this had gone on for some time, one bald gentleman who resembled no one so much as the bald, monocled man from Monopoly walked over and bent down close to Hank. "I say, Henry. What's this all about?" he asked, trying to sound genial. "All the club's abuzz."

"Thanks to my mother and the club's policies, a couple of my friends aren't allowed in the Old Ivy," Hank explained, his voice polite and informative. "So we thought we'd enjoy our evening out here."

"Oh, dear. Oh, dear." The man examined us all through his tiny little glasses, perhaps trying to pick out which of us might be the Jews. "That won't do at all. Surely your father, being on the board, could make an exception this once. This doesn't look good for the club at all. Not at all."

"We're not on club property," I pointed out. "This is the sidewalk."

"But my girl, that's not the point. Henry's father . . ."

". . . Is the one who endorses the club's policy of exclusivity," Hank finished for the man. "No thanks, Mr. Williams. We'll pass."

With a flurry of *oh dears*, the man trekked back up the stairs to the Old Ivy's interior, stopping only to pass on what Hank had said to the little gaggle of men and women outside the doors. Thanks to the holiday, there wasn't much traffic on Fifth, either on foot or in the avenue itself. A few passersby had regarded us with curiosity, then tittered to each other once they'd left us behind, but no one at all had really stopped to watch. Until, that is, Tilly nodded to a figure across the street, who was obviously interested. "Maybe he's a reporter!"

"He's a gawker." Miranda had kept her face pointed to the sidewalk during most of our protest, afraid to be spotted by any big-name Broadway producers who might walk by—as if that would happen. "Always looking for something to stare at. This city's lousy with them. Rich or poor."

"Are any of those people your relatives?" I asked Hank, nodding upward. Phil and Tom had opened up both of the Old Ivy's doors. A sizeable crowd stood within, chatting animatedly while they pointed and stared.

Hank studied them for a moment, then shook his

head. "Every Cabot is in the dining room right now, pretending nothing's happening. Trust me."

"That fellow looks familiar." Chester's statement was so unexpected that I took another look at the guy still hovering uncertainly on the other side of the street. He seemed to have come out of nowhere, I'd noticed earlier, which was unusual in itself, given our expansive view to either side. Chester put a hand to his brow and peered. "Is it—?"

"How strange!" Tilly seemed equally surprised. "You're right! What in the world is he doing here?"

"Who?" I tried scoping out the guy as well, but a passing car obscured him for a moment. Who in the world would Tilly and Chester both recognize? Someone from work? The funny singing lady with the Adam's apple from the Blue Parrot? The car cleared, and immediately I realized it *was* someone from work. Why hadn't I seen the monobrow right off? It was the single most identifiable characteristic on the guy's face from this distance. The word that flew from my mouth was most certainly not *gloriosky*.

Tilly kept shaking her head. "Does he live here?"

No, I knew. He'd been stalking me again. The thought that'd he'd trailed us from our townhouse to the Old Ivy gave me the shivers. It also made me want to leap to my feet, run across the street, and kick his ass. "Maybe he does," I said, trying to keep cool.

"That's your friend from The Flanders?" Hank asked, straining his neck to see.

"*Cathy's* friend," I stressed to him. "Not mine."

Merv must have noticed our interest in him. While we'd spoken, he'd darted forth into the street, where he stood in one of the far lanes. After taking a quick look for oncoming traffic, he jabbed his finger in my direction and started shouting something. "Crud." I held my head down like Miranda had been doing moments before.

She, in the meantime, was now looking up with interest. "Who's he?"

"He's a fellow from work," Chester told her, brushing a fleck of something from his pants leg. "Bit of a dipso."

"I simply don't understand why he's hollering at us," said Tilly. I wanted to groan. I had a definite suspicion. "It looks like he's yelling at . . . at you, Hank."

Huh? I looked up from the cradle I'd made of my hands. Tilly was right. Though many of his whole-arm jabs were in my direction, all Merv's attention was focused on Hank. "He's obviously inebriated," Hank said. "I recommend we ignore him."

Grateful as I was for that suggestion, Merv kept coming. He was on our side of the street now, still in the traffic lanes, and now we could hear every word he was yelling at the top of his lungs. "Yeah, *you*, mister!" he called to Hank. "That's right. I'm talking to you!" As if operated by one pivot, Miranda, Chester, Tilly, and Harold all swiveled their heads in Hank's direction, and then back to Merv again. "You think she's yours, but she'll turn on you! Oh boy, how she'll turn!"

"Hey." Hank's voice was loud, but calm. "Head home and sleep it off, buddy."

"Don't buddy me! You stole her from me!" Merv staggered a few steps closer. "S-T-O-L . . . L, her."

This confrontation was worse than our quiet little protest. Now we had not only the best of New York society watching this total lunatic shout at Hank, but a small crowd was beginning to gather on the sidewalks to either side of the Ivy Club stairs, afraid to cross in front of us. I couldn't take it any longer. This wasn't Hank's battle. "Merv," I shouted. "Go home. We can talk about this Monday."

"I—! You!" He clapped his hands to his ears and shook his head wildly, like a three-year-old told to go to bed. "Don't listen to her!" he roared. "She lies!"

"This is ridiculous." Though my legs were slightly numb after sitting so long on the sidewalk, I hauled myself up and marched to the curb. Standing was actually something of a relief, loath as I was to leave the compatriots I'd enlisted for the cause. "Listen, you," I called out to him.

Merv, however, still had his hands over his ears. "She'll tell you she loves you and then drop you like a hot potato!"

In the street's quiet I could hear Chester and both of my flatmates gasp. "Cathy?" Tilly asked.

An oncoming car honked its horn, sending Merv into retreat. From the road's center, he continued shouting while the driver edged his way around him. "You've got something she wants. Is it money? She'll tell you lies for money! Oh, she's good at lying."

"Shut up!" I yelled at him. "You're not impressing anybody."

"But he's *married!*" Tilly cried plaintively, behind me.

"I'm not talking to you," he said, vicious and spitting. "I'm talking to him. Your next mark. God knows what you've told him. It could be anything." By the stairs, Hank twisted and began to stand. The coat he'd draped around his shoulder opened, exposing his tuxedo. "Oh yeah, of course you're rich. No wonder she's latched on to you. Want me to tell you how to go all the way with her? You want to know?"

Merv was making such a drunken ruckus that by now the small crowds in the Ivy Club were spilling out the doors, and the sidewalks were full of genteel people dressed in their suits and good dresses for the holiday. "Go *home*," I shouted at him. I hated the way my friends were looking at me now. It hadn't been me who'd had an affair with the guy! Why should I have to bear the burden of blame?

"You heard the lady," said Hank, approaching. "Get out of here and leave her alone."

"I believed her, you see. She made up wonderful stories about herself to get me to feel sorry for her. Then I was hooked. She hook you that way? Cold as ice until she found out you had cash in your wallet, then a sudden thaw?"

This was ridiculous. But Merv had said something that obviously struck home, because Hank turned to me, eyes widening as he stared at my sin-bought outfit. "Hank, don't listen to him," I said. "You know it wasn't that way!"

"You couldn't . . . make it all up. Did you?"

"No!" I protested, stricken. How in the world could he believe such a stupid thing? "You know I didn't." He blinked several times. He wasn't buying it, was he?

Merv yelled on. "I bought her a few drinks and she let me kiss her. I bought her that dress!" He was close enough again that he could swat in its direction. "She let me touch her all over, then. And you want to know what she did for that mink she's got wrapped around those shoulders of hers?" The way he leered made me want to shuck my clothing—my dirty clothing—and run off screaming. "When I gave it to her, the bitch spread her legs so fast that . . ."

"Shut your dirty mouth!" Hank shouted, lunging forward.

For a minute, everything was all confusion. I remember hearing Tilly and Miranda scream, and I remember clutching Hank's shoulder and coat. I remember the coots from the Old Ivy doorway yelling and shouting like seventh-graders witnessing a cafeteria brawl. There was a rush of people from either side, and finally, the shrill sound of a whistle in my ear. I found myself being clutched by a police officer, fat-faced and red, the whistle still shoved in the side of his mouth. Hank was unharmed, it looked like; Merv stood out in the middle of Fifth Avenue again, panting.

"Oh, thank God," I said to the man in blue. "Officer, that man is stalking me!"

The cop didn't seem to be listening to a word I said. "Is this the one you wanted?" he said to someone standing nearby. I whipped my head around, expecting to find Hank's mother scowling me down. She was nowhere to be seen, though. Hank was right—she probably was inside, pretending nothing was happening.

"Yeah. We'll take over." A gruff male voice I didn't recognize spoke above my head, and I felt hands seize me from either side, dragging me away from the melee.

"Who in heck are you?" I demanded as the two men in dark suits and sharp hats hauled me onto the first of the Old Ivy steps. I didn't know either one of them. "I didn't start all this. Not the fight, anyway!" I was aware that everyone was watching me—Merv,

Hank, the crowds, my friends who were too stunned to move from their spots on the pavement. "Or is this about this sit-in?" I demanded to know.

"All right, folks," said the policemen to the two couples still seated. "I'm going to have to take you in for disturbing the peace. Come on. Get up." Stunned, my friends began rising to their feet.

"We have our rights! We weren't on their property. We were having a nonviolent protest on public property!" I yelled at the two thugs manhandling me. "If you want to talk about disturbing the peace, go after that guy!" I pointed at Merv, who still stood unsteadily in the avenue, gawking.

"Miss Cathy Voight?" said one of the suits, reading from a piece of paper. "Of 125 East 63rd Street, New York, New York?" I didn't say a darned thing. I knew my rights.

"Anthony Lewis, Federal Bureau of Investigation," said the other man in a suit, flashing a badge. My knees grew a little weaker at the sight of it. "We have reason to believe that in recent weeks you've sent messages through the U.S. Postal Service of a threatening nature."

"Cathy, who *are* you?" Miranda called out. "Married men? Threatening letters? What is this? Don't you *dare* put a hand on me," she snapped at the police officer, who was trying to corral the four of them together. "I *refuse* to be arrested!"

"I didn't . . ." I tried to say, but the words stuck in my throat.

Lewis took the slip of paper his partner carried, cleared his throat, and said, "The offices of Senator John F. Kennedy report receiving a handwritten letter from you stating that he would be assassinated by a

Mr. Lee Harvey Keitel in Dallas, when he was elected president. Does this sound familiar?"

I tried jerking my wrist free, but the other brute still held me tight. "That's not a threat. That was a warning!"

"You further indicated that his brother, Robert, would be assassinated by . . ." He consulted his notes. "To quote, '*someone whose name I don't remember but it's something like Boutros-Boutros Gahli,*' and to watch out."

"Hello!" I shouted. "Providing a public service here!" Where was Hank? There he was, standing by helplessly, looking as if he wanted to charge the FBI and the policeman and Merv, simultaneously.

The goon ignored me. "We also were informed that you sent a letter to the Reverend Martin Luther King, Jr., of Montgomery, Alabama, telling him . . ."

What I told the nation's greatest civil rights hero, nobody ever heard, because at that moment the man's voice was drowned out by a squeal of tires, the sound of a car horn, and then the awful noise of Merv slamming against the hood of a Cadillac, then sliding off its bouncing frame to the ground. "Ow," I heard him complain, sounding more confused than hurt.

All hell broke loose. From the club doors I could hear people demanding that someone call for the fire department, an ambulance, and the police. The crowds babbled, afraid to approach the accident. Even the FBI agents seemed a little surprised that something like that had happened on their watch. Hank was the only person looking in my direction, hands outstretched. I couldn't read his expression. He didn't really think I'd lied to him, did he? How could I have made up the Internet?

"Holy mother of God." The policeman, who had only moments before managed to pin my friends against the wall, seemed shaken. He crossed himself, forgot about my sit-in cohorts, and then rushed into the street. "Stand back, people!" he cried. "Is there a doctor in the house?"

Harold looked at Miranda. Tilly looked at Chester. Miranda bit her lip, grabbed Tilly's hand, and they both started running down the street as fast as their heels could carry them. "Cheese it," Harold suggested to Chester. Quick as a wink, they followed.

I, too, would have made a run for it if the FBI guys hadn't doubled their restraint. "Take her in," said Lewis, jerking his neck so that the forward brim of his hat pointed in the opposite direction.

"You're coming with us, lady," said the first agent.

"Wait! No! I didn't! I couldn't!" I yelled, as they dragged me away. "Hank! *Haaaaaaank!*"

When they stuffed me into the back of their government vehicle, parked half a block away, I was still calling his name.

Chapter Sixteen

Dear Cathy Voight,

Me again. Yeah, I don't mean to alarm you or anything, but if you had any plans to run for public office, I think I'd kind of lay them aside. You don't need the ulcers anyway. Anyway, because your fingerprints kinda sorta might be now in the FBI files for all eternity doesn't mean you're a criminal.

This might sound like an unusual request, but I have a favor to ask of you even though you don't really know me. Your boss, Mr. Richmond, paid you a fat bonus for an idea you gave him the other day. Five hundred smackeroos, in fact. Here's a tip from me to you: It's not going to fly, what with his name change and all. In another decade, take the idea to General Mills and don't settle for anything less than a percentage. You could retire early on that money, trust me.

Now, I've taken half of that bonus and put it

into your bank account. The other half I've put into an envelope that I'm enclosing with this letter. Please give the envelope to Miss Cherry Bradford, who works for you. Please. If you want, you can look at the short letter I wrote for her. It's just a list of stocks she might want to invest in.

Like I said, it might sound unusual, but you owe Cherry. Your friends were too scared to come back to the apartment the other night after the police and the FBI . . . well, never mind that. Let's say they kind of hid out in Cherry's parents' den most of Thursday night and Friday. And Harold broke her dad's television set. Don't worry, Harold paid for it. After all, he's the one who fell backwards on the thing after he anagrammed her dad Stan's name as "frond bastard" and her dad didn't take it too well.

So please, would you do that for me? Thank you.

—The other Cathy

P.S. You should really do some research on how they make mink coats. It's inhumane.

Chapter Seventeen

Tilly wore a checked bow in her hair that matched the pattern of her dress. Miranda had pulled her red mane back into a practical ponytail, to match the practical capris in which she liked to lounge around the apartment. I still had my curls, which by now I'd learned how to maintain all by myself, thank you very much. All three of us stood side by side with our eyes mere inches above the kitchen counter's surface, staring at the cooling rack. Our heads were all tilted to the left at exactly the same angle.

Tilly blinked first. "Well, Cathy sweetie, I don't know how you did it."

Miranda shook her head. "I thought that ovens had adjustable legs to prevent that sort of thing."

"They do. Ours does," Tilly assured her. "I baked a cake for Cherry's poor father in there yesterday and it was perfectly level."

"So is it a total wash?" I wanted to know. I straightened up and, as if on cue, the other girls followed suit. We all stared at my sad, cockeyed apple pie, overflowing at one end and oddly shallow at the other, as if we were hovering over the dearly departed at a memorial service.

"I'm sure it tastes fine."

"Yummy," agreed Miranda. Neither of them sounded particularly convinced. In fact, the moment I lifted the sticky pie from its rack, they scampered away. "What are we doing, Tills?" she called out. "A sandwich somewhere?"

"And a movie," Tilly called from her bedroom, where she was grabbing her purse. "Maybe a double feature," she added with a wink at me when she returned. "Do you have everything else ready?" she asked.

"World's smallest turkey is in the oven," I said, ticking off fingers. "The stuffing's inside—thank you for that, by the way. Succotash is in the pot, waiting to be heated. The potatoes are going." I pointed to the pressure cooker on the other burner, its wobbly cap chuffing away and spitting out steam enough that I'd cracked the outside window a little. Tilly had been very good earlier about not mentioning that I'd managed to put more actual potato in the trash bin with the peels than in the pot. "I'm skipping rolls. And there's pie. Of sorts." We both again cast mournful looks at my pathetic attempt at baking.

"You'll be fine." She smiled and rubbed my shoulder, which cheered me.

"She'll be fine," Miranda repeated from the living room. She pushed open the swinging door, busily wrapping herself in bumpy tweed. "This one's not married, right?"

"Shush!" Tilly swatted the redhead with her bag and went to choose a coat.

Miranda watched her go. "I don't want Tilly to

316

hear. She's . . . you know. Innocent. So between you and me," she said in a quiet voice, "are you planning to do anything with Hank tonight?" When I raised my eyebrows, wondering if she meant what I thought she meant, she sighed. "Anything *sexual*." She whispered the word as if it were dirty. "Because if you are, be careful, for pete's sake. When you told me that other . . . you know. The married one. Did you hear anything about him today, by the way?"

"A broken leg, is what they're saying around the office. And I heard his wife was by his bedside the entire weekend."

"That's a mercy. When you told me about how he thought you were with child . . ."

It was nice to know she cared. I smiled and laid a hand on her tweedy shoulder. "Miranda," I said loftily, "if Hank and I happen to do anything, I swear by all that is sacred and holy that the furthest I will go is the oral-genital kiss of love."

From the hallway I heard Tilly's shrill cackle. She appeared in the door, ready to go. She chucked Miranda's hanging jaw back into place and grabbed her hand. "Come on, princess. I'll tell you all about it on the way to the movies."

"Bye-bye, girls!" I called, listening to their cheery rejoinders before the door shut.

Chuff-chuff-chuff. The pressure cooker's steady pulse made me feel oddly competent. I had actually prepared an entire dinner by myself. From scratch! Okay, the succotash had been a package of Birds Eye from the freezer, and I'd managed to flatter Tilly into making me a batch of her world-famous pie crust so I could work on my stuffing. But by gum. This dinner was mine, all mine. Nothing was burning. I hadn't messed up the kitchen enough to give Tilly a conniption. It was going to be a perfect evening. And if there were any acts of love to follow . . . well, I certainly wouldn't object.

The scent of apples and cinnamon tickled my nostrils all the way down the staircase. "Knock knock!" I said, upon finding Hank's door cracked. "Sweetheart? Are you here?"

He sat the sofa. His hands lay on the cushions, limp. His shoulders were slack. Even his face seemed to have lost its elasticity. At the sight of me, he sighed deeply and let out a sound. "Ungh."

My heart went out to him. "Hank." In my soft checkered skirt and neat, white ironed blouse, sailing across the room to my man with homemade baked goods, I was the very image of 1950s femininity. "It's not that bad. Honestly."

"Not that bad!" He gaped. "I sold my soul to the devil! That's what it feels like!"

"I brought pie. It's a peep at the evening that is to come." I sat down on the coffee table and waved the dish under the poor guy's nose. "Mmmmm. Pie."

The grin he gave me was halfhearted at most. "What happened to it?"

"Nice. Thanks for the ego reinforcement. Get it while you can, big boy," I said, putting it down and standing up again. "In the future, pie is outlawed. Yeah, it's extinct. All we're allowed to eat in the future is flan. You know what flan is? It's a shimmery, snotlike . . . where are your babes?" He looked up at me, not comprehending. "Your Amazons. Your superior guides, your teachers with the big breasts. You know. Your babes!"

"There." He gestured to a stack of illustrations leaning against the wall beyond the dining table. "I'm not going to be needing them anymore. I'm not going to be *drawing* them anymore."

"You totally are!" I grabbed the illustration boards and began spacing the larger ones out on the mantel again. "You didn't promise your family anything. You said you'd *think* about taking more responsibility."

He buried his face in his hands. "That's as good as signing my name in blood to those monsters. I can't do it, Cathy. I know that my father knows people who know people who helped get you released quickly from that hellhole. . . ."

"It was not a hellhole," I interrupted. "They served me hot chocolate, and one of the agent's wives had sent along a pumpkin pie. In general, I think they thought I was a whack job. They would have let me go anyway."

"I didn't know that," he said, miserable. The Amazons were now back in their places, stylized swoops of power staring with both wisdom and serenity shining from their visages. And, you know, sporting huge knockers. I knew why Hank had offered a grudging servitude to his family in exchange for a few words in the right ear, but I still had problems believing that he'd done it. No, that kind of impulsive, decisive action was exactly what he was good at. I couldn't believe he'd done it for *me*. "I was so damned worried about you. I never should have mailed those stupid letters. I nearly ripped them up, when you gave them to me that night."

"You really love me, don't you?" I'd never felt so light, so delicate. So feminine. My skirt glided around me as I crossed back to him and sat down again. He looked like he was struggling for words. Poor guy— here I was, trying to get him to make a declaration he wasn't ready to make, in a decade when men weren't supposed to express their squishiest feelings. Of course, in what decade do they ever? "It's okay. You don't have to answer. But I love you." I took his face and pulled it to my own, kissing him softly. "I love you, Hank Cabot. Don't be down! The worst thing that's going to happen is that I won't be allowed near a presidental motorcade for, well, the rest of my life. I can live with it!"

A wry smile crossed his lips. "You don't know how much I wish I could escape. Remember a couple of weeks ago when you talked about how much you hated girdles and the tight waists of women's clothing? That's the way this feels."

"Tell them no." I picked up the pie and held it on my lap. I had to get back upstairs. I'd already left everything unsupervised for too long. "And don't give me any guff about how you can't. Our sit-in? That was one big in-your-face *no* from the get-go. You ought to be proud of that. Now, comb your hair, wash your hands, and haul your keister upstairs. We're going to have a nice, quiet, Monday-after-Thanksgiving, Thanksgiving dinner. *Capiche*?"

"You know," he said slowly. "I still don't understand half of what you say." I sprang up and, carrying dessert with me, crossed the room. "Cathy?" I turned around to find him standing, hands in his pockets as he said in a low, warm voice, "I'm not afraid to tell you I love you. I love you deeply. In fact." He shuffled awkwardly, giving a quick glance to the mantel. "You're all the Amazon I'd ever need."

"Damn right," I assured him with a wink. I floated back up those stairs, light as a feather and feeling swell. I was Miss U.S. Domesticity, 1959, and loving every minute of it.

Something was making a terrible racket inside our flat. "Tilly?" I called out, a little frightened at the noise. It sounded like a washing machine gone out of balance, crossed with a train rumbling over a bridge. What the hell? "Miranda?" I couldn't even hear myself over the racket.

Ping! I heard something pop. The metallic noise had come from the kitchen. It didn't sound good. That's when I realized that there was something I was supposed to have done with the pressure cooker. What was it Cherry had told me? I tried to remember as I sped through the living room. Not put too much water in? Make sure it had plenty of water? Run it under the tap?

I pushed open the swinging door with my shoulder, afraid of what I might see. What had happened to the cooker's comforting *chuff-chuff-chuff* sound? The thing had gone mad; it jerked on the burner like an epileptic gone into wild spasms, shuddering and heaving and . . .

Oh, no.

When the explosion came, with a blast of sound so intense I felt certain I'd be deaf forever after, I ducked, using the swinging door as my shield. It didn't close so fast, though, that I missed the heart-stopping sight of the pressure cooker ripping itself into pieces like a popping balloon, and the lid winging its way, Frisbeelike, toward me and slamming into the door, which flattened my face and sent me falling backwards into oblivion.

What was that noise of chirping crickets? I knew I should recognize it. My brain seemed slow to cooperate, but my hand automatically shot out and grabbed the telephone receiver. "Hello?"

"Cathy?"

I yawned, "Hey, Thuy, what's up?"

"Where are you? Are you running late? Did you

oversleep?" I heard her say, a little panicked. "Aren't you coming in early? Everything's under control, don't worry. I thought . . ."

"Come in where?" I was in a nightgown. A flannel nightgown. With gathered cuffs at the wrist. Printed with bluebells. And someone had replaced my royal blue sheets with the tiniest and most delicate of floral prints as well.

"Work? Duh?" My head throbbed and ached, and Thuy's attempts of humor gave me the same squirmy sensation of hearing someone rub their hands over an inflated balloon. "Motive? Wang Building? Ringing any bells? Listen, did you go out and party last night when I told you you'd need all the sleep you could get for the presentation today? Because if you went without me, I'm going to be seriously . . ."

The phone slipped out of my hands. I was in my bed. *My* bed. Staring at *my* telephone—the kind of telephone that made bleepy noises instead of clanging like a school bell. The sun streaming through the window fell onto my bedspread, through my blinds, in my apartment, as far, far away from East 63rd as a girl could get. I was back where I started, but without one crucial thing.

Hank.

"Cathy? Cathy? Don't yell like that! If you've got a hangover, you're only going to make it worse. Are you there? Cathy?" I could barely hear Thuy's tinny voice from the receiver, as I keened and cried at the sudden realization of everything I'd left behind.

Chapter Eighteen

11/24

Dear Cathy Voorhees,

Far be it from me to cast aspersions on the way you choose to live your life. If you want to live like a wild Indian who doesn't keep any food in the cupboards, or if you want to Martinize every single item of clothing you own at ruinous expense rather than use an economical capful of Woolite and your own laundry tub, who am I to criticize?

However, in case I find a way to get back to my own and more humble abode, I did want to note that I tired of your Better Crypts and Gardens approach to decorating and decided to spruce up your apartment a little bit. I don't care what year a person lives in. It's up to her to set an example of taste and style. The Salvation Army is quite grateful for your donations. I've filed the receipt in your new file cabinet, under "2006 Deductibles." It's really not so hard to be organized if you put your mind to it.

Yesterday I pushed a button on the monolith you call a television and now everyone speaks Spanish. I don't know if I have the patience to get it back. Would it really hurt to keep your instruction booklets?

Your sorry excuse for a doorman is a reprehensible person and I do not understand why you have not before sought to separate him from his source of employment. Of course, neither do I understand why you keep "panty" hose in the freezer.

I am leaving this note on your refrigerator. I don't know why, since the only food you've apparently seen fit to keep in there is a jar of manzanilla olives.

Sincerely and with best wishes for a
prosperous future,
Cathy Voight

P.S. The item in the bottom drawer of your left bedside table—you know the one I mean—appears to be broken, though I hasten to make clear I had nothing to do with it. I believe it has something to with its batteries.

P.P.S. I am acquainted with your CEO, I believe they call it. Isn't it the oddest coincidence?

Chapter Nineteen

Welcome Home.

The two words mocked me, but I couldn't turn my head in any direction without seeing them. Across a sky of blue and a field of waving wheat they drifted, warming the high-def plasma screens stretching across the front of the forty-fourth-story conference room. They greeted me from the front cover of every prospectus whipped up by Thuy and the gang from the graphics department. And they graced the front of every frozen-food package artistically arranged in a pyramid foundation on the conference room table: a gingham-clothed table set for two, with slices of breast meat on each plate, surrounded by stuffing and mashed potatoes and green beans, overlooking a field of ripening grains backed by a sunset. *Welcome Home,* read the two words in an inviting typeface. And then, underneath, *Turkey Dinner.*

"To sum up." Thuy Phan, confident and pert in her herringbone and velvet suit, took confident strides back to the center plasma panel, where presentation software splashed her summation points onto the screen as she announced them. "We propose a complete rebranding of the Maxwell Freezer Classics line. A fresh approach to the meals. An emphasis on quality ingredients. An emphasis on low-fat, lower-calorie foods. Simultaneous and coordinated launches of print, television, radio, and web advertising. And finally . . ." On the screen, the camera pulled back through a window into a country kitchen, where plates of wholesome-looking food sat on a kitchen table along with an open, checker-cover book. "Maxwell *Welcome Home* culinary guides—recipes to enhance the *Welcome Home* frozen dinner experience, for busy families who still crave that home-cooked touch." On the television, outside the window, the sunset deepened to a rosy hue; once more the new brand's name flashed across the screen. "Ladies and gentlemen . . . Welcome Home."

The applause was instant, thundering loud through-out the cavernous conference room. At my spot by the table's head, I watched as everyone rose to their feet in ovation. Everyone but me, that is. I didn't trust myself to rise. If I did, I'd probably walk right out of the conference room and keep burning foot leather until I reached my bed again. The problem was that people mistook my wry half smile and my reluctance to stand and take credit for my campaign as unnecessary modesty; scarcely had Thuy set down the remote controlling her PowerPoint presentation than I was mobbed. Maxwell representatives wanted to shake my hand; they babbled to me about how revolutionary the campaign would be for their entire product line and how truly heartwarming the entire promotion made them feel.

Only when one of the men from Maxwell jokingly asked if, after helming the creative aspect of the entire concept and presentation, I intended to write the cookbook as well, did I feel compelled to speak. "No!" I said with such ferocity that he backed away, more than a little frightened, until I followed it up with an entirely manufactured smile.

When the crowds eventually ebbed, Thuy frisked over, bobbing back and forth in a little aren't-you-proud-of-me dance. God, it felt like I hadn't seen her in years. Fifty of them, in fact. "Oh, my God, you are the most insanely popular woman in New York City right now," she said. "You actually single-handedly yanked an account from under Donny Deutsch's feet. I already heard the Maxwell CEO say he was ready to sign the papers."

"Honey," I said, squeezing her hand on the table. "You did all the work. You were magnificent."

"Thank you for letting me do the pitch. So much!" She squeezed right back. "I got to show off my presentational skills, and now everyone thinks you're the woman of mystery for sitting to the side and pretending you had nothing to do with it when everyone, *everyone* knows it's *totally* yours. Oh, my God, I'm going to cry." For a quick moment, she sucked in her lips and waved her outstretched hands in the vicinity of her eyes. "No, Martha Stewart says women in business don't cry. I'm all right. I'm okay." She took a deep breath and was all smiles again. "We'll talk later. You do your mingle thing. Mingle!" she encouraged me, twiddling her fingers.

But no. I didn't want to leave my seat. The conversation still raged around me for several minutes as I sat there, looking over Cathy's handiwork with appreciation and a little bit of envy. The girl hadn't had much sincerity going on in her personal life, but boy, in this venue she could have been a killer. I'd never considered, in all that time I'd spent in her shoes, that she might have jumped into mine. Now she was back at home, with her flatmates and her cookbooks and her sweater sets and minks. And my man.

I hoped she was happy.

Though the crowd had lessened, people still came up to thank me for my hard work—some of them from Maxwell, some of them our own men and women. I shook hands and smiled, but my heart wasn't in it. My eyes drifted to the Santayana quote painted in copper letters on the wall, and then to another even farther down the room, from someone named Gilson: *History is the only laboratory we have in which to test the consequences of thought.*

You know what really sucks about great thinkers? They're always maddeningly right.

I swiveled my chair from the quotations and gazed out over my city. In thousands of other offices like mine, WiFi routers hummed, fax machines whirred, computer servers processed e-mails too numerous to count—but the people were so very much the same. Some of us had worn gloves and girdles, while others sported flats and power cuts. A couple of us had done them both. Ambitious, silly, frightened, foolish, and sometimes granting ourselves the ability to see each other for who we really were, and who we could become.

I wasn't surprised to hear the soft *whoosh* of the executive suite doors after the last people had drifted from the room. I didn't turn around until I heard someone settle on the table nearby. I knew exactly who it had to be. "So," said old man Turnbull, his arms crossed. "How do you think it went this afternoon?"

He looked so old, so fragile. In less than twenty-four hours I'd witnessed his youth fly away, his skin slacken, his complexion darken and become uneven and speckled with age. He'd been a mere teen when I'd left. What would Hank—? I wouldn't let myself finish the question, not even in my head. "I'm not playing that game again," I told him. "Tell me what you thought."

He let out a long sigh before saying anything. "To be perfectly honest, I'm not at all certain what came over me, what was it, three weeks ago when I called you at home and asked you to come back in? I thought I must have been letting sentimentality get the best of me. But then again, I am an old man, and I am permitted to indulge myself now and again."

What unnerved me was that at the end of every sentence, I fully expected him to call me *mama* or make some cheap come-on. He didn't, and wouldn't. Fifty years of civilizing had taken place, and it was unfair of me to compare the guy to his adolescent self. Besides, I really didn't have the energy or will. "I can't imagine, either," I lied.

"The clients were very pleased. Quite a coup, my dear. Quite a coup indeed." He stood up. "I suppose I should congratulate you. Yet there are means of congratulations . . ." Turnbull reached into the pocket of his jacket with his index and second finger, withdrew a rectangle of white plastic with a black stripe across its top, and laid it on the table in front of me. "And means of congratulations."

It was an electronic swipe-key to the executive

suite. I'd coveted that card for such a long time. Now it sat within only a few inches of my fingertips. Without moving, I studied old man Turnbull. He didn't intimidate me any longer; I knew where he came from. I'd speak as freely as I liked with the guy from now on. What was most important to me had slipped from my fingers. What did I have to lose here? "You didn't tell me what you thought," I reminded him.

"What I thought? What I thought," he said softly, almost gently, "is that in a hundred years I would never have suspected, my dear, what an old-fashioned girl you could be at heart."

I thought it over. Yeah, I could live with that. After a moment, my fingers danced across the wood and plucked the card from the table. Any thrill it gave me was dulled by the heavy cloak that seemed to damp my every emotion.

Turnbull, while I looked hard at my key to the big time, nodded to me. "I'll have Ms. Caldwell meet with you about your new furniture. Congratulations, Cathy. You deserve to celebrate. Take the rest of the day off." He glided with long steps toward the other end of the room.

Celebrate what? Even the distant sound of animated excitement from the rest of the Motive crew in the break room was too nerve-wracking. I couldn't bear the sound of champagne corks popping, the caroling of triumph, the excited recountings of how we'd scored one of the biggest insurrections in the advertising business in years. I shut the door, fired up my laptop, and tapped out a query in my browser's search engine bar. My heart leapt into my throat with the very first result at the sight of a familiar name.

I Went to Vassar for This?

ACHIEVEMENT NEWS

<u>Matilda Sanguinetti</u> (Photo, courtesy of <u>Matilda Sanguinetti</u>). Matilda Sanguinetti is like lots of 10-year-olds. She likes sports, is an avid Harry Potter fan, and lists outdoor camping as her favorite . . .

That was obviously not her. Damn. I prowled through the small-print list of genealogists, bloggers, and a number of obituaries for Elise Sanguinetti, a well-known resident of Sitka, Alaska, who had passed away at the age of fifty-seven and was survived by her daughter, Matilda Fiers. It wasn't until I was on my second page of results that I found what I was looking for. I clicked through and was rewarded with a page from the Poplar Hills Retirement Community of Fort Lauderdale, Florida, dated six months before.

COUPLE CELEBRATES 40 YEARS OF MARRIAGE

It seemed like all the residents of Poplar Hills turned out for the big shindig to help Arthur Mills and his wife, Matilda "Tilly" Mills celebrate their fortieth wedding anniversary! Arthur (72), a local church organist and a frequent player in the Charles Winston Community Theater, cut the cake (vanilla sponge with chocolate filling from the local Costco) and remarked, "Marriage is the adventure of a lifetime! If you like adventures!" What a card!

"It was the happiest day of my life when Arthur proposed to <u>Tilly Sanguinetti</u> and made her into Tilly Mills," said Tilly (67), a favorite at the Poplar Hills bridge tables. "I just hope we can have another forty years together."

The pair have one daughter, who currently lives in Richmond, Virginia. They live in unit 240.

My fingers reached up to trace the face of an old woman with an impossibly young face, her blond hair grown white. Those blue eyes were as I remembered them, though—bright and funny and full of joy. But honestly, marrying a church organist and community theater actor? Poor Tilly. Some girls never really accumulated much of a gaydar. At least she looked happy.

I typed in another search. This time I had to wade through several pages devoted to a teen girl crusading to have the voting age lowered, but I found what I wanted on the fourth page.

HAROLD DAVID SILVERSTEIN

Harold Silverstein, president of Carolina First Credit Unions, passed away at St. Mary's Hospital in Greenville on January 25, 2004, from complications related to pneumonia brought on by Alzheimer's disease. He was 77.

Mr. Silverstein and his wife, both originally from New York City, have been Greenville residents for the last thirty years and have been highly active community philanthropists and patrons of the arts.

In addition to his wife, <u>Miranda Rosenberg</u> Silverstein, Mr. Silverstein is survived by a daughter, Barbara Silverstein Arntz and her husband Frederick, of Albuquerque, NM; sons, Harold Silverstein, Jr., and his wife Melody of Brooklyn, NY, and Henry C. Silverstein and his wife Sylvia, of Towson, MD; and seven grandchildren.

I Went to Vassar for This?

You know, screw Martha Stewart. Women in business do cry. At least, this one did, a little. It was no good consoling myself that poor old dopey Harold had lived a long and full life, from the sounds of it. He'd been a friend, and only a few days ago he'd been alive, and now he wasn't. Of course I mourned.

It was several minutes and a good few Kleenex before I could bring myself again to submit to the overwhelming urge to search. This time the results were plentiful; I didn't even have to pore through any of the entries. Instead, I clicked on the first, a profile from *New York* magazine:

To the children who know her, she's the plump, gray-haired, maternal icon who always has time to read a story or pour a cup of juice. To a sometimes-struggling family, she's many times been a sole source of support. To educators, she's known far and wide as the force behind the single largest community literacy foundation in the Northeast. In financial circles, she's known as a shark, a self-taught speculator who holds spots on the boards of several top Fortune 500 firms.

What does Cherry Anne Bradford-Parks think of these many sides of herself? She laughed when I asked. "I'm an old woman who's made the most of the one life I've been gifted." That's positive thinking from an African-American woman who admits, that at the peak of the great civil rights movement, her wages, more often than not, were the only income for a large family that included her parents, her two younger sisters, and an older brother. "It wasn't easy for any of us to get—or keep—a job, but we made do. We made do," she recalls.

How did someone with such an unassuming (some might say grim) background establish herself as a stock-market mogul? That's a secret she won't divulge. What she will tell me, however, is that she started small. "You would laugh at the amount I invested at first." How much? "Two hundred dollars," she admitted at last. "It was almost everything I had. I can't count the times in the early days I thought about cashing out my investments, because that two hundred dollars would have made all the difference in the world to my family. But I had faith that the future would bring better things, and faith won out."

"She's the shrewdest investor I know," says Bill Gates, chairman and chief software architect of Microsoft Corporation. "There were times in the 1980s and '90s when all of Wall Street would hold its breath to see where Cherry Bradford-Parks would invest next."

One of those investments was in Microsoft itself, in the days when the company was little more than

(NEXT)

Maybe my disastrous trip had done some good, after all. I didn't need to read more. Not now. Once again, I felt so helpless. I would have loved to see Cherry's ascent, and I hadn't been around for any of it. Damn! The only reassurance I had from any of this reading was that at least I hadn't dreamed it all. These people had been and were real. None of my friends had suffered untimely deaths; in fact, they'd carved out perfectly ordinary—maybe even extraordinary—lives for themselves. Why was that consolation so cold?

I tapped out the next name on my list: *Cathy Voight*. Nothing. Absolutely nothing. There was a Cathy Voight who was a track athlete at small high school in Indiana, and a clerical assistant for the physics department at the University of Windsor, and a biomedical science students' association Cathy Voight. There were pages and pages of the ubiquitous genealogy pages that had a Cathy and a Voight somewhere. But of my former life, absolutely nothing. I even switched over to eBay and tried looking up some of the titles to Richmond Better Homes Publications. Save for a battered copy of *Fast, Fun, Fondue!* on sale for a hot ninety-nine cents, nothing.

My fingers trembled as I typed in my final search query, the most important of them all.

Too many entries for a politician named Henry Cabot Lodge popped up; I quickly modified the search to remove all the entries with the word "lodge" in them. Lots of links to pages about some guy named John Cabot and King Henry the VII. Other than that, nothing.

Hank Cabot
"Henry Cabot" "New York"
Cabot Family "New York City"
"Henry Pew Cabot"

None of the searches I tried told me a thing. There were Henry Cabots aplenty in the online white pages for New York City, but how could I tell which might be my own? How did I even know he was still in the area? Both Tilly and Miranda had moved from the state. Cabots, Cabots everywhere. But not a sign of Hank.

What was happening with the two of them, now that I was gone? Had Hank arrived to my apartment—Cathy's apartment—to find her dumping the mutant pie in the garbage and cleaning up boiled potato from the kitchen walls? Did he rescue her from another kitchen accident? Had she woken to find him looking at her, as I had, and realized she'd had the perfect guy living downstairs all that time? What if he couldn't tell there was a difference? What if she found herself liking him . . . would he settle for her? Oh, my God, were they doing it? Right *now*?

"Cathy!" I was startled from my jealous thoughts when one of the guys from graphics opened my door and stuck his head in. "Come celebrate. You've worked so hard on this!"

I tried to smile. I must have looked as if I were in pain. I closed the lid of my office laptop, stood up, and started gathering the coat and bag already lying on my desk. "You know, I'm kind of worn out. I'm going to head home. But you guys have fun."

"Maybe we could all get together tomorrow night after work? Hit a club? Drink our asses off?"

The kid meant well. I nodded, knowing that I wouldn't be going anywhere, and let the door of my old office lock shut behind me.

The thing was, I realized on my trip home, that feeling antsy about anything Cathy and Hank might be doing was fruitless. It was in the past, dead and long gone. Probably no one remembered any longer what had happened in a run-down East Side townhouse one Monday evening in November, close to fifty years ago.

I Went to Vassar for This?

Fresh as its disappointments were in my mind, no one else was around to care.

The door of my building flew open before I could so much as grasp the handle. "Ms. Voorhees," said a familiar voice, his tone courteous.

I had to do a double-take. Even in my bleak mood, I couldn't help but be astonished by what I saw. "Kurt?"

Our "sorry excuse for a doorman," as Cathy had put it, nodded at me. His posture was erect, his jacket fastened. His buttons even seemed to shine. "Good afternoon, Ms. Voorhees," he murmured, bowing a little. I couldn't believe it. From behind his desk he produced an armful of blooms wrapped in green paper. "Delivery for you," he declared, cradling them. "I thought it might be best if I gave it to you myself. If you'd been much longer, I would have borrowed a vase and put them into water."

"That's, um." Freaky? Psychotic? I finished my thought with a lame, "Very good of you." The flowers were from Thuy, I knew—the usual congratulations from a friend for a job well done. I'd have to do something extra-special for her, once I was back in the saddle again. Why wasn't he giving them over, though? "Is there something else?"

"I thought I'd hold them for you while you collected your mail, Ms. Voorhees," he said.

Okay, someone had replaced Kurt with a pod person. For the moment, though, I was totally fine with that. Pod away! He waited until I'd scooped out some magazines from my box before presenting me with the bouquet. "Thanks."

He cleared his throat. "I hope I've been providing you with adequate service this week, Ms. Voorhees," he said quietly. "And your neighbors, too, of course. I'd hate for you to . . . report me again. I need this job. Especially since I don't think I'll get that cable gig again."

I actually wanted to laugh for the first time since I'd been back. So *that* was it. The kid was afraid of me! It was written plainly in his eyes. Of course, Cathy Voight would probably scare me pantsless, too. "See that you keep it up," I said with a touch of the grand hauteur that I associated with Cathy. I must have hit the right note; he scrambled to push the elevator button for me.

I didn't feel so grand on the trip to my floor. Had the whole experience, the entire terrible, wonderful time been just one of those random and cruel tricks fate plays on people? Did someone upstairs say, *Let's give Cathy enough time to fall in love with a guy, and then yank her away from him not to the other end of the earth, but to the other end of the century? Won't that be a blast?* Was that it? How long was it going to take me to recover from the unfinished business left between Hank and me?

Or was I supposed to rebuild and start anew? The thing about rebuilding for the future, though, was that it didn't happen in a vacuum; the New York of today wasn't the two-hundred-story city of skyscrapers Hank had envisioned. We lived continually surrounded by the architectural reminders of decades and centuries long gone by.

I simply couldn't picture a future in which I wouldn't be thinking of my past, and what I'd left behind in it.

Ding. The elevator bell brought me back to what I was doing. I stepped out and began walking slowly down my hallway. Unfinished business. Maybe the high priestess of Zohar still lived in the Village—or her daughter, or someone who'd taken over that ridiculous box. I couldn't stay here, not like this. Maybe Cathy wanted to come back, too. She might like switching spots on a permanent basis.

And if I couldn't find the Zohar freaks, what then? I could put a Welcome Home Frozen Dinner in the microwave. Did I cherish the thought of blowing up my kitchen again? No, but I'd totally take the risk. Even if it took a hundred dinners and a hundred microwaves, I'd find a way back. Even if it took a *thousand* microwaves, I'd . . .

Oh, man. One of the nice things about 1959 had been that my neighbors didn't play their stupid music at top volume. The creepy guy in 440 was at it again, blasting an idiotic doo-wop track so loudly that not only was his door vibrating with every pulse, but mine was as well. All I wanted to do was take a nap, but I knew the moment my head hit the pillow, I'd be gnashing my teeth and thinking of creative ways I could kill my neighbor.

Maybe there was a little Cathy Voight left in me. "Hey!" I shouted out, on the hallway side of the guy's wooden door. "Can you show a little respect and turn it down in there?" No answer. No surprise, really. There wasn't any way he could have heard me over the racket. "*Hey!*" In disgust, I tossed down my flowers and mail and bag in front of my apartment across the hall, and pounded with both fists. "*For the first time since you moved into this place, could you show a little bit of courtesy and turn down your God-damned . . .*"

BOOM! From the depths of 440 came a detonation so strong that I was thrown backwards into my own doorway, hitting the wood with such force that it knocked the wind out of me. And I'd thought the explosions with my microwave and the pressure cooker had been bad. At least for those I'd been knocked unconscious. The music stopped. During the near silence that followed, as over the high-pitched ringing in my ears I heard plaster sifting from the ceiling inside the apartment, my terrified mind bounced around for explanations, thinking of terrorists and bombs and exploding home crystal meth labs and all kinds of terrible things.

The door to 440 had swung open several inches. I looked up and down the hallway; maybe no one else had been home to hear the accident. I crawled to my feet. "Hey, mister," I called, stepping inside.

·There was no sign of smoke or fire, thank God. The place was a crazy mess, though whether that was normal or from the explosion I had no way of telling. An actual turntable still spun on a table farther in, its arm sticking straight up in the air and the record that had been playing jarred off the spindle. "Mister?" I called out again. "Are you okay?" Part of me kept telling myself to call downstairs for help, but if there was a guy dying in here, I didn't want to stay awake nights knowing that my hesitation had been the one thing that could have saved him. "Is there anyone here?"

"Help."

The sound was barely a mew, coming from the kitchen. I scrambled over the scattered sofa cushions and books and newspapers until I saw my neighbor lying on the floor, his hair askew, his face grimy with soot, rubbing his face with his hands. His oven door was open. He wasn't charred. None of his limbs stuck out at strange angles. In fact, the freak was rolling on his side as if about to try to sit up. "What the hell are you *doing* in here?" I demanded. "You could have burned the whole place down! I'm going to report you to the—" The guy dropped his hands and blinked at me, dazed.

My heart stopped beating for a second, then doubled its pace, pounding like a drum. It was Hank. His hair was longer and fashionably messy. He didn't wear glasses. His clothes were undeniably modern, in a retro hipster kind of way. But it was *Hank*, from the caramel depths of his eyes to the cleft in his chin. No, I realized. It was someone else. It couldn't be Hank, much as I willed it.

Then he spoke. "Cathy?" He squinted at me in the way people do when they've got contact lenses in their eyes for the first time, and aren't quite used to them. "Is that really you?" He looked around the room. "Where am I?"

There was no use in holding back. I was a mess. A big, blubbering, sniffling, snotty mess in a business suit, of whom Martha Stewart would never, ever approve. I dropped to my knees, shuddering and sobbing. "Sssh," he said in my ear, moving slowly as he tried to wrap his arms around me. "It's okay. It's me. I came to find you."

It took a moment for me to calm down enough even to look at him. It really was Hank. I couldn't stop touching his face, or kissing his lips, even though doing either too vigorously made him wince. "How?" I finally asked. "How did you know I was gone?"

"Oh, come on," he said, weak but still satirical. "Have you *met* Cathy Voight?"

"How did you get here, then?" I couldn't stop clinging to him. Sore and dirty as he looked, I wanted to hold his hands, his arms. I wanted to curl myself around him and never let go.

"This morning I tried a pressure cooker without enough water. That didn't work. Got this." He pointed to a red welt on his forearm. "Then I tried loading all my pots and pans in a high cupboard and letting them fall on my head. Yeah, ouch," he said, pointing to a bruise barely visible beneath the soot on his forehead. "Then finally this afternoon I got the idea of letting a little gas build up in the oven and trying to light the pilot light. Boom."

"No kidding, boom." I laughed through my tears. "Oh, my gosh! You escaped from your family!"

"No," he said, sitting up with a little more strength. "I came to you."

Hank must have been feeling better, because he squeezed me so tightly I almost couldn't breathe—but then again, I was doing the same to him. In the wreckage of the kitchen, which still smelled of smoke and gas and was littered with remnants of the light fixtures that had hung from the ceiling, we embraced so hard it felt like we might never let each other go.

"You know what I'm thinking?" he said at last, when we separated enough for him to have his first good look at the ruin he'd caused.

"How much you love me?" I asked, wondering what I'd ever done to deserve such a happy moment.

"Besides that."

"How you're never going to let me go again?"

"That, too. But no." I shook my head. "I'm thinking that we are *totally* going to have to spend the rest of our lives eating out."

I laughed, and planted a kiss on his sooty mouth. Already he was speaking the native tongue like a pro. He was going to get along fine. "You know what?" I said, grinning to have him near. "That'd be swell."

THE MILE-HIGH HAIR CLUB
NAOMI NEALE

When worlds collide: My life in a nutshell
By Bailey Rhodes, talent producer, Expedition Network

NYC and Dixie have little in common. In New York, I have a fabulous career in cable television, incredible friends, and exciting culture. In Dixie, there's relatives who are, shall I say, two bubbles shy of plumb crazy. New York has the boyfriend who can't commit; Dixie has the agronomist with the heart of gold and biceps by the pound. Shrill, talentless anchorwomen try to claw their way into my programming in New York, while loud, talentless contestants try to claw their way into the sixty-fourth annual Miss Tidewater Butter Bean Pageant in Dixie.

But there's one thing New York and Dixie have in common: Big mouths, big heads, and even bigger hair in...

THE MILE-HIGH HAIR CLUB
